Seventh Heaven

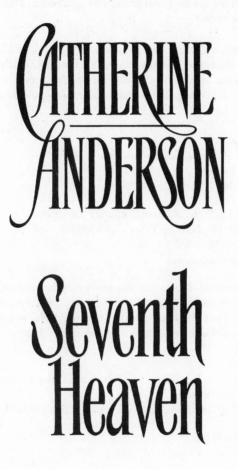

CATHERINE ANDERSON

Seventh Heaven

AVON BOOKS
An Imprint of HarperCollins*Publishers*

To Steven Axelrod, my agent, who always goes the extra mile and has earned my gratitude and respect. Since this book is about a football player, I'll put it this way: When I'm trying to run with the ball, you're always there as my cheering section, my coach, and my guard, intercepting and running interference so I can make my goal line. Thanks, Steve. You're the best.

AVON BOOKS
An Imprint of HarperCollins*Publishers*
10 East 53rd Street
New York, New York 10022-5299

Copyright © 2000 by Adeline Catherine Anderson
Back flap author photo by Terry Day's Studio
ISBN: 0-7394-1228-0
www.avonromance.com

Prologue

MONDAY, MARCH 20
SAN MILAGROS, CALIFORNIA

*B*efore leaving the cinema lobby, Joe Lakota paused well back from the double
doors to let his four-year-old son Zachary take a sip of
his newly purchased soft drink. The air around them
smelled strongly of fresh popcorn, the buttery odor filling
Joe's nostrils.

His hair shining in the muted lights, Zachary went after
the orange soda like a pint-sized siphon, his big brown
eyes watering at the sting of carbonation. *Too much
sugar*, Joe thought morosely. But he let the kid guzzle
pop anyway. This was a special occasion, after all. He
didn't want to become one of those dads so hung up on
rules that he never let his child have any fun.

After coming up for air, Zachary darted uneasy glances
at the people milling around the burgundy and gold lobby,
his expression reflecting a deep-rooted anxiety that would
subside only with time. Despite the advice of the child's
therapist, insisting on this visit to the theater had gone
against all Joe's instincts as a parent. What was so wrong
with letting the kid do things like this at his own pace?

"It's all right, son," Joe whispered. "Those people are just waiting in line to get food before they go in to watch the movie. I'm right here, and I always will be from now on."

Joe had fought long and hard to be able to say those words, and it felt damned good. So good, in fact, that he wanted to shout them to the world. His ex-wife Valerie would never get her hands on his son again. *Never.*

Joe smoothed Zachary's tousled hair, his gaze fixed on the small downturned face that everyone claimed so closely resembled his own. Aside from the Indian-dark complexion he and Zachary shared, compliments of their Sioux ancestry, Joe couldn't really see much resemblance. He supposed that could be due, in part, to the fact that he had spent nearly half of his thirty-one years playing football, breaking his nose a total of four times before a knee injury forced him to retire.

In all honesty, though, he couldn't remember ever having been that cute. Zachary's features were almost perfect, his mouth shaped in a classic bow with a generous lower lip, his high-bridged nose straight as a ruler. Just looking at him gave Joe a warm, achy feeling in the center of his chest.

"Don't overdo it," he cautioned, as he watched his son drink. "Remember what happened last time."

Zachary straightened and wrinkled his nose. "I won't do *that* again, Daddy. I'm a big boy now!"

"I know you are, but even us older guys can still have accidents. Let's not end our evening on a wet note." Joe gave the top of his son's head a playful knuckle rub. "Tonight's special, remember?"

" 'Cause the judge signed our paper today."

"That's right. A very *important* paper. From here on out, you and I are a team."

"For always and always?"

"You got it."

"You gonna be my 'fensive co'rdinator?"

Since visiting the practice field, Zachary had become

enthralled with every aspect of Joe's job as special coach for the San Milagros Bullets. As flattering as it was, Joe hoped his son's fascination with football didn't develop into a lifelong obsession. It was a physically taxing profession, for one thing, the injuries sustained on the field often permanent and debilitating. The sport could also be emotionally brutal, especially if fame and fortune came too easily to a young man unprepared to deal with it. Thirty-one years old, with a bad marriage behind him and inches away from bankruptcy, Joe had experienced the downside of stardom. He wanted more than that for his kid. A lot more, namely a life filled with things that endured and truly mattered.

"I'd like that," he replied huskily, thinking that most good fathers probably wanted to be an offensive coordinator of sorts, standing on the sidelines of life and offering sage advice before their kids went into the huddle.

He drew a folded black ball cap from the pocket of his blue windbreaker. After slapping the wrinkles out against his thigh, he put the cap on, tipping the bill low over his eyes to partially conceal his face as he bumped the door handle with his hip.

"You ready to scramble?"

Zachary grinned. "Ready!"

Cool night air washed over them as Joe pushed outside. Two teenagers stood off to the left, the girl a slender blonde, the young man dark with an athletic build. Arms locked, they studied a poster advertisement of an upcoming attraction and whispered softly, seemingly aware of only each other.

For a frozen moment, Joe felt the years fall away, and he could almost believe he was seeing himself and Marilee, his first love, a decade ago. There was something about the girl—the tilt of her head—or maybe the way her golden hair lifted in the breeze—that called to mind moments he'd worked hard to forget.

Joe seldom allowed himself to think of Marilee anymore, and he couldn't quite believe he was thinking of her now. Even more surprising was that the memories still hurt. God, how he had loved her . . .

Images of her moved through his mind, painted in such vivid strokes that he might have seen her only yesterday. Honey-blond hair, fathomless blue eyes, a smile so sweet it nearly broke his heart.

"Daddy?"

Joe jerked and refocused, feeling disoriented. His son was peering up at him with a perplexed frown, giving Joe cause to wonder how long he'd been standing there, staring off into space.

"I'm cold," Zachary complained.

It *was* chilly—par for the course in the Bay area in March. Gusts of wind molded Joe's open jacket to his torso, the coastal dampness cutting through the nylon. Zachary had been drinking ice-cold pop as well, which undoubtedly made it feel chillier to him than it actually was. Joe pulled the child close to him and quickly snapped the front of his small jacket.

"There you go. All better?"

Zachary shivered and eyed the soft drink askance. Joe smiled. "Let's just toss it." He moved toward a dome-topped trash receptacle near the island ticket booth. "When we get home, I'll make you some hot choc—"

Brilliant lights flashed in Joe's eyes. Harsh shouts and the unmistakable click of camera shutters erupted all around them. He heard the teenage girl squeal with fright.

"Daddy!" Zachary screamed, pressing closer to Joe's chest. *"Daddy!"*

Smashed between their bodies, the soft-drink cup popped its lid, and orange soda spurted over the front of Joe's shirt. The shock of icy coldness helped clear his head.

"It's all right, Zachary. It's just the press. Daddy's got you."

The child locked his arms around Joe's neck and emitted a thin wail of terror. Joe heard the theater doors slam closed and guessed that the two teenagers had escaped into the building. As his eyes adjusted to the stabbing brightness, he scanned the throng of advancing reporters.

"Mr. Lakota! We've learned that you were awarded sole custody of your child today. Would you care to comment?"

"Is it true you paid your ex-wife a substantial amount of money to get custody?" someone else yelled.

Condensation and spillage made the waxed cup slippery. Joe's fingers lost their grip, and the soft drink fell to the concrete. He felt the spray on the legs of his pants. One of the reporters stepped on an ice cube, slipped, and uttered a foul curse as he scrambled for footing.

Violent tremors coursed through Zachary's body. Joe considered escaping back into the theater. But, no—these bastards would just wait him out. Better to head for the car right now than to risk putting his kid through an experience like this twice.

Damn. Joe had done everything possible to avoid any run-ins with the press tonight, even going so far as to rent a vehicle, fearful that his own would be recognized. Now this. Couldn't a man take his son to see a movie without being hounded by reporters?

"Hey, guys," he tried. "Back off just a little. You're scaring my little boy. Let me get him in the car, and I'll be happy to answer your questions."

Ignoring the entreaty, the reporters continued to close in. All that mattered to them was getting their story, and if they drew a child's blood in the process, that was simply too bad.

Hunching his shoulders around Zachary to comfort him, Joe whispered, "It's all right, sprout. Just some newsmen. They won't hurt you."

"Is it true your ex-wife is doing drugs?" a man shouted.

A television reporter in the foreground shoved a microphone in Joe's face, carelessly thumping Zachary on the back of the head in the process. The child screamed. *Damn them.* He had to get his son out of here. Being frightened like this might be all it would take to push Zachary clear over the edge.

Between one breath and the next, Joe's temper reached the flash point. He shoved the mike away. "Get back and clear a path! I'm coming through."

The reporters didn't budge. In fact, it seemed to Joe they closed ranks against him. *Fine.* After five years of playing quarterback for the Bullets, he was no slouch when it came to breaking through a line.

Golden light from the overhead marquee and nearby street lamps illuminated the area. Joe's muscles snapped taut as he looked past the men to the silver Audi parked at the curb. He dived a hand into his trouser pocket for the keys.

"We've been informed by a reliable source that Valerie Lakota is addicted to alcohol and cocaine!" another newsman yelled. "Would you care to comment?"

Of course he didn't care to comment. Didn't they realize they were talking about his kid's mother? *Anything goes*—that was their motto. Well, he was about to give these dough-faced jackasses a taste of their own medicine. He just hoped his bum knee could take the punishment.

Much as he once had a football, he tucked his son under one arm, turning his opposite shoulder into the wall of bodies. Crouching low for balance and leverage, he burst forward, his aim to catch them off guard and run a scramble straight to the car.

The sheer force of his forward momentum, coupled with a hard-won surefootedness from years of colliding with larger players on the field, carried Joe out of the pocket, through the front line, and onto the sidewalk. He kept his gaze fixed on the door of the rental car. *Wham.* He scarcely felt the impact as he bulldozed his way on through.

A few feet shy of the automobile, his path was suddenly blocked by a stocky reporter in camel slacks and a white shirt. Peering at Joe through the lens of a flashing camera, the reporter cried, "Mr. Lakota, how much did you pay your ex-wife to—"

Joe slammed into the guy, knocking him sideways. He heard a thud of flesh and the clatter of equipment striking the cement. As he covered the remaining distance to the Audi, he jabbed at the remote-control keypad to unlock the driver's door.

"You son of a bitch, you broke my camera!"

The reporter leaped to his feet and made a wild lunge, trying to catch hold of Joe's arm. Missing his mark, the man grabbed Zachary's leg instead. The little boy bleated in fright. Joe wheeled and broke the man's hold with a sharp blow to his wrist. "Keep your hands off my kid!"

"To hell with your goddamned kid! What about my equipment?"

With one glance at the man's enraged face, Joe knew there was going to be trouble. His one thought was to get Zachary safely inside the car before anything happened. He sprinted the remaining distance to the curb. Just as he reached the door of the Audi, a hand clamped over his shoulder and jerked him to a halt. The key ring slipped from Joe's fingers, jangling as it bounced against the car and fell in the gutter.

Left with no alternative, Joe swung Zachary to the ground, placing the child between him and the car for protection. As he turned to confront the enraged reporter, beefy hands locked onto the front of his open jacket. "You're gonna pay for the damages. Got it, asshole? You can't go knockin' reporters down and get away with it! There are laws."

Joe might have pointed out that there were also laws to protect celebrities and their families from the press, but now wasn't the moment to debate the point. All he cared about was getting Zachary out of there. With a quick upward snap of his wrists, he broke the other man's grip and pushed him back a step.

"I'm warnin' you, mister, get out of my face. I've got a child with me, in case you haven't noticed. *Back off!*"

The reporter struck Joe's chest with the heels of both hands, putting enough force into the blow to knock the hat from Joe's head. Thrown off balance, Joe nearly staggered backward into Zachary.

That cut it.

Fierce protectiveness and a nearly mindless rage ignited within him. He doubled his fist and hammered the reporter's jaw with a right jab. Knocked off his feet, the man pitched backward, his tumble to the concrete broken only by the other newsmen who had pressed in behind him.

Ignoring the pain of barked knuckles, Joe turned and grabbed his child to thrust him inside the Audi. *The keys.* He bit back a curse as he bent to search the gutter. In a frenzy, Zachary clung to his neck, flinging his head and blocking Joe's vision. Finally Joe spotted the remote control keypad lying near a drainage grate.

As Joe bent to retrieve the keys, Zachary shrieked and cried, "Hurry, Daddy! I wanna go home! I wanna go home!"

As he opened the car door, Joe hugged his son more tightly. *Home.* Myriad images swept through his mind— of quiet tree-lined streets; of the city park on summer nights; of his mom in a floral-print housedress and apron, busily rolling out pie dough in her cheerful but dated kitchen. *Home.* The word meant far more to him than a second-floor apartment in the city, that was for sure.

"Please, Daddy? I wanna go!" Zachary cried. "They're gonna get us. Hurry! Please, Daddy? I wanna go. I wanna go!"

There was nowhere to go, no place to run. As long as they lived in San Milagros, occasional encounters with the press would be unavoidable.

Keeping his arms locked around his child, Joe slid in under the wheel, slammed and locked the doors, and then twisted onto his knees to put Zachary in safety restraints. The child refused to turn loose of Joe's neck. Both of them were shaking, Joe with anger, Zachary with terror.

"It's all right, sprout," he said, in as calm a voice as he could manage while he pried the child loose and buckled him in. "You're fine. I'm fine. It's going to be all right now." After turning back around, Joe jabbed the key into the ignition. "We're going home," he said, as the engine roared to life. "See? We're safe. The doors are locked. They can't hurt you."

A blinding light flared inside the car. Zachary flinched, his pale little face losing even more color as he stared at the reporter who had pressed close to the side of the Audi to take his picture through the glass.

"Hurry, Daddy! *Hurry!*"

Furious, Joe pulled the car out from the curb with a squeal of tires, refusing to brake for the reporters who leaped into his path. If the assholes got run over, that was their problem.

He was getting his kid out of this stinking hole of a town. Away from the madness. Away from all of it . . .

Home. Yearning hit Joe, fast and hard. Of all the places Joe could think of where he might take his son, Laurel Creek shone in his mind like a beacon in a storm. They could go there and be safe. Images filled his mind—of the slow, lazy pace; of the friendly, smiling faces. One person in particular stood out in his memory. *Marilee*, his one true love, the only woman he'd never been able to forget . . .

One

*J*t had been nearly a year since Marilee Nelson's last panic attack, and she honestly believed she'd never have another one.

Until she saw the football helmet.

As football helmets went, it was ordinary enough, gray and striped with crimson, the team colors of Laurel Creek High, her alma mater. Nothing very frightening about that. No, what struck terror into her was that the helmet lay in the back window of an unknown blue Honda with California plates that was parked in front of her garage.

That was enough to send Marilee straight past panic into full-blown hysteria.

After her car had rocked to a stop, she cut the engine and stared at that California plate until her eyes burned. *JOE*, it read. A very ordinary name. It was undoubtedly pure coincidence that some guy named Joe from California had parked his vehicle in her driveway. A kid working his way through college by selling magazine subscriptions, maybe. Or a census taker who'd wandered into the wrong state.

She might have convinced herself, only there was that helmet. Only one Joe from California would have Laurel Creek High football gear in his car. *Her* Joe. Six feet plus of muscular, lethal-edged male.

"Oh, God."

At the sound of her voice, her bloodhound Boo stirred awake from his nap on the passenger seat. Casting her a disgruntled, droopy-eyed look, he yawned and licked his nose.

"Don't look at me as if *I'm* a coward. You're the one who needs a Valium to get through an appointment with the vet."

Marilee dragged in a shaky breath, gulped, and tried to relax her body. *Slow, even breaths. Center your thoughts.* The routine came second nature to her now, and though sometimes ineffective, it worked this time to decelerate her heartbeat. Thank heaven. Having a panic attack at the mere sight of his car would be a dead give-away.

"This is silly. I mean . . . why be upset? He's moved home after ten years. So? We used to have a thing going. Big deal. After being back for almost two months, he's suddenly decided to drop by and say hello. *Why*, I have no idea. To make me miserable, maybe? Yeah, that works."

Boo whined, rested his massive head on his paws again, and closed his saggy red-rimmed eyes.

"Exactly. *Boring.* Like I care anymore." She dropped her keys in her purse. "I mean, really. I'm a self-sufficient twenty-eight-year-old in the dawn of an enlightened century. No matter how sticky the situation, I can handle it."

Gathering her courage, Marilee stepped from the car. All she had to do was take control and think up a really good lie to get rid of him.

Oh, God, why is he here?

Her hands shook as she walked around the car, opened the door, and rousted Boo from his nap. The hound groaned when she patted his broad, bony head. "Come on, you big chicken. For once, put that nose God gave you to good use. Sniff him out. Act vicious. Chase him away, and I'll feed you juicy top sirloin for dinner."

Boo grunted as he slid off the seat. Closing the door, Marilee turned to follow him, determined not to let this throw her. Everything had been going so well for her this last year. She'd be damned if she would let Joe waltz back into her life now and turn her world topsy-turvy.

No way. She had important things on her agenda for this afternoon. It mattered not a whit that it was only a huge pot of beef stew simmering on the stove. At precisely four-thirty, she had to put in the potatoes. *That* qualified as a pressing engagement, right? She'd simply act glad to see him again—*ha, ha*—and regretfully explain that he'd caught her at a bad time.

Situation handled.

Boo lumbered along in front of her, taking up most of the walkway with his rawboned frame, his loose skin rolling just above his protruding shoulder blades. At the Y in the concrete, he hung a left, taking the path that cut between the garage and house. Following on the canine's heels, she brushed nervously at the brown fur that clung to her white slacks and sleeveless pink cotton shell.

Oh, God. What was she doing? As if she cared how she looked. She absolutely would *not* suck it in. She puffed at her bangs to get the frizzy blond-streaked brown curls out of her eyes. Joe Lakota was the last man on earth she wanted to impress. He was dangerous to her well-being, and if she forgot that, even for a second, she'd find herself nose to nose with more trouble than she could handle, about two hundred twenty pounds of it.

Halfway to the house, Boo stumbled to a stop, his stance wary as he snuffled the air. Marilee saw Joe sitting on the side porch. Leaning forward at the waist with one leg bent and the other extended, he was massaging his knee.

Even from a distance, he was gorgeous—*if* you went

for bronze skin, tousled sable hair, and lots of muscle. He wore gray sweatpants and a matching athletic T-shirt with *Laurel Creek High School* printed in red block letters across the chest.

When he spotted her, he straightened. Like many canines, Boo was slightly myopic and evidently couldn't see Joe until he moved. Marilee might have laughed at the dog's reaction if she hadn't been so dismayed by their unexpected visitor herself. Boo's demeanor said, *"Holy smokes! An intruder?"* Almost instantly, long strings of white drool began to stream from the hound's floppy jowls.

"Hi there!" Joe called, his tone friendly and not at all threatening. Unfortunately, he looked dangerously capable of leaping to his feet at any given moment to twist a slightly overweight bloodhound into pretzel shapes.

Boo's big body snapped taut, all four paws parted company with the concrete, and he gave a soft *"Whoof!"* He failed to be a creature of dauntless courage, a trait made more obvious when he went into reverse and his rump collided with Marilee's leg.

Marilee had a good notion to run herself. That silky baritone had haunted her dreams for a decade. The blood rushed from her head, and little black spots danced before her eyes.

It was a ridiculous reaction. As long as she kept her distance, Joe Lakota posed no threat. As potent as his dark good looks might be, they no longer had any effect on her.

Well, maybe some effect. She wasn't dead, after all. His searing gaze made her skin tingle.

Barking nonstop, Boo shifted his get-along into attack mode, which for him was somewhere between a slow walk and a series of sudden stops, designed, Marilee felt sure, to be certain she was still behind him.

"It's all right, Boo," she said, bending forward as she walked to keep a comforting hand first on the dog's haunch, then on his spine, then on his shoulder, and last on his head as he fell farther and farther back to let her take the lead. *Dratted dog.*

"Let me guess. You got him for protection, right?"

Marilee forced a smile—one of those awful stiff ones that made her face feel as if it were smeared with egg white. So . . . this was how it would go. Both of them pretending that seeing each other again was the most natural thing in the world. Well, two could play that game.

"No insults, please. He's already had an upsetting afternoon at the vet's, and he's doped to the gills with Valium."

"Valium? Is *that* what's wrong with him?" Joe leaned forward, peered at the hound's droopy face, and then extended a hand that looked nearly as big as a dinner plate. "Come here, Boo. Why do I have a feeling the name suits you?"

Boo nearly knocked Marilee over, trying to escape being touched.

Joe chuckled. "Come on," he encouraged. "I like dogs. Ah, there, see?" he said as Boo sniffed his fingers. "I'm a good guy."

"He doesn't seem to realize the world is full of strangers. Except for visits from my family, we don't get a lot of company."

Boo inched forward to get another whiff of Joe's hand. Evidently the scent reassured him. He relaxed marginally and stepped closer to let their visitor scratch his ears. *Traitorous, worthless mutt.*

Marilee wondered yet again why on earth Joe had come over to her house. She only knew she wished he hadn't.

When he looked up at her, she pasted on another smile. "This is a nice surprise."

"I can tell you're thrilled." He stood up. "I hope you don't mind that I waited for you here. It's hotter than blazes out front."

Her memories and the newspaper photos hadn't done him justice. Why that surprised her, she couldn't say. Joe had always been so handsome he almost hurt the eyes, and the years had only enhanced his looks, lending character and definition to an already striking countenance.

Aside from the barely noticeable way he favored his right leg, his big, powerful body moved with easy grace, the play of his shoulder muscles visible under the gray cotton, the flex of his thighs stretching the legs of his sweatpants taut. Patches of shade and sunlight dappled his face, the flickering illumination accentuating the bladelike bridge of his nose and the muscular line of his square jaw. He looked alert and—aggressive.

Stop it, Marilee. Just stop it. Joe was one of the nicest people she'd ever known. On the tail of that thought, she found herself remembering the newspaper story she'd read about him back in March, claiming he'd struck a reporter and broken his jaw. She hadn't seen Joe in ten years. Since then he'd made it to the top in a brutal professional sport. He had been sweet and gentle once, but what was to say that he still was?

She frantically tried to remember the excuse she'd fabricated to get him out of here. One word hung in her brain, "agenda." Boo plopped down on the cool cement, releasing a sigh of unmistakable relief that he hadn't been called upon to protect her.

Joe shook his head. "I can see why you didn't name him Killer."

He settled his hands at his hips and cocked his right knee, the athletic stance displaying his rock-hard muscle. On another individual, the pose might have been for macho effect, but she suspected Joe was simply shifting his weight onto his good leg. Three years ago, a sack on the twenty-yard line had injured his right knee. According to her brother-in-law, Ron Palmer, who was also Joe's life-long friend, two surgeries and months of rehab had failed to repair all the damage. Joe wasn't crippled, but a man with less grit and determination might have been.

He plucked at his shirt. "Sorry about the threads. I didn't go home to change before I came over."

She realized she'd been staring. "Oh, no! I wasn't— you look fine, honestly. I, um—it's just—I'm surprised to see you. Pleasantly surprised, of course."

His dark gaze twinkled as it came to rest on her face. They stared at each other. For the intervening seconds, the years fell away, and she felt eighteen again. Just looking at him made old feelings surface from someplace deep within her and ripple outward to suffuse her whole body. Gladness, sorrow, wistful yearning—and a wariness that clenched her stomach.

He finally broke eye contact by glancing at Boo again. "The lowdown. How on earth did you tie up with a hound?"

The dog had already settled down for a nap and looked so silly that he did make for a great ice breaker. "I rescued him from death row." She decided he would think it strange if she remained standing such a distance away, so she moved closer to the steps. "He belonged to a man who raises and trains hunting dogs. Poor Boo didn't take a shine to tracking."

"Poor Boo was probably afraid he might tree something dangerous—like a squirrel. Is he always so aggressive?"

Sliding the strap from her shoulder, Marilee set her purse on the edge of the deck and bent to stroke Boo's ear. "The drugs lend him a little courage, actually." *Poor baby. Cowardice was a terrible cross to bear.* "He would have been put to sleep if I hadn't adopted him. Not everyone cares for hounds. Aesthetically speaking, they're rather—unique."

"You think they're gorgeous, of course."

Marilee forced another stiff smile. "I think he's so homely he's cute."

Responding to her touch, Boo stretched his spine, let loose with a rumbling snore, sighed in contentment, and farted. Marilee quickly straightened to avoid the blast.

"I think you went overboard with the Valium. He's one notch up from comatose." He arched a dark brow, stepped up onto her deck to avoid the odor, and turned to thrust out a hand. "Get on up here before you get asphyxiated."

She ignored his outstretched palm and climbed the steps, bending as she gained high ground to retrieve her bag. "You've just been treated to the reason we went to the vet. Diagnosis, nervous stomach." She patted her bulging handbag. "I got some drops to cure the problem."

He rubbed beside his nose. "We can hope."

"So . . . to what do I owe the honor of this visit?"

"Just wanted to stop by. Say hello. Do some catching up."

She glanced at her watch, thankful that her brain had finally kicked into gear. "Gosh, I feel so bad about this, Joe, but you've caught me at a bad time. I wish you'd called to let me know you were coming."

"Why? So you could conveniently be gone?"

He had her number. "Don't be silly. I'd dearly love to chat with you. It's simply that I have a pressing engagement."

"Come on, Mari. For old time's sake. Do you think it was easy for me to come over here? The least you can do is offer an old friend something cold to drink. I won't stay all that long."

He made her feel small. If he'd been dreading this encounter as much as she had, it probably hadn't been easy for him to come. "I, um . . . " She grabbed for a calming breath. "I suppose I can spare a couple of minutes. How about some iced tea?"

"I'd love some."

"Grab a seat." She gestured toward the sturdy white deck chairs. "I'll only be a minute."

She unlocked the French doors. As she entered the kitchen, Joe trailed in behind her. She'd meant for him to remain outside. Striving to hide her uneasiness, she set her purse on the oval oak table.

"Where's your little boy?" She wiped her clammy palms on her slacks. "My sister called last night after having you over for dinner. Gerry says he's the spitting image of you."

"Nah. He's much better looking."

"Zachary, isn't it?" As if she didn't know. The child's name was one she would never forget, for reasons she didn't care to remember. "Gerry says he's four?"

"Four and a *half*. Forget to tack that on, and he's deeply offended. He's still over at my mom's. I swung by here before going to pick him up."

"Oh. Next time, I'd love for you to bring him along." Not that there would be a next time if she had anything to say about it. "I'd enjoy meeting him."

"He's pretty shy with strangers."

Marilee had heard as much from her sister. "I understand he's been through a rough time?"

"You could say that. His mom's a mess."

She knew about that as well. "I'm sorry."

"Yeah, well, marriage on the rebound. I had my head up my—" He broke off and cleared his throat. "Valerie just isn't cut out for motherhood."

She avoided looking at him. "Some women aren't, I guess. Gerry says you moved back because of your son?"

"Small-town atmosphere, no reporters or fans to hound me. I couldn't stand life in the limelight anymore. Here in Laurel Creek, I'm just Joe, a homegrown boy who had a knack for throwing a spiral." He shrugged. "That makes it easier for Zachary."

"Well, I hope it works out for you here." *Liar, liar, pants on fire*.

She fetched two glasses from the cupboard, then poured and served the iced tea. Her big, country kitchen didn't seem all that roomy with him standing in it. Even worse, he leaned a shoulder against the end cupboard, boxing her into the U-shaped work area. His dark gaze swept over the gleaming oak, then took in the crisp blue Priscilla curtains, her collection of ceramic farm animals that brightened every available spot on the ivory-tile counter, and the hand-braided rag rugs that she'd made last winter.

"Still an incurable animal lover, I see," he observed dryly.

"Dyed-in-the-wool. You know exactly where you stand with animals."

He chuckled. "Which, with certain species, means you're the entrée."

"True, but at least they're up front about it. With man, it's a guessing game, isn't it?"

"Speaking from experience?"

What did he mean? Sweat beaded on the nape of her neck. That had always been the way of it with Joe. He knew her too well and made her feel as easy to read as block print. All the more reason for her to stay away from him.

"I like your place. It has a homey, welcoming feeling."

"Thank you. I've been very happy here. Do you take sugar?"

"No, thanks. Just stick your finger in it."

Startled by his reply, she glanced over her shoulder to find him watching her. His firm mouth twitched with suppressed humor, his eyes gleaming with appreciation as they moved lazily to her face.

"You're looking great. I was praying you'd be fat and ugly by now, with a couple of big warts tossed in for good measure. There is no God in heaven."

Fat and ugly? Why on earth had he been hoping that? Because he still had feelings for her. The thought scared her half to death.

"You're looking pretty good yourself." And she hated him for it. At thirty-one, the least he might have done was develop a bit of a paunch. Perhaps she could suggest he come back in another ten years. Give them both a chance to deteriorate physically just a little more.

Her throat burned. He pushed away from the wall and sauntered toward her, his gaze never leaving hers. With every step he took, her legs felt a little weaker. She couldn't handle it if he touched her, and she feared that was exactly what he meant to do.

When he drew to a stop, she felt as if he were standing almost on top of her and hogging most of the available oxygen. The scent of him surrounded her—a not unpleasant blend of sun-dried cotton, spicy aftershave, freshly cut field grass, and clean, male sweat that filled her mind with chilling memories. The heat radiating from his big frame penetrated her knit top and linen slacks, warming her skin, making her head reel, and causing her breath to hitch.

Even breaths. In and out. Concentrate on the conversation. Don't let yourself think about anything else.

The twitch of humor at the corners of his mouth slowly became a full-fledged grin. That was another thing about him she remembered with painful clarity, the lazy way he smiled. His eyes always started to twinkle first. Then his dimple winked as that devastating grin took hold. It had never failed to make her knees feel weak, and it didn't now. The only differences she could detect were that his mouth had grown firmer, the twist of his lips had become a little cynical, and the dimple had chiseled a permanent crease.

Seeing the changes in him hurt, for each represented the thousands of days and nights since they'd seen each other last. They had both once believed that nothing on earth could keep them apart. Unfortunately, Marilee had learned the hard way that a whole life could turn in the blink of an eye, changing everything and every plan.

He reached past her to pick up one of the glasses, his arm lightly grazing hers. Then, with her still trapped between him and the counter, he took a long drink. She stared at his throat, watching his larynx bob and the muscles work. The tea was nearly gone when he came up for air.

"Ah," he said softly as he licked his lips, "that hits the spot."

"More?"

"A gentleman wouldn't show up uninvited and drink all your tea." He held out the glass. "But, then, when did I ever claim to be a gentleman?"

"It only takes a second to make more." She lifted the pitcher to refill his glass. Her hand was shaking so badly that she slopped some of the liquid. "Oops. Sorry about that."

"No problem." He switched the glass to his other hand and wiped his wet fingers on his pants. "It's so hot out there today, you could dump the whole works on me, and I wouldn't complain."

To her relief he moved to the table, where he leafed through the rough sketches she'd been working on for a children's book she was writing. "A posy with a face and long eyelashes?" he said with a chuckle.

"It's supposed to be a pansy."

"Don't be offended. The closest I come to flowers is when I call in an order."

For one of his many lady friends, no doubt.

"Who's the little guy with the sad face?"

"His name is Blue. He's the only pansy of that color in the garden, and he's an outcast, the moral of the story being that our color isn't important. In the end, scorned by the others though he has been, he saves the entire flower garden from destruction because he's a rare subspecies."

He smiled thoughtfully, then went to stand before her curio, bending to study the framed photographs and snapshots that took up two of the glass shelves. "Ah, I remember that day. The whitewater races at the city park."

If she'd known he was coming, she would have hidden all the pictures of him. She remembered every detail of that afternoon, and they'd spent very little time watching boat races. Joe had taken her under the bridge, spread a blanket, and tutored her in the fine art of French kissing, which she'd found utterly disgusting—for all of about three seconds.

"The races are still an annual event here the last part of August," she told him.

"Really?" He sent her a mischievous glance. "Maybe we should take a stroll down memory lane and go together this year."

"I have to help Gerry corral kids these days. You'd be bored to tears."

"I seriously doubt that. Not with seven kids running every which way. Seeing Ron again made me almost glad I never married you and became a Catholic."

She carried her tea out to the deck and went to stand at the railing, one arm hugging her waist, her glass clasped in her other hand. When he joined her, he stood so close the fine hair on her bare arm tingled. She inched away to give herself the buffer zone she needed and then tried to block him out, to concentrate on the birds singing, on Boo's snoring, on the ice chinking in their glasses. Joe Lakota was difficult to ignore.

She soothed her throat with a sip of tea. He turned his dark head, bringing his face so close she could see the pores of his burnished skin, the strands of his long, sable lashes, and the flecks of gold in his brown eyes. Her gaze shifted to his mouth, and she resisted an urge to move farther away.

"I'm sorry for barging in on you like this, but I needed to get this first meeting over with. Living in the same small town, we're bound to bump into each other. I don't know about you, but I've been dreading it."

"Flattery will get you nowhere."

"You know what I mean. We didn't part company under the best of terms." A sheepish expression came over his dark features. "I'm ashamed to admit it, but I hid out at first, hoping to avoid you. That seemed ridiculous after a while. It got so I was paranoid every time I saw a blonde. When I almost hunkered down at the supermarket to hide behind the oranges, I knew I had to come face you."

Marilee couldn't help but giggle at the image his words

conjured. Joe Lakota, cowering behind the oranges? It helped somehow, knowing he felt nervous, too. "I nearly rammed a parked car the other day when I thought I saw you crossing the street. I know the feeling."

He sighed and glanced at her hair. "The color has changed. That's scary. I was watching for pure blond, and you've got streaks. We would've been nose to nose before I recognized you."

She fingered a frizzy curl at her temple. "It started to turn brown as I grew older, and Mother Nature went on hiatus before completing the job. I wound up with the present mess."

"Same old Marilee, putting yourself down. Some women pay a fortune to streak their hair with blond like that. It's beautiful."

"Yeah?"

"Yeah," he assured her warmly. "You really don't realize, do you?"

"Realize what?"

The breeze picked up, and he pushed at a lock of hair that trailed across his forehead. "How pretty you are."

"Oh, please."

"Hey, you've got to know I wouldn't pay you a compliment just to make you feel good."

She laughed again, aware as she did that some of the tension had eased from her shoulders. "Thank you. I think."

"Hey, I'm being brutally honest here. I resent the hell out of you, honey, but that doesn't mean I'm stone blind."

"Thank you," she said again.

"Some people just have a special glow," he went on. "You look at them, and they just—I don't know how to describe it, but you feel the sweetness in them. It's almost like a hug. Have you ever experienced that?"

"Yes, with Aunt Luce."

"*Aunt Luce?*" He threw back his head and barked with laughter. When his mirth subsided, he wiped under one eye and said, "Oh, God, I'm sorry. She's a sweetheart, really. It's just—" He gave in to laughter again. "She's such a corker! Does she still tint her hair outlandish colors?"

"Pink, last count. And she's into earrings that twinkle now. Little lights powered by watch batteries. She looks like an alien that just landed. A very sweet one, though. Whenever I need someone to love me no matter what, I go to Aunt Luce. She doesn't pass judgment, you know?"

"What have you ever done—*aside* from breaking my heart, of course—that anyone could pass judgment on?"

If only he knew. "We all mess up, Joe."

"Like I said, I resent the hell out of you, honey. But I still think you're as close to perfect as anyone can get."

"Don't be absurd." More of her tension eased away. Why that surprised her, she didn't know. That was the most treacherous thing about Joe, his ability to work past her defenses. "I'm the girl who split your head open. Remember? Got mad and pushed you off the high dive."

"It was my own fault I hit the cement."

She gave a startled laugh. "Good grief! You always did make excuses for me."

"Well, it's true. I twisted in midair to catch myself. Besides, I untied your swimsuit top and had it coming."

"I was a *brat*. Eleven years old and flat as a board. If I'd been older, with something to hide, it might've been understandable."

He swirled his glass, making the ice chatter. "Girls that age are painfully modest. *I* was the brat. Somehow, I just couldn't resist teasing you."

Marilee smiled nostalgically as the sweet memories curled around her. "You did go through an ornery stage."

"I was flirting with you. You were still too naïve to appreciate my efforts."

"Oh, go on. Not way back *then*. I was way too young."

"And what was I, Methuselah?" He shook his head. "I always loved you. You know that. Just last night, I was lying awake, trying to remember when I first caught the fatal disease. I think you were about five and I was eight."

Somehow they had ventured onto dangerous ground. But, then, wasn't all ground dangerous with Joe? Nevertheless, she couldn't resist saying, "As I recall, you had a hot thing going with Jane Ellen Rawls when I was eleven. And what about Beth Patterson and Suzy Fischer?"

"I never messed with Suzy Fischer, and the other two were just test runs."

"You sure did a lot of testing."

He winked at her as he took another sip of tea. "I had to get my technique perfected so I wouldn't blow it with you."

Definitely dangerous ground. He'd never gotten to try his technique on her. *If only.* She might have been okay then, better able to cope and put things into perspective. Ah, but there was the heartbreak. Life had thrown them a curve ball.

Marilee took a quick drink of tea, her movements so jerky she spilled some down her front. It was ice cold and made her gasp. She grabbed the neckline of her top to hold the wetness away from her skin. Joe's gaze dropped like a rock. She flattened her hand over her chest. They stared at each other.

She looked away first. "So why . . . you just came by to talk?"

"Yeah, just to talk. Mainly to clear the air." His expression grew thoughtful. "I can't hate you anymore, Mari. It's time to turn loose of it, put the hurt behind me. I said some terrible things to you that night. I didn't mean any of them. I just wanted to hurt you as badly as you were hurting me."

A searing sensation washed over her eyes. She really didn't want to get into this. On the other hand, perhaps he was right. Maybe they'd both feel better if they buried their ghosts together. "I'm so sorry, Joe. You're the last person on earth I ever wanted to hurt. Please know that."

He nodded, but said nothing. She had a feeling he had a lump in his throat just as she did, and that he couldn't speak. Quiet fell between them. The smells on the air reminded her of lazy summer days long since past.

When he finally broke the silence, he said, "Yesterday when I went over to Ron's, we did a lot of catching up. He mentioned that you didn't finish college. It seems such a shame you never got your degree. As far back as I can recall, you wanted to be a teacher."

"Yes, well . . . writing for children is a form of teaching."

"The sketches on the table are wonderful. You have an affinity for children and really feel passionate about reaching them, don't you?"

"Yes. I love my work."

"I'm glad. It must have been an agonizing decision to quit college."

Her stomach knotted. Dangerous ground again.

He set his nearly empty glass on the railing and rubbed his palms together. "How long did it take you to reach the decision?"

"Gosh, I don't know. A while." That much wasn't a lie. Anything from an hour to a year could be termed a while.

"The last time we talked you were still hot to get your credentials."

"Yes, well, as time wore on, my enthusiasm waned. The classes bored me. Psychology, and all that. I realized teaching wasn't for me."

"It took you a while to realize, then? Did you finish out the year?"

He'd left her no room to sidestep this question. She either had to lie or tell him the truth. She hugged her waist more tightly with the one arm, remembering the time they'd slashed their palms, mingled their blood, and made an eternal pact to be best friends forever. Friends didn't lie to each other. She turned her glass to stare pensively at the ice as it caught the sunlight. The girl who'd made that vow was dead.

"I finally quit during my spring term. I never went back after the break."

He fell silent for an interminable time. Then he said, "I took a little psychology myself."

"Oh? And did you like it?"

"I learned a lot. Did you ever study body language?"

"No."

"I didn't think so. You'd know better than to assume a defensive posture so much of the time."

"A defensive posture?"

"Hugging yourself like that. It says, 'Don't touch me.'"

She drew her arm from around her waist and clenched both hands on the glass, overlapping her fingers at the far side.

"Trying to compose yourself, Marilee?" He gestured at the glass. "Clasped hands. A subconscious attempt to hold yourself together."

She moved back a bit from the railing.

He turned to watch her and smiled. "Now the chin comes up. Classic."

Her pulse picked up speed. She set her glass beside his and wiped her palms on her slacks. "Classic what?"

"Defiance. You're starting to feel angry, and you'd like to tell me where to stuff it. Politeness—or possibly good sense—or maybe a bit of both, prevents you from going quite that far, so you're saying it with the angle of your head." He studied her for a moment. "You don't carry it off very well. That look in your eyes ruins the whole effect. Mixed messages." He smiled again. "Never give a man mixed messages, sweetheart. It'll get you in trouble."

"I don't care for your tone. Perhaps we should end this discussion."

"Not a chance."

"You're not making sense."

"Sure I am. And you know it."

A glint appeared in his eyes. "Do you really think you can lie to me? Think again. I know you too well."

"I haven't lied to you."

Marilee didn't like the way he was looking at her. She glanced at her watch. "Oh, my gosh, it's nearly four-thirty! I need to get the potatoes in the stew. Gerry's feeling under the weather today, and at eight-and-a-half months along, that's a worry. I'm taking the stew over to them for dinner."

He chuckled, the sound deep, silky, and dangerous. "You aren't going to avoid this conversation."

She locked gazes with him. Retreated a step. "I don't know where this is coming from, Joe, but I don't like it."

"Seeing that fear in your eyes is no picnic for me, either." He looked coiled and ready to spring. "Can you explain that to me, Marilee? Name me one thing I've ever done to make you feel afraid of me."

"Don't be absurd. I'm not afraid of you. You've implied that I'm lying to you, and I don't appreciate it!" She hugged her waist again, this time with both arms. "And I am *not* afraid of you. I've known you since I was little. I—I would trust you with my life!"

"Prove it," he said with a smile that looked nearly as lethal as his laugh had sounded. "Step over here and kiss me."

"*What?*"

"It's not like you never have before. We've kissed each other dozens—hell, probably *hundreds* of times. Back when we were dating, kissing was as far as we could go, remember? We got so creative, I can't think why you look appalled now." He crooked a finger at her. "Come on."

"I—I think it's about time for you to leave."

"Like I did ten years ago? Sorry, honey. I'm not reeling with shock this time around. I'm thinking with my head, not my heart, and I've got the blinders off."

He continued to advance on her, his movements slow and measured.

"Remember when we were kids," he said softly, "and they told us honesty is always the best policy? It definitely would be in this case. The truth, Marilee. So simple and easy. You owe me that much. Don't you think?"

"Don't threaten me."

He advanced another step. "I never make empty threats. You know that."

"Don't do this," she whispered. "We were making a nice fresh start. I was even hoping that maybe we could be friends again. Now you're acting ugly. Why can't you just accept and turn loose of it?"

"Accept what? That you stopped loving me?"

"Yes!"

"And how long did you agonize over that decision? Was it like your decision to drop out of school? A revelation that came to you overnight?"

"I didn't decide about school overnight. I told you, it was something I realized over time, that—"

"You're lying." He advanced another step. Her feet felt as if they'd become glued to the deck. He lashed out a hand and caught her by the wrist. "Yesterday, Ron told me how it really went, Marilee. That you quit school abruptly. Came home. Stayed in your room. Wouldn't eat. Wouldn't talk. Lost so much weight your folks were worried sick. Everyone believed it was *my* fault, that I was the world's biggest jerk and had dumped you. And you *let* them believe that. Never said a word to set anyone straight, not once in all these years. *Why?*"

She tried to speak, couldn't. *Oh, God, oh, God . . .* she gulped for breath.

"I wouldn't mind so much if it they'd been people I didn't like. But Ron is my best friend, Gerry like a sister to me. And you knew how much I respected your folks." He laughed bitterly. "Ron acted strange for—God, it must have been three or four years. I thought he felt bad because you dumped me. But the truth is, he was pissed at *me* for jilting you. You almost ruined a lifelong friendship. Can you explain that to me? Or justify it? Name me one reason I deserved that?"

Tears sprang to her eyes, and she shook her head.

"Me neither," he said, his voice pitched barely above a whisper. "And you know what else? It's out of character for you to be that cruel. In fact, out of all the people I know, you're the last person I'd ever expect to do me dirty. The very *last* person I'd suspect of lying, that's for sure. You simply don't have it in you. Yet, by your silence, you allowed people I loved to think the worst of me, and you stood there just now and told me a bald-faced, out-and-out lie. Why? Something tells me that when I learn the answer to that question, everything else will fall into place as well."

"I never meant for anyone to think badly of you!" she finally managed to say. "I swear it, Joe. No one ever said a word about it to me. I didn't know Ron was mad at you. Honestly, I didn't."

"I believe you," he assured her. "You know why? I think you were so focused on something else that you never really stopped to think what your silence might lead people to think about me. All that mattered—all that was on your mind—was keeping them from guessing the truth about you—the *real* reason you quit school and came home to hide. Isn't that right?"

Marilee felt as if she might faint.

"I think that's the same reason you just lied to me, because if you tell me too much, I might start putting things together and guess the truth."

"I—I don't know what you mean. And besides, what earthly business is it of yours?"

He just kept talking as though he hadn't heard her. "So, you quit school. What's the big deal? Lots of people quit school. Why would you want to keep me in the dark about *when*? What would knowing tell me?"

She felt the blood drain from her head. He *knew*. The knowledge was written all over his face. She didn't know how, but somehow he knew.

Two

"Joe, please. Don't do this." Marilee had experienced too many panic attacks not to recognize the warning signs. She twisted helplessly, trying to break his hold. "Let me go. I mean it."

Though his grip inflicted no pain, it was relentless.

"What would knowing the truth tell me?" he asked again. "All last night, I thought about it, circled it, took it apart and put it back together. Why would Marilee not want me to know she quit school the Monday morning directly following our breakup?"

"It happened a decade ago. What difference does it make now?"

"If it makes no difference, why did you just lie to me about it?" He tapped his temple. "What about the other guy? The one you let me believe you dumped me for? From what I gathered talking to Ron, there was never another guy. Not before you broke up with me. Not after. *Never.* And if there was never another guy, why did you break my heart?"

Marilee had the awful feeling he already knew—or at

least suspected. "I mean it, Joe. I've had enough of this. It's time for you to go."

"There's a solution. If I leave, you won't have to deal with me."

"I don't have to deal with you now. You're making a big mistake if you think you can just waltz back into my life after ten years. I don't have to put up with this."

"Waltz? I didn't waltz out. I was *shoved*. Now I'm back and finding out that nothing, *nothing* was what it seemed to be back then. You lied to me that night, and you're lying to me now."

"So what?" she said, her breath coming in shallow pants. "I let you think there was another guy, and it turns out there wasn't. Big deal. I didn't love you. That was all that mattered then, and it's all that matters now."

"Is that the truth or another lie? Look at me when you say it." He caught her chin and forced her face up. "You *look* at me, dead in the eye, and then you say it. 'I don't love you, Joe.' "

Marilee felt as if she were caught in a plastic bubble. With every breath she drew, it pressed closer, leaving her with less and less oxygen. A surreal brightness limned everything, making it difficult to focus. She squeezed her eyes closed. "Joe, I don't love you!" she cried brokenly. She lifted her lashes and glared at him, her vision so affected now it was like trying to see him through heat waves. "Right now I *hate* you for doing this!" With a strength born of desperation, she tried to break away from him, but even with panic to lend her impetus, she was no match for him. His hand remained locked on her arm. "Go home. Just leave me alone." Afraid she might collapse right in front of him, she pressed her other fist to the center of her chest and grabbed for breath. "I don't want you here."

"I'm not leaving without answers."

"Do you think you're the only one who got hurt?"

"No, I don't think that," he whispered. "Not anymore."

A part of her knew she should say nothing more, but

he'd pushed her past caution. "When I watched you walk away, it *hurt*! And later when I heard about all the girls you dated, it *hurt*! And when you got married, it *hurt*, damn you! And when you had a baby?" Her voice went shrill, seeming to resound inside her head. "It was supposed to be *me* who had your babies! *Me*! How do you think I felt? 'Zachary James.' Did you think I wouldn't remember we chose that name *together*?"

Oh, God, she could barely think. Running her hand into her hair, she made a tight fist. "What's the point of this? Why go back over things ten years dead?"

"Because it isn't dead. Not for me. I still love you, damn it!"

Hearing him say that was the final little push to send her plummeting over the edge. The bubble had shrunk to the danger point. She felt like a hunk of meat that had been vacuum-packed, the film sucking tight over her mouth and nose every time she tried to draw breath. Spinning, spinning, the whole world was spinning. Air. She had to get some air.

"Mari? Are you all right?"

His voice sounded as if it came from a great distance. And for the life of her, she couldn't reply.

Joe had wanted desperately to get the truth out of her, and now he wished he hadn't. Her face had gone deathly pale and shiny with sweat. She stared fixedly at his chest as her own heaved violently. With slowly dawning horror, he realized she was having a problem breathing. He gripped her shoulders and stooped to peer at her waxen features.

"Mari?"

She flattened both hands on her breasts, her mouth open, her eyes filled with frantic urgency as she fought to drag in oxygen. Quick little panting intakes that didn't appear to reach her lungs. What was this, asthma? Or a severe anxiety attack, maybe? Sweet Lord in heaven. Her legs nearly buckled, and she looked as if she might collapse. She was suffocating right before his very eyes.

Acting purely on instinct, he stepped behind her and locked her in a hug, his arms around her waist, his mouth next to her ear.

"It's all right, Mari. I'm right here. Calm down. Slow, deep breaths. Just relax. Stop fighting it. Let your muscles relax."

She jerked when he curled a hand over her ribs. Then she flung her head back against his shoulder and struggled to free herself from his hold. Believing she might fall if he let go, he stayed with her as she shoved hard with her feet against the cedar, her legs pumping convulsively. He tried to blank his mind to the frenzy of her struggles, both against him and the betrayal of her own body. He just kept talking, losing track of what he said, his main goal to keep his tone soothing and get her to stop fighting to breathe.

She had to be getting at least some oxygen, he realized, as they moved in a macabre dance across the deck. If not, she would be unconscious by now. Even so, it seemed to him that every second lasted an eternity, and if it was like that for him, he could scarcely imagine how horrible it was for her.

At one point, she curled a hand over his wrist as though to push his hand from her midriff, but the lack of oxygen had robbed her of the strength. Nevertheless, it gave him cause to wonder. Had he caused this, maybe by grabbing her arm? He didn't want to believe that, couldn't believe that. No matter what had happened to her, they'd been friends most of their lives. He'd taught her to ride her first bike.

But what else might have brought it on? She'd been breathing all right before he grabbed her. A bit too rapidly, maybe, but nothing pronounced. Then he'd seized her wrist, and bang. *Idiot.* After talking with Ron yesterday, he'd had his suspicions. He should have heeded them and kept his distance. But, oh, no. He'd been so bent on digging the truth out of her, he hadn't stopped to think of the possible consequences.

He remembered the wary look he'd seen in her eyes when she spotted him on her deck, how she had fallen back a step every time he got a little too close. *Sweet Jesus*. She couldn't bear for him to touch her.

Twisting her in his arms and catching her behind the knees, he carried her to a chair and set her down. The instant he felt sure she wouldn't pitch off the seat, he released her and backed away a bit, still prepared to catch her, but allowing her the distance she so desperately needed.

He didn't know how long the attack lasted after that. When it finally subsided, she slumped over her knees, her mouth yawning as she dragged in huge, ragged breaths. Knowing he'd caused this, he could have wept.

"There's a girl," he whispered. "Just concentrate on breathing. Don't think about anything else. Let your lungs do their job. You're going to be all right now."

He braced a hand against the house, needing the support. *Oh, God*. He'd been so blind, so incredibly blind. *Do you think you're the only one who got hurt?* He'd seen the dismay cross her face as she said that and knew damned well she'd never meant to tell him.

"I'm sorry, Mari. So sorry. I never meant to make that happen."

She shuddered and rubbed her arms.

Taking care to keep his distance, he hunkered in front of her, his arms on his knees, his gaze riveted to her fragile cheekbones.

A crazy urge to laugh came over him. Suddenly it all seemed so clear. So brutally clear. The abrupt way she'd broken their engagement without any explanation. Even the way she'd kept her distance and hugged her waist that fateful night came back to haunt him now. *I don't love you anymore!* she'd cried. And he had believed her, turning his back on her the one time when she'd needed him the most. *I never want to see you again, Joe. It's over between us. Do you understand? It's over.*

"Oh, Mari." He searched her pinched expression for answers to questions he was almost afraid to ask. "Why didn't you tell me?"

Her lips parted as if to speak, but no sound came forth. She swallowed. Her lashes fluttered. "I just couldn't, Joe. That was right after it happened, and I was—" She licked her lips and shrugged. "Some things you just can't share, not with anyone."

A part of him had been hoping she might say he was wrong—that his guess was way off mark. But, no. He saw the truth of that written all over her face. He bent his head and watched the shadow play of his dangling hands on the deck, taking a moment to let it sink in. *Mari, his sweet, precious Mari.* For all the three years they'd dated, he'd driven her to religious education class every Wednesday evening. Every Saturday night before going out on a date with her, he'd parked his butt on a church pew, bored out of his mind for thirty minutes to an hour, depending on the line, while she went to confession. She'd been his Mari girl—young and sweet, with stars in her eyes, and he had toed the mark whenever he was with her, fiercely guarding her innocence.

To *think* that some creep had taken advantage of her— that the bastard had *dared* to put his hands on her—hazed his vision with rage. The shadows cast by his own hands on the deck knotted into fists.

"Who did this to you?" he whispered tautly. "I swear to God and all that's holy, I'll kill the son of a bitch."

She just sat there for a moment, staring blankly, her trembling fingers massaging her throat. When she finally looked up, her thick, luxurious brown lashes unveiled eyes so blue they struck a vivid contrast to her pallor. "What earthly good would that do?"

"It'd make me feel a hell of a lot better."

He bit down so hard on his back teeth that his jaw joint throbbed. He burned to put his fist through the side of the house, to take the deck apart in a wild rage. Poor substitutes. What he really wanted was to curl his hands around the son of a bitch's throat and slowly squeeze the life out of him.

She cupped her hands over the ends of the armrests. "I'd like for you to go now," she said tonelessly. "These spells leave me drained. It's been so long, I'd nearly forgotten how exhausted they make me feel."

"You've had a lot of them, I take it."

"None over the past year."

If that was subtle, he hated to see blunt. "I'm sorry, Mari. When I came over here, my aim was to get to the truth, not make you sick."

"I know."

"What are they, some kind of anxiety attack?"

"For want of a better term."

She flicked the tip of her tongue over her full bottom lip, making him recall the many times he'd done that himself. The sweet, heady taste of her was engraved on his memory tracks. She'd been an elegant little package back then, the kind of girl who filled a guy's head with thoughts of steamy sex and wedding bells because he knew damned well he couldn't have one without the other.

She was still elegant—so dainty and golden she took his breath. "I'll leave in a few minutes—as soon as I'm sure you're going to be okay."

"I'm fine," she assured him, a quiver in her voice belying the words. "All I need is to lie down. I'd like for you to go and leave me to it. Why can't you understand that?"

The urgency in her tone went a long way toward helping him understand. She looked cornered—her lovely eyes glistening like polished windows to a tortured soul and darting from side to side as if she sought a way to escape. In that moment, Joe knew she couldn't talk about this further, that if he pressed her or got too close to her, she might have another attack.

He pushed erect and backed away, this time nearly to

the deck rail. "If it's space you need, you've got it." He settled his hands on his hips. "See?"

She nodded even as she hauled in breaths a little too rapidly for his peace of mind.

"No more questions, no more crowding you, I promise. All that really matters to me is you. Once I'm sure you'll be okay, I'm out of here."

He didn't add that it would be only a temporary retreat. He still loved her; and she had as much as admitted she still loved him. He'd been granted two miracles in his life, one being his son, the other this woman, and he'd nearly lost both of them. He'd fought long and hard to regain custody of Zachary. Now he was faced with another kind of battle entirely, one that called for intricate planning and carefully executed strategy. No matter. She would be well worth the effort.

"While we're waiting, is it all right with you if I clear the air about a couple of things?"

Her expression conveyed weary resignation. "I guess."

"All these years, I thought I was the only one who got hurt," he said huskily. "Now I realize that I was more successful than I imagined all those times I did my damnedest to hurt you."

She said nothing, simply sat there, listening with a stony cast to her pale features.

Joe bent his head, digging at a deck board with the toe of his running shoe. "I wish now that I could undo it all, Mari, but I can't. The Almighty hands out very few erasers. All I can do is ask you to forgive me."

He sneaked a glance at her to see if she was paying attention. Her deadpan expression gave him no clue. The muscles in the back of his neck bunched and throbbed with tension. It wasn't easy to lower his guard and make himself vulnerable to her again.

He swallowed, his throat feeling as if a cruel fist was clenching his larynx. Fleetingly he wondered if this was how she felt when an attack was coming on.

"About all the other girls I slept with after you gave

me back the ring," he said. "None of them—not a single one—ever meant anything to me. I know that's a favorite line with men, damned near a cliché, and if you choose not to believe me, I can't really blame you. But it's the truth."

Silence.

"It sounds like you kept a diary on my love life," he went on. "With every entry, you should have included a footnote, that I still loved only you, and that I couldn't get you out of my head, no matter what I did."

Still nothing. She just sat there, staring at the deck, the warm breeze ruffling her sun-kissed curls. Joe had an unholy urge to grab her by the shoulders and give her a shake.

"For two years after we split, I got tears in my eyes every time I poured *milk* on my cereal. Two *years*, Mari." Okay, so it wasn't romantic. He had her attention, at least. She fixed a bewildered gaze on him. "You always sang, 'Snap, crackle, *pop!*' as you poured the milk. Remember?" He stepped slowly toward her. "After you ate, you always drank the milk left in your bowl." Still at arm's reach, he traced the delicate bow of her upper lip with a fingertip. "It gave you a mustache, just there. Every damned time I had cereal, I thought of that, and I missed you so bad it about killed me."

He withdrew his hand and sighed.

"The other thing you brought up that I've got to address is my son. The first time I realized how much he looked like me, I turned off the light and rocked him in the dark because tears were streaming down my face. You always said our first child would be a boy and that he'd be exactly like me. I remembered that every time I looked at him. That was *six years* after our breakup. Six! I was a married man. I had no business thinking about another woman, let alone crying over one. But to me, *you* were my one and only, the girl I'd loved all my life, the girl I'd always love, and, God forgive me, in my mind, Valerie was the interloper.

"I'd feel really guilty about that, but she didn't love me, either, so it made us even. I knew when she married me that she was mainly attracted by the big bucks and the flash of the cameras, a fact that became blatantly obvious when she bailed out after I blew my knee. But at the time, I hoped we could build a life together. We got along pretty well, and the sex was good, if not fantastic. I took a gamble, I lost, and my little boy paid for it. He's still paying for it, a fact that keeps me awake nights because I know I'm responsible for every tear he sheds."

"Oh, Joe . . ." Her gaze clung to his, and she caught her bottom lip between her teeth. "I guess I'm responsible for that, too."

"I didn't tell you all this to make you feel guilty. I just want you to understand that—"

"I know. But I do feel guilty, all the same. I've always known I hurt you. I just never thought past that to wonder about the impact of my actions on a little boy I've never met." She brushed at her cheeks. "I wish I could've written to you, explained, at least in part. But I just couldn't talk about it with anyone. Not even in a letter."

Joe sorted through what she'd just said. One point stuck in his mind, that she'd never talked to *anyone* about this. He could scarcely credit his ears.

She pushed unsteadily erect and then just stood there as if her feet had become disconnected from her brain. When she swayed slightly with dizziness, he held himself under tight restraint, not stepping forward to grasp her elbow as he yearned to do. A bird began to sing in her yard. She fixed her gaze on the tree where it was perched.

Watching her, Joe marked every breath she drew, every pulse beat in the hollow of her throat, and every fidgety movement of her slender hands. God, how he loved her. Slowly, the color began to return to her delicate cheekbones. He could almost see the strength flowing back into her limbs.

"Do you remember the time I used the sunless tanning

lotion a few hours before my junior prom?" she suddenly asked.

Where that had come from, he didn't know. He smiled slightly. "The time you applied it too heavily, didn't blend it in, stopped halfway up your neck, and forgot to wash your hands? Yeah, I vaguely remember something like that."

She continued to stare at the tree where the bird twittered so prettily. "My dress had spaghetti straps. I looked like a zebra."

"I always have loved zebras."

She ignored that. "I was so upset I cried until my eyes were almost swollen shut, and when you came to pick me up, I had red splotches all over my face."

"Beautiful splotches. They went well with the brown stripes."

She sighed. "I wore Mama's blue lace mantilla around my shoulders to hide the worst of it, and you pinned the ends together with my corsage. I knew I looked horrible, but you kissed the end of my nose and said, 'All fixed, Mari mine. You're the prettiest girl in three counties again.' "

"I thought you were. More importantly, I still do. You're beautiful, Mari. So beautiful. And I've never stopped loving you. I don't think I ever will." He swallowed and let his gaze trail away as he carefully chose his next words. "I know this isn't on the same plane as brown streaks and red splotches. We've both become adults, and our problems are a little more difficult to solve these days. But difficult doesn't equate to impossible, Mari. Not if we face those problems together. Years ago, we faced *everything* together. Remember? If we do that again, we can get past this. Not overnight, and maybe not easily, but together, we can do it. I know we can."

She turned the most beautiful eyes in the whole state on him, and in their depths, he saw how deeply she still loved him. Unfortunately he also saw hopelessness that ran so deep it frightened him. "You can't fix this, Joe," she said tremulously. "Not this time. You can't fix *me*. Oh, how I wish that you could."

With those parting words still ringing in his ears, she turned her back on him and disappeared into the house.

Three

*A*t three the next morning, Marilee was awakened from sleep by the nightmare that had haunted her for the last ten years. The dream, choreographed on the stage of her mind in slow motion and full color, seemed so chillingly real that it always left her in a state of sheer terror, and she knew from experience that the only way to shake it was to walk it off.

She knew the routine by heart. Beginning in her bedroom, she invariably turned right as she exited the doorway to check the other three bedrooms up the hall and then the front door. U-turn. Back along the hallway to the living room, then into the adjoining family room. From there, she walked back through the main part of the house to the kitchen, nearly jumping out of her skin every time the floor creaked.

All secure. Every sliding window was latched and braced closed with a length of wood. Except for the new French doors, which had no extra security latch as yet, every door was double locked, its deadbolt engaged.

Limp with relief, her body clammy, she stood in the middle of the kitchen. *Safe.* Just a bad dream. Her little world remained inviolate.

With a sleep-blurred gaze, she caressed the familiar, much-loved things she'd placed around the kitchen. Her grandmother's cookie jar—a plump piglet in a sprigged pinafore—the family of ceramic ducks that paraded across the floor. Familiar things. Good memories. It had only been a dream, and she was safe.

With that thought still embracing her, she caught movement from the corner of her eye and whipped her head around to stare at the oversize broom closet beside the louvered doors that separated the utility room from the kitchen. Even as she watched, the already slightly ajar closet door inched farther open and—*oh, dear God*—she saw four fingers of a large, gloved hand ease out the opening.

A man . . . hiding in the closet. She stood a mere six feet away, trapped in the U-shaped work area of the kitchen with him between her and the rest of the house. After gauging the distance to the opposite end of the room and possible escape, she started moving in that direction. Before she could take two steps, the fingers reached farther out and curled slightly as though to grip the edge of the door.

Mindless prayers formed in her head, a litany of terror. Her slamming heart felt as if it would climb right up her throat into her mouth. She couldn't feel her legs. *Oh, God—oh, God—oh, God.*

And then the hand plopped on the floor. Poised to run, she gaped at it. Disembodied, pathetic, it just lay there on the air-conditioning vent, fingers fluttering as if in death throes.

It was only her brown gardening glove, which had been hanging with its mate on a cup hook inside the door. Caught in the draft coming up through the crack, it had drifted sideways and out the opening.

Marilee's legs buckled. She went down hard, her knees

cracking on the waxed oak. Feeling separated from the pain, she wrapped her arms around herself and sobbed. A glove. Only a glove. Dear God. If she'd had the presence of mind to lunge for the phone on the counter behind her, she might have called the police. She could just imagine the looks on their faces when they discovered they'd raced here to save her from a marauding gardening glove.

When the strength returned to her legs, Marilee pushed to her feet and started over to pick up the glove and return it to its hook. As she crossed the room, the closet door moved again, making her nerves leap. *Stupid, so stupid*. It was just a draft, that was all.

Even so, she stopped dead. Ten years ago, she'd thought, *He's just trying to help me*. Explanations she qualified with "just" tended to be her undoing.

Just a draft? It was the only reasonable explanation, but could she be positive of that? What if she opened the door to hang up the glove and a man was standing in there?

It was madness, and she knew it, but she grabbed a butcher knife from the block on the counter, just in case. *Just in case. Just in case.* She was losing it. Going off the deep end.

She gingerly hooked a finger over the door handle and swung the closet open with such force that the door smacked the front of her refrigerator. Except for the usual assortment of cleaning tools, the closet was empty. *Woman inflicts multiple stab wounds on dustmop.*

Her gaze moved to the louvered doors of the utility room. She'd looked in there once and checked the back door to make sure it was locked. But had she looked good? She couldn't remember opening the pantry, which was definitely roomy enough to hide a man.

She reminded herself that all the doors and windows in the house had been locked when she checked them. She told herself that to go in the utility room again was obsessive, compulsive, and repetitive behavior. She recalled all the years when she'd been so sick—how her life had gotten so out of control. If she allowed herself to start behaving irrationally, she could escalate.

No matter. She had to go in the utility room. No choice. Absolutely had to. She opened the doors, stepped inside, and jerked open the pantry. *Nothing.* She should have felt relieved, but just then the refrigerator kicked on and the house creaked. She turned, her heart pounding, a small voice at the back of her mind saying, *What if it wasn't just the house creaking? What if it was the floor giving under someone's weight?*

Chiding herself, she went back through all the rooms again to check the windows and doors. With every step, she told herself that her real-life demons were ten years in the past, that Laurel Creek was as crime free as a town could get, and no intruder could possibly be in the house. What was she afraid of?

When her second search unearthed nothing, she refused to let herself fall into the trap of doing it yet again. Instead, she forced herself to return to bed. After tossing and turning for nearly an hour, she finally dropped off to sleep, only to be revisited by the dream almost immediately. She jerked awake and could still feel the huge hand clamped over her mouth, the meaty thumb blocking the air flow to her nostrils.

She scrambled off the mattress and stood hunched over in the middle of the room, hyperventilating and staring at the rumpled covers as if they were crawling with snakes. *Oh, God.* This hadn't happened to her in almost a year. *Just a dream.* It hadn't been real.

But it had *felt* real, *seemed* real.

She groped for her rosary, which lay on the nightstand. Kissing the crucifix with numb lips, she crossed herself and began to whisper prayers between panting intakes. *Oh, God. Help me. Help me. I can't do this. Can't let it happen again. If I once let it get hold of me, it may never turn loose.*

Too terrified to heed her own voice of reason, she hurried from room to room, double-checking the locks on every door and window, turning on every light, jerking open every closet, looking in every cupboard, and peeking under every bed.

And then she repeated the process.

The third time around, she realized what she was doing. *Déjà vu.* She couldn't let this happen. Wouldn't let this happen.

She halted in the living room, her arms locked around her waist, the rosary still clenched in one fist. Her heart was hammering, not a normal accelerated heart rate, but a rib-cracking beat that she remembered with sickening clarity. If she didn't stop this, the next thing she knew, she'd be barricaded in the bedroom, afraid to even answer the phone.

No. It wasn't going to play out that way. She had worked too hard, suffered too much, to let these feelings take over. After all, she was Marilee Nelson, the successful writer and illustrator. They'd done a feature in the paper about her last year. She had a career most women could only dream about.

But as she stood there, she wondered, *Why?* She'd been doing so well for months. No nightmares, no attacks. Now she was on the verge of her second bad spell in less than twenty-four hours. *Why?*

The answer was terrifyingly simple. *Joe.* Having him pop up on her doorstep had frayed her nerves and sent her emotions into a tailspin. All last evening, she had refused to let herself think about the possible ramifications of his visit, but her subconscious wasn't so easily controlled. Deep down, the revelations of the afternoon terrified her.

Oh, God, he had pried the truth from her, and if he honestly still loved her as he claimed, she was in big trouble, no maybe to it. She knew him too well to believe he'd take no for an answer and simply back off, not if he still cared about her. He was one of the most tenacious individuals she'd ever met. If he set his sights on a goal, he attained it or nearly killed himself trying. His success in football bore testimony to that. The very fact that he now walked with barely a limp bore testimony to his iron strength of will as well. If he wanted something, he never gave up.

Knowing him, he'd contact her tomorrow. When he did, she would lay it on the line—explain in no uncertain terms why she could have nothing more to do with him. It would be difficult—and humiliating, but she had to make him understand what might happen to her if he persisted.

If he loved her—really loved her—he would stay away.

The following afternoon, Joe kicked back in his creaky office chair, planted the heels of his Nikes on the desk, and slapped an undersize ice pack on one side of his knee, wondering who the hell had decided to make the buggers so small. Not that he didn't appreciate the genius. Jelly that got freezing cold when you smashed it inside a plastic bag was a fantastic idea and wonderfully convenient for a closet cripple who didn't want his players to see him gimping around. But right now he would've appreciated a pack large enough to cover all of his knee at once.

Sighing, he stared at the locked metal door. Painted a high-gloss gray, it was chipped and gouged in places to reveal an old coat of baby-poop brown. Thousands of boys had thrown open that door over the years, Joe himself included. He knew exactly what had caused all those chips and gouges, not to mention the painted-over dents. When the door swung too wide, which it tended to do when a hundred and ninety pounds of high school kid was behind it, the damned thing hit the file cabinet. Why no one had ever moved the cabinet was a mystery.

Blessed relief. Ice always took the edge off. He leaned his head back and closed his eyes, letting the coldness do its work. When the worst of the pain had eased, he glanced at the wall clock, which ran twenty minutes slow because the second hand kept sticking. *One o'clock, give or take a few stuck seconds either way.* Zachary would be up from his nap.

He leaned over, hooked a hand over the phone, and pulled the old relic onto his lap. A rotary dial. He never used the damned thing without wondering what the school board spent the annual budget on. At least they supplied him with a cell phone. Crappy reception, but hey, it worked. He carried it in his sweatpants when out on the field, not so much because he wanted to be available if the principal called to get his daily update on the team's progress, but because his mom might try to get in touch. He needed to know he was only a phone call away if something went wrong with Zachary.

He dialed the number that hadn't been changed since he'd been required to memorize it in kindergarten, a safety precaution in case he ever got lost. *My name's Joey Lakota. My mom's name is Faye Lakota. I live at 362 K Street. My phone number is 555-3231.*

He had only one question: How in the hell could a kid get lost in Laurel Creek? Joe felt sure he could damn near piss across the city limits. Not even Mrs. Grimes' basset hound had ever gotten turned around in this little burg, and the poor mutt had been so dumb, that was saying something.

Just before the phone started to ring, Joe broke the connection, his gaze returning to the clock. He had over an hour before double-day practice resumed. Why not use his lunch break to drive over to his mom's for a short visit? He could put ice on his knee over there while he enjoyed a cup of coffee with her. Now that he'd started his job, he didn't get to see her nearly as much as he'd like, and Zachary would enjoy the surprise as well.

Grabbing his car keys from the center drawer, Joe tossed the disposable ice pack into the trash.

Less than ten minutes later, he was pulling his Honda to a stop in the driveway of his childhood home, a rambling old relic of a farmhouse with rough cedar siding that had turned dark brown with age. He'd barely cut the engine when his mother stepped out onto the wide front porch, looking for all the world as if she'd been expecting him. Joe sometimes wondered if she stood at the window, keeping tabs on her neighbors as so many elderly people did. She'd never struck him as the nosy type, but there was no denying that she always knew the exact moment when he pulled up at her house. Her curly, grizzled brown hair framed her face with soft waves that seemed to have lost their luster, and gazing through the windshield at her, Joe thought she looked a little pale.

"Hi, Mom. How's it goin'?" he called as he swung from the car.

"Fine, sweetie, just fine."

She wiped her hands on her ever-present apron, which protected her floral housedress. Joe thought there must be a "timeless" catalog that old ladies ordered their clothing from. Moving across the spotty lawn toward the steps, he marveled at how unchanging she was. Except for the ravages of age that had lined her face and made her frail, she looked exactly as she had when he was a boy, right down to the chunky black pumps and brown support hose she wore.

"I'll bet you're here to see that son of yours," she said. "He's sleeping right now, dear heart. He went down for his nap a little late."

Joe suppressed a shudder, relieved that none of his players would ever have occasion to hear his mother's pet names for him. *Sweetie* and *dear heart*? Ah, well. They were a step up from doll face, another indignity she inflicted upon him.

She looked so tired. That worried him. Lately it seemed to him she always looked tired, giving him cause to wonder if watching Zachary was too much for her. She was no spring chicken anymore, and a four-year-old made for a lot of extra work.

"You okay, Mom?" he asked as he mounted the steps.

"You look a little worn out around the edges. Maybe you should lie down yourself for a while."

"Nah. I'm going to bake him a 'punkin' pie."

"In this heat?" His mother's Scotch soul cringed at the unnecessary expense of running the air conditioner. Gaining the top step, Joe bent to kiss her soft, wrinkled cheek. "You'll cause yourself to have a stroke."

"I rested for a bit while he was watching an old *Lassie* rerun. I'm fine, Joseph. You fret too much."

"Maybe so." He just loved her, was all, and it seemed to him she pushed herself more than was wise at her age. "*Lassie*, huh? The kid wants a dog, Mom. You aiding and abetting?"

She laughed as she opened the screen door. "Every boy should have a dog. It was the regret of my life that I could never afford to get you one."

She'd given him everything else a kid needed and then some, cleaning houses eight hours a day to supplement her measly widow's pension. Except for the occasional racist comment about his Sioux ancestry, he'd never once felt second rate during his childhood and teens. In high school, he'd always worn name brand shoes, designer jeans, and had plenty of spending money. He'd had to work to buy a car and pay for his own insurance, and later he'd gone through college on scholarships, but so had a lot of other boys. All and all, it had been a good learning experience. Somewhere deep in his memory banks, he still knew how to stretch a buck.

"I'll get him a dog, Mom. Promise. I just have to build a fence first."

Joe followed her into the living room, tossing his keys on the console television he'd bought for her three years ago. That and the blue recliner, which he'd also purchased, were the only sticks of furniture in the room that weren't vintage 50s or earlier, the only positive point being that some of the pieces were now miraculously back in style. He'd seen an overstuffed sofa similar to hers when he was shopping for furniture last month.

"Don't put off getting him a dog for too long," she cautioned as she led the way into her antiquated but cheerful kitchen, the floors creaking every step of the way. Every creak and groan irritated Joe. He'd given her tons of money back in his glory days, and for the life of him, he couldn't figure out what the hell she'd spent it on. He only knew she hadn't used it to repair the house. "First thing you know," she went on, "he'll be graduating from high school, and the last thing he'll want is a puppy. Regrets are like soap and water; they come real cheap."

"It's cruel to chain a dog all day, Mom, and no way am I leaving one in the house. It'd take a dump on my new carpet, sure as God made little green apples."

"That carpet!" She stepped to a cupboard, grabbed a dessert plate that was the same blue and white pattern he'd eaten off of at sixteen, and served up a huge piece of what looked like spice cake with homemade caramel icing. Joe's mouth started to water. As she poured a tall glass of milk to go with it, she said, "You must have had a case of temporary insanity to buy that rug. I'll never understand why you chose off-white."

His whole house was off-white. Rug, walls, drapes, and upholstery. So? Nothing clashed, at least, and selecting the colors hadn't taxed his patience. "It looked good to me at the time."

Interior decorating wasn't his forte. Thinking about the bare walls in his new house, Joe took a gallon-size plastic bag from one of the kitchen drawers and then went to the ancient Frigidaire to fill the bag with ice cubes.

Taking a seat on one of the wooden kitchen chairs, he laid the ice pack over his knee and gazed at a plaster handprint above the recipe-book shelf. He'd given his mom the handprint for Mother's Day back in first grade. Soon, Zachary would start to school, and the wall-decoration problem would be solved. Joe would have bean mosaics, handprints, silhouettes, and all kinds of other stuff to hang everywhere, so why worry about it?

His mom cut his mental meandering short by thrusting

the piece of cake under his nose. "Eat," she said.

"Is that for *me*?"

"Of course it's for you," she replied, setting the milk next to his elbow. "If I ate like that, I'd weigh three hundred pounds."

Personally, Joe thought she could stand to gain a few pounds. He took a bite of the cake, closed his eyes, and nearly moaned in ecstasy. It *was* homemade caramel frosting, the kind she simmered on the stove and then whipped until it got creamy. The stuff was damned near as good as sex.

"Oh, Mom," he said with an appreciative sigh. "This is fantastic. Did you make it for Zachary? You'll spoil him."

"You survived it." She sat down across from him and smiled. "I enjoy spoiling him. You've no idea what a treat it is to have him here every day."

While Joe finished his cake and kept the ice on his knee, they chatted about nothing in particular. It felt good to be able to sit in her kitchen on a sweltering July afternoon and talk about nothing important, Joe decided, yet another reason he was glad he'd moved back home.

"Well, Mom," he finally said. "I should probably go back to work."

He put his dishes in the sink. Then, slipping an arm around his mother's shoulders, he walked with her to the front door, grabbing up his keys as they passed the television.

"I love you, angel mine," she said, as he bent to kiss her forehead.

"Do me a favor? Lie down for a few minutes while Zachary's still asleep."

"Oh, posh!" She pushed open the screen door for him. "You just be careful driving back over here this evening. Keep that foot of yours off the accelerator."

Joe descended the front steps, then turned to walk backward. "I don't speed anymore, Mom."

"Uh-huh. I know you, my little speed demon."

Mothers. Her little speed demon? She made him sound as if he were barely out of diapers. He hadn't received a speeding ticket since the divorce, when Valerie had gotten her greedy mitts on his Lamborghini. The Honda he'd purchased to replace it provided comfortable, reliable transportation for a reasonable cost, but it didn't have the horsepower to break any speed records.

He was smiling as he backed the car from her driveway. At the corner, he hung a right turn onto a main thoroughfare, taking care to keep his speed at twenty-five, on the nose, as he drove in the residential area. He passed kids on bikes, saw people out walking, and had to drive around a dog that had decided to take a nap in the cool shade of an elm.

Everywhere Joe looked, he saw reminders that he'd left the harried pace of city life far behind. Laurel Creek was an entirely different world. Zachary would have a great childhood here, with far more freedom to roam than would have been possible in San Milagros. Being in the same town with Marilee was a definite plus as well.

He passed the street she lived on just then. Glancing at his watch again, he saw that he still had a little time to play with before he was due in the locker room. He'd been worried sick about her all morning. What harm could it do to stop by and see how she was doing?

He decelerated and grabbed second to turn and circle the block back to her house. Her green Taurus was parked in the driveway, telling him she was at home. He nosed his Honda into the space beside her car.

Boo met him on the front walk, taking up so much of the path that Joe stopped for a moment to pet him. "You remember me, do you?" he said, scratching behind the dog's floppy ears. "Here's hoping your owner welcomes me with the same enthusiasm."

Fat chance. Joe climbed the front steps and rang the bell. Her double front doors had paned glass at the tops. When she entered the hallway to answer the summons and saw who was on the porch, her footsteps faltered.

Joe flashed her a grin. She covered the remaining distance to the entryway with obvious reluctance and then opened the door only as far as the chain guard allowed.

"Hi," she said tonelessly.

"It's me, the bad penny. I just wanted to stop by and check on you."

"Oh."

That wasn't exactly "Go to hell," but close. He braced a hand on the top rail of the stationary door, crossed his ankles, and leaned closer to better see her face, which looked waxen and pale. "How are you feeling today?"

"Fine," she said in a monotone.

An itch ran up the back of his neck. "Fine? You don't look fine, honey."

"I was napping."

"Oh, I'm sorry. I didn't mean to wake you."

She stared blankly at his chest. The itch crept up to his scalp. "Mari, honey, are you sick?"

Long silence. Then her lashes fluttered, and she said, "Joe, yesterday when you said you still love me, did you mean it?"

There was something wrong. He'd never seen her like this, completely emotionless, her voice flat, each word spaced.

"I love you so much I'd lay down my life for you." He glanced at his watch and decided his assistant coach could handle things until he got there. "Just tell me what you need."

"I need for you to stay away from me, Joe," she said tonelessly. "Just, please, stay away. Don't come here again."

That was as close to dying for her as he'd probably ever get. Never to see her? He closed his eyes and listened to her breathing for a moment, relieved beyond measure that she didn't seem to be having a problem. No quick, shallow intakes. He lifted his lashes to gaze at her sweet face. He couldn't help but be concerned by her pallor.

"I know you don't understand," she said softly, this time with at least some inflection, which eased his mind a little. "And I don't want to get into a detailed explanation because it's embarrassing. Just, please, accept, Joe. I can't be around you. I've worked really hard to piece my life back together, and I can't let it be destroyed."

"I'd never do that."

"Did you know I used to have to order my groceries over the phone?"

"No, I didn't know that. Mari—"

"Just listen, please." When he tried to speak again, she cut him off with another "*Please?*" He fell silent, and she continued. No thoughtful pause. He had a feeling she'd memorized what she planned to say. "I bought this house so I could have my own space." She waved a limp hand. "Living at home was just—I can't explain it—stifling somehow. You know how regimented my parents are."

Joe knew very well. Karl Nelson was the salt of the earth, and his wife Emily was a dear heart, but they gave a whole new meaning to the word "fuddy-duddies." Eight o'clock mass every weekday morning. A family rosary every evening after dinner. They seldom watched movies on television because of the bad language. If Marilee hadn't rebelled as a teenager, she'd still be wearing long skirts, ankle socks, and black-and-white oxfords.

"Anyway," she went on, "I thought I'd like living alone and being a home owner. I had the money Mama and Daddy had saved for my college as a down payment. Gerry used her college money to help buy her and Ron's house, so I figured, why not me? But after I moved in here, I regretted it. I felt really uneasy living here all by myself."

His throat went tight as a picture began to form in his mind of what her life had been like.

"Act in haste, and all that. This was too nice a place to rent out or leave empty, and I was stuck with the mortgage payments. I thought about selling it and moving back home, but—I don't know—I think my folks were secretly glad to have me out of their hair, and I was ashamed to admit I was such a big coward. So I was determined to tough it out and stay. A bad mistake, that. I started getting really sick—a lot worse than I'd been at my folks' place. Even with two deadbolts on each door, I leaned pizza pans against the jams so they'd clatter if anyone came in. I strung those little round Christmas bells on long pieces of twine and hung them in the door-ways. When the phone rang, I felt like my skin was being peeled off with a grater. The only places I went were Sunday mass and to see my folks or sister, and I nearly had a heart attack just getting to my car, even in broad daylight. I suppose you could say I was semi-agoraphobic."

Like Zachary, he thought. Hiding from the world.

"I can't go back to that," she whispered dully. "I never knew what might bring on an attack. Can you imagine being in a grocery line and having it happen? Or going for a drive to calm down, getting sick, and not being able to get home? One time I had one at a family gathering, and Daddy called an ambulance. It was terrible. The doctor in the ER said I had asthma, and after that, my folks bugged me to death about not carrying my inhaler. It didn't help, so why carry it? Only I couldn't tell them that. If I had, they would've asked questions."

Joe shifted his weight onto his other foot, wishing she'd unfasten the damned chain guard and let him in. "And it would've been bad if they'd asked questions?" he prompted. "Maybe talking to someone might help, Mari. Did you ever consider that?" When she didn't answer, he said, "Isn't there treatment available for anxiety attacks? The least you should do is see a doctor."

"I went to my primary caregiver and told him I was a nervous wreck and had anxiety attacks. Evidently, they're quite common, and he didn't pry. He wrote me a prescription for mild tranquilizers. In a week, I called him back and told him they weren't helping, so he increased the strength."

Despite her flat delivery, Joe could almost feel her anguish. "Oh, Mari, if you were having that rough a time, why in the hell didn't you tell me? You had to know I would come. Screw the football, screw everything." He reached through the crack of the door to trail a fingertip along her cheek. "I would have parked on your doorstep, slept on the sofa. Whatever it took. I was never more than a phone call away."

She made an exasperated little noise and moved her head to escape his touch. "Don't you see, Joe? You were the *last* person I could call. The very last."

"Why, for God's sake? I guess that's what blows my mind the most. We were always so close. I told you everything, you told me everything. And suddenly you couldn't talk to me?"

"I knew what would happen if I was around you, what you'd expect from me. I couldn't deal with that, and I still can't."

An airless pounding began in his temples. "Sex, you mean?"

"Don't sound amazed." She fell silent for a moment, which told him she had finished her well-rehearsed speech and was now searching for words. "We were waiting until we got married, but how long would that have lasted? We were engaged. It was harder and harder, every time we were together. I knew it was coming, and probably soon."

A chill raised goose bumps on his arms.

"We'd waited three whole years, and I was finally eighteen. After that happened, I couldn't go through with it. I just couldn't!"

Joe lowered his hand from the door. Resting his fists on his hips, he paced in a tight circle on her porch, his gaze fixed on his feet. He had grass stains on his Nikes, he noticed inanely. Finally he said, "*That's* why you broke our engagement? Because you thought I'd expect you to have sex with me?"

She ran her hand over the chain that prevented the door

from opening wider. "No think to it, I *knew* you would."

"Give me some credit," he told her gently. "I'm not that insensitive."

"You didn't know, and I couldn't tell you. I couldn't even talk about it!"

"And that wasn't good," he pointed out. "I would have taken you up to Eugene. Even back then, I'm sure they had a rape crisis center there."

She winced when he said the word aloud. Joe ached with sadness for her. She was obviously in denial, not only unable to talk about what had happened, but pretending on some level that it had never actually occurred.

"You needed some counseling, Mari. I think you still do. I would have seen to it that you got some."

"I couldn't talk to you about it, Joe. Why can't you understand that?"

"So you cut me out of your life instead. What were you thinking, honey, that you'd just miraculously get well, all by yourself? Sweetheart . . ." He moved back to the door, reaching through to touch a hand to her beautiful hair. The wisps curled over his fingertips like threads of silk. "People don't always bounce back after something like that happens. They need help to cope, and unless they get that help, they have problems. You aren't alone, you know."

She began to sob softly. Joe pressed his shoulder against the other door, as if by doing so, he might somehow get closer to her. "Ah, Mari, don't." He seriously considered breaking the damned chain so he could hold her and comfort her. "I'm sorry for preaching. I know it wasn't an easy time for you, that you felt all alone and probably didn't know what to do." She'd been a small-town Catholic girl. Back then, Joe doubted she'd even heard the word "rape" very often, let alone what to do if she ever became a victim. "Please, don't cry. What we need to focus on is the present. Right? I know about it now. I can help you, if you'll let me."

"Help me?" she echoed shrilly. "I can't be involved in

a relationship, Joe, and being around you is pressure I don't need right now."

She made him feel like a contagious disease.

"Nothing's changed over the last ten years. You're still Joe, and I'm still the same old messed-up me. Being around you yesterday? Now I feel like I'm locked in a cage and being poked with sticks."

"I'd never hurt you. Surely you know that."

"What I know and what goes on way deep in my head are two different things. The dream came again last night, Joe."

The dream?

"It's the first time I've had it in ten months. I had to take tranquilizers just to sleep. More this morning. That's why I was napping when you called. I'm spacey, out of it. If you love me, *really* love me, you'll stay away from me."

He really loved her. Always had, always would. But leaving her alone didn't strike him as the smart thing to do. If she could just see him regularly in unthreatening situations, she wouldn't have any panic attacks, and eventually she'd get over this. He knew she would. "Marilee, will you do just one thing for me?"

She sniffed and finally nodded.

"Let me take you to a doctor. Not here in town where anyone will get wind of it. Bedford, maybe. I'll bet they've got a couple of good psychiatrists there. I'll drive you. If you want me to wait in the car, I'll do that. Or if you need moral support, I'll go in with you. I'm sure the doctor will understand if I stay with you the first few sessions."

"*What*? And have you hear all the dirty details and sit in judgment?"

"*Judgment*! What the hell would I judge you about?"

She huffed softly, the wounded look in her eyes nearly breaking his heart. "What if the woman asks for it, Joe? Did you ever think of that?"

He swore under his breath and closed a fist over the

chain, thinking how easily he could rip the damned thing loose. "No woman *asks* for that. I don't care if she parades naked down Main Street, she doesn't have that coming."

"You don't know the whole story!"

"I don't need to. I know *you*."

"I did the *stupidest* thing, Joe." Her gaze clung to his, the blue of her eyes so dark and filled with shadows they looked bruised. "So stupid. I walked right into it! You told me never to go to frat parties. Remember? You warned me, over and over."

"I remember," he said tightly.

"Well, I didn't listen. I went to one with my big sister in the sorority. A lot of other girls did it, and they never had a problem. I figured you were just being overprotective."

He had been overprotective. Growing up in Laurel Creek with strictly religious parents, she'd been sheltered all her life, and with three years of college under his belt, he'd known the dangers she might encounter on a large university campus.

"Everyone in the sorority used the buddy system. That was the rule for parties, and my big sister couldn't get anyone else to go with her. Her boyfriend was going to be there, and she really wanted to go, too. She kept pleading with me to buddy up with her that night, and finally I gave in. We were supposed to stay together, look out for each other, only she took off."

He was going to be sick. *Damn it*. "Mari, you were only eighteen. Eighteen-year-olds do dumb things sometimes. It's part of growing up, sweetheart. Making mistakes is par for the course. Do you think I never did anything stupid? Think again."

"Not everyone pays for their mistakes like I did."

She'd never talked to anyone about this, and now, when she finally decided to, it was through the crack of a door? He supposed the tranquilizers had loosened her tongue, but regardless, he needed to be in there with her.

Standing out on her porch like this when she so clearly needed his arms around her was sheer torture. "Mari, honey—"

"You know that stuff—the high-proof alcohol? Evergreen or something like that? Someone put a truckload of it in the punch."

"Everclear, you mean?" The stuff was a hundred-eighty proof and could knock a big man on his ass faster than a mean right hook.

"Yes, Everclear, that was it. The fraternity house was packed, the music blasting. I was hot, and my sorority sister's boyfriend offered me a glass of punch. I thought it tasted funny, but I'd never had any alcohol."

Oh, God. He remembered how incredibly naïve she'd been then. He wanted to kill the guy who'd done this to her. There was no statute of limitations; not in his books. The bastard might well be married and have kids, but that didn't entitle him to have a life unblemished by this while she struggled with the memories every waking moment.

"Is that all you had, just one glass?" he asked, hoping to keep her talking.

"It was a big plastic one, and I drank *all* of it."

Joe knew the type of cup she meant, and if the bastard had been trying to get her drunk, he had undoubtedly laced her punch with additional alcohol. Joe had known guys like that in college, some of them in his own fraternity. They were conscienceless jerks.

"I got really dizzy at first," she said raggedly. "Then I started to feel sick. Horribly sick. He said there was a place where I could lie down."

Joe passed a hand over his eyes. He knew what was coming—practically could have finished the story himself. He pictured her, barely able to keep her feet and feeling nauseated, then trusting some "nice guy" to help her out.

"I should have called a cab to get back to the sorority!" she cried, her voice going thin. "Instead—oh, Joe, I was so *stupid*, so unbelievably stupid. I knew him, and I thought I could trust him, so I—went with him. I went with him!"

She started to weep in earnest then. He stood there and helplessly watched for as long as he could bear it. Then he grasped the doorknob, put his shoulder to the door, and said, "Step out of the way, honey. This is nuts. I'm coming in."

"*No!*" She threw her weight against the door to brace against him.

"Just to talk, I swear."

"I told you, I can't talk about it."

She'd been doing a fine job of it a moment ago. It didn't escape his notice that when the dike finally broke, he'd been the one she chose to pour her heart out to.

"Fine. We won't talk, then. I just want to be in there with you. As your friend. Strip everything else away, honey, and we still have that. Friends always, remember?"

"Oh, Joe."

"I can stay for a while." Screw the locker room pep talk. If he lost his job, he'd get two more pumping gas. Except for his son, there was no one on earth who mattered more to him than this woman. "I'll fix you some tea. Listen. When you're feeling better, I'll leave. Okay? Just unfasten the chain."

"No . . . please. Don't come in. Please, don't, Joe." She dragged in a shaky breath. "I'm fine. Really. And I don't want you in here. I was doing okay until I saw you yesterday. I was practically well."

"You got something against entirely well? You don't want me going in with you, fine, but the bottom line is, you need to see a doctor."

He refrained from mentioning that he'd stopped by the library after leaving her place yesterday, picked up several books, and had started educating himself about her problem last night after putting Zachary to bed. He'd focused his attention mainly on anxiety attacks and posttraumatic stress disorders, and though he was still far from well-informed, he'd marked several pages that described her symptoms to a tee. Practically every passage was preceded by "*In severe cases.*" She needed help, and if it was the last thing he did, he intended to see that she got it.

"You think I'm crazy."

"Sweetheart, I didn't say that. Did I say that?"

She made an exasperated sound. "You're right. I am crazy. But I can't go for counseling. Talking about it will only make me worse. Even *thinking* about it makes me worse."

She'd been pouring her heart out until he mentioned going inside, and he had a sneaking hunch it had done her a world of good to get even that much off her chest.

"Mari, I—"

"I have to go now, Joe. Please, don't come back over here. I won't open the door next time."

He couldn't let her close the line of communication between them like this. Just in case she ever needed to talk, he didn't want her to feel hesitant about picking up the phone. "Can I at least call you sometimes? Just to see how you are?"

She stared at him for a long moment, her eyes filled with yearning that told him she wished with all her heart that she could say yes. "Don't call, Joe. I can't take a chance. If I start getting sick again, I may never get well. I need you to stay away, and I'm sorry to say that includes talking on the phone."

She needed his arms around her, but for the moment, he wouldn't argue the point. "Just remember, the line is open both ways."

"I will."

"Good-bye for now, then," he said, his voice husky with feelings he couldn't express. He settled for saying, "I love you, Mari. If you ever need me, please don't hesitate to let me know. I'll be here in a blink, and I won't arrive with any expectations, I promise."

Another long silence. Then, so softly he almost didn't catch it, she whispered, "I love you, too," just before she closed the door in his face.

 *Four*

*B*y late the next afternoon, Joe made himself concentrate on a group of boys who
couldn't play football to save their souls. Only a month
remained before school started and football season began.
He didn't have much more time to whip them into shape,
and the task became more daunting by the second.

Standing on the sidelines with his assistant coach, Ted
Ridgeway, he watched the team execute a practice play.
When the quarterback made the pass, the wide receiver
not only fumbled the ball but somehow managed to trip
over his own feet.

Ted swore under his breath. "Man, Bedford High is
going to slaughter us this season. I'm going to end up
flipping burgers for a living unless these kids get it together."

Bedford had been Laurel Creek High's fiercest competitor for as long as Joe could remember. Over time, the
rivalry between the two schools had become the primary
focus of this community each football season, turning
what should have been a fun game into a grueling scram-

ble for victory. Sometimes the crop of boys who turned
out for football made winning against Bedford a possibility. This wasn't one of those years. Joe had never seen
so many uncoordinated kids in one place in all his life.

He had tried to talk with Jim McCalister, the high
school principal, about the team's overall lack of athletic
ability, but Jim had turned a deaf ear. Whipping Bedford
High was an absolute must, amen. Why else did Joe think
the last coach had been fired and Joe had been hired to
replace him? Because high school football was damned
important in this town, that was why, and if anyone could
take Laurel Creek High to the state playoffs, it was Joe
Lakota.

Big problem. Joe wasn't sure these boys had it in them.
Every time they ran a play, one of them screwed it up
without fail.

This morning, Joe had grown so frustrated that he'd
caught himself about to scream at a kid, something he'd
sworn never to do. With his job hanging in the balance,
it was all too easy to get sucked into the madness and
start thinking that winning was everything. Well, damn
it, winning *wasn't* everything. Those boys were working
their hearts out for him, and that had to count for something even if they never won a single game.

Joe jotted down a quick note, then tucked the clipboard
under his arm and moved out onto the field. As he ran,
he blew two sharp blasts on the silver whistle that hung
on a shoestring around his neck.

Looking crestfallen and ashamed of themselves, the
boys shuffled their feet, some of them hanging their
heads, others removing their mouth guards to spit on the
grass. Joe could see a pep talk was in order. If their spirits
plunged any lower, their bottom lips would be dragging
the ground.

He drew up and patted the wide receiver's shoulder.
"You kept your eye on the ball this time. Big improvement!"

His blue eyes suspiciously bright, the red-faced youth

glanced at Joe and shrugged. "I fumbled the play again. How's that an improvement?"

It wasn't easy to praise a kid when he'd messed up so badly, but Joe was motivated. Over the course of his football career, the coaches who'd had the most profound effect and gotten the best performance out of him had been the ones who made him believe in himself. Thinking quickly, he said, "Because this time you fumbled doing it *right*, Petersen! Now all you have to do is learn to relax your hands when you make contact with the ball."

Laying the clipboard on the grass, Joe signaled at a player to throw him the ball. "Like this," he said as he threw the ball in the air and then caught it. "See how my hands give at impact?" He patted the youth's shoulder again and slapped the ball into his hands. "Pretend it's an egg."

"A what?"

"An *egg*. You don't want it to break, right? So when it comes into your hands, give with it. You'll be amazed at what it does for your catching. Once we master that, you'll be well on your way to becoming a champion wide receiver."

"Me?"

Joe had to admit that it took a stretch of imagination. "Of course, you. Why else do you think I picked you to play this position?"

"Because there was nobody better who turned out?"

"Damned right there was nobody better," Joe shot back. "You think I'm going to select second best? I know potential when I see it, and trust me, Petersen, you're unique."

That much wasn't a lie. Joe did know potential when he saw it, and Petersen ranked in the top ten percent for his utter lack of it.

"Same goes for the rest of you guys!" he said gruffly. "I handpicked each and every one of you. So get those glum looks off your faces. Becoming the best is no cakewalk. It's going to take hard work! You willing to give me a hundred and ten percent?"

"Yes, Coach!" a few players yelled.

"Louder!" Joe yelled back.

"Yes, Coach!"

"Come on. A bunch of sissies can do better than that!"

"*Yes, Coach!*" they all roared.

Joe just wished they could play football as well as they could yell. "That's what I wanna hear," he cried. "Now, run it again! We're gonna do it until we get it right!"

The cell phone in Joe's sweatpants pocket rang just then. He drew it out and flipped it open. "Lakota here."

Joe expected the call to be from his trainer, who'd just taken one of his players up to the locker room a few minutes before to wrap a sprained wrist. Instead it was some woman. He plugged one ear and stepped away from the group of boys, straining to hear what she said. She sounded elderly and in a tizzy about something.

"Excuse me," he interrupted. "Who is this?"

"Sarah Rasmussen, your mother's neighbor! She's very sick, Joseph. I called an ambulance, and they're here now, taking her to the hospital. I think it's her heart."

Joe felt as if the earth had suddenly vanished from under his feet. "Oh, Jesus, no," he whispered. Fear made the blood pound in his temples. "How bad is it?" He started from the field, then realized he couldn't just walk away without telling his assistant coach why he was leaving. He wheeled back around. "Where's my little boy, Mrs. Rasmussen?"

"He's under the table. Poor little guy's scared to death. I'd offer to watch him so you could go straight to the hospital, but I honestly think it'd be better if you came by here first. All this commotion, I guess. He's screaming and horribly upset. I can't even touch him."

Even with the wind making it difficult to hear, Joe caught the sound of Zachary's shrieks. "I'll be right there. Will you tell him that for me, Mrs. Rasmussen? I'll be there in five minutes or less."

"Yes, I'll tell him."

Joe ended the call and jogged back to the sidelines to apprise his assistant coach of the situation. Less than a minute later, he was racing for the faculty parking lot.

It was nearly eight o'clock before Joe got home that night, and his feet were dragging as he carried his sleeping son from the car to the house. *Man, what a day.* With rest and treatment, it looked as if his mother would be all right. Her EKG showed no abnormalities, and although the results on the enzyme test hadn't come back yet, the doctor believed the severe pain in her neck and arm had probably been caused by angina pectoris, not a coronary. As a safety precaution, they were keeping her in the hospital for more tests and observation, much to Joe's relief. He'd been scared half to death when he saw how ghostly pale she was.

Your mother's not as young as she used to be, Dr. Petrie had told him later. *Keeping up with a four-year-old is simply too much for her. I suggest that you make other arrangements for childcare. Once she goes home, she can watch her grandson for short periods of time— a couple of hours unless she has help, in which case she can keep him longer—but no more all-day stays if she's caring for him by herself, and never on a regular basis again.*

As relieved as Joe was that his mom was going to be all right, her unexpected collapse had placed him in one hell of a spot. Making other arrangements for childcare was no simple matter, not with a kid like Zachary. There was no way Joe could leave his little boy at a daycare center as other parents did.

Damn. Joe didn't know what he was going to do, and he had a bitch of a headache from worrying about it. No way around it, he had to be on the field for practice in the morning. Missing work when he was still so new on the job was a good way to get his ass fired.

Zachary woke as Joe drew back the covers to tuck him into bed. "How come you're still sad, Daddy? Grandma's better, right?"

Joe forced a smile and bent to press a kiss to his son's forehead. "I'm not sad, sprout. Just a little tired, that's all. And worried."

" 'Cause Grandma Faye might die?"

"No, no . . ." Joe smoothed Zachary's hair back. "Grandma Faye is going to be fine."

"Unless I make her sick again."

Frustrated by the shadows in the semidark room, Joe leaned closer to search his son's big, frightened eyes. "You didn't make Grandma sick, Zachary. Where'd you get that idea?"

"The doctor said."

Joe winced, wishing Zachary hadn't overheard that conversation. But, there again, without a sitter, Joe had had no choice but to keep the child with him at the hospital. "No, tyke, that isn't what the doctor said at all. Grandma Faye got sick because she's old, not because of you."

"The doctor said taking care of me wore her out."

There was little point in denying it, so Joe didn't try. "You're an active little boy, and Grandma Faye is an old lady with a bad heart. Lots of things she really likes to do can wear her out—working in her flowers, baking pies. If her heart started to hurt because she got tired from going to church, would you blame God for making her sick?"

"No," Zachary said, his voice wobbling.

"Well, then, you shouldn't blame yourself, either." Joe gathered his son into his arms and drew him onto his lap. "Silly boy. You love your grandma, and you work hard over at her house, doing all kinds of things for her. She just loves you so much that she doesn't lie down as often as she should when you're there. That's all."

Zachary hid his face against Joe's chest and said in a high, squeaky voice, "I never meant to make her heart hurt, Daddy. She was just making me my snack like she does every day, then her face went all funny and she asked me to bring her the phone. After she called the neighbor lady, she fell on the floor and couldn't talk anymore. I though she was gonna die."

Joe closed his eyes and began to rock slowly back and forth. Sometimes he felt so pitifully inadequate as a father. Why hadn't he realized how his child had been feeling? All these many hours of waiting for news about his mom, and Zachary had been blaming himself the entire while. That was a mighty heavy load for one small boy to pack around all afternoon and evening.

"Oh, Zachary . . . I'm so sorry. Listen to me. You listening?"

"Yup."

"What happened to Grandma Faye wasn't anyone's fault. Her heart is old and weak, and she's been having the angina pain for a long, long time—way before she started watching you. Almost anything can bring on an attack. You know how she loves to go walking in the evening? Even that can do it. It had nothing—absolutely nothing—to do with you."

"For sure?" the child asked in that same squeaky voice that told Joe he was about to cry.

"Absolutely for sure. Cross my heart—" Joe quickly broke off. Not a good choice of words. "Scout's honor," he settled for saying. "Grandma Faye *loves* you, and she really has fun watching you. It's just that she's old." Joe kissed the top of the child's head, breathing in the little boy smells he loved so much, traces of shampoo and bath soap, peanut butter and jelly, crayons and glue. "If she knew you were feeling bad, she'd tell you the exact same thing, that it wasn't your fault and you're a silly boy for thinking so. Before we know it, she'll be up and around, feeling fit as a fiddle again. Just you watch and see."

"I can't stay with her anymore," Zachary said forlornly.

"Not like before," Joe agreed.

"Where'll I go while you're at school for football practice, Daddy?"

"I'll figure something out," Joe said with far more confidence than he felt. "And you'll be happy with the arrangement, I promise. Until then, it's nothing for you to be worrying about. How about a bedtime story?"

Zachary smiled and scooted off Joe's lap to dive back under the covers. *"G'night Moon."*

Joe stifled a groan. He'd read that book so many times he knew it by heart. He flipped on the bedside lamp. *"Goodnight Moon* it is."

Zachary snuggled deeper under the lightweight covers and yawned. "Daddy?"

"Hmm?" Joe replied as he sorted through the collection of favorite books in the nightstand drawer.

"What if you can't make a 'rangement for me? What'll we do?"

That was a question Joe couldn't answer, and he was as worried about it as Zachary was. "You ever known me to fail when I put my mind to something?"

"Nope."

"Well, then? I'll come up with something, sprout, and you'll like it. I promise."

Marilee was in the laundry room feeding Boo when the phone rang. It was nearly nine and she seldom received calls this late, so her first thought was that Gerry might be having the baby. She raced to the kitchen and, grabbing up the receiver, said breathlessly, "Don't tell me you're in labor."

A deep, masculine voice came over the line. "Pardon me?"

Heat rushed to her face. "Joe?" She was so unsettled by his call that it took her a moment to collect her wits.

"Please, don't hang up."

"I thought we decided that we wouldn't talk."

"I need your help, Marilee."

Something in his voice made her hesitate to break the connection. Her hand tightened on the plastic. "Help from me?"

"My mom's in the hospital. It's her heart. She collapsed this afternoon."

Marilee's stomach dropped. "Oh, no." She had always been fond of Faye Lakota. "Her heart, you say? Oh, Joe! She's so *young*."

"Seventy-six next month. That's not really so young."

Seventy-six? Marilee stared out the kitchen window into the darkness of her yard. Where had the time gone? "I'm so sorry. Is she going to be all right?"

"The results of the enzyme test aren't back yet, but her EKG looked pretty good." He sounded emotionally drained, his voice oddly hollow, yet laced with tension. "Doc Petrie thinks it was only severe angina, not an actual heart attack."

"What can I do to help?"

"I hate to presume upon our friendship, honey, but I don't have a choice. I need to ask a favor."

"Don't be silly. Your mom is a dear person. When things like this happen, you set all the other stuff aside. When does she come home? I can go over and change the bed linen, tidy the house. As far as that goes, I could work over there for a few days and watch after her."

"I've already got that covered. Remember Mrs. Rasmussen, the lady next door? She's still pretty spry, and she's offered to help out. She and Mom are pretty tight, so they'll enjoy the time together, I think."

"Oh." Marilee traced the lines of brown grout between the creamy counter tiles. "What, then?"

"I need someone to watch Zachary. The doctor says my mother can't keep him anymore. A child his age is just too much for her."

That thought hadn't occurred to Marilee. She closed her eyes. *Zachary.* "For how long?"

Long silence. "Probably for several weeks. I'd ask Gerry and Ron, but they've already got so many kids, and she's due to drop again any time. In addition to that, Zachary's painfully shy and it would take him weeks to adjust to all the commotion over there."

"Several *weeks*?"

"Only until I can get him acclimated to a daycare center. Once he settles in with you, I can start taking him by a center once a day during my mid-morning break. Slowly get him used to the caregivers and all the other kids. When he feels at ease, I can start leaving him. Maybe just mornings, at first. Then pretty soon, all day."

Weeks? If it had been any other child, Marilee would have said yes in a heartbeat. But Zachary? Her sister Gerry said he was a darling little boy, and she'd probably adore watching him. Only in order to keep him, she'd have to see Joe every day as well. There would be no way to avoid it.

"I, um . . ." She thought quickly. "Actually, Joe, it would work out better for me to help out at your mom's and let Mrs. Rasmussen watch Zachary. That way, I can squeeze in a little work while your mother's resting." *And I can carefully arrange the schedule so I never bump into you*, she silently added. "Keeping track of a four-year-old would take up most of my day."

"I know. It's just—" He swore under his breath, the words unintelligible. "Damn, Marilee. I wouldn't ask if I weren't in a hell of a fix. Zachary isn't like other kids. I can't leave him with just anybody. For some reason, he doesn't like Mrs. Rasmussen. Today when Mom had the attack, he freaked. He was hiding under the table and screaming when Mrs. Rasmussen called me at the school. Poor little guy was scared to death."

"But, Joe, he doesn't even know me."

"He'll love you. I know he will. Kids aren't dumb. You have a special affinity for children, Mari. Just seeing some of your work tells me that. You're also sensitive. Zachary's been through a tough time, living with his mom. He's been reticent about the details, telling me very little. He won't even confide in his therapist. I think he finds it difficult to talk about it. You'll understand him, honey, maybe better than anyone does."

She thrust her fingers into her hair. "Dirty pool. Don't tug on my heartstrings like this. You *know* I don't want to see you. Watching Zachary, I'd have no choice."

"Do you really think I'd use my kid in such an underhanded way? I still love you, Marilee. I've been up front with you about that. If I could think of some way to do it, *any* way to do it, I'd take up right where we left off, complete with a ring and wedding date. But you can't accuse me of being sneaky about it."

That was true. Frighteningly true. Joe had never been the sneaky type. He always laid his cards on the table and played fair. If the moment ever came for a confrontation between them, he'd stand toe-to-toe and nose-to-nose with her. Just the thought made her knees weak.

"I'd love to help out with Zachary," she admitted. "But I just—can't. I don't want to see you. I thought I made that clear."

"Marilee, I'm desperate. I can tell him you're my friend, that I've known you forever. It won't be like leaving him with a total stranger."

She blinked and rubbed her suddenly throbbing temple. "I'm sorry, Joe."

"Marilee, please . . . I'm going to lose my job if I start missing practices. I either have to leave him with somebody or lose my income, and contrary to what everyone thinks, I'm not sitting pretty with tons of cash in the bank. Valerie almost cleaned me out when we divorced, and she finished the job when I bought her off to get custody. I had enough money to put a small down on this house when I moved here, with a little left over as a nest egg. That's it. Lose the job, and I'm up shit creek without a paddle."

"So you're asking me to wade in up to *my* eyebrows?"

He was silent for a moment. "You feel that strongly about seeing me? I'd just be dropping my son off and picking him up."

And tearing her heart out every time she saw him. "I'm so sorry, Joe. I'd love to help. But that's the one thing I simply can't do."

He made a low, breathy sound that she knew was pure frustration. Then he fell silent, a rapid tapping noise marking off the seconds. She envisioned him striking the tip of a ballpoint pen on the kitchen counter. "I almost hesitate to ask this for fear of what your answer may be. Are you actually *afraid* of me, honey? Is that what this is about?"

"It's not that cut and dry." Her hand tightened convulsively on the phone. "When people are in car wrecks, do they feel afraid of cars? No. It's going somewhere in the car that unnerves them, especially at high speeds."

"So we'll take it at a snail's pace. I've got no problem with that."

"It isn't that *simple!*"

"Marilee . . . what is it, exactly, that you're afraid may happen?"

"You know very well what I'm afraid may happen."

"Sex, only that makes no sense. It takes two to tango."

"Does it?"

"With me, it does." His voice went husky with tenderness. "So where's the worry? Nothing will ever happen between us that you don't want to happen. Surely you know that."

"It's not just that. It's way more complicated. I can't dissect my feelings and lay them all out for you." She pinched the bridge of her nose. "The bottom line is, seeing you, being around you will upset me, and I can't risk getting sick again."

"Marilee, think about it. Is that a rational fear?"

"Joe, if *rational* had anything to do with it, I wouldn't own twelve pizza pans."

"Twelve? You don't have that many outside doors."

"I propped one up and laid two on the floor to make sure there would be a loud clatter. That in addition to two deadbolts on every door. Rational? You ask me if I'm *rational?*"

"Actually, you're brilliant. A makeshift and very effective burglar alarm."

She rolled her eyes. "You know very well it was crazy. Don't pretend otherwise. After moving here, I lived like that for several years, and it took me another three to get where I am now."

"And I jeopardize that?"

"Yes."

"How? I'm trying really hard to understand, but frankly, it doesn't make much sense. First and foremost, we're best friends, and best friends don't hurt each other."

"News bulletin. That's why crazy people are crazy, because we make no sense."

"The very fact that you believe you may be crazy tells me you aren't. Crazy people think everyone else is nuts."

"I'm convinced you're nuts for suggesting that I see you twice a day. Does that count?"

He chuckled, and the sound conjured images in her mind of the crease deepening in his lean cheek as his firm mouth slanted slowly into a lopsided grin. If just picturing him wreaked havoc with her nerve-endings, how could she possibly hope to keep her distance when she saw him all the time? Even worse, she stood to lose everything. Including her mind.

She moved the receiver out from her ear and said into the mouthpiece, "I'm sorry, Joe. I hate to let you down like this. I really do. But my watching Zachary for you is out of the question. If I can help in any other way, don't hesitate to let me know."

"Marilee," he said, his voice faint. "Don't hang up!"

She dropped the receiver into its cradle and then stood there, staring at the phone, counting to ten. At seven, it rang again. She closed her eyes, knowing very well that it was him. Every peal of the ringer jolted her. She clenched her hands at her sides, determined not to answer. She'd end up saying yes if she did. As much as she would have liked to help and as badly as she felt about letting Zachary down, she had to look out for herself.

Oh, God, how long was he going to let it ring? She considered unplugging the phone. But what if Gerry went into labor and needed her? She was due to have the baby in less than two weeks, and sometimes she delivered early.

Finally, Marilee could bear it no longer. She jerked up the receiver and cried, "Won't you *please* take no for an answer? Do you think it's easy for me to refuse when I know Zachary could end up in a daycare center?"

"Marilee?"

Oh, *no*. "Gerry? Are you having the baby?"

"Don't I wish. No. I just called to see if you'd mind some company. I need to return your stew pot, and Ron offered to hold down the fort so I can get out of the house by myself for a few minutes. Have some hot chocolate with my sister, maybe, and do something really wild, like have an uninterrupted conversation with another adult."

Coming so soon after Joe's call, the prospect of having company wasn't high on Marilee's list, but Gerry got away from her kids so seldom that she didn't have the heart to tell her no. "I'd love some company. And you're in luck. I have fresh brownies."

Gerry made a sound that was half moan, half sigh. "I'll be there in five minutes. A chocolate brownie? Ah, man. My mouth waters just thinking about it."

Marilee chuckled. "See you in five, then."

It took Gerry closer to ten minutes to get there, undoubtedly because pregnancy had slowed her down considerably. When she entered the kitchen, she did so belly first, her back slightly arched as if to maintain her balance. She wore a pink floral tent dress their mom had made for her, the rose tones complementing the flush on her cheeks. Her blond hair, as wildly curly as Marilee's own, framed her delicate features in soft, glimmering wisps, making her blue eyes look big and startled.

Now that they were older, people often mistook Marilee and Gerry for twins. Though she could definitely see a strong resemblance, Marilee secretly thought Gerry was by far the prettier woman. Even in the advanced stages of pregnancy, she looked beautiful and seemed to glow with an inner sweetness.

"Sorry I took so long," Gerry said a little breathlessly. "I had to make sure the air bag was off before I could drive over, and some fool put the doohickey in the center of the dash. You have to lean sideways and forward to turn the thing. Major problem. I no longer find it easy to lean, plus it was hard to see the little dial thing to tell if it was on or off. Then, after doing all that grunting and squirming, I got stuck between the seat and steering wheel."

By this time, Marilee was laughing. "Oh, no. *Stuck*? Not really?"

"Ron keeps lowering the steering wheel tilt and forgets to put it back the way I had it. The darn thing has to come down a notch before it'll go back up. Our baby boy is going to be born with finger grips on his head."

Marilee laughed again. "You poor darling," she said, taking the pot from her sister's hands, then giving her a quick hug. "You look so uncomfortable."

"Uncomfortable? I passed that two weeks ago and have now reached the miserable stage." Gerry grasped the table's edge and clumsily lowered herself onto a kitchen chair, a maneuver she accomplished by leaning backward slightly and then simply plopping. She sighed and fluttered her lashes. "Did you know I've spent almost eight of the last fifteen years pregnant? It seems almost normal, not being able to see my toes."

"It's nearly over. You'll be skinny again before you know it." Marilee put the stew pot on the counter next to the sink and then sliced some brownies to put on a plate. As she set them on the table, she asked, "Do you want hot chocolate or a tall glass of cold milk?"

Gerry grinned. "You're kidding, right? Ron never lets chocolate pass my lips while I'm expecting. He read somewhere that it's bad for the baby."

"Is it?"

"Maybe. I vaguely recall Doctor Holt saying I shouldn't eat too much of it, which is why I'm sure Ron read it somewhere. I'd never be dumb enough to tell him something like that and risk being deprived of my chocolate. I *crave* the stuff. You just don't know. Last night I dreamed I had an affair with a chocolate Easter bunny."

Marilee grinned. Her sister never failed to brighten her mood, even when she was complaining. "Hot chocolate, coming up."

"With marshmallows."

"With marshmallows," Marilee agreed. "Yum. By the time you go home, you'll be so wired from chocolate and too much sugar, Ron will have my head."

As Marilee heated mugs of water in the microwave for their instant hot drinks, Gerry chattered nonstop about her husband and kids. "It was so sweet of you to fix that stew for us, Marilee. You'll just never know. You not only saved me from having to make dinner that night, but I had enough left over to make a big casserole with it again tonight. Added a couple cans of chili, threw some refrigerator biscuits on top, baked it for ten minutes, and, bingo, we had dinner ready. Ron made a big salad to go with it."

Feeling one of her tension headaches coming on, Marilee rubbed her temple as she joined her sister at the table. "I'm glad it came in handy."

Silence ensued as Gerry bit into a brownie and smiled dreamily as she chewed. After swallowing and taking another bite, which she tucked into her cheek, she asked, "When I telephoned, was I imagining things, or did you think I was Joe?"

Marilee shrugged. "Um—yeah, something like that."

"You've seen him?"

"Yes."

Gerry's wide blue eyes sparkled with curiosity. "You've been holding out on me. Did he grovel and beg for forgiveness?"

Marilee swallowed, hard. "Forgiveness for what?"

"For *what*?" Gerry gestured with her half-eaten brownie. "The guy dropped you like a hot potato when he got drafted for the pros. He broke your heart."

Marilee pressed her finger to a crumb that had fallen on the table, avoiding her sister's gaze as she admitted, "Actually, Gerry, it was Joe that got his heart broken."

"*What?*"

"You heard me. I was the one who broke the engagement, not him."

Long silence. "You broke the—" She broke off and sat there staring for a long moment with her mouth agape. "*Why?*" She licked a bit of marshmallow from the corner of her lips. "You never told me that. All these years I thought you worshiped the ground he walked on. Why on earth did *you* break it off?"

"I just did is all." In that moment, Marilee knew why she'd kept silent all these years, allowing everyone to believe Joe had dumped her. She hadn't wanted to be put on the spot like this. Rather than take the heat, she had sacrificed him on the altar of self-preservation, knowing, deep down, that no one in her family would ever feel quite the same toward him. The realization made her feel so ashamed. Joe was right; he'd never done anything to deserve that from her. "I had my reasons, Gerry. Please, accept that and don't ask questions. All I'll say is, it had nothing to do with anything Joe said or did."

Gerry raised her eyebrows. "And that's all I'm getting?"

"That's right."

"Are you aware that burning curiosity can send a woman into early labor? It'll drive me crazy. Tell me."

Marilee shook her head. "It's none of your business, sis. I had my reasons. Let's leave it at that. Okay?"

"Was there another guy? That's it, isn't it? You

thought you'd fallen in love with someone else and broke up with Joe for him. Then he dropped you. That's why you quit school and came home, because you were destroyed over it."

"I'm not going to discuss this with you."

"I'm your *sister*."

She was also a big mouth and told their folks and Ron practically everything. "I really, *really* don't want to talk about this, Gerry, and if you keep on, I'm going to leave you to eat your brownies by yourself while I go fold a load of clothes."

"All *right*! All right. No more prying." Gerry polished off that brownie and grabbed another one. "So what's the deal about Zachary going to a daycare center? Can you tell me that much?"

Marilee sighed and related the story about Faye Lakota's heart problems. When she finished, Gerry said, "Jeez, Marilee, under the circumstances, how can you tell the guy no?"

"It wasn't easy."

"It's not like you."

"Yeah? Maybe you don't really know me."

Gerry laughed. "Uh-huh, and pigs have wings." She took a loud slurp of hot cocoa. "Boy, will Ron have a cow when I tell him you were the one who broke up with Joe, not the other way around. He was so mad for a couple of years that I had to do some serious talking to keep him from jumping Joe about it. Now I'll have to talk myself blue to keep him from wringing your neck."

Marilee wished she could have kept mum for another ten years. Only that wasn't fair to Joe. "Tell Ron I'm sorry. Joe wasn't the skunk you all evidently thought."

"Hey, sweetie?" Gerry reached over to touch Marilee's hand. "Are you all right?"

"Yes, I'm fine," Marilee said tightly. "I, um—I just feel a bad headache coming on." She rubbed her temple again.

"Tension. Joe's call upset you." She sighed. "I wish

you'd unload on me, get whatever it is bothering you off your chest. Since when do you keep stuff from me?"

Since ten years ago. "I'm not keeping stuff from you. I just—"

"Bull hockey." Gerry set down her mug with a sharp click. "Come on. Out with it. I guessed it right. It was over another guy, wasn't it? That's the only explanation. He broke your heart and humiliated you, turned you off men. That's why you don't ever date. Right?"

"No." Marilee's head suddenly felt like a pumpkin that had splattered on cement. Blinding pain exploded behind her eyes. "No other guy. Who in her right mind could even *look* at another guy when she had someone like Joe?"

"He is gorgeous," Gerry agreed. Then she nibbled on her lip, studying Marilee bewilderedly. "He's nice, too. An unbeatable combination. Except for breaking up with you—which now I discover he didn't do—I've never known him to do a mean thing to anyone unless he was pushed into it or he was defending you."

Marilee sighed at the mention. "He did get into a lot of scrapes over me. Didn't he?"

Gerry grinned. "Remember the time he stuffed Brady Pritcher in his locker for squirting ketchup in your hair and all over your new dress?"

"The stain never did come out, and Mama had just made it. That was the first day I wore it."

"And your hair was pink on top for days!" Gerry giggled. "Gosh, that Brady was a mean kid. You know what's funny? He's the nicest guy you'll ever meet now. Weird, huh? I think he got rid of all his mean during childhood. I think he had a crush on you. He always picked on you more than anybody else."

"Joe got suspended for three days for fighting with him in the hall." Marilee sent her sister an agonized glance. "I feel so rotten for letting him down, Gerry. I know he'd never let me down if our roles were reversed."

As she said that, Marilee struggled with a crushing

wave of guilt. It was true. Joe had never been anything but wonderful to her, including recently, yet she had just turned her back on him when he needed her. Even worse, she knew very well that if anything ever happened and she needed him, he would be there for her, no questions asked. And Zachary. If he was as troubled as Joe claimed, how could she let him go to a daycare center?

"Do you really think I can waddle home now and sleep with this swimming around in my head?" Gerry asked. "God! I can't believe this. You're still in love with him. I see it written all over your face." All trace of teasing mischief had left Gerry's expression, and her blue eyes darkened with sympathy. "Ah, honey, don't do this. That's what sisters are for, to talk to. You're really torn up about something. Tell me about it."

"This is one subject I simply can't discuss." Marilee hauled in a bracing breath, knowing her decision about Zachary had undergone a sudden reversal. Oddly, the pain in her head dissipated the moment she reached that conclusion. "Um, Gerry, do you happen to have Joe's phone number? I imagine he has it unlisted, doesn't he?"

"Of course it's unlisted. Someone like Joe can't have his number available to just anyone. People would drive him nuts, calling all the time."

Marilee waited a moment. "So do you have it?"

Grumbling under her breath, Gerry struggled up from her chair. "Not on me. I'll have to call Ron and have him look through the Rolodex." She placed the call, then jotted the number down for Marilee on a notepad beside the phone.

"Thanks," Marilee said as she joined her sister at the counter. She stared at the phone number for a moment and then boldly underlined the digits. "I hate to cut this short, sis, but I need to call him back, and I'd like to talk to him privately."

"You're going to keep Zachary, aren't you?" Gerry said knowingly.

"Yes, I think I will."

Gerry leaned closer. "Can you tell me just one tiny, little, itty-bitty thing?"

Marilee smiled in spite of herself. "No." She ushered her sister to the French doors and kissed her cheek before shooing her out. "G'night, sis. Love you. If you need me in the middle of the night to come watch the kids, just give me a jingle."

Gerry leaned back in to return the kiss and grab another brownie. "For the road," she said, a dimple flashing in her cheek as she smiled impishly. "Hopefully Ron won't smell my brownie breath. Like occasional chocolate will hurt anything? He's such a fussbudget, and on top of all the modern stuff, he still believes all the outdated things as well. Won't let me hang clothes on the line or reach over my head. When he painted the nursery, I couldn't step foot in the room and smell the fumes. He drives me nuts."

Marilee helped her sister down the steps, and then, not allowing herself time to change her mind, hurried back in to the phone and dialed Joe's number. A few seconds later when he answered her call, she didn't bother to identify herself. "Hi."

If he was surprised to hear from her, he gave no indication of it. "Hi."

She could hear a smile in his voice. "I'm sorry, Joe. I shouldn't have told you no. I'll do it, but only under certain conditions."

"I knew you wouldn't let me down," he said huskily.

"The conditions?" she reminded him. "Otherwise, it's a no go."

"Right. The conditions. What are they?"

"No funny business."

"Funny business? What, exactly, do you mean by that?"

"I want your word you'll keep it strictly on a friends-only basis. In plainer terms, no pressuring me in any way, and absolutely no twinkles and grins."

"No what?"

"You know, twinkles and—" She realized how absurd that sounded. "Don't play innocent. You grin at me like that on purpose, and you know it."

"Grin at you how?" There was definitely a smile in his voice now. "You need to be more specific."

"You know. And if you do it, out the door you and Zachary go. The same for long, heated looks. No heated looks, period."

"Heated?" He chuckled warmly. "Do you check with an atmospheric thermometer, or is yours a finger in the wind gauge?"

"Joe, you know what I mean."

"I can't *look*? Ah, come on. A guy can't—"

"No long looks," she said firmly.

"All right, all right, no long looks. Anything else?"

"No doing your lost puppy act."

"My lost puppy act? That's my only surefire. When I was sixteen, I spent half my life in front of the mirror, practicing. Damn, you drive a mean bargain."

She laughed in spite of herself. "So you *do* give me those looks on purpose!"

"Sweetheart, with you, I leave nothing to chance."

"And no terms of endearment," she said with finality.

"How do you spell endearment?"

"Are you making a list?"

"No, I just wanna keep you on the phone. I love hearing your voice."

Marilee closed her eyes. "Keep it up, and we're doomed before we start. I mean it, Joe. Friends only."

"This *friend* loves your voice."

"You're impossible. Do you want me to keep Zachary or not?"

"You know I do. Friends only, honey. You've got my word."

"Honey's an endearment."

"You can also pour it on pancakes. Honey stays. I've always called you that, and I'll do it without thinking. You have to at least be fair."

He *had* always called her honey. She nodded, then realized he couldn't see her. "Okay, honey stays. But at least try not to use it often. So what do you think?"

"Am I allowed to negotiate these conditions?"

"No. Do we have a deal?"

"It's a deal. Friends only."

"You're sure?"

"I know what you're thinking. That I'll try to make this arrangement work in my favor."

She was afraid of that, yes. "Will you?"

"I've never broken my word to you yet, have I?"

"No."

"Why would I start now?"

"I don't suppose you would."

"Do you know what I've been doing while I waited for you to call me back?"

"You were that sure I would call?"

"Pretty sure." His voice thickened and dipped low. "When have I ever asked you for anything and had you turn me down?"

"Never, I guess." Didn't he see that her inability to tell him no was what made him so very dangerous? "So . . . what were you doing while you waited for me to call?"

"Holding my breath."

"Holding your—" She broke off and squeezed her eyes closed. "Oh, Joe."

He sighed, the sound coming over the line, ragged and weary. "It's pretty horrible, not breathing, and the hell of it is, I know how I feel is nothing compared to what you go through. At least I know I can make it stop any time I want."

She couldn't think what to say, so she said nothing.

"I would never—and I do mean *never*—deliberately do anything that might make you go through that, honey."

"I know," she whispered. And the heartbreak of it was, she really did.

"So stop worrying. For one thing, I've got my son to think of. I won't risk blowing it with you. Where would that leave him? Secondly, the way I see it, if there's any hope at all for us, we've got to start over as just friends, anyway."

"That's just it, Joe. There isn't any hope."

"I know you believe that."

She wrapped the phone cord around her finger and watched her flesh darken as the circulation was cut off. "Don't make me regret agreeing to do this before we even get started. One wrong move, and the deal is off. I mean it. No second chances."

"I know it's pretty scary business, seeing me every day."

If any other man had made that comment, she would have denied it. But she'd already admitted as much to him and could see no reason to pretend otherwise. "Yes," she said hoarsely, "really scary."

"Seeing me under these conditions won't make you sick again, Mari," he assured her gently.

"I hope you're right."

"I'll make damned sure of it. And here's another thought to hold on to. If, by some chance, you ever do get sick again, you won't go through it alone. Zachary and I will move in and take care of you."

Just what she wanted to hear.

"If you need groceries, I'll go get them. If you need to go for a drive to calm down and can't get home, I'll have a tracking beeper installed on the car so I can go find you. And instead of pizza pans, you'll have me to stand guard at your doors."

The picture that formed in her mind made her smile in spite of herself. "Having you in my house when I'm like that would push me right over the brink."

He chuckled. "I'll buy you a high-voltage cattle prod."

She smiled again, for she could almost believe he would go that far, which was only another reason for her to question her sanity. How could she fear a man when he clearly loved her so much?

"Oh, Joe . . ."

"Don't worry about getting sick again. Please, don't, honey. If it happens, you won't go through it without me. I'll be there for you next time."

Tears filled her eyes. "You and Zachary going to help me string my little bells on twine?"

"You bet. Whatever it takes."

He made it sound so uncomplicated. Only it wasn't, and she couldn't think how she might better describe it so he would understand.

A long silence fell. Then he said, "You're an angel for agreeing to help me out. Zachary will love it there. I just know he will."

Thinking of the child, some of the tension eased from Marilee's shoulders. "Will you bring him in the morning, then?"

"How's seven-thirty sound? The first day, I should stick around for a half hour or so to make sure he's going to handle it all right."

She wasn't thrilled at the thought, but if she was going to watch Zachary, that was to be expected the first day.

"Seven-thirty will be fine," she agreed.

"You really *are* an angel, honey. I'll see you in the morning then."

After saying good-bye, Marilee hung up the phone and stared at the receiver for a long moment. He'd called her honey even while saying good-bye. They were off to a great start. She hated to think what he could do with hello.

She had a hysterical urge to laugh. One wrong move, and the deal was off? Joe Lakota could make moves on her from across a room.

Five

riends only.

Marilee had high hopes of enforcing that dictum. Big problem. The very next morning, Joe showed up on her doorstep at six o'clock with a pajama-clad Zachary asleep in his arms. Still tying the sash of her robe, Marilee listened in drowsy befuddlement as Joe apologized for waking her. Then, dropping a paper sack of his son's clothing at her feet, he rushed on to explain that his mom was being transported by ambulance to the cardiac center in Bedford.

"Problems during the night," he said softly so as not to waken the sleeping child he put into her arms. "Doctor Petrie thinks there's some severe blockage. They're going to do an emergency catheter test—you know, one of those procedures where they shoot dye into the heart?" He glanced at his watch. "She's scheduled for half past eight, and I want to be with her for a while before they take her in. Doc Petrie says it can be dangerous, especially when she's already having problems. They have to do the test to see what's wrong, but there's a chance—"

He broke off and passed a hand over his eyes. "They could lose her on the table."

"Oh, Joe, I'm so sorry." Starting to come awake, Marilee shifted his child to get a better hold on him and said, "How will Zachary react, waking up with a stranger?"

The muscles around his mouth tightened, drawing down the corners of his mouth. "He'll be upset." He reached inside the red polo shirt he wore and drew out a chain. After tugging it off over his head, he enfolded it in her hand. "Give him this. I don't part with it often, but sometimes I let him wear it. I told him it'll keep him safe, and sometimes it makes him feel better if he has it. Failing in that, at least he'll know you're somebody pretty special to me simply because I gave it to you."

Marilee tightened one arm around the sleeping little boy to twist her other wrist and open her hand. On her palm lay the St. Christopher medal that she'd given Joe some twenty years earlier. Tears filled her eyes. "I don't know if he's even considered to be a saint anymore. I can't believe you still wear it."

He gave her one of those lost-puppy looks she'd dreaded so much. "The only time I take it off is to let my son wear it. I honestly believe it's saved my life more than once."

"I'll give it to him when he wakes up then."

"Good. It'll make him feel better. The rest you'll have to play by ear. If you can't get him calmed down, call the hospital, and I'll get back here as quick as I can."

"And leave your mom?"

"Zachary comes first. She understands that."

Nevertheless, she wouldn't have him paged unless she absolutely had to. "Just go, Joe. I'll manage some way."

"I'm so sorry about this! I meant to stay a while. Honestly, I did."

"I can handle it." Marilee knew it would take him over an hour to make the drive to Bedford. Every minute he wasted talking to her was a minute he wouldn't get to spend with his mom before they took her in for the procedure. "Give your mother a big hug from me. All right?"

He gave her another of those looks that always melted her heart, and she found herself thinking that he was the one who was badly in need of a hug. He looked worried half sick, and she could tell by the circles under his eyes that he hadn't rested well.

"Thanks, Marilee. I don't know what I'd do without you. I really don't."

Before she could think about it and change her mind, Marilee freed one arm, stepped over the threshold, went up on her tiptoes, and hugged his neck. "Don't worry. She's going to be all right, Joe. I just know she will."

She glimpsed a startled expression crossing his face, and she could almost feel his hesitance. Then he sighed, cautiously returning her embrace as he bent to kiss her hair. To her surprise, it was wonderful to feel his strong arm around her again. Wonderful and utterly bewildering because she'd meant the hug only as a caring gesture to an old friend and hadn't expected to like it.

His arm still lightly encircling her and his son, he drew back slightly to kiss the tip of her nose and both cheeks as well, then pulled her close again. "You really are an angel, you know it? When Zachary wakes up, tell him I love him, and that I'll call every hour on the hour to check on him."

Her cheeks still tingling, Marilee nodded. "I—I'll tell him."

She could feel him shaking, and by that, she knew she'd been right in thinking he needed a hug.

"Would you do something else for me?" he whispered near her ear.

Anything. "What?" she asked.

"Say a rosary for her. If anybody has a hotline to God, it's got to be you."

"Not really. But consider it done," she promised. "I'll call Mama and Gerry and ask them to pray for her, too."

"Thank you."

His mouth grazed her ear in a whisper of warmth. Then

he was gone. As she watched him run through the lemon-yellow morning sunlight toward his car, she nearly wept at the way he favored his right leg. He had to be in constant pain.

Joe. Some things simply never changed, and her love for him was one of them. In retrospect, she couldn't quite believe she'd actually hugged him. What on earth had she been thinking? If she expected him to keep his distance, she had to do the same. *Friends only*? Right. They were off to a marvelous start.

She pushed the door closed, watching through the paned glass as he backed his Honda from the driveway. When he'd driven from sight, she rested her cheek against Zachary's soft, dark hair, knowing even before she tried to sort through her tangled emotions that she already loved this little boy because he was Joe's son. It was as simple as that.

Only, of course, it wasn't simple at all. What in life ever was? This was the child she'd once dreamed of having herself. *Zachary James.* It made her heart hurt, holding him like this. Relaxed in slumber, he lay against her so trustingly, as though he belonged there, the press of his warm little body soft and heavy. She ached with sadness and regret and jealousy, yet having him in her arms also satisfied a need that she had tried hard to believe no longer existed. *Zachary*, the child that might have been hers. Should have been hers. She felt so cheated. Robbed of everything she'd ever wanted.

How was she supposed to deal with that? More importantly, how on earth would she hide her feelings from Zachary? Children were far more intuitive than many adults gave them credit for being.

She made her way to the living room and sank onto the rocker with the child still clasped to her breast. He murmured something in his sleep. After putting her beads and Joe's medal on the end table, she smoothed his hair with a light touch and gazed down at his darling little face. *Oh, God.* He was so precious, and Gerry was right; he looked exactly like Joe.

She began to rock, soothing him back to sleep even as she soothed herself. *Jealousy.* What a waste of energy. Zachary couldn't help who his mother was, and if she allowed thoughts of Valerie to taint her relationship with this little boy, she was a moron. She lifted his hand, marveling as he made a loose fist over one of her fingers. His fingernails were so tiny and absolutely perfect. She rubbed her thumb over his knuckles, her smile deepening as she recalled the many times she'd watched Gerry examine her new babies in much the same way.

Well, so? For this little while, Zachary James Lakota was *hers* to love. It was an unexpected gift, and she was determined to enjoy every minute of the time she had with him. It didn't matter who his real mother was. For now, he was hers.

An hour later when Zachary began to come slowly awake, Marilee was still rocking him. When his eyelashes fluttered, she braced herself, knowing he might be startled to see her and grow frightened. Instead he opened his eyes, focused blearily on her face, and smiled sleepily.

"Are you the story lady?"

Marilee's throat tightened. "The what?"

"The lady who writes little kid stories. My dad said he was bringing me here. I fell asleep in the car."

"Oh. Yes, I'm the story lady.

"Hi."

"Hello, Zachary," she replied softly.

"My dad says you're his best friend ever, that he's your best friend ever, and you'll like me lots, just 'cause."

"That's right," she murmured.

"How come?"

She smiled in spite of herself. "Just because."

He smiled back—a slow, crooked grin that warmed

his beautiful brown eyes before it slanted over his mouth. A deep dimple flashed in his cheek.

He snuggled close and looped a thin arm around her neck. "I like you, too."

She tightened her embrace around him and rested her cheek against his silky head. Child of her flesh . . . child of her dreams. In that moment as she hugged Zachary close, she wasn't sure there was a measurable difference.

So began her stint as a daycare provider, with her falling a little more in love with every breath she drew.

As the morning progressed, Marilee asked herself at least a dozen times how on earth she could be such an airhead. Had she been kidding herself? Lying to herself? Or was she just plain stupid? How could she have believed, even for a moment, that she could do this for Joe and survive with her heart intact? Love didn't come with an on-and-off valve. She had loved Joe almost as far back as she could remember and still did. By taking Zachary into her home, she'd set herself up. Next step, heartbreak and possible catastrophe. *Several weeks*? That was just long enough for her to become addicted to this child . . . just long enough to fall so in love with him that she'd want to die when Joe started taking him to a daycare center.

True to his word, Joe called shortly after he reached the hospital. Wearing a mustache of milk, Zachary eagerly grabbed the phone, grinning from ear to ear as he listened to his dad's voice. Watching him, Marilee smiled. He was such a little guy that even the telephone receiver seemed mammoth in his hand.

He suddenly began darting glances around her kitchen, finally spied her spotted-cow wall clock, and said, "Yup, I can see it." He frowned. "Little hand on the nine, big hand on the twelve." He flashed Marilee an excited grin. "My dad's gonna call me again at nine o'clock!"

Marilee nodded, thinking to herself that most fathers in Joe's situation might have forgotten to call altogether. He had to be worried sick about his mom, yet he intended to keep his promise and telephone his little boy at pre-arranged times. *Every hour, on the hour.*

"Okay. Yup, she gave it to me. But I don't need it. She's real nice, and she has a dog! I love you, Daddy. Tell Grandma I love her, too." He thrust the phone at Marilee. "My dad wants to talk to you."

"Hi," she said softly.

"Hi, honey. How'd it go? Did he cry when he woke up?"

"No, not a drip. Evidently he went to sleep in the car expecting to come here, so when he woke up and saw me, he wasn't surprised."

"I told him, but he was so sleepy, I wasn't sure anything I said sank in. He sounds happy as a clam."

Marilee watched Zachary as he climbed back onto the kitchen chair to finish his breakfast cereal. Her hound sat patiently beside him, ever on the alert for dropped tidbits. "He and Boo are already pals. I think he's going to be fine, Joe. Concentrate on your mom and don't worry."

"I'm not worried," he assured her. "Not when he's with you. Just in case you need me, though, I'd better give you the number to the nurse's station."

Marilee quickly jotted down the information. "How's your mom?"

"Scared. I keep telling her she'll come through just fine, but that's easy to say. She's in a lot of pain."

"Can they give her something?"

"I think they have. It's just not working yet."

Marilee heard voices in the background. Joe quickly said good-bye, promising to keep in touch, and hung up. Marilee drew the phone from her ear and hugged it to her for a moment, her eyes squeezed closed as she struggled to make sense of her feelings. Dread, yearning, fear, and excitement.

It was the excitement that worried her the most. Hearing his voice. Seeing him. Looking into his eyes. She might be a giddy teenager again. This was dangerous. She felt like a wader, toe dipping to test the water. If she entered this particular pool, she might wander into the deep end and go under.

Friends only, she assured herself. She had stipulated the conditions, Joe had agreed to them, and she intended to enforce them, to the letter.

She had to.

Joe called back every hour to speak to Zachary, and each time he wanted an update from Marilee. She tried to keep their conversations brief and impersonal, but Joe's obvious concern for his son weakened her resolve, and she found herself staying on the phone with him longer than was necessary, giving him particulars to ease his mind. They were coloring—playing games—making lunch. At the end of each phone conversation, Joe's voice grew husky and he thanked her with a sincerity that made her feel hugged.

"You're one in a million," he whispered when he called while his mom was in the surgery. "It's the strangest feeling, hearing your voice on the phone again. I feel like I've been lost for ten years and just found my way home where I belong."

"Joe," she whispered warningly.

"I know—I know. I promised."

He sounded so forlorn that Marilee instantly felt guilty. "You're under a lot of pressure right now," she tempered. "I understand."

"Forgive me?" he asked with strained jocularity.

Marilee knew she would forgive him almost anything, and that was yet another thing that worried her.

When Joe called shortly before noon, it was to tell Marilee that Faye had been scheduled for an emergency angioplasty the following afternoon. "It's going to be a risky procedure. Doc Petrie was right; she's got some severe blockage. No permanent damage to the heart yet, though."

"That's good news," Marilee pointed out, trying to be positive. "I'm sure she'll come through it with flying colors, Joe. Try not to worry so."

"I'm not worried," he assured her, which was obviously a lie because his voice sounded shaky. "I, um . . . just have tons on my mind. This afternoon, I absolutely have to make an appearance at work because I'll be taking off most of tomorrow. And I'd really like to come back here and be with Mom tonight. Will it be a problem for you if I don't show up to get Zachary until about ten?"

"Not at all. Got you covered. You just do what you have to do and don't give it another thought."

"Tomorrow, I—"

"Same goes for tomorrow and over the weekend. You'll want to be with her Saturday and Sunday as well, I'm sure. I'll wash his pajamas each afternoon and just put him to bed here. Things will smooth out next week, and we'll be able to establish a routine. Until then I'll expect him to come early and leave really late."

"Are you sure you don't mind, especially Sunday? He'll freak if you try to take him to mass. He doesn't do well in crowds."

"I can miss one Sunday, Joe. It's not a problem. Really."

Marilee scarcely saw Joe until well into the following week. He was so busy with the demands of his job and trying to be with his mother at the hospital every possible moment that he barely had time to breathe, let alone stay for any length of time at her place. He did call every hour, though, keeping his promise to Zachary, regardless of where he was or what he happened to be doing.

The child seemed to take his father's steadfastness for granted, which told Marilee that Joe was the wonderful parent she'd always believed he would be. Many men made promises to their children and then promptly forgot all about them. Not Joe. If he promised Zachary anything, he stood behind his word.

The long days gave Marilee plenty of time to enjoy

having Zachary, and keeping her vow to herself, she set out to make the most of every minute, working only while he slept. During his waking hours, they whiled away the time, doing things they both enjoyed. Zachary's favorite pastime was coloring, and he greatly favored Marilee's sketches over regular coloring books. Luckily she had heaps of drawings she'd done over the years that weren't up to par for publication. Zachary, however, thought they were wonderful.

Zachary. No way around it, he was far too easy to love. By the end of the first day, she was already so far gone that it was hard to turn loose of him when Joe came to pick him up. Midway through the second day, she found herself looking down at his expressive little face and getting tears in her eyes just at the thought of anyone ever hurting him. By the end of the third day, she wanted to find Valerie Lakota and rip out her hair.

Not a rational reaction, especially for Marilee, who seldom indulged in violent fantasies. But her sense of outrage made it difficult to care if she was being rational or not. Someone had cruelly mistreated this child, and the very thought that the individuals responsible might go unpunished made her seethe.

Naturally, her anger became centered on Joe's ex-wife. As Zachary's mother, it had been Valerie's responsibility to protect the little boy from harm while he was in her custody, and the pathetic creature had failed miserably in her duty. Though Marilee saw evidence of that infrequently, each incident had a devastating impact on her.

One day when Zachary spilled his milk at lunchtime, his face turned as white as the liquid he tried so frantically to stop from dripping on the floor.

"Hey, it's all right, Zachary," Marilee hastened to assure him. "Accidents happen to everyone."

But the child didn't seem to hear her. With small, cupped hands, he formed an ineffectual dike to block the flow of milk, his eyes growing huge when the liquid seeped under his fingers and trickled over the edge of the table onto her waxed floor. He had obviously spilled his milk on some other occasion and been severely punished for the offense.

Boo came to the rescue. When the hound had finished licking up the mess, Marilee raised an eyebrow at her frightened lunch guest and said, "I think he'd like some more if you wouldn't mind spilling what's left."

Zachary blinked. Then he shifted his gaze to the small amount of milk that remained in his glass. He clearly couldn't believe she meant for him to spill it on purpose.

"The floor will survive," she told him. "Since we've already got to mop, where's the harm?"

"You don't care?"

Marilee pursed her lips. "Will you help me clean up?"

"Yup."

"Well, then?" She shrugged and smiled. "Go for it."

With a trembling hand, Zachary picked up his glass. Giving her a last wondering glance, he poured out the rest of his milk. The hound hurried over, happy to lap up the spillage. Zachary giggled and relaxed somewhat. "He sure likes it a lot!"

Marilee pushed up to get the jug of milk from the refrigerator to refill the child's glass. "Boo likes people food, period. He's always on hand to do accident cleanup." As she poured more milk, she softly added, "It *was* an accident, Zachary. I know you didn't knock over your glass on purpose. At my house, you'll never be punished for anything you didn't mean to do. All right?"

"All right," he acknowledged faintly, his tone conveying doubt.

Marilee returned the milk to the fridge and resumed her seat, her interest in eating taking second priority to her concern for the child. "As far as that goes, Zachary . . ." she went on cautiously, "I don't really believe in punishment at all."

The child's soulful gaze became fixed on hers, his expression of incredulity changing to stunned disbelief. "Not ever?"

"Nope, not ever," she assured him. "I think punishing little boys is dumb and mean."

"Me, too!" he was quick to agree.

She struggled to hide a smile. Toying with the crust of her bread, she explained, "I think we all learn more from our mistakes if we have to make up for them in productive ways." By his nonplussed look, she guessed he wasn't certain what that meant, so she went on to clarify. "For instance, if you make a mess? I'll ask you to clean it up. If you do something that's not very nice to someone else, I'll ask you to do a good deed to make up for it. That way, you've not only learned that you've made a mistake, but you've learned how to make it right. Being sorry is nice, but it seldom fixes anything."

He mulled that over for a moment. "You don't ever spank?"

She shook her head. "I don't think spanking is very productive."

He looked greatly relieved to hear that. "My dad doesn't spank. He says he will if I play in the street, though."

"I guess playing in the street is a pretty serious offense, at that. You could be hit by a car, and that could hurt you very badly or even kill you."

He nodded. "That's how come he said he'd spank me. 'Cause he loves me. I don't feel scared, though. I'm never gonna play in the street." Picking up his sandwich, he cast a sidelong glance at Boo, who had taken up squatting rights beside his chair and was eagerly awaiting more fallout. "Poor Boo. He didn't get any lunch."

"When we're finished, you can feed him our leftovers," Marilee promised.

That said, she returned her attention to the meal and let the subject of punishment drop. In time, Zachary would grow to trust her and feel safe with her. Until then, she could only reassure him and do her best not to frighten him.

The only problem was that Zachary grew frightened

for no apparent reason. One afternoon after working up a sweat while sweeping the deck, Marilee announced that she needed a drink, whereupon Zachary ran and hid in a bathroom cupboard. Another time when she asked the child to go fetch a shoebox of color crayons from the hall closet, he hid under her bed. Both times when Marilee discovered the child's hiding place and tried to coax him out, he grew so terrified he wet his pants.

Each time this happened, Marilee felt absolutely sick with worry. To make matters worse, Zachary clearly believed she might fly into a rage because he had soiled his jeans. Instead she carried him to her chair where she rocked him until he calmed down. Afterward they both had to change their clothes from the skin out, and she ran a load of wash to right the damage.

"Now no one will know," she told Zachary with a wink.

"That's good," the child admitted. "It makes my dad real, real mad."

Marilee's neck prickled. "At you?"

"No, at my mom, I think. His face gets all funny and his lips turn gray."

Marilee imagined that her lips had turned gray, too. To see the fear in Zachary's eyes—to watch him clutch at his jeans, clearly horrified because he'd lost control—it nearly broke her heart. It also made her want to find Valerie Lakota and punch her right on the nose.

Oh, God—oh, God. She'd gone from hair pulling to punching? What in heaven's name was happening to her?

Zachary was happening to her, she realized. She had wandered into the deep end and was drowning, after all. And Joe hadn't even been around to give her a push.

Zachary.

For such a little boy, he had an enormous appetite. Those first few days when Joe came so late in the evening to retrieve his son, Zachary ate dinner at Marilee's, and each time she started to cook, she could have sworn she saw his mouth watering.

"Don't you ever eat pot roast at home, Zachary?" she asked one afternoon.

"Nope. Just hambugger, and Daddy always burns it."

"Not much of a cook, huh?"

The child shrugged and wrinkled his nose. "He's gonna go to school."

"School?"

"Yup. To learn to cook. He says he can't raise me on canned stuff, that I'll grow up puny."

Marilee cautiously questioned Zachary to learn exactly what his father fed him. She discovered that Joe's culinary talents extended only to ready-to-eat or easily prepared foods that came in cartons, cans, or foil packets, the only exceptions "burned hambugger" and "blowed-up potatoes."

"How, exactly, does one blow up a potato?" she asked.

"In the microwave. Now Daddy just leaves 'em until they get hot, and we eat 'em sort of raw." At Marilee's appalled look, Zachary quickly added, "A hot, sort of raw potato is better than a poke in the eye."

That was Joe's motto, she felt certain. She could almost hear him saying it. *Burned hambugger*? Good grief. When Joe began picking the child up at four each afternoon, she was going to feel just awful for letting them leave hungry, especially knowing as she did that they'd probably go home to a can of chili for dinner.

Stop!

She gave herself a hard mental shake. She was *not* getting sucked into this. No how, no way. Plenty of kids survived quite well on far less healthful fare. Zachary would be just fine.

Once Faye was released from the hospital, the demands on Joe's time relaxed, and after that, he was finally able to bring Zachary at eight each morning and pick him up at four as they'd originally agreed. The first morning drop-off went well, with Joe saying a quick farewell to his son and not even coming inside because he was running a little late. Unfortunately Marilee doubted things would go as smoothly when he came to get Zachary that afternoon. For the first time since the start of their arrangement, he would be in no hurry to get anywhere, and she feared he might invent a dozen excuses to linger.

Alarmed at the thought of spending time with him, Marilee decided to nip it in the bud before it got started. She called Gerry in the early afternoon during Zachary's nap and made arrangements to go over at a quarter past four for a coffee klatch. Now, she assured herself, she could tell Joe in all honesty that she had an appointment to make and hurry him on his way.

Tomorrow . . . well, hopefully tomorrow would take care of itself. She'd think of something. The trick, she felt certain, was to get him into the habit of leaving quickly. Once a pattern was established, he'd be less likely to break it.

Unfortunately, just minutes after speaking to her sister, she inadvertently frightened Zachary again by suggesting they play a game of hide-and-seek. The child turned pale and started backing away from her, shaking his head.

"I don't wanna!" he said with a sob and promptly raced to the dining room, where he dived under her table, curled into a ball, and crossed his arms over his head.

They'd been getting along so well for a couple of days, with Zachary showing every sign that he felt safe and completely at ease with her. Marilee couldn't think what on earth she'd done or said to frighten him.

Pulling away the chairs, she dropped to all fours and crawled under the table. Afraid to touch him for fear he might lose it completely, she sat hunched over beside him instead and hugged her knees.

"If you don't like the game of hide-and-seek, sweetie, we can play something else."

Zachary shrank away. "I don't wanna play nothing!"

"That's fine. We can color for a while instead. Or I can tell you a story."

When he gave no sign that he intended to leave his hiding place, Marilee decided the story was her only option. She rested her chin on her knees and began a tale about a small boy who went to stay with a babysitter.

"The little boy didn't know for sure what to expect from the babysitter," she said carefully, "and sometimes, without meaning to, the lady said and did things that made him feel afraid."

Zachary moved one arm to peer out at her. Marilee smiled at him.

"The poor lady . . ." she went on. "She loved the little boy *so* much, and all she wanted was to be his good friend. The very *last* thing she set out to do was frighten him. But somehow she did.

"Afterward she wasn't sure what she had done that was wrong and she couldn't even say she was sorry. So she climbed under the table with him and got a crick in her neck from sitting all bent over."

Zachary hid his face again.

Marilee waited a beat, and then she gently said, "Won't you please tell me what I did wrong, sweetie? I promise that I'll never do it again."

"I don't want you to jump out at me," he said so faintly she almost couldn't catch the words. "Out of closets and stuff."

"Ah." She thought about that for a moment. "I guess that would be really scary, wouldn't it?"

"Yup."

"Has someone jumped out at you before?"

"Yup. It happened lots when my mom had parties. People got drunk and put stuff in their nose. Then they played mean games, turning off the lights and jumping out like monsters."

A burning sensation washed over Marilee's eyes. Zachary was only four now, and Joe had gotten custody of him last spring. He couldn't have been much over three when that sort of thing had occurred. "Did they actually jump out at you, sweetheart, or just at each other?"

"At *me*!" he replied angrily.

Marilee didn't blame him a bit for feeling bitter and mad. How could responsible, decent adults do something so horrid to a little boy in the name of fun? "You said they turned out the lights. Was it was all dark in the house when they jumped out at you?"

"Yup," he said in a squeaky voice. "They thought it was funny, and they laughed."

"That couldn't have seemed very funny to you."

"Nope," he admitted thinly. "It scared me real, real bad. I went and hid."

"I would have, too!"

"Not my mom. She said hiding was naughty, and she got real mad when she couldn't find me."

"Uh-oh." Marilee hugged her knees more tightly. "What did she do when she found you, sweetie?"

"Spanked me until her hand hurt. That made her mad at me, too, so she'd tell Frank to do it with his belt."

"Oh." Marilee's throat felt as if it were closing off. "That must have hurt awfully bad!"

"Yup," he said with an audible gulp. "My mom said for Frank to do it easy, but he didn't. He always did it real, real hard, and if I tried to wiggle away, I got more licks. He'd hold my arm and spank me around in circles."

Spank? In Marilee's book, lashes with a belt didn't qualify as a mere spanking. It was a whipping. "Did he bruise you?"

"It made blue marks."

Marilee didn't want to hear this. The pictures that formed in her mind made her sick. "Oh, Zachary . . ." She reached over to lightly rub his narrow back, not certain what to say.

"You won't tell, will you?" he asked.

Her hand froze on his brown-and-yellow striped T-shirt. "Tell who, sweetie?"

"My dad."

Her heart caught. "You haven't ever told your dad about this?"

"Nope," he said shrilly. "And you can't, either. Promise? My dad would get real, real mad. At my mom and Frank."

Marilee bit her lip, realizing in a flash that this little boy was experiencing some of the same fears she'd had ten years ago, namely that Joe might fly into a rage if he learned the truth and do something crazy.

"Oh, Zachary . . ." she whispered. *Don't do this to me!* she thought frantically. *Don't ask me to keep secrets from your father.* "Your daddy needs to know these things."

The child rolled onto his back and fixed her with an accusing look. "You said you wanted to be my *friend!* You *lied!*"

"No, no . . . I'm trying to be your friend, Zachary. Really, sweetie, I want nothing more."

"Then you can't tell my dad!" Tears filled his eyes. "My daddy loves me lots and lots!"

"I know he does."

"And he'd get really, really, *really* mad if he found out. He'd go to my mom's house and yell at her, and she'd call the cops! And they'd put him in jail for beating up Frank, and they might never, never, *never* let him out."

"Oh, honey, I'm sure your dad won't be put in jail."

"Uh-huh! Just like before!"

"Before?"

"When he came and yelled at my mom and hit Frank, my mom called the cops! They came and 'rested him."

That was news to Marilee. "They *did*?"

Zachary stared up at her, tears spilling over his spiked lower lashes onto his pale cheeks as he nodded. "They put handcuffs on him and took him away in a white car with lights on top."

"Oh, *dear.*"

Marilee was shocked. Joe had been arrested for assault? Dear God in heaven . . . *Joe*? Her incredulity quickly waned. She knew how fiercely protective he was of those he loved. Besides, who was she to pass judgment? She couldn't count the times over the last few days that she'd entertained the notion of punching Valerie on the nose.

"Oh, Zachary . . ."

He rubbed furiously at his cheeks, scowling at her from behind his fists. "My mom was afraid to let him in, so he kicked in her door and came in anyhow!"

"Oh, my." The list of charges against him grew in her mind. Breaking and entering, destruction of property, assault . . . no wonder he was broke. He must have paid a fortune just in fines.

"He was real, real mad. He got Frank on the floor and pounded his face."

Marilee forgot the lack of headroom and bumped her crown on the table. Cupping a hand over the smarting spot, she asked, "Was he so mad because he found out Frank spanked you with a belt?"

"Yup. And also 'cause Frank said I told him a lie and made me gurgle hot sauce."

"*What?*"

"Hot sauce. It's red, and it burns. That way, you don't never forget and tell more lies."

Marilee couldn't conceive anyone doing such a thing to a small child. Horrified, she said, "If you were living with your mom, how did your dad find out what was going on?"

Zachary's chin started to quiver, and the tears fell more quickly over his cheeks. "I called him up on the phone."

"Oh." The picture became clearer and clearer.

"I thought he'd just come get me. I didn't know he'd get so mad he'd kick my mom's door and hit Frank."

Marilee sighed, scarcely able to imagine how enraged Joe must have been. Receiving a phone call from his sobbing child. Being told that some jerk had whipped him and forced him to gargle with hot sauce? She closed her eyes, grabbing for composure and uttering a quick, silent prayer for wisdom.

"If they put my dad in jail again, my mom'll get me

back," Zachary told her in a jerky voice. "I don't wanna go back, not ever again!"

"I can see your dilemma," she confessed.

"So you can't tell him I got more spankings or about the monster games. You gotta promise."

Marilee rested her chin on her upraised knees again, her troubled gaze fixed on Zachary. "Now I understand how come you haven't told your dad much about what happened while you stayed at your mom's," she said softly. "You're faced with a double whammy."

"What's that?"

"A double whammy? That's when two really bad things might happen, in this case, getting your dad in so much trouble that they might put him in jail and, as a result, you having to go live with your mom again."

"Yup, a double whammy."

"Well," she said, thinking carefully before she spoke, "we can't let either of those things happen."

"Nope. So you gotta promise."

Marilee looked him directly in the eye. "I'm honored that you trusted me enough to tell me, Zachary."

He dropped his gaze. "I didn't mean to. I just—when I talked about the monster games, I forgot and talked too much."

She drew in a deep breath and slowly released it. "You know why, don't you? Because you've kept ugly secrets all locked up inside of you for way too long, and they need out. And you'd like a friend to talk to. Someone who won't tell your dad or anything." She smiled at him. "You feel pretty confident that *I* won't go to your mom's and hit Frank. Right?"

He smiled slightly, then pushed to a sitting position and crossed his legs. "You aren't big enough to hit Frank."

"I'm not brave enough, either," she admitted with a humorless laugh. She sighed again. "Your dad is, though. I bet he'd fight lions for you."

"Yup. He loves me lots."

"Yes, he certainly does, and you're absolutely right in believing he would get really, really mad if you told him what Frank did to you."

"Frank did lots of stuff. Other people did, too. People that came to my mom's parties."

Marilee nodded. "I sort of thought maybe so. People who drink and put stuff in their noses get all funny in the head, Zachary, and they do things they shouldn't." She thought for a moment. "The other day when I told you I needed a drink—you thought I was going to get drunk and be mean, didn't you?"

He nodded, looking ashamed. "Just for a minute was all."

"I was just thirsty for some tea."

"I know that now."

Marilee sighed. "Sometimes I drink alcohol."

"You do?" He gave her a worried look.

"Not very often. Usually only wine at a special dinner," she assured him, "and never enough to get drunk. And even if I did get drunk, I'd never be mean to you. I promise."

"That's good."

Marilee swallowed and gazed at the crease in her jeans. "Is that why you're afraid of my crayon closet?" she asked. "Because you think someone may jump out and get you?"

He nodded. "Or put me in it."

Her stomach lurched. "In it?"

He shrugged. "Yours doesn't got a lock, though. I looked."

"Someone locked you in a closet?"

"Sometimes my mom did 'cause she was having fun and didn't want to watch me. She said I couldn't get hurt in the closet. She gave me my pillow and a blanket, but I didn't like it in there. It was dark and I couldn't get out."

To Marilee's dismay, she felt her mouth start to quiver. She took several fast breaths, determined not to cry.

When she regained her composure, she said, "I wouldn't like it in a closet, either, Zachary, and I won't ever lock you up in one. All right?"

"Not even if you have a party?"

"Not even then."

"I *hate* parties."

"Not all parties are like that. But I understand why you might feel that way. Now I think I know how come you feel afraid of strangers, too."

He swiped at his wet cheeks. "Not of you, though." He looked up. "You got smiles in your eyes."

"Oh, Zachary . . . thank you. That's the nicest thing I think anyone ever said to me."

"Do you promise not to tell my dad?"

Marilee circled that question cautiously. "You know, Zachary, I think you may be underestimating your dad. You're right to believe he'll feel very angry with Frank when he finds out, and angry with your mom as well. But not so angry he'll do something stupid. Keeping you with him is the most important thing in the whole world to him. He won't do anything to mess that up, no matter how mad he gets."

"My dad can get really, *really* mad."

Marilee couldn't blame Joe for kicking down Valerie's door and storming into her house. She might have done the same thing herself. "Yes, he can," she agreed. "And I understand why you feel reluctant to tell him all this. At the same time, though, I think it's a big mistake for you to keep secrets from him. He's—" She broke off and considered carefully before she went on. "Your dad is a Mr. Fix It. Did you know that?"

"He can't fix the garbage 'sposal."

Marilee chuckled in spite of the seriousness of the conversation, imagining Joe with the sink torn apart. "I suppose his talent for fixing doesn't extend to everything," she conceded. "But he's great at fixing feelings. He's what I call a good listener, and he understands how people feel. You know all those scary feelings you've got?

Your dad would figure out a way to make them stop, I think. But he can't unless he knows why you're feeling them."

Zachary grew pale again. "You're gonna tell."

"I didn't say that. I said it's a big mistake for *you* not to tell him." Marilee stretched out a hand to cup his small chin. "Did you know it hurts your dad's feelings because you won't talk to him about what happened at your mom's?"

"It does?"

She nodded. "He told me you won't talk to him, and he sounded so sad. I think he's very, very worried about you. That's why he takes you to the doctor, you know. In hopes that you'll tell the doctor what's troubling you because you won't tell him."

"I can't tell the doctor nothing, either. He always talks to my dad afterward and tells him everything I say."

Marilee gave another appalled laugh. "My goodness, what a *tangle*. You're between a rock and a hard spot, aren't you? You can't talk to anybody."

"Nope. And if you tell, I'm gonna be real mad at you."

She smiled and tweaked the end of his nose. "I'll tell you what. I promise not to tell your dad a single thing you've told me unless he promises and crosses his heart first that he won't yell at your mom or hit Frank. How's that?"

Zachary looked dubious.

"Your dad *always* keeps his promises. He's never broken one he's made to me yet."

"Never to me, either," Zachary admitted.

"Well, then? Get him to promise! Then you can talk to him about anything you want with no worries."

This was obviously an option Zachary had never considered. "Do you think I can make him promise?"

Marilee thought for a moment. "I can't think why not. Would you like me to talk to him about it? I think I can probably wrangle a promise out of him."

Zachary nodded. "And if he won't promise, you won't tell him nothin'?"

"Not a single word." She held out her hand. "I give you my solemn oath, Zachary. Not a word unless he promises and crosses his heart not to lose his temper and do something dumb."

They shook on it, then and there.

Six

For the remainder of the afternoon, Zachary talked nearly nonstop. Now that the little boy could confide in someone, all the ugliness he'd kept bottled up came rushing out. The stories, by turn, brought tears to Marilee's eyes, sparked her anger, or made her feel heartsick, and all of them, without exception, drove home to her just how much this child had endured.

A line of communication absolutely had to be established between Zachary and his father, she realized. This child needed to heal, and, in her estimation, that would never start happening until Zachary felt he could confide in Joe. The child naturally looked to his dad for comfort and protection. A hug and reassurance from him would go a long way toward helping the little boy deal with the myriad feelings that roiled within him.

As reluctant as Marilee was to initiate any personal interaction with Joe, this was one time she felt compelled to make an exception. To that end, she called to cancel her visit with Gerry and added more vegetables to the weekly pot roast than she normally might have.

When Joe showed up at four, she left Zachary watching television while she walked out to the car to meet him. Sunlight reflected off the windshield, partially obstructing her view of him inside the Honda, but she could see enough detail to make out his broad shoulders, breeze-tousled hair, and dark eyes, which seemed to study her and miss nothing as she approached.

Bending down as he lowered his window, she said, "I was wondering if you and Zachary might stay for dinner tonight."

He immediately arched an eyebrow, his gaze searching hers and filled with question. "Dinner?"

He was so clearly incredulous that she smiled in spite of herself. "Tonight the special is pot roast simmered to a turn with potatoes, carrots, and baby onions, accompanied by salad, homemade biscuits fresh from the oven, and warm apple crisp à la mode for dessert."

He narrowed an eye, the mischievous twinkle belying his scowl. "You really shouldn't tease a starving man. You're liable to get too close and draw back a stub."

She laughed. "Will you stay or not?"

"Offer me a meal like that, and the question isn't if I will stay but whether or not I'll ever leave. Cooking isn't my forte."

"Zachary has mentioned that a time or two."

He plucked his keys from the ignition and opened the door. As he swung from the car, he seemed to tower over her, the roof of the Honda barely clearing his bottom rib. Marilee retreated a step, feeling minimized by him, even outdoors. The wash-worn cotton of his gray athletic shirt clung to his upper torso, showcasing the powerful contours of his chest. The short sleeves revealed bronze arms bunched with muscle and roped with tendon. Even his running shoes dwarfed hers.

"I know it's rude to look a gift horse in the mouth," he said, "but I have to ask. Why the dinner invitation? The last I knew, you didn't want me hanging around."

Marilee had hoped to ease her way into this conversation, but now everything she'd planned to say fled her mind. "I decided to make an exception this once. I need to have a talk with you about Zachary, and it's not something I can get said with you standing on the porch."

His eyes narrowed. "Zachary?" He glanced worriedly toward the house. "Is he all right?"

"He's fine. Well, actually, he isn't fine. We both know that. He's a very troubled little boy." She nibbled her bottom lip, trying to think how best to say this. "He opened up to me this afternoon, Joe. Told me everything that happened to him over at Valerie's."

"He did? Marilee, that's *wonderful*! Why the glum face? I've had him in counseling going on five months. If he's finally starting to talk, it's a major breakthrough."

She nodded. "Yes, well, he's talking to *me*, not his doctor." She waited a beat. "More importantly, not to you. That's a state of affairs you need to rectify."

"In a heartbeat."

He slammed the car door and started to move past her. "Not so fast, Joe. There are things you need to know, things we need to discuss."

He halted and turned to search her gaze. "Like what?"

"Before I start, let me say this. As I listened to your son talk this afternoon, it was all I could do a few times to stay calm. I had an unholy urge to punch Valerie in the nose by the time Zachary wound down."

"Oh, God. The stuff he told you was that bad?"

"Pretty bad, but that isn't my reason for bringing it up." She held his gaze for a moment, trying to say with her eyes what she couldn't possibly convey with words, that she would never stand in judgment of him. "I just want you to know before I say anything that I understand exactly how furious you must have been a few times, and that, for the most part, I admire your restraint."

He sighed and raked a hand through his hair. "Shit. He told you about Frank." The shamefaced expression that came over his features made Marilee want to pat his shoulder. Because she didn't wish to establish that kind of familiarity between them, she managed to resist the urge, but only just barely.

"There were extenuating circumstances," he rushed to assure her.

"I know that, Joe, and the truth is, had I been in your situation, I might have done the same thing. I find it incredible that you were the one arrested. In my estimation, Frank was the villain. They should have locked *him* up."

"Yeah, well, at that point in time, there was no evidence to corroborate my story. Zachary didn't get it with the belt until afterward, his punishment for calling me and getting Frank in Dutch, so the cops never saw any welts."

"Oh. I understood him to say Frank had already spanked him when he called you."

"He's four and has his sequence of events messed up." He shrugged. "Just hearing about the hot sauce was enough to get me steamed. Nasty stuff, and Zachary swallowed so much, he vomited, which was extremely painful. Unfortunately, it left no outward signs of abuse. I was the more obvious villain. When I got to the house, I could hear Zachary screaming, and I kicked in the door to reach him. When I found Frank in the living room, shaking him, I rearranged the bastard's face, end of story."

"Not quite," she said softly. "We haven't written 'The End' for Zachary."

Very carefully, Marilee related parts of her conversation with Zachary, her main focus Zachary's need to exact a promise from Joe that he wouldn't grow angry and retaliate if his child talked to him. With every word she spoke, Joe's expression grew grimmer.

"Dear God," he whispered when she finished. "My child's afraid to confide in me? That's what you're saying. All this time, with me doing everything I could to make him open up to me, and the entire time, *I've* been the problem? He can't even talk to his doctor, for Christ's sake, for fear the doctor will tell me what he says?"

Seeing his distress, Marilee set aside her reservations and reached out to touch his arm. "Oh, Joe, please, don't think of it like that. Zachary isn't afraid *of* you. He's afraid *for* you. He doesn't want his daddy to do something crazy in defense of him and get thrown in jail again. That's all."

He winced. "How do you think that makes me feel? Who's the dad and who's the kid? My four-year-old, looking out for me? *Damn.* I feel about two inches tall. Losing my temper like that has kept him from getting better."

"Okay, so you let your temper get the best of you, and Zachary is afraid it might happen again. So? Overall, you're his dragon slayer. Only think how good that must make him feel, knowing how you love him and that you'll break down doors to reach him."

He put his hands on his hips, glanced over her neatly manicured front lawn, and sighed. "Well, I guess I've got some fences to go mend. I'd best get to it."

"Yes."

He scratched beside his nose, then lowered his gaze to the cement. Spying an ant that was trying to cross the driveway, he entertained himself by tormenting it for a few seconds, blocking its path one way and then another with the toe of his shoe as the poor thing tried frantically to get away. When he finally tired of teasing the insect and let it escape into the grass, he glanced up.

"Thank you, Marilee," he said in a low, silky voice. "It isn't enough, I know. I'd hang the moon for you, if I could. You've given me back my son. Thank you."

Her eyes burned with tears as she watched him stride toward the house. At the top of the steps, he paused to glance back. "How much time do I have before dinner?"

"All the time you need. The pot roast is on low, so it'll keep as long as necessary, and I saved the biscuits to go in last."

"Do you mind if we commandeer your living room for a while?"

"Make yourselves at home. I can find plenty to keep myself busy while you talk."

Joe carried his son to the living room for a long-overdue chat. Once they were situated on Marilee's sofa, he let Zachary talk for a few minutes—about anything and everything but his experiences while living with his mother. The child asked about Joe's workday, about when they might go fishing, and then he pulled out the big gun, putting in a request for a dog of his own, preferably one just like Boo.

Joe smiled, settled more comfortably against the hunter-green cushions, and then, with no warning, flipped Zachary onto his back to give him a playful whisker rub on the belly, sending the child into gales of laughter.

"I think you're beating around the bush," Joe accused with a teasing growl. "A dog? A *dog*! I'm waiting to eat dinner so you can ask me for an ugly old slobbery *dog*? I thought we came in here to talk about serious stuff!"

As Zachary's mirth subsided, his big brown eyes filled with shadows, and he gazed up at Joe with a pleading expression. "I wanna talk about serious stuff, Daddy, but I got squiggles in my tummy."

Joe's smile faded as he helped his son sit up. "Squiggles, huh? That sounds pretty awful."

Zachary nodded. "Scary squiggles that make me feel like I might urp up my lunch."

"Not all over me, I hope."

"Yup."

Joe sighed. "Well, I guess before we can talk, we need to make those squiggles go away. You must have some real bad stuff to tell me."

"Yup, and I'm afraid you'll get mad even if you try not to."

"At you?"

"Nope. At my mom and Frank and some other people."

"And that gives you squiggles?"

The child nodded. "It's gonna make you real, *real* mad, Daddy. Maybe even mad enough to smash a car."

"Wow, that's pretty mad." Joe thought for a moment. "As I understand it, you did quite a lot of talking to Marilee today. Did that give you squiggles?"

"Nope. Marilee isn't big enough to go hit Frank."

"Ah." Joe smiled sadly. "I guess you've got a point there."

Zachary made a fist on the front of his little T-shirt and started twisting the knit every which way, his forehead pleated in a troubled frown. Joe had a feeling the child had talked himself into a corner.

Gathering him close for a reassuring hug, Joe set himself to the task of helping the boy talk his way out of it.

After listening to his son for nearly an hour, Joe suggested that they save the remainder of their conversation for later that evening when they got home.

"I think we should probably go eat before dinner gets ruined. Don't you?"

Zachary straightened and blinked. "Yup. I'm really hungry."

"No news to me. Your tummy's been growling nonstop for the last thirty minutes."

"Yours, too."

Upon entering the kitchen, Joe found Marilee sitting at the table, her elbows bracketing a writing tablet, her head in her hands. He knew the feeling. Balancing Zachary on one hip, he gazed at her for a long moment, wanting nothing more than to deposit his son on a chair and take her into his arms. She would weep with him, he knew—sharing his pain and his sorrow over what had happened to his child—and then she'd talk with him until the nausea in his stomach went away and the ache in the center of his chest abated.

Only he couldn't touch her, let alone take her into his

arms, and, oh, how he resented the constraints. Funny, that. In his late teens and early twenties when they'd been dating, practically all he'd ever thought about while they were together was making love to her. Now he longed just as much for other kinds of intimacy entirely, those that transcended the physical. To simply hold her close to his heart. To talk with her long into the night. *That* was what love was all about, sharing. Sex was wonderful, and he sure as hell didn't discount it as unimportant, but with maturity, he wanted more, so very much more, and he instinctively knew that the only person on earth he could find it with was Marilee.

She was such a sweetheart, this woman. He doubted she had any idea just how very special she was. In a little over a week with his son, she had accomplished what Joe and two different doctors had failed to do in almost five months.

Unaware of their presence, she had dropped her usual façade of cheerfulness, and without the mask, she looked as dejected and utterly hopeless as he felt, her shoulders slumped, her delicate knuckles white from the press of her fingertips on her scalp. He wondered if she had a headache—or, worse, if he'd said or done something to upset her.

"Mari?"

She jerked erect and then came up off the chair as if he'd jabbed her with a pin. "Oh! I'm sorry." She gestured at the tablet and then rubbed her palms on her jeans. "I was, um—trying to make out my grocery list." She gave a nervous laugh. "At the end of the day, I go sort of brain-dead."

She did look tired. Judging by some of the stories Zachary had just shared with him, Joe guessed he couldn't blame her. He had a feeling she'd heard many of the same stories over the course of the afternoon. It wasn't in her to be made aware of such things and go on with business as usual. She was too caring a person for that. He imagined that Zachary's confidences would haunt her, just as they would him, and that over the next few days, she'd be constantly thinking about them.

"I'm feeling a little brain-dead myself," he said. "The heat, I guess. It takes something out of you."

Her gaze clung to his, asking questions she didn't dare voice and he couldn't answer.

"Zachary and I decided to talk more when we get home." Joe forced a grin and glanced down at his son, whose small face was mottled from crying. "The delicious smells in here were making our stomachs growl. Right, sprout?"

Rubbing one eye with his fist, Zachary nodded. "Daddy says mine sounds like a hungry wolf."

"Uh-oh. You must be really hungry," Marilee said.

"Yup, and Daddy's is growling like a lion."

"My goodness. I'd better get the food served up before one of you takes a bite out of me!"

Watching her move across the kitchen, Joe decided she definitely looked good enough to eat. Her snug blue jeans showcased world-class legs, and she wore a red cotton blouse tucked in at her slender waist, accentuating the flair of her hips. Just looking at her made his blood pressure shoot off the chart.

She grabbed a potholder to remove the lid from the Dutch oven. "You've got twenty minutes to wash up and set the table. Chop-chop!"

Joe waggled his eyebrows at Zachary as he swung him to the floor. "Last one back is a monkey's uncle."

The four-year-old took off like a streak. On the pretense that he didn't know the way, Joe followed more slowly. Upon reaching the bathroom, he found Zachary already standing on a stepstool at the sink.

"Are you stylin', or what? You've got your very own perch."

"Marilee got it for me." Zachary pursed his mouth as he clumsily scrubbed his face with a drippy washcloth, getting more water on his shirt than he was on his skin. His cheeks still bore traces of the tears he had shed while talking with Joe about his mother. "There's a stool in the kitchen for me, too."

Joe assisted with his son's ablutions. Once the scrubbing session ended, the child quickly dried off and then scampered from the bathroom, intent on winning the race back to the table. Once in the hall, he cried, "You're gonna be the monkey's uncle, Daddy!"

"I guess I am, at that. You're just too fast for me."

An instant later, Joe heard his son telling Marilee that he'd won the race. Judging by her response, she was pretending to be suitably impressed.

As Joe thrust his hands under the flow of warm water from the tap, his gaze came to rest on a Mickey Mouse toothbrush that poked up from a matching toothbrush holder sitting at the edge of the sink. A soap dish and glass sporting the same Disney design sat beside it. Given the fact that Mickey Mouse ranked second only to Barney in Zachary's estimation, Joe had a hunch that Marilee had purchased the bathroom accessories especially for his son.

Seeing how much trouble she had gone to in order to make Zachary feel at home brought a lump to Joe's throat. *Marilee.* She was the perfect wife for him and the ideal mother for Zachary. Couldn't she see that? And whether she wanted to admit it or not, she needed them as much as they needed her.

As Joe dried his hands, he gazed at some pastels hanging on the wall opposite the vanity. He suspected that Marilee had painted them herself. They were all of animals and delightfully whimsical. Pink-nosed bunny rabbits with long eyelashes, fluffy tails, and comically overlarge snowshoe feet. Spotted cows with soulful brown eyes. Playful tabby kittens tangled in webs of brightly colored yarn. Everywhere he looked, she had created a fantasy world for children.

Children she obviously yearned for and would never have if left to her own devices.

He gazed solemnly at a corner curio shelf that held a

collection of miniature mice, one in overalls and a straw hat, another a granny mouse in a long flowery nightgown and nightcap with spectacles on her nose.

He smiled and shook his head. Little wonder Zachary loved it here. Marilee not only created make-believe worlds in her stories; she lived in one. He couldn't help but wonder if she felt safer somehow, surrounding herself with the fanciful. He didn't suppose he could blame her, if that was the case. Reality hadn't been kind to her.

Joe sighed, knowing that his thoughts were taking a dangerous, one-hundred-and-eighty-degree turn where she was concerned. He had agreed to her conditions in order to have her watch Zachary, but with each passing day, he questioned the wisdom of that decision a little more. No long looks, no flirting, and absolutely no touching. *Damn.* How could he possibly make any headway with her? The bottom line was, he couldn't.

That was how she wanted it, he knew. To be left alone. To never be forced to deal with her problems—or her feelings for him. After witnessing one of her panic attacks, Joe could certainly understand her reluctance to have another one, but even so, he didn't believe that allowing her to wrap herself in cotton for the rest of her life was the answer. Knew that it wasn't, as a matter of fact. With that milk-white, velvety skin of hers, she was far better suited to a lover's embrace and silk sheets.

He felt certain he could work his way around the panic attacks, if only she would trust him. He had been reading the books from the library every chance he got. Granted, working his way through the psychiatric tomes didn't qualify him as an expert, but at least he had a far better understanding of her attacks now. Patience and a slow hand were the tickets. If only she would take a mild tranquilizer regularly for a while, he could accustom her to his nearness, one small step at a time. Eventually she'd realize there was nothing to fear and be able to relax with him. All he had to do was convince her of that.

Therein lay the problem. Trying to penetrate that wall

she had erected around herself was like walking face first into solid concrete. *Friends only.* Joe was loath to break his word to her, especially knowing as he did that she trusted him to keep it. But sometimes a man found himself confronted by two evils, and he had to choose between them.

Which was worse, to break his word or to let her throw away what might be her only chance at happiness?

Marilee was about to put the roast on a platter when the phone rang. She quickly wiped her hands and leaned across the counter to grab the receiver. An instant later as she hung up, she started pulling off her apron. Joe walked into the kitchen just then.

"That was Ron. Gerry fell down the stairs. They're doing an emergency Cesarean."

"Oh, God. Is she going to be all right?"

"I don't know." Marilee's heart was pounding. She pushed a hand into her hair and cast a worried look around the kitchen. "I'm sorry, Joe. Can you take it from here? The biscuits are in the oven and should be taken out. I, um . . . have to get over to Gerry's place. A neighbor is with the kids for now. Ron asked me to go over and hold down the fort."

"Go," he said. "Don't worry about anything here."

Marilee tossed her apron on the counter and ran over to get her purse down from the top of the refrigerator. As she frantically fished for her keys, which always seemed to hide when she needed them in a hurry, she said, "Please, go ahead and eat. I did promise you dinner, after all. Just stack the dishes in the sink when you're done. I'll take care of them when I come home."

She started for the French doors, then stopped and turned. "Could you feed Boo and make sure he goes out for a quick run before you leave? Zachary knows where the bag of food is. I have no idea what time I'll be back."

"Sure. Just drive carefully, all right? Getting in a wreck won't help Gerry."

She stopped again before going out the door. "There's a spare key there on the cup hook under the cupboard. Would you mind locking up for me?"

"No problem. Got you covered. Just go."

An hour later, Marilee was in one bathroom trying to bathe the eighteen-month-old Amanda while Derek, the twelve-year-old, waged war with Jacob in the upstairs bath, trying to scrub his ears.

"Aunt Marilee, Jacob's being a brat!"

Marilee rocked back on the toes of her sneakers, craned her neck, and yelled as loudly as she could in the hope that her voice might carry. "Jacob Robert Palmer, you behave yourself!"

"Aunt Marilee, Derek's pulling my hair!"

"Nuh-uh! You little liar!"

Marilee heard a crash. Then Jacob started to cry. She groaned and pushed to her feet, resigned to the fact that she'd have to pluck a dripping Amanda from the tub, wrap her in a towel, and dash upstairs to see what on earth had happened.

Just as she reached for a towel, the doorbell rang. "Holy mother," she whispered under her breath. Then, "Mary, can you get that?"

The ten-year-old yelled back, "Sure, Aunt Marilee!" That was quickly followed by a wail from Tracy, the six-year-old. "I want Mommy!"

"I'll finish the story in a minute," Mary promised.

Tracy wailed louder. Marilee heard Mary's footsteps thudding through the house as she raced to answer the door. The next instant, a deep and wonderfully familiar voice drifted to the bathroom.

"Joe, is that you?" Marilee called.

"It's me," he replied, sounding closer. "Where are you?"

"In the bathroom. I need you to hurry and come help!"

"I'm on my way!"

A second later, he appeared in the bathroom doorway, holding Zachary in one arm. He looked big and capable and fabulously *adult*. She could have hugged him. Instead, she slapped a wet washcloth in his hand. "Her hair still needs to be shampooed, and everything below the bellybutton still needs scrubbing. I have to get upstairs. I think Derek is killing Jacob."

As if on cue, Jacob screeched again. Joe laughed, swung Zachary down to the floor, and advanced on the tub where Amanda sat, eating soap. Lather streamed from the corners of her mouth.

"Oh, God!" Marilee cried.

Joe laughed again. "Hey, there, sweet cheeks," he said as he went down on one knee in the lake of standing water next to the tub. "Do you remember me? My name's Joe."

"The no-tear shampoo is in the rack!" Marilee called as she dashed into the hall.

A few minutes later when Marilee finally made her way back downstairs, she found Joe still trying to shampoo Amanda's hair. He looked diminished somehow, not to mention very wet, and when he glanced up, he no longer looked quite as capable as he had upon his arrival.

"Thank God you're back. She urped from the soap. I had to run fresh water."

Marilee waded through the puddles to the tub and knelt to finish rinsing Amanda's hair. "Thank you, Joe. You saved my life. I'm sorry about your shirt."

"It'll wash." He plucked the bar of soap from Amanda's slippery little hands. "No more snacks for you, kiddo. You're cut off."

Amanda grinned, displaying yellow globs of Dial packed between her baby teeth. Marilee grabbed a fresh washcloth and tried to get it out.

"I already tried that," Joe informed her. "I think we'll have to use a toothbrush. Just pray she doesn't get sick again. I think she ate blackberries."

"I almost urped, too!" Zachary said proudly.

Joe looked a little green, now that she studied him more closely. "I don't know how Gerry and Ron do it," she confessed.

"They're both insane. I talked to Ron right before I drove over. Gerry's in recovery, and the doctor says both she and the baby are going to be okay."

"Praise God. The last time I spoke to Ron on the phone, he still hadn't seen the doctor. I've been so worried."

"Everything's looking good," he assured her. "Ron sounded drained but happy as a clam. He was glad I was coming over to see if I could help you out. Now I know why."

Marilee gathered her plump niece into a fluffy towel and lifted her from the tub. After drying the child's hair, she handed her off to Joe. "Now for the soap removal."

Two hours later, Joe and Marilee, both still damp from bathing kids, were collapsed in the living room, she in the easy chair, he on the couch facing her. All but Gerry and Ron's older children were finally down for the night. Zachary was asleep as well, his dark head resting on Joe's lap.

He absently stroked the child's hair and sighed wearily. "Does this mean if I ever convince you to marry me, I can look forward to bathing eight kids every night?"

She smiled sweetly at him. "Actually, I want an even dozen."

Joe narrowed an eye at her. "Figure to scare me off, do you?"

"Is it working?"

He winked and grinned. "Not on your life."

Marilee was saved from making a reply by the door-bell. Before she could rise to go answer it, the front door opened and what looked like a cloud of pink cotton candy poked through the crack. "Hello, darling! Reinforcements have arrived!"

Smiling, Marilee pushed to her feet. "Aunt Luce? I thought you were at the hospital with the rest of the family."

Lucy tottered across the tile entry on high heels with dainty ankle straps that perfectly matched her voluminous caftan, a rose-colored satin creation with a chiffon over-lay that billowed around her. As she stepped down into the sunken living room, she looked for all the world like a pink schooner in full sail with all her clearance lights flashing.

"I got to see the baby, which is more than I can say for you. I've come to relieve."

The smell of Lucy's perfume preceded her. Marilee sniffed, not at all surprised her aunt wore rose scent to complement her ensemble. When Aunt Luce wore apple green, her silvery-white hair was always tinted in a co-ordinating shade and she smelled of apples. When she wore lavender, she invariably had purple curls and smelled like a lilac bush in full bloom.

"It was sweet of you to think of me," Marilee said, her gaze diving to the pendant that nestled in her aunt's con-siderable and artfully exposed cleavage. Like Lucy's ear-rings, the ornament winked on and off, the overall effect that of a light series display. "I hope you didn't cut your visit short at the birthing center."

"Oh, piddle. If you've seen one red-faced, wrinkled baby, you've seen them all." Lucy gave Marilee an ex-uberant hug. "The poor little fellow has a cone head and absolutely no chin. I swore he was the most beautiful infant I'd ever clapped eyes on and then hurried out of there before I said something honest and offended Ron."

Marilee laughed in spite of herself. "All babies are a bit misshapen immediately after birth, Aunt Luce! He'll pretty up in a few days and be beautiful, just like all the others."

"We can pray. This is a Cesarean baby, remember. They're supposed to be pretty when they're first born. I think the funny head may be permanent." Lucy turned, finally saw Joe, and beamed so brilliantly with gladness she rivaled her light display. "*Joseph?*" She pressed a hand over her heart. "Oh, my dear, sweet boy! It's so *good* to see you!"

Joe eased Zachary's head off his lap and pushed to his feet. "It's good to see you, too, Aunt Luce." He shot Marilee an amused glance. "You still brighten a room like nobody else I've ever known."

"Oh, go on." She flapped an arthritic hand so laden with cubic zirconia, Marilee was surprised she could still lift her arm. "I know who your sunshine is, young man, and it certainly isn't me." She reached up to grasp Joe's broad shoulders, then leaned back to peer at his face. "Still as handsome as ever, you poor darling. It's a terrible burden for a young man when he's cursed with good looks. Too much temptation and all of that wonderful testosterone dulling his wits." With gnarled, acrylic-tipped fingers, she grabbed Joe's cheek and gave it a little shake. "I always feared you'd snap the leash and run wild for a while. Shame on you! It's about time you came to your senses. Stay put this time, you naughty man. Only a fool goes for the brass when he's got pure gold waiting at home."

Joe arched an eyebrow, glanced at Marilee, and then smiled good-naturedly. "You're absolutely right, Aunt Luce, and rest assured, I've learned my lesson."

She gave his jaw a loving smack. "Don't break her heart again, do you hear? I'll find you and make you sorry."

Joe grinned. "I won't, I promise."

Just then, a thumping noise came from the entry. Marilee turned to see her aunt's latest significant other coming in the front door. A tall, robust sixty-six-year-old,

Charlie Wade was loaded down with Lucy's gear—a pink straw handbag large enough to qualify as a suitcase, her ornate walking cane, which she seldom used, a huge white sack of something that smelled like donuts, a rose-colored crocheted shawl, and a gray overnight case. Marilee hurried over to help him, rescuing the donuts first and placing them on a pedestal table, then grabbing the overnight case.

"Goodness, Charlie. You're going to rupture a disk!"

"Damned woman carts around so much stuff, it makes me poor to carry it."

Aunt Luce hurried over to relieve Charlie of her purse. "Dear heart, why on earth didn't you make two trips?"

"I'm tired of walking. Got turned around in the hospital. Up this hall, down that one. But did we ask for directions? Hell, no. You know your aunt. Always sure she knows where she's going until she gets there." Charlie leaned the cane in a corner and cocked his head as if to listen. "Where are all the little creatures?"

"Mary and Derek are watching television in the family room," Marilee explained. "Joe and I finally managed to get the others down to sleep."

Charlie's beefy face relaxed in a smile. "Praise the Lord. I won't have to share all my donuts!"

"Oh, yes, you will!" Aunt Luce said. "Your cholesterol, remember. You can have one, and that's all. We'll save what's left for the children in the morning."

"Ah, come on. One is barely a taste."

"Maybe two if you behave yourself."

"Are you planning to stay all night?" Marilee asked.

"Well, of course," Aunt Luce replied. "You have that horrid hound to let out. Charlie and I have no pets." She rolled her eyes. "Teaching a man new tricks is all the frustration I need."

Charlie stepped across the room, a hand extended in greeting to Joe. "Charlie Wade. Good to meet you."

Joe reached out to shake the man's hand. "Joe Lakota."

"I know who you are. I'm a big fan of the Bullets.

Quite a throwing arm you've got there, son. Damn shame about the knee and having to retire so young."

"I enjoy coaching nearly as much as being on the field."

"How do you think Laurel High's going to do this year?"

While the two men fell into a conversation about football, Marilee updated her aunt on the children. Lucy's enthusiastic input finally awakened Zachary, who blinked, sat up, and stared in sleepy bewilderment at the flashing pink lady in their midst.

"This is my aunt Luce, Zachary," Marilee said by way of introduction.

Zachary gaped at Lucy's pink hair.

"Aren't you the image of your daddy!" Aunt Luce bent low to smile at the child. "My goodness, I see the handwriting on the wall. He'll leave a string of broken hearts in his wake. We should hang a danger sign around his neck."

"Zachary's a little shy, Aunt Luce," Joe quickly explained. "You'll have to give him some time to relax around you before you get too friendly."

Joe returned to the sofa, gathered his son in one arm, and began to rock him while he visited with Charlie. Marilee ran interference by guiding her aunt to the kitchen.

"Are you sure you want to spend the night, Aunt Luce? This crew can be a big handful, and I'm perfectly willing to come back after I run over to the hospital."

"With the younger kids already down, I can handle it from here."

"Mandy may wake up," Marilee warned. "And sometimes Jacob has nightmares. Only a story puts him back to sleep."

"Got it covered. I'm not quite in the grave yet, darling. I just have my reservation confirmed."

A few minutes later, Marilee found herself sitting on the passenger seat of Joe's Honda, her arms cradling Zachary, whom Joe had rocked back to sleep. When they left, Charlie was enthroned on a stool at the breakfast bar about to enjoy a donut and a cup of microwave hot cocoa. Big problem. The older gentleman had parked his car behind hers in the driveway. Somehow it was collectively decided by everyone but Marilee that Charlie would move his vehicle later and that Joe would drop her off to pick up her Taurus.

"You okay with this?" Joe asked as he backed from the driveway. "It's not out of my way or anything to come back by here, but if you feel uncomfortable—"

"I'm fine." As Marilee spoke, she realized she actually was fine. No racing pulse, no feeling of breathlessness. She was acutely aware of Joe's looming presence beside her, but for reasons beyond her, for once it wasn't making her feel tense or claustrophobic. "Let poor Charlie enjoy his snack. Aunt Luce runs the man's legs off."

Joe chuckled as he shifted into drive and headed up the quiet, tree-lined street. "She *is* spry. How old is she now?"

Gazing through the summer evening dusk at the neatly manicured lawns they passed, Marilee replied, "She and Mom turned seventy-four in May."

"You'd never know it. Spike heels? I kept wanting to grab her arm so she wouldn't do a face plant."

Marilee turned to look at him. "You should see her high-heeled cowgirl boots. Bright red with gold rivets and lots of fringe."

"Cowgirl boots?"

"Which complete her cowgirl outfit, also bright red. She calls it her Dale Evans suit. One Sunday, she wore the entire getup to mass. My mother nearly fainted and fell off the pew."

Smiling and shaking his head, Joe hung a right. "Amazing, isn't it? That pair is proof positive that identical twins can still be as different as night and day. Your mom is so conservative, and Aunt Luce is—" He broke off, evidently unable to think of a suitable adjective. "Delightful. She makes the golden years seem like a promise instead of a death sentence."

Marilee sighed. "She definitely enjoys life."

"What's the scoop on Charlie? He seems genuinely fond of her."

"Head over heels in love, more like. He wants her to marry him. Aunt Luce won't because her first marriage was in the church."

Joe shot her a startled look. "Aren't they—you know—intimate?"

Marilee grinned. "I haven't asked. Feel free, if you'd like."

He chuckled. "Point taken. The important thing is that she's happy."

"Tell that to my mother. Aunt Luce's unorthodox approach to life drives her up the wall." Marilee shrugged. "My take is this. Aunt Luce made a terrible mistake when she was very young, and if she had stayed in an abusive marriage, that would have been wrong for her. By divorcing the guy, she brought no children into a nightmarish situation, at least. If she wished, she could petition the Vatican for an annulment of her first marriage, leaving herself free to remarry in the church. The first marriage was ill-fated from the start, very short-lived, and she's been divorced for over fifty years. I can't believe she couldn't get a papal dispensation."

"Why doesn't she do it, then?"

"Old school, I guess. Aunt Luce is liberal in her thinking in most ways, but there's a puritanical, old-fashioned streak running through her as well. In her day, annulments were practically nonexistent. Holy Matrimony was forever, amen. She believes with all her heart that her mistake can't and shouldn't be rectified."

"I believe a spiritual union should be for forever myself," he confessed. "Sounds bad, coming from a divorcé." He drew to a stop at an empty intersection, glanced both ways, and then applied the gas. "Sometimes I lie awake nights, going back over that time in my life, wondering where the hell my head was at. Such a stupid decision! When I make a vow, I think I should keep it. You know?"

Marilee cuddled Zachary closer and stroked his hair. "Something very precious resulted from your mistake, Joe. You're so very lucky in that, to have created something so sweet and perfect, even when you were messing up."

He flashed the child a warm look. "Yeah, and for that reason alone, I can't really regret the marriage. I do regret any pain he has suffered over my bad judgment, though. For that, I can never forgive myself."

Marilee pressed a kiss to Zachary's forehead. "We all make mistakes. If we can understand that and cut other people slack, then why do we find it so hard to forgive ourselves? And how can we believe that God, in His infinite wisdom, doesn't forgive us?"

"Good point."

"You used bad judgment one time in your life," she said softly. "It's done, and because of Zachary, you wouldn't change it, even if you could. Forgive yourself, put it behind you. I'm sure God has."

He was silent for a long moment. When he finally cut her a glance, his eyes gleamed with intensity. "Thank you, Mari. You're right. I should forgive myself and put it behind me." He waited a beat, and then he huskily added, "Now do me a big favor? Take your own advice."

 *Seven*

*O*ver the next two weeks, even though Zachary drooled every time Marilee put something on the stove in the afternoon, she resisted the temptation to invite him and his dad for dinner again. She did, however, allow herself the pleasure of preparing him and his dad desserts, which she sent home with them at night. The following morning, Joe never failed to wax poetic about her culinary skills, making her feel wonderfully appreciated.

He also took every opportunity to tell her how well Zachary seemed to be doing. The child's therapist had been raving about his progress, a turn of events Joe attributed solely to her. She was, he told her, "the answer to a prayer." The praise and gratitude left her feeling thoroughly hugged for hours afterward, and often when she least expected it, she found herself thinking of Joe and smiling.

With the last part of August came a sharp rise in temperature, turning the long summer days sweltering and muggy. To escape the heat, Marilee began taking Zachary to the city park where they could lie in the shade and wade in the shallows of Laurel Creek. The outings brought back memories, for she'd spent many a long summer day with Joe along these banks as a kid, and she couldn't help but take journeys into the past while she played there with his son. She soon found herself falling into the habit of sharing those memories.

"There used to be a rope hanging from that tree," she told the child one afternoon as she pointed to a gnarled limb at the edge of the creek. "Your dad would give his version of a Sioux war cry, swing out over the water, and turn a somersault as he dove in."

Another day, she told Zachary stories about the times when she and Joe had danced under the trees to the music of bands playing in the pavilion.

"You were best friends, huh?" he said, his small face rapt with wonder.

Feeling suddenly sad, Marilee hugged her knees and gazed at the leaves that rustled above them. Remembering . . . remembering . . . always remembering. "Yes," she said softly, "he was my very best friend."

Before Marilee could say more, she caught movement from the corner of her eye and glanced around to find a stout little boy standing near their blanket. His freckled face was smeared with what appeared to be chocolate ice cream, and his carrot-red hair looked as if someone had stirred it with a whisk. He stared long and hard at Zachary, then hooked his grubby thumbs over the waistband of his denim shorts and said, "My name's Jimmy."

Zachary moved closer to Marilee. "Hello," she replied. "I'm Marilee, and this is my friend, Zachary Lakota."

Jimmy squinched up his round face and scratched his head. "You like to play on the seesaw?" he asked Zachary. "I wanna play on it, and I need a kid at the other end."

Zachary pressed even closer to Marilee. "I don't like seesaws."

Jimmy gazed up the slope at the seesaw. After shoving

his finger so far up one nostril that Marilee worried he might do himself brain damage, he said, "I won't jump off and let you hit the ground or nothin'. I promise."

Marilee glanced at Zachary. "I need to go up and get a drink from the fountain. We may as well have a look at the seesaw while we're there." She pushed to her feet, refraining from offering her hand to her small charge. She'd been around Gerry's boys enough to know that fussing in front of other kids was a major bad move. "What's your last name, Jimmy?"

"Bratt."

Marilee stifled a startled laugh, hoping the name didn't suit the child's personality. As she'd known he would, Zachary fell in beside her as she walked toward the playground area. Once at the seesaw, Jimmy showed Zachary the way it worked, then he plopped at one end, grabbed the handlebar, and said, "Well, come on, kid. Get on!"

Zachary reluctantly did so, and within minutes, he was giggling and having a wonderful time. "Look, Marilee!" he cried once, turning loose of the bar and raising his arms. "I'm not holding on."

"Don't fall!" she warned. "Your father will have my head."

"I won't. I'm not a baby!"

Marilee went to sit beneath a nearby tree to watch. The boys soon abandoned the seesaw in favor of the swings. As they trotted away, Zachary glanced back only once to be sure Marilee was still in attendance. After that, he became so engrossed in play that he seemed to forget all about her.

Smiling softly, she experienced a confusing tangle of emotion, feeling both joyful and sad at once. This was a good-bye of sorts, she knew. Zachary had depended on her so much. Now he was taking his first small step away from her. As his confidence grew, he would become bolder and more self-sufficient, needing her less and less. The strong maternal instincts that she'd developed toward this child made her mourn the loss before it even happened.

She stiffened her spine and straightened her shoulders. *Ninny.* Love always came with a price. Who knew that better than she? She'd understood from the start that allowing herself to love Zachary would eventually end in heartbreak, and this was only the beginning. She hated to think how was she going to feel when Joe began taking him to a daycare center.

Devastated, that was how she'd feel. Completely and utterly *devastated.*

Maybe this was a blessing in disguise, she decided. A gradual separation, with Zachary weaning himself away from her a little more each day.

A good-bye was inevitable, after all, and in the end, it would be best. She had scarcely worked at all for a month. If she didn't get her act together soon, she'd be late on her contract deadline. That would put her behind schedule and might be detrimental to her career. Zachary needed the company of other children, and he'd get that at a daycare center. As much as she would miss him, she'd soon become engrossed in her work, and in time she would get over it.

Late that same evening, Marilee had just dressed for bed and was about to have her nightly mug of hot cocoa when the doorbell pealed, catching her by surprise and startling Boo, who jerked awake and scrambled frantically across the hardwood floor. After snuffling the air, however, the dog grew calm and lay back down, telling Marilee more clearly than words that their visitor was someone familiar.

Glancing at the clock, she noted that it was twenty of ten, far too late for any of her family to be paying her a visit. Who on earth would be coming by this late?

When she went to answer the summons and flipped on the outside light, she saw through the paned glass that it was Joe standing on her porch, holding a sleeping Zachary in his arms. Despite the fact that he looked irresistibly handsome in a pink-and-gray striped oxford shirt and khaki chinos, he projected an air of bone-deep weariness, his burnished face drawn, his dark eyes lusterless.

She quickly disengaged the security bolt and opened the door. "Joe?" she said softly so as not to awaken the child. "What on earth are you doing here? Is your mom sick again?"

He shook his head. "No, Mom's fine, honey. Can I come in? I need to talk to you."

She stepped back to allow him entry. The spicy scent of his shaving cologne teased her nostrils as he moved over the threshold. "Is it Zachary?" she asked worriedly, lightly touching a hand to the sleeping child's forehead to check for fever. "He seemed all right when you left this afternoon."

"No, no. He's fine. For the moment, anyway."

Marilee didn't like the sound of that. "For the moment?"

Joe swung his head at the nearest doorway. "Is that a bedroom? I'd like to lay him down so we can talk without waking him up."

She didn't like the sound of that, either. The almost toneless exhaustion in his voice told her he had come bearing bad news. "Yes." She hurriedly closed the front door and led the way into the guestroom. "You can put him there," she said, stepping to the opposite side of the queen-sized bed to draw back the comforter.

When Joe had gently deposited the sleeping child where she indicated, she drew the cover back up. Zachary mumbled something in his sleep and turned his cheek against her hand as she tucked the comforter around him. Marilee caressed his baby-soft skin with her knuckles and then lightly smoothed his hair, her heart twisting with fierce protectiveness.

"Oh, Joe," she whispered. "I'm in big trouble with this

little guy. I've let myself grow to love him way too much."

"Good," he replied hoarsely. "I'm counting on it."

A chill ran over her skin. She straightened to peer across the bed at him, frustrated by the shadows that cloaked his features. "Do you have to be so mysterious? You're frightening me."

"I guess it's contagious," he whispered hoarsely. "I'm scared to death myself. My little boy's in big trouble, Marilee."

"Trouble?" she echoed, her pulse suddenly pounding.

He drew a legal-sized envelope from the pocket of his slacks and handed it to her. "Read it," he said grimly.

Bewildered, Marilee led the way to the kitchen, opening the letter as she went. She sat at the table, her gaze going first to the letterhead of a California law firm. As she began skimming the body of the text, her heart caught.

"Oh, dear God." She glanced up at Joe, who stood in the center of her kitchen looking for all the world as if he were shell-shocked. "Does this mean what I think it means?"

"Yeah. She's petitioning the court to regain custody."

"She can't *do* that!"

"Oh, she can do it." Thrusting both hands through his already rumpled hair, he laughed softly, the sound hollow and bitter. "I've been on the phone with my divorce attorney half the evening. He says she can not only renege, but there's a damned good chance the judge may rule in her favor."

The letter slipped from Marilee's suddenly numb fingers and fluttered to the table. She pressed a palm to her waist, feeling as if she might lose her dinner. "I thought you paid her a bunch of money to get custody. Now she can just up and change her mind without paying you back? That isn't fair."

"I can tell you've never been through a divorce. Very little about the whole process is fair, especially if you're dealing with a money-grabber like Valerie." He laughed again. "Our agreement didn't specifically state that I was paying her for my son. A child can't be bought. The precise legalese escapes me now, but essentially the money was referred to as a post-decree cash endowment and mentioned only in an addendum. We both understood that I was buying her off, but it wasn't spelled out."

"So she can just change her mind?"

He curled a hand over the back of his neck. "It won't be quite as simple as that. She has to go to the court, and if I counter-file, which I certainly will, it'll go before a judge. But, yeah, the bottom line is that she can change her mind. 'A change of heart,' my attorney calls it. She's his natural mother, and even though she signed away her maternal rights, the bond between mother and child is considered to be almost inviolate in many states. You see the same sort of thing happen all the time with adoptions, the natural mother changing her mind after a few months and getting her kid back."

"And your attorney didn't warn you of this before you paid her all that money?"

He sighed and rested his hands at his hips. "Oh, yeah, he warned me. I knew it was a gamble, but for Zachary's sake, it was one I had to take."

Gazing up at his haggard face, Marilee could have wept for him. The pain in his eyes was terrible, the awful hopelessness that accompanied it even worse. He was about to lose his child, and there might be nothing he could do to prevent it. She couldn't begin to imagine how he must feel.

"Given the situation Zachary was in," she said tightly, "I guess taking a gamble was better than doing nothing at all. You had no real choice."

"No." He shrugged. "My hope was that the expense of taking me back to court would be a deterrent and she'd never do this. What I didn't figure on was her getting so chummy with a wealthy state senator."

"A *senator*? She's dating a politician?"

He nodded. "When I got the notice this afternoon, I contacted a good friend of mine down in San Milagros who's still with the Bullets. Mac says the guy's name is James Patterson. I remember reading about him in the newspaper. A middle-aged man. Fat around the middle, starting to go bald, and rolling in dough. Mac says that since Valerie hooked up with him, she's been spending money like there's no tomorrow. Evidently, he's the proverbial sugar daddy."

"So she can afford to hassle it out with you in court now to get Zachary back?" Marilee encapsulated. "In the end, she gets everything, practically all your money *and* your son. How very clever of her. Where I come from, we call it treacherous, but I'm sure my opinion won't keep her awake nights."

"I wish I were dealing with someone as fair-minded as you are." He gazed at the ceiling. "I've had hours to assimilate this, but I still can't believe she's doing it. It's not as if she's got a strong maternal bent. Having Zachary around will just cramp her style."

"Oh, Joe, I'm so sorry," Marilee whispered. "So very, very sorry."

His voice sounded as taut as a fiddle string when he spoke again. "Mac thinks she and the good senator are thinking about getting married, that she wants Zachary back for appearances' sake."

"Appearances? I'm not following."

"Patterson's career was nearly destroyed a couple of years ago by a sex scandal that resulted in a nasty divorce from his first wife. Male menopause, at its worst, the older man trading in his thirty-year marriage for a sexy blond and a sports car."

Marilee frowned. "I still don't see how that relates to Zachary."

He leaned a shoulder against the flank of oak cupboards that lined the wall. "For several months after the story broke, Patterson was hot news, with pictures of him and his bombshell girlfriend plastered on the front page of the paper. He either had to clean up his act or lose the next election. He chose to clean up his act." He arched an eyebrow at her. "A classic case of whitewash, if you get my drift. In front of the camera, he behaved himself. Lost the sports car. Stopped being seen in public with bimbos. But behind the scenes, he was still seeking the Fountain of Youth, a regular good-time Charlie."

"It sounds like Valerie's found the perfect mate."

"Exactly. She's young, beautiful, and loves to party, with the added bonus that she's something of a celebrity and has a little class. With a woman like her, Patterson can have his cake and eat it, too, keeping his nose clean in public, partying hearty behind the scenes. His marrying Valerie is undoubtedly what the spin doctor ordered, a way to put a good face on an unsavory situation."

"With a reputation like Valerie's? It seems to me that having his name associated with hers would do his image more harm than good."

Joe snorted derisively. "You'd think so. But if the right spin is put on it and the press runs with the story, you can pull off almost anything. Mac claims the slant is 'fairy-tale romance' in bold caps, which is always an easy sell. Middle-aged senator with checkered past meets wayward younger woman. Love changes their lives, blah, blah. Together they turn over a new leaf and become Mr. and Mrs. Respectability."

"Who'll believe tripe like that?"

He smiled grimly. "The American public. You see it all the time. Camouflage the truth with enough frill, and we'll believe almost anything."

"You make us sound like a bunch of naïve imbeciles."

"Not that so much. It's just that we're inundated with grim reality, day in and day out—in the paper, on television, over the radio, at the movies. It's a relief to hear something good for a change, and we eagerly embrace it. What better than a real-life love story?"

She mulled that over for a moment. "And Zachary will complete the picture of respectability and marital bliss?"

He shrugged and lifted his hands. "If Valerie marries a senator, it'll be extremely important for her to look settled and quash all hint of scandal ever connected with her name. When I got custody, the press ran with every angle, hinting more than once that she was into drugs and that I paid dearly to get my son away from her. If she gets Zachary back, it'll refute those rumors, not to mention that a cute little boy clinging to Patterson's hand will be great window dressing."

"That's *horrible*! Window dressing?"

"Well, it's only speculation, Mac's best guess as to what may be motivating her. Knowing Valerie, though, I'd say he's right on track."

"What kind of person does such a thing? Using her child to feather her own nest? That's despicable, Joe."

"She isn't thinking clearly, Marilee. She hasn't been for a long, long time." He shifted his weight against the cupboard. "When I'm not furious with her—which isn't often these days—I pity her. What a sad waste. She used to have so much going for her. She was smart, beautiful, ambitious. Now her drug habit has taken over her life, and it's damned expensive. I think she's already gone through most of the money I coughed up. Marrying a rich boyfriend will save her ass."

"For a time," she inserted. "At the rate she goes through money, what's-his-name—Patterson, did you say?—won't be rich for long."

Marilee was starting to get one of her tension headaches—a beastly stab of pain that began above her left eye and felt as if an ice pick were being shoved into her brain. Hoping to stave it off before it became any worse, she stepped to the cupboard near the stove for some ibuprofen and then to the sink for some water.

As she returned to her chair, she said, "Have you considered letting Zachary testify? He's much more willing to talk now and could be questioned by the judge in private chambers. If he were to tell him even a portion of the things he's told us, Valerie would never have a prayer of getting custody again."

"True. But what would it do to Zachary?" Joe shook his head. "I called his doctor tonight and had a long heart-to-heart with him. Except as a last resort, he strongly advises against involving Zachary in any of this. In fact he's concerned about Zachary's even knowing about it. The kid's only just now starting to get his emotional balance. He'll be terrified if he finds out his mom's trying to get him back. The doctor is worried that it'll send him into a tailspin."

She remembered Zachary's panicky expression when he thought about being returned to his mother. "I suppose that's a strong possibility."

"If there's any way around it, I don't want to take the chance."

Marilee kept picturing Zachary, frightened and alone in a dark closet. "What on earth are you going to do then?" she asked, her headache growing worse by the second. "Did your attorney offer you any hope at all? We can't just let her take him, Joe. Living in those conditions will destroy the poor little guy!"

"That's why I'm here—to talk to you about what can be done."

The tic of his jaw muscle and the determined glint that suddenly came into his eyes told her she wasn't going to like what he was about to say.

Evidently Joe felt fairly certain she wasn't going to like it either. He lowered his gaze to the floor, scuffed the toe of his shoe over the polished surface, and then scratched beside his nose, all habits of his when he got nervous. "I, um, don't know exactly how to approach this," he admitted in a gravelly voice, "so I'm just going to be straight out with it."

Marilee braced herself.

He glanced up. "My lawyer says my chances in court will be two, maybe three times better, if I'm no longer a single father when I go before the judge."

She circled that cautiously, her mind shying away from the obvious implications.

"If my wife could be a stay-at-home mother to my son, my chances would be even better," he added gruffly.

A heavy silence fell over the kitchen, the quiet broken only by the rhythmic ticking of the clock and Boo's soft snores coming from under the table.

" 'Stay at home'?" she repeated, her voice little more than a squeak.

"It only makes sense. The way it is right now, I'm at work the giant's share of each weekday, and Zachary has to stay with a sitter. Valerie will argue that she can be a full-time mother and give him better care. My best defense in court will be a home environment for Zachary that's damned near without flaw."

"Nothing's without flaw."

"A figure of speech. Don't get upset, Marilee. You asked, and I'm just telling you what the lawyer said."

She had a hysterical urge to laugh, only she was afraid the top of her aching head might blow off if she did. "You can't possibly be suggesting what I think you're suggesting."

When he said nothing, she clenched her hands into fists. "That's why you came over here so late—why you couldn't leave this for tomorrow—because you wanted to discuss getting *married*?"

He started to speak then fell silent, his gaze holding hers for a long and interminable moment. "All right," he finally said. "You want it straight to the point with no lead-in? Marriage is what I'm suggesting. Hell, I'll go you one better. How's that? I'm pleading. Would you like me on my knees?"

Rubbing her throbbing temple with trembling fingertips, she closed her eyes. "Don't lay this on me. Please, Joe. Stop before you start and, please, just don't."

"I wish to God I had that option. Unfortunately I don't. You said it at the start. I can't just let her take him. She'll destroy him if I do."

"Oh, *God!*"

"Honey, you know I'd never pressure you like this if I had a choice. I've honored the terms of our agreement up until now. Haven't I?"

"Yes," she whispered.

"But when I gave you that promise, I never in a million years anticipated this. Now I'm faced with a situation bigger than both of us. This isn't about you. It's not about me. Not about *us*. It's about a little four-year-old boy whose life is about to be turned upside down, and you're the one person on earth who can prevent it. What would you have me do? Ignore that? Not discuss it with you? There's a possible solution to this. What kind of father would I be if I didn't at least give it a shot?"

Marilee's pulse was starting to race, and her windpipe felt as if it were closing off.

"Do you think I've been lying awake at night, plotting ways I can get you to marry me?" he asked incredulously. "This was dropped on me, out of the blue. I'm fighting to save my son, damn it, and you're my only ace in the hole." He huffed in frustration. "Zachary's doctor is willing to give a deposition describing Zachary's condition when he first began seeing him and testifying to how rapidly he has improved since he started staying with you. Just think how good a report like that will look to a judge, *especially* if he knows we're happily married and this will be a permanent arrangement."

"Happily married? You and I?"

"I'm not saying it'll be easy, honey."

"Impossible, more like."

"I know you believe that. But you know what? I think the two of us can overcome anything if we face it together. I'll go to counseling with you. We'll chip away at the problems, one at a time, together. Hell, if it's necessary, we'll get a doctor to prescribe you some tranquilizers to get you over the rough spots."

He hunkered down in front of her and cupped her face between his hands. "I can give you babies, honey. Your very own babies." At her look of dismay, he winced. "Not right away, of course. All in good time—when you feel ready for that sort of thing. We'll take it slow. One step at a time. I love you enough to wait, and I think you love me enough to try with everything you've got. That's an unbeatable combination, if you think about it. A hell of a lot more than most people have."

"Most people don't have my hang-ups," she reminded him.

"And that's exactly what they are, hang-ups. We can work past them eventually."

Marilee would have given almost anything to believe it was that simple.

"Once we work our way past those difficulties, we can start working on having children. A whole brood, if that's what you want. Zachary will be safe from Valerie, and we'll have the family we always used to dream about." He slipped his fingers into her hair, his face moving closer to hers, his eyes imploring her. "Give me half a chance. Please, won't you trust me enough to at least let me try?"

"I can't, Joe. I know you don't understand, but I just can't."

His gaze held hers. "There's no such word as 'can't.' You *can*. Remember when you were little, and I taught you to skate? Remember how you counted on me to keep you safe, to make sure you didn't get hurt? Why did you trust me so much?"

"Because I knew how much you loved me," she whispered, the admission a torture because the memories made her feel so ashamed.

"I *still* love you that much," he assured her. "Trust me like that again—just one more time. I'll get you through this, I swear to God, and you'll never regret it. Not for a single moment."

She could barely see him now through the blur of tears. "I can't," she whispered raggedly. "I can't. And if you love me—*really* love me, Joe—you won't ask it of me."

He drew his hands from her face, his gaze still holding hers as he pushed to his feet. For a long moment, he simply stood there, staring down at her.

"Well, I guess that's that," he said hollowly.

She closed her eyes and nodded. "I'm sorry. I want to help. Really, I do. If you need money, I have about seventy thousand in savings. It's yours. Just say the word. If you need more than that, I can get a second mortgage on the house. I'll do anything. *Anything*, Joe. Just name it, and it's yours."

He said nothing for several seconds. "As much as I appreciate the generous offer, honey, it's not your money I need."

With that, he turned and left the kitchen, his footsteps resounding on the hardwood floors as he walked the length of the hall. The hollow echoes made the house feel so empty and cold. She hugged herself to ward off the chill.

Suddenly she saw herself thirty years from now—alone in her kitchen late at night, hugging her waist and staring at the floor. No husband, no children, no grandchildren. Just an endless string of lonely nights.

Joe was offering her the chance to have a life. A *real* life. Not what she'd had to settle for because she was afraid to take risks. Not what passed for normalcy. He could give her everything she yearned for—a husband who loved her, a house filled with kids, people who would love her when she grew old. A *family*.

Oh, how she longed for the courage to run after him, to grab this opportunity before it passed her by. *Joe*. She loved him so much. How could it be that the one thing that could make her happy was also the one thing she couldn't have?

She heard him go into the bedroom to collect his son. Then the front door opened and closed, the mechanism making a soft, ominous click. *Silence*. Asleep under the table, Boo snored on, completely unaware as she sobbed softly into her cupped hands.

Joe. He was leaving. Again. And this time, she doubted he would ever come back. Even worse, she couldn't blame him.

Eight

No longer bothering with a shot glass, Joe poured straight from the bottle, the chugging sound of the whiskey as it sloshed over ice seeming to whisper, *Idiot, idiot, idiot.*

He'd pulled a few stupid stunts in his life, but the one tonight took the prize. In the morning, he was going to wonder what the hell had come over him. He kept remembering how enormous Marilee's eyes had gotten when she realized he was suggesting she marry him.

Gazing into the tumbler, he gave the whiskey one brisk swirl before tossing it down. Eyes watering from the burn, he poured himself more, determined to reach a state of total numbness. Halfway there didn't quite cut it, not tonight. With his thoughts still racing as they were, he'd never get a wink of sleep unless he was pie-eyed. Zachary was safely tucked into bed, so why not? It wasn't as if he made a habit of it, after all. The film of dust on the whiskey bottle gave testimony to that. Since getting custody of his son, he seldom indulged in even so much as a glass of wine with dinner.

He sighed and moved with exaggerated care from the built-in bar to a window where he stared out into the darkness. At this late hour, most of his neighbors had already gone to bed, and if he were smart, he'd follow their lead. It was already well after eleven, and even though tomorrow was Saturday, one of his days off, Zachary would hit the floor running by seven o'clock.

Would Marilee even watch Zachary again? If she told Joe to take a hike, he guessed he wouldn't blame her. They'd made an agreement, and he'd given his word to abide by it. *Friends only.* He'd blown that out of the water.

Of all the ill-advised, stupid, wildly crazy things to do. It would have been bad enough if he'd just asked her to marry him, but why in God's name had he offered her a whole *brood* of babies while he was at it?

He closed his eyes, wishing he could call back every word he'd said to her. True, Zachary's future was at stake, and Joe was desperate. But that wasn't Marilee's concern. She'd been so wonderful up to now, watching Zachary at no small emotional risk to herself—loving him, making him feel secure, being his confidante. Joe knew damned well she had set aside her work for well over a month, devoting her time almost entirely to his son. Zachary wasn't even her child. How could he reasonably ask more of her?

The answer to that was, he couldn't.

Joe turned from the window to gaze at the telephone, knowing he owed her an apology, but unsure how to phrase it. *I'm sorry for being such a selfish jerk?* Yeah, that'd be a good start.

The doorbell rang just then, startling him so badly that he jumped and slopped a little whiskey on the rolled-back sleeve of his shirt. *Who the hell?* On his way from the family room, he set the tumbler on the bar. When he reached the entry, he flipped on the outside light and drew open the carved mahogany front door.

Looking like a waif in a pair of faded blue jeans and

an overlarge green shirt with pastel smudges of paint on the front, Marilee stood on his brand new welcome mat. Framed by an artless tangle of platinum-streaked curls, her cheeks were white and her big blue eyes shimmered up at him.

"Joe," she said shakily, "I, um . . . need to talk to you."

She was the last person on earth he had expected to see. "I was about to call you."

"You were?"

When she made no move to step inside, he gently seized her elbow and drew her over the threshold. "Yeah, I was. I had no business dumping on you like I did or expecting you to bail me out, and I wanted to apologize."

When he pushed the door closed, she cast an uneasy glance around. "I, um, called Gerry to get your address."

Joe nodded, wondering if she was simply explaining how she'd found his house, or if she was taking the added precaution of letting him know her sister knew where she was. The second possibility nearly broke his heart. "Smart thinking," he managed to say in a light tone. "At this hour, it's foolhardy to be out and about without letting someone know where you went."

She intertwined her fingers, gave her hands a twist, and popped her knuckles. She was coiled tighter than a spring.

"Sweetheart, you're perfectly safe here."

"Oh, I know that." She touched the tip of her tongue to the indentation above her lip. The fine blond hair growing there glistened in the entryway light like a sprinkling of fairy dust on her flawless skin. "It isn't—I'm not really . . ." Her voice trailed away, and she fixed him with that nervous, big-eyed gaze again. "It smells strongly of alcohol in here. Have you been drinking?"

"Oh, that. I have had a few drinks, yeah." He brushed at his shirt sleeve. "I also spilled a little on myself."

"Are you—drunk?"

"Not *drunk* exactly." He flashed a grin he hoped would ease her mind and tried his best to look harmless, which wasn't one of his talents. "I'm just feeling mellow, is all. I don't get cantankerous, if that's what's worrying you." She didn't look reassured. "Marilee, I really do want to apologize. It's great that you came over so I can do it in person." Suddenly nervous himself, Joe rubbed the back of his neck. "About that marriage business. I stepped way over the line suggesting something like that to you, and I want you to know if it weren't for Zachary, I never would have. It's just that I'm desperate, you know?"

He no sooner spoke than he wanted to kick himself. A man didn't tell the woman he loved that he'd proposed to her only because he was desperate. Maybe he *was* a little drunk. If he were smart, he'd postpone this conversation until tomorrow. Small problem. She was standing in his entryway right now.

She straightened her shoulders, brought her chin up, and hauled in a bracing breath, her manner reminding him of someone gathering the courage to take a flying leap off a cliff. "I came over to talk to you about that, Joe. I, um . . . after you left . . . I got to thinking, and I've decided it's really not such a bad idea."

"What isn't?"

She fiddled nervously with the open collar of her shirt. "Getting married. I thought we might talk about it, anyway."

He leaned slightly forward, fairly certain the booze was muddling his brain. "Come again?"

In a slightly louder voice, she said, "I've decided maybe it's not such a bad idea. Brilliant, in fact. As you pointed out, it's the perfect solution for Zachary, and I really do want to help in any way I can. It'd break my heart to see Valerie regain custody of him." She nervously licked her mouth again and took another deep breath. "I also can't deny wanting a baby. If I could have a child like Zachary—my very own little boy, exactly like him—I'd be the happiest woman alive."

Oh, yeah. He was brilliant, and she wanted to have his

baby? He could scarcely credit his ears. At the same time, he had to resist an urge to grab her, hurry her to the closest soft surface, and get right to work on the project before she changed her mind.

This was his fondest dream come true. Marilee, agreeing to become his wife? Maybe he had drunk himself into a state of oblivion, after all, and was dreaming all this.

"Honey, are you—" Joe broke off, half afraid to complete the question. "Would you mind pinching me? I'm either drunker than I thought or hallucinating."

"You're not hallucinating."

"Hallucinations always say that."

She rolled her eyes and laughed softly. Then she reached out and pinched his arm. "Satisfied?"

He stared at her wonderingly. "You can't be serious."

"Serious enough that I'd like to discuss it with you. If the offer is still open, that is."

Still open? If he had his druthers—which he knew was out of the question—she'd be pregnant with Zachary Number Two in less than an hour. "Oh, the offer's definitely still open." Afraid she might bolt, he was sorely tempted to lock a hand over her wrist. Instead he took her gently by the arm. "Come into the family room where we can be more comfortable while we talk. I'll fix you a drink." A *triple*. The more relaxed she was, the less chance she might get cold feet.

"Oh, no drink, thanks. Not when I have to drive home."

She was strung so taut, he could damn near pluck notes. "Just one won't hurt, will it?"

"Actually, except for a glass of wine on special occasions, I seldom indulge. Another hang-up of mine, I'm afraid. I don't like feeling muzzy-headed."

Joe guessed he didn't blame her. Getting muzzy-headed had cost her dearly at one point in her life.

Once in the family room, he steered her over to the cream-colored leather sectional, helped her to sit down, and then retrieved his drink before taking a seat on the ottoman facing her.

She stared at the whiskey for a long moment. Joe considered setting the glass aside, but then he discarded the thought. He never became ill-tempered when he drank, and he sure as hell didn't force himself on women. If she didn't already know that, it was high time she learned.

"I, um . . ." She folded her hands, her pointy knuckles going white with the force of her grip. "As I said, I've been thinking about your proposal. I think we might be able to make a marriage work if we proceed much as we have been up to now. As a temporary arrangement, anyway."

That tripped him up. "What do you mean, 'as a temporary arrangement'?"

"Well, you know—long enough to get you through this custody issue. A couple of years, maybe?" Her gaze flitted from his. She frowned slightly as she glanced at his bare family room walls. "Once there's a track record proving Zachary has done well in the home environment you've provided, I don't think Valerie will stand a chance in court. What judge would want to cause unnecessary turmoil in the child's life if he's been happy living with you?"

Joe realized he was starting to sound like an echo, but he couldn't seem to stop himself. "Did you say a couple of years?"

Plucking at the front placket of her shirt, she nodded. "I know it's an unconventional way to go about things. But given my difficulties, I can't make the commitment otherwise, and what will happen to Zachary if I don't?" Her large blue eyes grew moist, making him feel as if he were drowning in drenched velvet. "After you left, I couldn't stop thinking about him. I kept remembering that day he talked to me about his mom, how terrified he was of going back to her. He's so little and helpless, Joe. What kind of person could just turn her back on him?"

Joe had loved Marilee Nelson for so many years that

he'd nearly forgotten when he first lost his heart to her, but never had he loved her more than now. He couldn't quite believe she had worked up the courage to do this.

"I should never have asked you for help," he said, his voice going thick with regret. "It's not your problem, and it was wrong of me to dump it in your lap."

She shook her head. "No, no. Please don't think that way." Her smile was overbright. "It's not an entirely unselfish gesture, after all. There's a possibility that I may get a baby out of the deal. Not that my offer hinges upon your agreeing to that part, and please know that if you should agree, I'm perfectly willing to draw up some sort of contract to protect both of us after the divorce."

After what he'd been through with Valerie, Joe would have told any other woman to go whistle Dixie if she'd asked him for a baby in one breath and mentioned divorce in the next. But Marilee wasn't another woman, and in that moment, he was so touched by her concern for Zachary that he would have found it difficult to deny her anything. Besides, he didn't believe she would ever actually get a divorce, anyway. Right now, she was extremely nervous and her emotions were running high. She obviously hadn't taken the time to really think this through. Zachary was already attached to her, and the child's feelings for her would only intensify if he came to think of her as his mother. When the two years were up, she wouldn't have the heart to leave.

Armed with that knowledge, he smothered a tender smile as he studied her pale face. He loved her so much that he ached. She was such a sweetheart, this woman, and only a lowdown skunk would consider accepting her offer. It was tantamount to luring her into a trap and dropping the hatch closed.

He guessed he was a lowdown skunk. He hated himself a little for that, but there it was, an ugly truth about himself he couldn't deny. He wanted her, and the bottom line was, fair or not, noble or not, he'd take her any way he could get her. To have that baby she wanted so much she would have to be physically intimate with him, which would remove the one obstacle that stood between them, her abhorrence of sex. He harbored not a single doubt that he could make it a pleasurable experience for her, one she'd want to repeat after she discovered she had nothing to fear.

Warming to her idea of a "temporary arrangement" more by the moment, Joe took a slow sip of his drink, savoring the taste of the whiskey as it rolled over his tongue. Maybe it was the booze dulling his wits, but he couldn't think of one good reason to pass this up.

"Honey, are you absolutely sure you want to do this?"

"Oh, yes."

He waited a beat, allowing her a moment to change her mind. When she didn't, he said, "Then, sweetheart, you've got yourself a deal."

"Just like that?" Her eyes widened. "You do understand that I'm not suggesting a *normal* marriage. I suppose we'd share meals together and stuff like that, but otherwise, I'd keep to my own corner most of the time, working at night while you were home to watch Zachary and sleeping in my own room. My house is fairly large, so I probably wouldn't see all that much of you."

In order to get that baby she wanted, she'd see enough of him to suit his purposes. What was she thinking, that they could get the job done with an occasional handshake? He frowned slightly. Surely not even Marilee was that naïve. Few women got pregnant immediately. He might have to make love to her a half-dozen times—hell, they might try every night for six months straight—before she finally turned the stick blue.

Joe wanted to marry her so badly that he hated to look for flaws in her offer, but loving her as he did, there were practical concerns he couldn't ignore.

"How do you plan to control your panic attacks?" he asked.

She shrugged as though that wasn't really a concern. "I'm hoping I won't have any. Since that first afternoon,

I've been around you several times with no ill effect."

He hadn't made love to her any of those times. Joe refrained from pointing that out. If he was gentle and patient, he could surely help her to get over her wariness of him.

"Why borrow trouble?" she said brightly. "I've done well around you so far. Right? If we continue in the same vein, why would I suddenly start having problems?"

"True," he settled for saying. "Why borrow trouble? If problems crop up, we'll handle them as we go along."

"So it's a deal?" She smiled incredulously. "You truly don't mind working with me so I can have a baby?"

Mind? "Mari, I'd love to give you a baby."

Her cheeks flushed a pretty pink. "Oh, Joe, truly? I thought sure you'd balk at that idea." Her eyes shone with happiness. "Most men would tell me to go fly a kite." She hugged her waist, clearly so excited she could barely contain herself. "Oh, Joe . . . a baby? I just can't believe it."

He couldn't either, actually. Visions of Marilee in his arms filled his mind, the details of which definitely had to be alcohol induced because his thoughts immediately ran to black lace and steamy sex, which wouldn't be in the cards for a long, long time.

"Where will we do it?" she asked.

About to swallow more whiskey, he nearly choked at the question. He gulped and stared at her with watery eyes. She couldn't be asking what he thought she was asking.

"I don't really care, one way or another, as long as we do it right away," she added, giving a nervous laugh. "If I think about it too long, I'm afraid I'll chicken out."

Joe definitely didn't want that. *Damn.* As for where— he loved her so much and wanted her so badly that the floor was starting to look pretty good. *Hold it.* He was a little intoxicated, not completely brain-dead. Something wasn't right with this picture.

After studying her sweet features and guileless blue

eyes for a second, he smiled slightly. "Sweetheart, back up for a minute. What, exactly, are we talking about?"

She gave him a bewildered look. "Getting married, of course."

His smile deepened. "Of course. I don't know where my head was at."

She chafed her hands together as though she were chilled. "Reno's the only place I know where we can do it immediately." Her brow pleated in a questioning frown. "It is imperative that we do it soon, isn't it? Not just because of me. What with Valerie and that custody issue hanging over our heads, I think we need to get your new marital status established as quickly as possible."

"Absolutely. The sooner, the better," he agreed. "Otherwise when I go to court, it may look as if we got married at the last minute simply to sway the judge in my favor. And you're right. Reno is the perfect solution." Though he refrained from expressing the thought aloud, Joe sincerely hoped she would agree to marry him in the church later. "In Nevada, we'll encounter no red tape, and there's no waiting period."

"My thoughts exactly."

"When do you want to go?" he asked.

"I could probably be ready to leave by nine tomorrow morning. If you want to do it this weekend, that is."

"The weekend is definitely best for me. That way I won't miss any work." He thought for a moment. "I can probably be ready to go by nine."

"What'll we do with Zachary?"

"If Mrs. Rasmussen will agree to help out over at Mom's, I can drop him off there."

"It wouldn't be too much for your mom to keep him?"

"Dr. Petrie says that as long as Mrs. Rasmussen is there to do most of the actual work, Mom can have him more frequently and for longer periods of time. Zachary doesn't seem to be afraid of Sarah as long as Mom's around, so no problem on that score, either."

"I'll feed and water Boo before we leave, and he can

stay outside in the yard for the day. I was thinking we could make a fast round trip, leave tomorrow morning and come back tomorrow night."

Joe nearly agreed, but then it occurred to him he'd be missing an opportunity to be alone with her one entire night. "Actually, ten hours of driving is a bit much for one day, and that's not counting how long it may take to get everything done once we get there. Let's just stay over and head home early Sunday."

Judging by the expression that crossed her face, she was none too certain she liked that plan.

"If we're going to do this, you have to trust me, Marilee."

"Right," she said with a determined nod. "Staying the night just hadn't occurred to me, is all." She wiped her palms on the knees of her jeans. "We'll get separate rooms, of course."

She looked so disconcerted by the thought of sharing a room with him that it gave Joe pause. He had a nagging feeling that he was overlooking something. "Honey, are you absolutely certain you really want to do this? Marriage is a big step."

She nodded decisively. "I'm sure. Our getting married will safeguard Zachary, which is, of course, my primary concern, and having my own baby will be a dream come true."

He relaxed slightly, swirling the remains of his whiskey. He'd given her the chance to back out. She was twenty-eight years old and knew her own mind. He shouldn't have to list the pros and cons for her and point out every possible pitfall. He lifted the glass to his lips to finish off his drink.

"I'm just surprised you're willing," she went on. "Most men would balk at the very mention of artificial insemination."

Joe choked. Whiskey went up his nose and down his windpipe. *Fire.* Marilee jumped up and whacked him on the back.

"Are you okay?"

He was *not* okay. Dear God. "Artificial insemination?" he croaked.

"The nurse at the clinic called it 'creative procreation.' That has a much nicer ring to it." Her voice quavered slightly. "From now on, we can use that term if you like."

She could call it whatever she wanted. By any name, it spelled trouble for their relationship. She had no intention of trying to work through her problems and eventually have a normal marriage. "What clinic?"

"The fertility clinic in Bedford. I, um, went there last year to check out the possibilities."

Joe felt as if his brain had gone through a fast-freeze process. He stared up at her, trying to grasp this situation and accept the implications.

"I never really got that far into it," she went on. "A sperm bank seemed so—I don't know—iffy, I suppose is the word. Picking the father of my child by computer."

"By *computer?*"

"Yes. You sit and read computer profiles on the available donors." Color flagged her cheeks. "Physical characteristics, sketchy personal details. Most of the donors were Bedford Community College students. To ensure privacy, the clinic offered no photographs." She wrinkled her nose. "Essentially, I would have been playing genetic roulette, and I knew I'd be stuck with the outcome, for better or worse. Before I got into it too deeply, I backed out." She smiled beatifically. "This way will be much safer. I've known you most of my life. Our baby will have everything going for it—intelligence, athletic and artistic ability, good temperament, and from your side, at least, far better than average looks."

Joe was still reeling from shock. To her credit, she had told him she didn't intend for this to be a normal marriage. He'd just been so focused on his own agenda, her meaning hadn't sunk in. Finally he found the presence of mind to say, "I thought things like artificial insemination were against your religion."

"Well . . ." She sighed and sat back down. "It may be, I suppose. As far as that goes, so is our getting married out of the church."

"A civil marriage ceremony isn't quite on the same par as artificial insemination. Are you sure you want to go that route? Your folks are pretty stodgy. How do they feel about things like that?"

She turned her hands to gaze at her palms. "Daddy calls it 'newfangled madness,' and he doesn't approve. Whether that's a personal judgment or a religious conviction, I'm not sure, and I've purposely avoided asking."

"I see." This didn't sound like the Marilee he knew.

She kept her gaze downcast. After a long moment, she finally looked up, her eyes sparkling with tears. "I just want a baby so much, Joe. I can't explain. Sometimes you just want something so badly, you can't think past it, and that's where I'm at, not really caring *how* I get one, just as long as I do." She shrugged. "As for the church's stance on artificial insemination, Father has never chosen that topic for the homily, and I've never actually asked anyone about it." She looked a little shamefaced. "I figure if the church is against it, maybe it won't really be that bad a sin if I don't know for sure I'm doing anything wrong."

Joe's heart caught as he searched her gaze. Just the fact that she was willing to ignore a ruling of the church to have a baby told him how very much she wanted one. Marilee lived by the precepts of her faith and had never, to his knowledge, flouted the rules.

"For once, I'm going to do what *I* want," she whispered fiercely, "the devil take what anyone else thinks. Do you think I'm terrible?"

He thought she was the sweetest, most precious person God had ever allowed to draw breath, and it broke his heart to think how devastatingly lonely and empty her life had been up until now.

"Ever since I was little, I've tried to please my parents. But what about pleasing myself? I've watched my sister have eight beautiful babies, and every time I ached to hold one of my own. Now I've got this chance, and I'm taking it."

"And you feel going to a clinic is the appropriate choice?"

"At this point in time, it's the *only* choice for me. I thought you understood that."

By way of explanation, Joe held up the tumbler of whiskey. "I guess I was a little slow on the uptake. I thought—" He broke off and gave a weary sigh. "I don't know what I was thinking. All the wrong things, obviously."

The picture was coming into clear focus for him now. She did plan to stay in her own corner—to live in the same house with him, have his baby, and never get within ten feet of him in the process. No wonder she wasn't worried about having a panic attack.

He nearly told her to go fly that kite she'd mentioned earlier. He *loved* her, and, damn it, she still loved him. How could she possibly expect him to go along with this?

In that moment, Joe faced a fact he'd been avoiding up until now. She'd never confront her fears about sex and or try to overcome them unless she was forced into it.

Disappointment and concern for her became a crushing weight in his chest. Then, before he knew quite what hit him, the disappointment and concern turned to a burning pain. Could he just stand aside and watch while she threw away her one chance for happiness, not to mention his own, simply because that seemed to be what she wanted?

He'd be damned if he would. True love didn't come calling often. If you were lucky, you got one shot at it. *One.* He had let this woman slip through his fingers once.

He wouldn't again.

 *Nine*

*M*arilee's hands trembled as she pushed the key into the ignition and started her Taurus. She'd been so afraid Joe would refuse her proposal that her heart was still pounding like a trip hammer. As she backed from his driveway, she could see him watching from the porch. Even in the moonlight, the powerful lines of his body were evident. He stood with his hands on his hips, one knee slightly bent, his tall frame casting an elongated and broad shadow against the house. He looked so big and solid and deliciously handsome standing there that she could scarcely believe he would soon be her husband.

Her emotions seesawed violently between relief, joy, nervous jitters, and waves of sheer fright that made her feel as if she were drowning. No matter. For the first time in ten years, she was going to press forward without weighing the risks. She had loved Joe nearly all her life, and being separated from him for so long had not diminished her feelings for him. The very fact that she'd come chasing after him tonight proved that. She couldn't bear it if Zachary had to go back to his mother, and she'd die if she lost Joe again. Her unusual marriage proposal to him had been the only way she could think of to stop either of those things from happening.

Joe. Until she broke their engagement, he'd been the canvas on which she stitched the whole pattern of her life, past, present and future. After she sent him away, there'd been nothing left—no direction, no design to anything, just an awful, horrible emptiness, as if she were floating in a void. She couldn't go through that again, *wouldn't* go through that again, not if she could prevent it. No more sitting in her kitchen, staring at Boo and thinking of the empty years that lay ahead. No more passive acceptance of whatever life dished up. She was taking action this time, grabbing hold of what she wanted with both hands, the devil take caution.

Joe Lakota was all that she'd ever wanted, and by this time tomorrow night, he would finally be hers. She refused to think about the possible consequences, and she wouldn't allow herself to feel guilty for not being completely candid with him. Marriage under her terms would protect Zachary from Valerie, which had been Joe's primary concern, and as an added bonus, Marilee would have Joe in her life another two years. It was the *perfect* solution for her. No expectations on Joe's part. No prior agreements that would bind her to him if the arrangement didn't work. If her greatest fear became a reality and she began to get sick again, they would both have an easy out.

Thank you, God. Thank you. This gave her a chance at happiness that she'd never hoped to have. Granted, maybe it was only a slim chance, but it was a chance all the same, and it would be entirely up to her what she made of it. *Two whole years.* That gave her plenty of time to test the water with Joe and work at getting well. No pressure from him. No goals for her to reach within specified blocks of time. No promises she wasn't certain she could keep. She could relax, enjoy his company, maybe even go to counseling on the sly so he wouldn't insist on going with her. And maybe, just maybe, at the end of the two years, she'd be able to be a real wife to him.

Tears of relief nearly blinded her as she backed her car into the street. After shifting into first, she beeped the horn in farewell. In response, Joe lifted a hand, not actually waving, but bidding her good-bye all the same, the gesture as masculine as he was. For just an instant, she sat there staring at him, her heart twisting because she knew he wasn't happy with her proposal. But how could she possibly agree to his terms? He wanted a commitment from her to work toward their having a real marriage, which undoubtedly would involve intimacy by graduating degrees, with him calling all the shots. The very thought made her feel as if a hand was closing around her throat.

At precisely nine o'clock the next morning, Joe rang Marilee's doorbell. As he stood on the porch waiting for her to answer, he tried not to think of how much he loved her and what he was about to do. Nevertheless, talons of desperation and panic clawed at him with every other breath, urging him to ignore the voice of his conscience. His hands shook, and he knotted them into fists.

He gazed through the window glass of her door, wondering what was keeping her. Maybe she'd come to her senses and decided to run like hell. A part of him almost wished she had. Then he'd be spared the ordeal of having to explain this to her, at least. *Damn.* What was he going to say to her? He'd been the one to first suggest marriage, after all, and now he was doing a sudden about-face.

He hauled in a deep breath and tried to concentrate on the beauty of the late August morning. The perfume of dew-kissed roses floated on the air, and at his feet, sunlight pooled. As wedding days went, this one would have been picture perfect. *It still can be*, a wicked voice at the back of his mind taunted.

Through the glass, he saw her hurrying up the hallway. When she finally opened the door, she said, "I'm sorry! I was in the bathroom." She fluttered a fine-boned hand over her hip, smoothing a wrinkle from the formfitting skirt of her dress. "I was afraid you'd get tired of waiting and leave."

Her voice rang shrill, telling Joe she was a bundle of nerves. She pushed at her hair, her wide blue eyes searching his for approval. "Do I look all right?" She glanced at his casual attire, a pair of neatly pressed khaki chinos and a blue Oxford shirt. "I'm too dressed up, aren't I? Oh, man, give me just a minute!"

About to step over the threshold, Joe nearly got his nose smashed when the door closed in his face. He had barely assimilated the fact that she'd left him standing on the porch when the door flew open again. The flush of embarrassment on her cheeks made him smile, and tenderness welled within him. God, how he loved her.

"I don't know what I'm thinking! Come on in. There's fresh coffee in the kitchen. Do you mind just helping yourself?"

"Mari, don't go change," he said, his voice reminding him of a toad croaking at the bottom of a barrel. "You look beautiful."

She reeled to a stop, blinked, and glanced down at herself. "Do you really think?"

"I really do," he assured her and meant it. *So very beautiful.* Just looking at her nearly brought tears to his eyes.

She wore a simple ecru dress that skimmed her figure, a yoke overlay of antique lace drawing his gaze to the scoop neckline where the barest hint of her cleavage peeked out at him. Her pumps matched the dress perfectly, a pearl choker glowed softly at her throat, and a pair of dainty pearl-drop earrings winked at him through her sun-kissed curls. *Sweet.* That was how she looked, like a delicate concoction of spun sugar, created expressly to whet a man's appetite. *Oh, God.* He needed divine intercession to get through this.

A sense of urgency filled him. If he didn't get this said in damned short order, temptation might get the best of him. "Mari, honey, I need to talk to you."

She glanced at her watch. "Thanks to me, we'll already be running late. Can't we just talk on the way?"

"No." He said the word with more vehemence than he intended, and she threw him a startled look. "No," he said more gently. "What I need to say won't keep."

"Oh." She nibbled her bottom lip with small, perfectly formed white teeth, the shape of which he'd once traced with the tip of his tongue. The memory made his guts knot. "I, um . . ." Her voice trailed away, and her happy, nervous expression clouded with disappointment. "Oh, Joe, you've changed your mind, haven't you?"

With the same froglike gruffness, he said, "I'm sorry, honey. I know you went to a lot of trouble, getting ready. But unless we can come to a compromise and alter our course a bit, I've changed my mind."

"I see."

Only, of course, she didn't see. Not at all. And he was so very glad she didn't. He only wished he could leave it that way. "I almost called to save you the hassle of packing, but this is something I need to say in person."

Her arms fell limply at her sides, her beautiful eyes shimmering in the dim light. "Joe, if it's the business about the clinic, we can just forget about it. I understand it's an unconventional way to go about things, and I knew when I asked that you'd probably turn me down. The primary concern is Zachary's well-being."

"It's not that." That wasn't entirely true, of course. *Creative procreation?* Every time he recalled her saying that, he nearly cracked a molar clenching his teeth. He stepped inside, pushed the door closed, and gestured toward the kitchen. "How's about we sit down over a cup of that coffee you mentioned?"

"All right." She turned to lead the way back up the hall. "If we're not going to Reno, I guess we've got all the time in the world."

Hardly any time at all, actually. If he carried through with the decisions he'd reached this morning, he'd say what he had to say, wait for her reply, and if it wasn't what he hoped to hear, he'd get the hell out of here.

Following behind her, Joe fixed his gaze on the tantalizing swing of her hips and then her well-turned ankles. It was the first time he'd seen her in a dress since coming back home. The sight chipped away at his willpower, which had been on a downhill skid for weeks as it was. Seeing her every day, wanting her so badly his bones ached. *Damn.* He was no saint. Far from it. He had as much self-control as any man, and out of regard for her, he'd exercised it constantly, but now he had reached the end of his rope.

He could still change his mind and go through with the marriage. He hadn't said enough yet to take them past the point of no return.

Stop it, he ordered himself. He loved this woman, and as difficult as it might be, he had to put her well-being and happiness before his own.

Her heels tapped a tattoo on the hardwood floor, the light, feminine rapidity striking a marked contrast to the slower, heavier resonation of his own. As he followed her through the house, he noted other differences between them: the graceful glide of her movements as he lumbered in her wake, the fragility of her frame in comparison to his own, and the marked difference in their height. Even in three-inch heels, she barely cleared his chin. Much to his dismay, he also noticed the delicate, ivory skin revealed by her sleeveless dress, creating a flawless canvas for the stroke of his dark hands.

God help him, how he wanted her. So badly his hands were shaking. So badly that he'd been tempted to take her any way he could get her, even if it involved trickery. The realization of how close he had come to dancing with the devil made his stomach roll and filled him with disgust. What kind of a man married a woman, agreeing to keep the relationship platonic, and then pressed her for more than she'd bargained for after the fact? Only a bastard, plain and simple.

There was something to be said for being a happy bastard, he thought grimly. Better that than a miserable nice guy. Right? *Wrong*, he told himself firmly. He had to stop waffling and get this finished.

Oblivious to the treacherous train of his thoughts, she crossed the kitchen to a cupboard, pushing up on her tiptoes to pluck two mugs from a top shelf. The motion hiked up the hem of her dress, displaying world-class legs he knew would be milk white without the hosiery and silky to the touch. He envisioned himself trailing his fingertips up her inner thigh, territory he had yet to explore. Who needed memories when imagination painted such a vivid tableau? He knew his way around a woman's body, and Marilee's was exquisite, softly padded to give her a tempting roundness in all the right places. Her skin would be warm and slightly damp with passion as he made love to her. Her breath would quicken when he suckled her breasts. Her muscles would quiver in the throes of orgasm as he teased that sweetest, most guarded part of her.

Joe's own breath quickened, and he tried to shove the images from his mind, afraid of what he might do if he continued to entertain them. Love, desire, compulsion. It seemed to him in that moment that there was little difference between the three, and it would be so horribly easy to take advantage of her. Her love for his son made her vulnerable, less than cautious, and wide open for a scoring pass.

His hands trembling, his throat taut with repressed yearning, Joe forced himself to sit down at the table and gazed out the French doors into her yard. When Marilee brought him a mug of coffee, she set it gingerly before him and then moved away, taking a seat at the opposite side of the table.

He cupped his hand around the mug, his heart squeezing when he glanced down and saw that the handle was a three-dimensional elf. From there, his gaze moved to the mice salt-and-pepper shakers on her lazy Susan. Was there nothing in her home that depicted reality? Everywhere he looked, he saw fantasy elements. A family of sweet-faced, ceramic ducks paraded single file across the hardwood floor. A spotted-cow on the wall doubled as a clock, its heavily-lashed, merry brown eyes shifting back and forth with each movement of the second hand. Even her cookie jar, a plump piglet dressed in a pinafore and black high-top shoes, reflected the fantasy theme.

Her hold on emotional stability was so frighteningly fragile, he realized, whimsy and make-believe forming an insubstantial barrier between her and the outside world. It shamed him to realize he had actually contemplated shaking her carefully fabricated existence clear off its axis.

In the pocket of his chinos, the tattered and smudged velvet box that held their decade-old wedding set seemed to burn a hole in his thigh. To find the rings, he'd stayed up half the night, tearing into boxes he'd never had time to unpack, and God forgive him, he'd brought the rings with him this morning, just in case he no longer felt in the mood to be decent once he got here.

Decency. It was going to make for a very cold bed partner.

Marilee fiddled with the pearls at her throat, her gaze fixed on Joe's dark face as she waited for an explanation for his sudden change of heart. Instead of giving her one, he seemed unaccountably interested in her coffee mug. He turned it in his hands, studied the elf, and then stared morosely into the depths of his coffee.

When he finally looked up, her heart caught at the

anguish she saw in his eyes. She had the most awful feeling that he was about to tell her good-bye.

His voice husky with emotion, he said, "Sweetheart, I'm really nervous, so I'm just going to jump in and say this as best I can." A muscle began to tic in his lean cheek, and he swallowed, his Adam's apple bobbing. "I, um—" He broke off and looked away. Then he laughed under his breath, the sound humorless and oddly hollow, and rubbed a hand over his face. "Damn. I'm not even sure where to start."

"When I feel like that, I always just start at the beginning."

"And when was that?" he asked softly, his eyes glistening with what looked like tears. "This started for me a lifetime ago—the first time I ever pulled your pigtails."

It wasn't the most romantic proclamation she'd ever heard, and yet it touched her in ways nothing else could, calling to mind a host of memories and tumbling her backward through the years. She knew exactly what he was attempting to say, that he loved her, that he'd always loved her, that it seemed to him his feelings for her had no beginning and would never have an end. Oh, yes, she understood, because she loved him in exactly the same way, with every beat of her heart.

In that same hollow voice, he went on, every word he said bringing tears to her eyes. "I want it all, Mari mine, a real marriage, all wrapped up in a package called forever. I want to make love with you long into the night and show you magic. I want to give you my babies the old-fashioned way. I want to be the guy who dries your tears when you're sad and holds your head when you're sick. When you grow old and gray, I want to be the old man there beside you—so I can hold your hand and tell you you're still beautiful and that I love you more than life itself. I want to watch you play with my grandchildren. Forever, Mari. Or forever and a day if you can manage it. But I can't settle for two years."

Nerves attacked Marilee's stomach, sending her muscles into spasms, and her nylon slip did a ticklish jig over her belly. She had a crazy urge to jump up and clamp a hand over his mouth so he would say no more. The tortured expression on his face told her she wasn't going to like what he'd come to tell her.

"I'd like that, too, Joe," she inserted, her voice taut. "Forever and a day—with you. But I—"

"No buts." He smiled slightly. A beautiful understatement, Joe's smile, always moving slowly across his face and filling her with warmth. It reminded her of the feeling she got when she watched the sky slowly brighten at daybreak. "I know you love me, honey, and that deep down, you want the same things I do." He studied her for a long moment. "But that isn't what you're offering me, is it?"

"No," she admitted tonelessly.

"I can't settle for less."

"But last night, you—"

"I wasn't thinking straight last night. Call it a case of temporary madness or whatever else you like, but I wasn't thinking straight. If I marry you, I want it to be a real marriage eventually, and in order to be fair to you, I need to make that clear from the start. I can't play the game by your rules. When I suggested marriage last night, I had every intention of our working toward having a normal relationship, not a meaningless coexistence that would end two years down the road with a divorce. As for giving you a baby, I'd give my right arm to have the honor, but not your way, knowing in advance that we'd separate. Ideally, I think a child should live with both its parents."

"I see."

He searched her gaze, his aching with sadness. "Somehow, I doubt that, and I'd really like to keep it that way. Unfortunately, for you to understand what I'm about to say, I can't leave it at that. Last night after you and I talked at my place, I came face-to-face with a dark side of my nature I never even realized existed. I truly don't believe it's possible to love too deeply, but sometimes a man's feelings get in such a tangle, the first thing he knows, he can't separate his feelings of love from his own selfish needs and desires.

"When that happens, what should be a beautiful, sweet emotion becomes ugly and hurtful to the one person on earth he loves the very most. Last night, I decided to hell with everything, that I'd take you any way I could get you, even if it involved trickery and lies. Something is way out of whack when a man starts thinking that way, and he's got one of two choices, changing course or walking out. Do you understand what I'm saying to you?"

"I'm trying."

He rested his arms on the table and leaned slightly forward, as if by getting closer, he might lend emphasis to his words. "I love you, Mari mine. More than I can say, and probably more than you'll ever know. So much that I'm not sure I can live through losing you again. And therein lies part of the problem, my fear of losing you. When I think about your leaving me in two years, I get to feeling a little desperate. Then I start thinking about doing things I normally wouldn't, namely marrying you, pretending to go along with your conditions, and then telling you the plans have changed after the fact."

Marilee's insides lurched, and for an awful moment, she feared she might be sick. The look on his face. Oh, God. It nearly broke her heart. *Shame.* He didn't look away or bend his head, but she could tell that making this admission was the most humiliating experience of his life.

"In my own defense, I need to tell you that my intentions were good. I believe with all my heart that our lovemaking will be a beautiful, pleasurable experience for you." A twinkle of mischief came into his eyes. "If you'd only give me ten minutes and half a chance, I'd prove it to you, and then all of these feelings you have would be nothing but a memory."

Ten minutes. Rationally Marilee knew that was a short amount of time, but she also knew every second might drag on for an eternity. She suppressed a shudder and averted her gaze, unsettled by the teasing invitation in his eyes.

"I'm not ready for that yet, Joe. I may never be."

"I know," he whispered. "And where does that leave us, Mari? I am ready. More than ready."

"I don't know where it leaves us. I only know where it can't possibly take us."

Silence. It hung there between them, the only sounds the muted ticking of her wall clock and the hum of the refrigerator. Finally he said, "And there we have it, don't we? We're poles apart on this issue, and unless we can find a happy meeting ground, I have to back out. If I don't, I'll only end up hurting you. As things stand, I'm a panic attack waiting to happen. I don't want to be responsible for making you sick again, and without trust between us, that's exactly what'll happen."

He tapped his fingertips on the table, a nervous gesture that told her how tense he really was. "It wouldn't be a decision on my part, or even deliberate. Please, know that. I'd never hurt you on purpose. But at a certain point in a relationship, a man's libido takes over, and his better judgment goes out the window. Sooner or later—probably sooner, judging by the way I'm feeling—I'd start making moves on you, pressing you for more than you're ready to give, and before we knew it, we'd be up to our eyebrows in more trouble than either of us could handle."

Marilee sat more erect, straightening her shoulders and raising her chin. "And if we can't find a happy meeting ground, what about Zachary? I thought our getting married was your only hope of protecting him from Valerie."

"It was. It is. But at what cost? I love both of you. To ensure Zachary's future, I can't put you through hell. That wouldn't be fair to you."

"No." She smoothed a wrinkle from her skirt, then met

his gaze again. "I just love him, is all. I don't want anything bad to happen to him, and I especially don't want to feel in any way responsible if it should."

"I'll protect Zachary," he said with solemn determination. "I'll fight Valerie with everything I've got, and if it begins to look as if the legal system may fail me again, there are always other options. If push comes to shove, I can always skip out."

"Where would you go?" she asked thinly.

He ran a hand over his hair and sighed. "I haven't really thought that far ahead yet. Out of the country, certainly. My face is too well known for me to fade into obscurity here in the States."

If it was possible for bones to turn to water, Marilee's did. She stared at him incredulously. "Out of the country? Oh, Joe, if you do that, I may never see you again."

"Unless we can reach a compromise, you won't be seeing very much of me anyway." At her shocked expression, he arched an eyebrow. "What do you think I've been saying to you, Mari?" he asked gently.

"I didn't think you meant to end our friendship," she said, unable to quash the frantic feeling that welled within her. "Surely we can go on much as we have been, with me keeping Zachary and our seeing each other every day."

He gazed out the window for a long moment. When he finally looked back at her, there were definitely tears in his eyes. "As friends only?" he asked, his voice gravelly. "That isn't working for me, Marilee. I wish with all my heart that it was, but I'm a healthy young man with an equally healthy sex drive. I'm crazy in love with you, and my body tells me about it every time I'm around you. I can't go on as we have been. This situation with Valerie just brought things to a head a few days sooner, is all. I'd already decided we needed to change course. I first started thinking along those lines the night Gerry had the baby."

"That long ago?"

"Yes."

She raked her nails over her skirt then knotted her hands into tight fists. "Friends forever. Isn't that what you said?"

"Yes, and I still mean it. Friends forever, Mari mine. But I need more from you than just that. Last night was a danger signal, and I'd be a fool to ignore it. Friends don't hurt each other, and I'll eventually hurt you unless we make some changes in our relationship. I won't intend to, but I will."

Her throat felt as if it had been scoured with a bottle brush. She swallowed to steady her voice. "You need more from me than I can give, Joe."

"Do I?" He pushed up from his chair and moved around the table to hunker beside her. Cupping her chin in a big hand, he drew her face around. Then with a blunt fingertip, he spent a moment tracing her features, as though to commit them to memory. "I don't expect you to have an overnight recovery. I don't care if you come to me with a truckload of fears and hang-ups. We can work our way through those by going to counseling together and having long heart-to-heart talks. As for making love, I can move forward with that at a snail's pace if I know every slow inch of progress is leading us toward forever."

Tears spilled over Marilee's lower lashes and onto her cheeks. "I might get sick."

"Yes, you might," he admitted. "And maybe I'll get cancer. Life doesn't come with any guarantees except for the ones we give each other, Marilee, namely that we'll be there for each other, no matter what happens. If you get sick, I'll be there, and I'll help you get through it. I believe there are some new medications available now that may help you. We can check into that. Chances are, you won't get sick again. But that isn't really the point, is it? This is about being willing to take a few risks. It's about your taking a gamble on me and trusting me to love you more than I love myself."

He looked deeply into her eyes, imploring her. "Trust me, Mari mine. Trust me, just one more time. No conditions, no limitations. Will you marry me?"

Marilee could barely see him now through her tears. "This feels very much like an ultimatum. You're asking me to make a commitment to you that I'm not ready to make, and if I refuse, you're going to walk out. I need more time."

"How much time?" he asked, rubbing his thumb over her mouth. "Will you be completely well in, say, another ten years?"

"That isn't fair."

"Life isn't fair. It sure as hell hasn't been fair to you. Don't think I'm blind to that fact, or that I'm making light of what happened to you. I just don't think you're going to get better by yourself, Mari. Ten years, twenty. You won't get any better than you are right now until you move forward from here. You call this an ultimatum? I call it an invitation to take those small steps forward with me beside you."

"I'm not *ready*."

"You'll never feel ready," he whispered raggedly. "Never, Mari. You have only one point of reference, a really horrible one. How can you ever feel ready to go through that again? You can't. Instead, you have to believe in me and trust that it won't be like that with me. Just gather your courage, put your faith in me, and step into my arms."

"You make it sound so simple, but it isn't."

"Do you love me?"

Her chin started to quiver. "I never stopped. You know I love you."

"What can be more simple than that?" His eyes clouding with tenderness and warmth, he clumsily brushed at the wetness on her cheeks. Then he flashed her a crooked grin. "Just go with the feeling, Mari girl. Forget everything else, and just go with it. Let me worry about the rest."

The words he wanted to hear were locked behind a lump of dread at the base of her throat. She ached with the yearning to do as he asked and simply throw herself into his arms, to feel his heat and strength all around her. *Forever.* Oh, God. He was every dream she'd ever had, every hope and aspiration. She'd shrivel up and die if he walked out.

"I can't," she whispered. "I can't, Joe."

He remained crouched beside her for several endless seconds. Then, with a sigh that rang with exhaustion, he stood. "I guess that's my answer."

She gulped back a sob, hating herself for being such a coward, but unable to find her courage. She'd had some once. A lifetime ago, she'd had plenty. But somewhere along the way, she'd lost it along with all her dreams.

He stood there a moment longer, as if he were waiting. Waiting for something that didn't come. "I should never have come back around," he whispered. "You're the last person on earth I'd ever intentionally hurt, and I know I have. I'm so sorry, Mari mine. I should have just stayed away and left you alone."

With that, he turned and walked away.

Marilee nearly called out for him to come back, but she didn't have the courage to do that, either. Instead, she clamped a hand over her mouth to stifle a sob. *Joe.* Oh, God. Feeling as if her heart was being torn from her chest, she sat there, staring sightlessly through a blur of tears at the louvered doors of the utility room, all her senses riveted to the sound of his heavy footsteps going through the house. As had happened last night, an awful desolation filled her, and she clenched her hands into fists, her nails lacerating her palms.

The floor trembled slightly beneath her chair when he stepped out and closed her front door, a shuddering punctuation to something that hadn't yet begun. She should be grateful that he'd chosen to back out, she knew. Grateful that he'd had the strength of character to end this before it got ugly. Only she wasn't grateful—and she wasn't glad. Instead she felt as if she were dying, inch by slow inch.

She pressed her shaking hands over her face. *Ten minutes.* He'd asked her for only ten minutes. *Trust me, just one more time.* Instead of agreeing, she'd just sat there with her tongue stuck to the roof of her mouth and had let him leave.

"Oh, Joe . . ."

Sobbing uncontrollably, Marilee lay across the table, her arms outstretched toward where he'd been sitting. *Joe.* Her cowardice had cost her dearly over the last ten years, but never had the price been so steep.

As Joe drove away, he kept fighting the urge to make a U-turn and go back to her. *Marilee.* If he lived to be a hundred, he'd never forget that awful look that had come into her eyes. He'd done his best not to upset her, but he had. Worse, he had a very bad feeling he'd broken her heart. *Oh, God.* He felt like a slug.

He slammed the heel of his hand against the steering wheel and swore under his breath. He'd done some difficult things in his time, but walking out on her had been the hardest, every step he'd taken a decision. He only hoped that later she'd understand he'd done it for her. Because he loved her. Because he didn't want to hurt her any more than he already had.

If only she'd found the courage to run after him and ask him to stay. But she hadn't, and he had to accept that. Looking at it logically, he knew it was probably for the best, anyway. She had a heap of problems, and they wouldn't be easily solved. He had enough on his plate, trying to raise an emotionally messed up kid. The last thing he needed tossed into the mix was a troubled wife.

Not that he wouldn't have leaped at the opportunity.

Tears burned at the back of his eyes, and he blinked them angrily away. Did a guy's testosterone levels start depleting once he hit thirty? Maybe that was it. Just what he needed, a male hormone deficiency. Next, he'd start sniveling at sad movies.

Damn it. He swiped at his cheeks, telling himself it was just sweat running into his eyes. Oh, how he loved her. Maybe even more now than he had ten years ago. There was something so very vulnerable about her now, and it brought out all his protective instincts.

As he started into the intersection, he fancied for an instant that he heard her calling his name, a wistful cry so faint it barely reached him. His heart leaped with hope, and he glanced in the rearview mirror, chiding himself for being such a fool. Oh, sure, he knew she loved him. But just loving him wasn't enough. She'd never in a hundred years work up the nerve to come after him.

He caught movement in the mirror just then and brought his foot down hard on the brake. The car came to such a sudden stop that his chest hit the steering wheel. He stared stupidly at the mirror, scarcely able to credit his eyes. Skirt hiked well above her knees and minus the high heels, Marilee was running straight up the center of the street, one hand pressed to her chest, her shoulders heaving with exertion.

Joe almost jumped from the car with it still in first gear. The Honda's engine chuffed and nearly stalled, the resultant jerks snapping him back to his senses. He was sitting in the damned intersection.

"Joe!" she cried, the peal of her voice still faint.

He shifted from first into reverse, slammed on the gas, and backed the car from the intersection over to the curb. The vehicle lurched and sputtered when he killed the engine. He threw open his door and jumped out. His heart felt as though it might burst with happiness as he watched her cover the remaining few feet to reach him. The feet of her nylons were tattered from the rough asphalt, wide runners shooting up her slender legs.

He wasn't prepared for her to take a flying leap into his arms. The impact of her weight, slight though it was, sent him staggering back a step. Luckily, the car was there to help him catch his balance. He wrapped his arms tightly around her, aware that hers clutched frantically at his neck.

"I love you, Joe. I *do*! Please, don't leave me again. *Please!*"

He gathered her close, aware in some distant part of his mind that she was trembling violently, and by that he knew how very deeply she did love him.

"Oh, Mari . . ."

"Forever," she cried brokenly. "You win. After the Reno ceremony, I'll marry you in the church if you want. And I'll go to counseling. Not with you. That's something I need to do by myself, but I promise to go. Forever, Joe. Just, please, don't leave me."

Oh, God . . . he'd dreamed of this, wished and prayed for it, but he'd never really believed she'd find the courage to do it. He wanted to hold onto her with all his might and never let go.

"Are you sure? Please, be sure, Mari. If you change your mind later, it'll kill me."

"I won't change my mind." A sob caught in her throat, and her slender frame jerked with the force of it. "You're the one who needs to be sure. I can't promise you anything, Joe. Only that I'll stay and try with everything I've got."

"I can't ask for more than that," he whispered.

"Just understand, there'll be no easy way out doing it your way," she said in a quivering voice. "If I get sick again—you'll be locked in." Her voice rose to a shrill squeak. "Pizza pans and bells on strings. A loony wife who's an embarrassment to you and your little boy." She made a mewling sound low in her throat that was pure heartbreak. "I didn't want to put you through that. That's how come I suggested two years, not because I don't love you, but because I didn't want you and Zachary to be stuck with me if things went wrong."

Joe's heart twisted, and an awful ache filled his chest. Tears scalded his eyes and streamed down his cheeks into her hair. "Oh, sweetheart, no. Stuck with you? You listen to me. You listening?"

She nodded, the movement rubbing her nose and chin against his shirt.

"I *love* you, and nothing will make me prouder than to have you as my wife. You'll be the best mother on earth to my son. The very best."

"Bells and all? You just don't know."

"Oh, yes, I do, and I'll take you, bells and all. If you need pizza pans again, we'll paint them so they look pretty sitting by the doors. And we'll hang the bells so people think it's a decorative touch."

She laughed, the ring of it laced with hysteria.

"It's going to be all right," he assured her, his voice throbbing with love for her. "It's going to be all right. You'll see. We'll get through this, Mari. You and I, together. We'll get through it. No regrets. No easy outs. Just you and me, Mari mine, all the way."

"Oh, Joe . . . I'm scared," she admitted in that same squeaky voice. "Scared to death. It won't be that easy. I'm so messed up inside. It's going to take time for me to get my head on straight."

"We've got forever," he reminded her, smiling against her curls. "And try not to be scared. Best friends, remember? I'll be there. You're never going to regret this decision, Marilee. I promise you that."

She smelled of soap and shampoo and talcum—the blend forming a scent he remembered well and that he associated only with her. No other woman in his memory had ever smelled as sweet. *Marilee.* Where his palm curled over her hip, he could feel the soft warmth of her. He wanted nothing more than to test that softness with his fingertips, but warning bells went off in his mind, and he kept his hand anchored where it was.

He hugged her fiercely. For a moment, she grew so rigid he feared her bones might snap. But then she slowly relaxed and melted over him like a dollop of sweet butter, her slender arms tightening around his neck.

Joe lost track of time and had no idea how long he stood there, swaying with her in his arms. Dimly he was aware that they were in the middle of the street, and that her neighbors were probably watching them. Not even that could induce him to turn loose of her. He just thanked God it was a quiet street and there was little traffic.

Trust. He'd asked for her trust, and she'd given it to him. No ground rules this time, no stipulations. And being able to hold her like this after ten long years was the sweetest gift he'd ever been given. He didn't care that she came to him with misgivings. He didn't care if they had miles of rough road ahead to get her past this. All that really mattered was that they'd walk that road together.

All his life, he'd heard people say they were so happy, they were in seventh heaven, and he'd thought them silly. *Seventh heaven?* Where the hell was that, six flights up from regular heaven? Well, he was no longer laughing. Seventh heaven did exist, and now he knew exactly where it was.

In Marilee Nelson's arms.

Ten

$\mathcal{B}$y the time they reached Reno, Marilee felt as if she were soaring one minute and about to crash and burn the next. She was relieved beyond words that she had convinced Joe to go through with the marriage, not just for her own sake, but for Zachary's as well. But at the same time, she felt as if she'd grabbed a very large bull by the horn. Until now, Joe had kept his distance and seldom touched her. Now all that had changed in a twinkling, and she wasn't sure how to handle it. Even while driving, he frequently reached over to touch her cheek or squeeze her hand, as if by making physical contact, he could assure himself that she was actually there with him.

She understood how he felt. This was like a dream—a wonderful dream, for the most part. It was just that Marilee knew firsthand how quickly a dream could become a nightmare.

"Stop worrying," Joe ordered, the teasing twinkle in his eyes warming her. "It's going to be okay."

"Can I have that in writing?"

He grinned and returned his attention to the traffic. "Seriously, no worrying allowed. We've made our decision, and now all we can do is handle each problem as it comes. If you worry, you'll only make yourself needlessly tense, and that'll just create problems, not solve any."

He was right; she knew he was. But some things were far more easily said than done. She couldn't help but think of all the things that might go wrong, and for once, all of her concerns weren't for herself. Zachary deserved a wonderful mother, and it terrified her to think she might fail him.

"Mari," Joe said softly, calling her back from her dark musings again. "Just trust me. All right? You're not alone anymore. You've got me. Whatever it is that's worrying you, I'll take care of it. Just relax and try not to think bad thoughts."

"I'm trying."

He slanted her a concerned look. "Is everything okay right now?"

"Yes."

"Well, then? Right now—this moment—that's all that matters."

The chapel in Reno had pink hearts plastered all over it, and even worse, they were lighted hearts that pulsated. The ceremony itself was cheap, tawdry, and meaningless. Marilee felt more depressed than married after Joe slipped the plain gold wedding band on her finger.

"This is a legality, nothing more," he whispered as he bent to kiss her. "We'll be married by a priest as soon as I can arrange it."

Marilee tried to cling to that thought, but Joe kept her so completely off balance for the remainder of the evening that just keeping her emotions under tight rein became a challenge. He rented a suite at the Hilton, which seemed frivolous to her when they might have gotten by with a much smaller room at a roadside motel. However, when she voiced that opinion, he firmly vetoed the idea by saying, "No way. Not on our wedding night."

Their wedding night? It was that, she supposed, but she'd been hoping he might give her some time before he insisted on celebrating the occasion.

After getting them settled in the room, he proceeded to call room service and order a candlelight supper for two, complete with two bottles of very expensive champagne.

"I thought you said this ceremony was just a legality," she reminded him nervously, nearly leaping out of her skin when the first cork smacked the ceiling.

Joe flashed her one of those grins that always made her knees feel funny. "Honey, would you relax?" With a masterful flourish, he filled two goblets, then put the bottle back on ice. Offering her a glass, he said, "Come here, Mrs. Lakota. I'd like to make a wedding toast."

Marilee's stomach sank. This was making her very uneasy. A wedding toast? He suddenly looked a yard wide across the shoulders to her and twice that long in the legs. She pressed a quivering hand to her waist. Instead of accepting the goblet, she wanted to run shrieking from the room.

His gaze sharpened on her face, which she feared was probably bloodless. She also had a bad feeling he could read her every thought and feeling in her expression, none of which were very complimentary to him. His smile dimmed, and a concerned look came into his dark eyes. He glanced down at the two goblets he held, a thoughtful frown pleating his high forehead.

"Have I done or said something to upset you?" he asked.

"No!" she said faintly. "Nothing."

He gave her a long study. "Then why do you look as nervous as a long-tailed cat in a roomful of rockers?"

She wiped her damp palms on her skirt. "I, um . . . do I look nervous?"

He narrowed one eye at her. Then he set aside the glasses of champagne to move toward her. Marilee's heart leaped when his big, warm hands settled on her shoulders, his hard palms touching the bare skin of her upper arms. He bent slightly at the knees to meet her gaze.

"Out with it. You're upset about something."

Admitting the truth would make her feel foolish. She was twenty-eight years old, she was with the man she loved, and she should be taking all this in stride. "I'm just a little jumpy is all." She lowered her gaze to one of his shirt buttons. "All this wedding-night business, I guess. It makes me feel uneasy."

"It is our wedding night," he pointed out. "And I've been waiting for this moment for over twenty years. I'd like to make it an evening we both remember."

"Yes. I was just hoping we might—well, you know— wait a bit before we marked the occasion."

A glint of understanding entered his dark eyes, and he gave her arms a gentle squeeze, which she assumed was meant to comfort her but only succeeded in reminding her of his strength.

"I didn't say our wedding night has to be a conventional one." He grasped her chin, his fingers gentle on her lower jaw as he lifted her face to look deeply into her eyes. "Nothing will happen between us that you don't want to happen, Mari. I give you my word on that." He turned to retrieve the goblets and handed one to her. "Maybe a few sips of champagne will calm your nerves a little."

She needed something to calm her. Just *looking* at him made her pulse pick up speed. As if he knew exactly what she was thinking, he smiled and linked his wrist with hers. His voice dipping to a husky timber, he made a wonderfully romantic toast, the entirety of which completely escaped her. When it came time to drink her champagne, she drained the glass without taking a breath.

Having taken only a sip of his own champagne, he watched her drink with a raised eyebrow, his eyes reflecting wry amusement. "Thirsty?"

"Absolutely parched."

The corners of his mouth twitched.

She forced a smile and held out her goblet for more. "Now it's my turn to make a toast. Right?"

He nodded and gave her a refill.

"To us," she said without preamble, almost forgetting to touch her goblet to his before she chugged the second glass of champagne. She licked her lips and held out her goblet for more. "Your turn."

He laughed as he poured each of them another measure of wine. "I didn't think getting drunk was an experience you cared to repeat."

"Maybe I've changed my mind."

"You're drinking this stuff like it's soda pop. It may not taste that potent, but believe me, it's got a kick."

"Good. Calming my nerves suddenly strikes me as being a very good plan."

He raised his goblet to hers. "To my Mari girl, who never ceases to surprise me."

"Here, here!" She finished off the third glass in three gulps. Then she stood there, holding her breath to keep from belching. It felt as if the champagne was bubbling back up her throat. She swallowed, burped despite her efforts not to, and said, "Oh, my. Excuse me."

His eyes twinkled mischievously when she extended her glass again. "No way," he said. "I don't want you getting sick."

She pressed the glass closer. "I won't."

"Mari," he said softly, "there's nothing for you to feel so nervous about." He bent close, his gaze holding hers. "Look at me."

Looking at him was part of the problem. But she did as he ordered because he'd left her little choice.

"What do you see?" he asked.

"A tall half-breed Sioux warrior with a dangerous glint in his eyes and so much muscle, I'm in peril of having a heart attack. A woman expects to find guys like you in historical romance novels. But you're a little unsettling in a Reno hotel room."

He gave a startled laugh. "Does the Sioux warrior have a name?"

"Joe." The tender scolding he gave her with his eyes brought a lump to her throat. "My Joe," she added shakily.

"Yes, your Joe," he agreed, "the guy who loves you with every breath he takes." He gave her a questioning look. "Who held the seat of your bike while you learned to ride so you wouldn't take a spill?"

"You did."

"Who kept you from going under while you learned to do the dog paddle and float on your back?"

"You did," she whispered softly.

"Who held your hand and took the leap with you the first time you went off the high dive?"

Tears filled her eyes. "You did," she whispered, sweet memories drifting through her mind as she gazed up at him.

He leaned closer to kiss the tip of her nose. "Who beat the hell out of Danny Groves for unfastening your bra in the eighth grade?"

She gave him a watery smile. "You did," she managed to say, even though her throat ached with tears. "I never needed a brother to watch out for me and fight my battles. I always had you."

"You still do." He pressed closer yet to rest his silken lips against her forehead, where he whispered with husky sincerity, "No nasty tumbles tonight, Mari mine. No unpleasantness. Please, don't be afraid of me. It breaks my heart. I'd rather die than hurt you. If you can believe in nothing else, believe in that."

She squeezed her eyes closed. "Oh, Joe, it isn't you. It has nothing to do with you. It's me. I'm a mess."

"You're not a mess, honey. You're just—" He leaned back and gave her a measuring look. "Well, maybe you are a little bit of a mess," he said with a wink, "but you're a gorgeous mess. Definitely a keeper." He smoothed back her hair. "If you'd like more champagne later, that's fine. But let's eat a little something first. All right?"

"All right."

He lifted the leaves of the room service table, arranged their place settings, and then began uncovering dishes. "I ordered you a New York steak."

With all the bubbles churning in her stomach, she wasn't sure she'd be able to swallow. "Oh, thank you. Steak! My favorite. Yum."

He drew over two chairs from the round wooden table in the corner of the room, helped her to sit down, and then smoothed her napkin over her lap, every pass of his fingertips on the linen making her leap. She needed another glass of champagne. On second thought, straight into the vein might be better.

After lighting the candlewicks and turning down the lights, he sat across from her and applied himself to his meal while she picked at her own. The way his jaw muscle wiggled as he chewed was fascinating, she decided. Flickering amber from the candles played over his burnished face, delineating the sharp angles with shadow, which made the play of tendon in his lean cheek seem all the more pronounced.

"What?" he asked as he poured them each another glass of bubbly.

"Nothing."

"It must be something. You're staring as if I just grew a third eye in the middle of my forehead."

"Your jaw," she finally admitted, pointing at the offending body part with her fork. "Do you realize it ripples and bunches every time you chew?"

He arched one eyebrow, an ability of his that she'd always envied. "Damn. You're already tipsy," he said softly. He glanced at her glass. "Maybe you've had enough."

She took a quick sip. "I'm fine. Really. How do you do that?" She pulled a face, trying to lift only one brow, which made him chuckle. "What did you do, practice that in front of a mirror?"

"No. I did practice wiggling my ears, though." He demonstrated and grinned. "Bet you can't do that."

"Bet I can." She set aside her wine, grabbed her ears by the lobes, and gave each three tugs.

"Easy with those ears, lady. I may want them for dessert."

She nearly knocked over her goblet with her elbow. He grabbed for the glass, righted it, and settled a warm gaze on her. "More champagne?"

"Very funny. And, yes, thank you, I believe I will."

"I believe you've reached your limit. Your aim was to relax, not be unconscious."

"Says who?"

"Me. You're worrying about nothing. Even if we do reach a unanimous decision to make love tonight, it's nothing for you to be feeling nervous about." He thought for a moment and shrugged. "Between two people who care deeply for each other, lovemaking is a beautiful experience."

"Maybe so. But I'd still rather sleep through it the first time and wake up later with the entire ordeal behind me."

"The very fact that you use the word 'ordeal' in reference to sex tells me you haven't a clue what you'd be missing. Sensation, for instance. If you've had too much to drink, your nerve-endings will be desensitized. That isn't to say it's going to happen tonight," he hastened to add when he glimpsed her expression. Finished with his steak, he rested his elbows on the table and gazed steadily at her over the flickering flames. "Do you have any inkling how fantastic it feels to have your bare skin lightly caressed? Or kissed?"

A piece of meat lodged behind her larynx, and she gulped to get it down. "No, I can't say I do."

"The bend of your arm, for example, or the back of your knee. There are hundreds of sensitive nerve-endings in both those spots, and they respond to the slightest touch. With the tip of one finger—or the tip of my tongue—I could raise goose bumps over your entire body."

As he spoke, he was trailing his fingertip around the edge of his goblet. Unable to pry her gaze away, Marilee stared, and she started to get goose bumps without his even touching her. Worse, when she finally pried her attention away from his hand and looked into his eyes, she suspected he knew exactly how he was affecting her. There was a definite twinkle in those chocolate depths. He smiled lazily and took a sip of champagne, slowly—very slowly—blotting his lips with the tip of his tongue afterward.

She grabbed up the champagne bottle to pour herself more wine, only to find that the bottle was empty. "I'm ready for more now."

"Eat your steak and roll first. No more on an empty stomach."

Motivated as she was by goose bumps, Marilee did as she was told, dutifully stuffing steak and bread into her mouth while he looked on. When she had eaten half the meat and most of her roll, he finally popped the cork on a second bottle and poured her more champagne, which she greedily consumed. She was miles away from being numb yet, and that gleam in his eyes told her time might be swiftly running out.

When she couldn't swallow another morsel of food, he put the champagne and candles on the other table, then rolled the cart from their room into the hallway to await pickup. When he returned, he flipped on the television. Marilee was gratefully thanking God and hoping he'd find a football game to entertain himself when lilting, romantic music filled the room. As if he knew exactly what she'd been hoping, he merely grinned and turned down the lights even more.

As he walked slowly across the room toward her, she looked first at his face, a burnished sculpture of sharp features topped by gleaming sable hair. Then her gaze settled on his shoulders, which shifted under his shirt as he moved, muscle bunching and then relaxing, the overall effect one of leashed power. Lower still, she took in his flat belly and narrow waist.

Stop. If she allowed herself to watch the way those long, tendon-roped legs drew the cloth of his trousers taut as he moved, she really was going to have a heart attack.

When he drew up in front of her and rested one hand at her waist, she felt numb. And then he drew her into a waltz, his big body guiding hers in liquid sweeps around the room. After two complete circles, he bent to kiss her hair, murmuring, "Sweetheart, trust me. Nothing's going to happen between us that won't be wonderful for you. Not tonight, not ever. I promise you that. Just relax and enjoy yourself. All right?"

Her legs nearly buckled. "I trust you, Joe. I do."

His silken lips moved over her curls to find her ear. "Then dance with me. Close your eyes, and just dance with me."

He swept her in another wide arc, pulling her hips hard against him so she rode the steely column of his thigh. Even wearing heels and lightheaded as she was from champagne, it was easy for her to ride along without stumbling. And soon she felt as if she were floating. She didn't even mind that her dress had inched up to accommodate his leg.

The next song on the stereo was slow and languid. Releasing her hand, he enfolded her in both arms, hunched his shoulders around her, and barely moved his feet to keep time. A thousand memories slipped into her mind as she leaned into him. *Joe*. Years ago, she had danced like this with him in the park pavilion, the summer night a dark embrace around them, both of them so in love that the rest of the world seemed miles removed. *Joe*. Though the years had added breadth to his shoulders and back, the angles and planes of his body hadn't changed.

She rested her cheek against his chest and smoothed

her palms over his shirt, reacquainting herself with the way he felt. The same, she thought dreamily, only so vastly different. He wasn't a kid anymore. The Joe who held her now was a mature man. She could feel the masculine need that emanated from his rangy frame, a blanket of warmth and longing that engulfed her. To her surprise, the heat of him melted some of the tension from her limbs.

At some point, he loosened one arm from around her and began trailing his fingertips from her shoulder to her wrist, the feather-light caresses tantalizing her bare skin. When he lingered at the bend of her elbow and tortured her nerve-endings there, she did indeed get goose bumps, which he smoothed away a moment later with a caress of his hard palm. Within seconds, he moved on from that activity to nuzzling her ears, which made her smile against his shirt. *Dessert*. He savored her as though she were a delicious treat, nibbling her lobes, then tracing the shell of each ear with the tip of his tongue.

He knew exactly what he was doing to her, she realized. Perhaps it was the champagne, making her mellow and beyond caring—or maybe it was simply that she loved him so very much—but she didn't mind. They were still dancing—sort of. As long as they remained on their feet, what could possibly happen?

Only a few minutes later, that question was answered. She got sick. Too much champagne on a nervous, empty stomach didn't go well with one waltz after another, especially with an expert partner like Joe, who swept her in fluid circles around the room. Pretty soon, the walls seemed to be leaning inward, and when she looked down, the carpet had waves in it.

"Joe?"

"Hmm?" He tightened his arm around her waist and executed another swing.

Instead of answering him, Marilee gulped to keep her dinner down.

"What, honey?" He tucked in his chin to look down

at her. Then he stopped dancing abruptly. "You okay?"

"I need to—" She swayed on her feet. "I, um, feel a little queasy."

"Uh-oh." He loosened his arm from around her, then immediately caught hold of her again to keep her from toppling. "Easy."

Marilee closed her eyes.

"Don't do that," he advised. "Bad move."

It really was. The instant her lids drifted shut, her head started to spin even more.

Keeping an arm around her, he led her slowly to one of the beds and helped her to lie down. "Keep one foot on the floor," he instructed.

"Why?" she asked weakly.

"So the room doesn't whirl."

"You've been through this."

He gave a low laugh. "A few times. It'll pass if you lie still for a bit."

Trying to keep one foot on the floor as he'd suggested, Marilee struggled with her straight skirt, the confines of which prevented her from spreading her knees too widely. Joe glanced down, saw her dilemma, and promptly solved the problem by shoving the hem of her dress way up her thighs. The brush of his hard hands over her nylons set off alarm bells in her reeling mind, but before she could protest, he jerked the other side of the bedspread down and drew the chenille over her legs.

"All covered," he assured her, then sat beside her and gazed worriedly at her face. "You're quickly turning an interesting shade of chartreuse," he said with a gentle smile.

She angled an arm over her eyes. "Oh, *God.* I can't believe I did this. I'm sorry, Joe."

"Not a problem," he assured her. "You just don't know your limit yet. That's all. It happens to the best of us."

"How embarrassing."

"There's nothing to be embarrassed about. You've been a little silly, but very charming."

"You know the worst part? All that champagne, and I'm still nervous."

He chuckled and tucked the bedspread under her hip to anchor it. "There's nothing to feel nervous about, either. I'd never take advantage of you in this state. Not my style. When I woo a lady, I prefer her to be sober."

" 'Woo,' " she repeated. "That's an old-fashioned word."

"I'm an old-fashioned fellow."

Marilee groaned. "I'll never drink again. Never, ever." She tried taking a deep breath, and that didn't help. "Joe? Remember saying you wanted to be the guy who held my head when I got sick?"

Silence. And then in a cautious tone, he said, "Yeah, I remember."

"You're about to get your wish."

He scooped her up from the bed with amazing speed and got her to the bathroom in the nick of time. Afterward Marilee hugged the porcelain while he swiped at her face with a cold cloth and then pressed it against her throat.

"Oh, Joe, I'm so sorry. This is the most humiliating experience! I'm so very sorry. What must you think?"

Kneeling on one knee, he slipped an arm around her waist to help support her weight. "That plying you with booze definitely isn't the ticket." He waited a beat. "Somehow, seeing you on your knees before the porcelain god wasn't what I had in mind for this evening."

Marilee giggled, the sound echoing back at her. She realized she was feeling a lot better. Getting rid of some of the champagne had helped.

Joe stayed with her until the nausea and dizziness passed. Then he brought her luggage into the bathroom. "I'll go catch a little television while you get ready for bed. If you need me, don't hesitate to holler."

"I'm fine now," she assured him. "Much better, anyway. But thank you for offering."

*   *   *

There were six hundred and eighty-eight loops of yarn in the expanse of carpet between Joe's feet. Sitting on the edge of the bed, he stared morosely at them, sighed, glanced worriedly at his watch, and started counting them all over again. When he reached one hundred, he lost patience, cursed under his breath, and pushed to his feet.

"Mari?" he called as he advanced on the locked bathroom door. "Are you all right in there?"

"Fine," she said faintly.

He sighed and leaned a shoulder against the door frame. Hands shoved in his pockets, he stared at the doorknob, willing it to wiggle. *Nothing*. She'd been in there for nearly an hour, and forty minutes of that time had elapsed since he heard the shower turn off. What could she possibly be doing? Counting bumps in the wall plaster, maybe?

"Are you feeling sick again? I'm starting to get worried," he admitted.

"Don't. I'm fine. Really."

Joe listened, hoping to hear noises to indicate she was still performing her nightly ablutions. "What'cha doin'?"

"Oh . . . just thinking."

Thinking? He rubbed his jaw. Shoved his hand back in his trouser pocket. Dug his heel into the nap of the powder room rug. "What're you thinking about, honey?"

Silence. A very long silence. Then, "Oh, Joe. I'm so miserable. Would you do me a huge favor?"

"Anything. Just name it."

"Bludgeon me into unconsciousness."

He gave a startled chuckle. *Mari*. Her indomitable sense of humor had always been one of the things he loved most about her. She truly was frightened, yet she still had it in her to crack a joke. "Why don't I just shoot you and get it over with?"

"There's a thought. Only then I'd be dead, and coward that I am, I don't want to actually *die*."

"That's probably just as well. I didn't think to bring my six-shooter." He sighed and pressed the flat of his hand against the door. "Mari?"

"What?" she asked, sounding frustrated.

"Why don't you come out so we can discuss this?"

"Methods of putting me out of my misery, you mean?" He heard her sigh. "Oh, Joe. I'm sorry. This is childish and stupid and unforgivable. You should have just kept driving this morning. I'm a *mess*!"

Her voice rose to a high pitch on that last word.

"Come out, and maybe we can talk you through it."

"Every time I start to open the door, my heart starts in, and I can't breathe. I'll have an attack if I come out."

"Why? Nothing unpleasant will happen if you open the door."

"I know. Mostly. I don't make sense, Joe. I told you, remember? This isn't a reasonable problem. If I open the door, I'm going to be sick, end of subject. I don't even know why."

He considered for a moment. "You can't stay in there all night."

"No. My legs are already asleep from sitting here on this stupid toilet."

He smoothed his hand over the wood. "There's a way around this."

"What is it?"

"Let me open the door for you. You just unlock it."

"Well, *that's* dumb!"

"I know." He grinned. "That's why I thought the idea might appeal to you."

"Oh, thank you. Just what I need, a smart ass."

"Hey, it's just dumb enough to work. Try it. Get up and flip the lock. Nothing to it. I promise not to come in without an invitation."

No response. He waited. After what seemed a small eternity, he heard the latch turn. Waiting longer yet, he allowed her time to resume her seat. Then he cracked the door open a scant inch. "How you doin'?"

"My feet have turned purple."

He pushed the door farther open and poked his head in through the crack. "Purple feet are not a good sign."

She cast him a miserable look. "We shouldn't have done this, Joe. I can't go through with it."

"It's rectifiable."

She blinked. "You'd let me back out?"

"Can't stop you. If that's what you want to do, what choice do I have?"

"It's not what I want."

"I know. Otherwise, I wouldn't offer."

She laughed hollowly and pushed at her hair. She was wearing a thick, pink chenille bathrobe over her gown, the only bare parts showing her face, hands, and feet. Steamy air wafted through the cracked door to bathe his face.

"You're going to melt. What're you wearing under that robe, anyway, a string bikini?"

"Don't you wish."

"Uh-huh."

"No such luck. It's a flannel granny."

"Honey, that's nuts."

"We've covered that ground. Remember? I'm crazy. You can't say I didn't warn you."

"Crazy people have no idea they're crazy."

"They don't?"

"No. And that means you're not. Your behavior is irrational, but you realize it. That means you're just—"

"What?"

"Normally abnormal."

She shoved at her hair again, which had gone all kinky from the steam. He yearned to let the curls drift through his fingers. Feminine scents drifted to him on the moist draft—talcum powder perfumed with rose petals, lotion, a hint of cologne. She smelled good enough to eat.

"I like that. Normally abnormal. It's much nicer than plain old nuts."

Joe toed the door open more widely and without moving his shoulder from the jamb, shifted around to face her. "You're just scared, honey. It's a weird thing, fear. The longer you leave it to fester, the bigger it gets. Ten years is a hell of a long time. You need to talk about it. Get some help to deal with it. You've kept all these feelings bottled up for way too long."

She took several deep breaths, her hands curling over her well-covered knees. "You know what?"

"What?" he asked softly, wishing with all his heart he could hug her.

"Don't have me committed, all right? But I think maybe my panic attacks are a reenactment."

"A what?"

"A—" She broke off and swallowed. "Not really panic attacks. You know? More an awful reenactment, the memory not just a memory at all, but sort of a—reliving it, maybe. Does that make any sense?"

He supposed that was possible. "Is that how you feel, like it's happening all over again when you have an attack?"

"Yes. Sort of. And I can't make it stop, just like then. That night, one of them put his—" She passed a shaky hand over her face and blinked again. "One of them put his hand over my mouth, and I couldn't—" Her fingers fluttered down to lay at the base of her throat, and her shoulders rose and fell in rapid succession. "His thumb, over my nose. I couldn't *breathe*. They were holding me down. I couldn't move his hand. He didn't know, and he just held it there, *suffocating* me."

Joe felt as if a horse had kicked him in the guts. *They?* His legs turned to water. He barely managed to bite back a curse, the flash of rage that flared through him so searing he felt as if he were being consumed in the conflagration.

It was all he could do to regain control. But he knew if he didn't that she'd stop talking. *They.* It was the first time she'd shared much of anything about that night with him. He couldn't start barking questions. She might never find the courage to tell him more if he did. *They*? Oh, God.

Hands clenched, he watched her, aware that her breathing had grown rapid. She stared straight ahead, evidently lost in her memories. Afraid she might indeed have an attack if he didn't stop this before it went farther, he broke his promise about not entering the bathroom without an invitation and moved to hunker in front of her.

"Mari? Honey, look at me." *Nothing*. "Mari!" he said more loudly.

She jerked and focused, her face filmed with sweat and ghostly pale.

"It's not happening now," he said softly, trailing a fingertip over her damp upper lip. "See? No hand. You can breathe fine."

She gulped and closed her eyes, turning her head to follow when he started to draw his finger away. He smiled sadly and traced another half moon under her nose. "Nothing there," he whispered. "You're all right."

She took a deep, quavering breath and nodded, her throat still working as she struggled for calm. Joe ran his hand up into her hair. Even her scalp was beaded with sweat. A cold, clammy sweat he knew wasn't from the steamy air. He drew her toward him and rested his forehead against hers.

"It'll never happen again," he vowed gruffly. "If anybody dares to lay so much as a finger on you, I'll be there to kick ass and take names. You hear? No one's ever going to hurt you again."

She nodded once more and looped limp arms over his shoulders, leaning more heavily into him, her narrow forehead centered on his, the tip of her small nose flattened against his bridge. "I'm so tired, Joe. So awfully, horribly tired."

He could hear the utter exhaustion in her voice. "You need some sleep. We're both running on adrenaline at this point."

"Not that kind of tired," she whispered. "I'm just tired. I feel like a bunch of marbles in a basket that has holes in the weave. Little pieces of me keep falling out, and no matter how hard I try, I can't keep all the holes covered."

"I've got an extra pair of hands." He leaned back to meet her gaze, and this time, he didn't care if she saw the tears in his eyes. His heart was breaking for her, and maybe she needed to know that. "One of the benefits of having a guy love you so much. I don't want to lose any of you. Every part's precious."

"Even the loony ones?"

"I especially love the loony ones." A tendril of hair had stuck to her cheek. He smoothed it back. "If you don't want the loony parts, hand 'em over, and I'll keep track of them."

She smiled slightly. "I can't sleep with you tonight."

"We've got two beds." He pushed to his feet, and without giving her any warning, scooped her up from the commode and into his arms. "One of which you're going to occupy in about three seconds."

She gave a startled squeak and hugged his neck. "Oh, God. I forgot."

"What?"

"How strong you are. No *wonder* looking at you gives me a heart attack."

He chuckled and carried her from the bathroom, shifting her weight in his arms when he reached the bed to reach quickly down and fold back the covers. "In you go." He lay her on the crisp bottom sheet, then positioned the pillow under her head. Her eyes drifted closed when he spent a moment arranging her hair in a golden fan of curls over the white pillowcase. "Have I mentioned recently that you're the most beautiful woman I've ever met?"

"No, but this one time, it's okay if you lie to me."

He grinned and trailed the backs of his knuckles along her cheek, marveling at how fragile her cheekbone felt.

"You're the most beautiful woman I've ever met. You're also the hottest little number I've ever seen. The robe has to come off."

"I really think—"

"No arguments." He tugged the sash loose and pushed the heavy chenille from her shoulders, an endeavor foiled by the frantic clutch of her hands. He pretended not to notice, hooking a palm over the base of her neck to sit her up and then tugging her arms from the sleeves. When he jerked the chenille out from under her rump, her night-gown twisted, the hem riding up to her thighs. Before she could straighten it, he shoved her back onto the pillow. "You're a cute little marshmallow, but I'd rather not roast you."

He drew up the sheet to cover her legs. She grabbed the top edge of the linen and pulled it to her shoulders. "I am rather like a marshmallow, aren't I? White and blobby."

"White and soft," he corrected as he straightened. "Not to mention sweet."

"You're like caramel. Lots of it. Partially melted and still lumpy, then cooled again to make you all hard."

"Yum." He forced a laugh, his gaze tracing her face. *They.* He wanted to do murder. "I hope you like lumpy caramel. As I recall, chocolate's your favorite."

"Actually, my absolute favorite is a blend of chocolate and caramel. I never eat a chocolate-caramel candy bar that I don't think of you. Your hair and eyes are chocolate brown."

Joe wished she'd have a taste of the real thing. He sighed and started unbuttoning his shirt.

"What're you doing?"

"Time for lights out." He stripped off the Oxford and flung it at a chair. "Anything I can get you before I go to sleep?"

She stared at his chest for a long moment. "Do you know CPR?"

Joe decided then and there that he'd better keep his pants on.

Eleven

*O*n Sunday afternoon, the first stop Joe and Marilee made was at her parents' house. Karl Nelson wasn't overjoyed at the news of his daughter's marriage to Joe. The man refused to shake Joe's hand or congratulate the couple. Though Gerry had wasted no time in telling her parents that Joe had not been responsible for ending the engagement ten years ago, Karl still seemed to hold Joe accountable. That being the case, Joe supposed he couldn't blame the older man for having reservations about the marriage. The way Karl saw it, Joe had broken his little girl's heart, and now he'd come back to have another go.

After leaving her parents' house, Joe drove to his mom's to pick up Zachary. He hoped this visit went better than the last one had.

The Honda no sooner rolled to a halt in the driveway than Zachary bolted out the front door and down the steps. "Hi, Daddy! Hi, Marilee!" he cried.

Joe climbed out of the car and bent to catch his son in his arms. Swinging him high, he said, "Good grief, you've grown an inch."

"Nuh-uh!" Zachary giggled.

"He ate enough to have grown a foot!" Faye called from the porch. Her gentle blue eyes settled on Marilee and she opened her arms. "Come here, daughter. I've been waiting well over fifteen years for this day. He finally landed the right fish."

Marilee laughed as she hurried across the lawn and climbed the wide front steps. The brown farmhouse, like its owner, showed its age, the wood planks creaking slightly under her weight. "So you think I'm the right one, do you?"

"I know you are! Never had a doubt. This is one of the happiest days of my life."

"Thank you. That's a lovely compliment."

"Sincerely meant. He may be a grown man, but he'll always be my baby. I want to see him happy, and now I know he will be."

Tears stung Marilee's eyes as she hugged Joe's mother. Faye had always been a slender, fine-boned woman, and the ravages of bad health had left her frail. Marilee was shocked when she felt the older woman's ribs through her floral-print dress.

"You're looking good today," Marilee fibbed. She leaned back to study her mother-in-law's drawn features. "What did you do, get your hair cut?"

"Just a trim and new perm." Faye patted Marilee's arm as they drew apart. Then she touched her graying brown hair. "Unlike you, I've got no natural curl."

Carrying Zachary on the bend of one arm, Joe bounded up the steps. As he passed his mother on the way into the house, he stooped to kiss her cheek. "Zachary says there's apple pie. Can I have a piece?"

Faye laughed and turned to follow the Lakota males inside. To Marilee she said, "It's one surefire way to make sure that boy stays to visit for a while, baking him a pie."

A few minutes later, Marilee glanced up from the kitchen table where she sat with Joe and Zachary, enjoying a piece of apple pie, still warm from the oven. "I've never tasted such a flaky crust."

Faye finished pouring Zachary a second glass of milk. En route back to the table, she said, "It's a Lakota family recipe. Joe's paternal grandmother shared it with me forty years ago. If you'd like, I can pass it on to you now that you're an official member of the family."

"I'd love it." Marilee glanced at Joe. "He never goes after my pie like that."

Joe winked at her. "Your chocolate chip cookies are incomparable."

Faye took a seat, smiling as she watched Zachary drink his milk. "He's going to shoot up, Marilee. Be prepared. You'll blink, and his britches will be too short. He's been eating like this all weekend."

Marilee settled back in her chair. She couldn't forget how frail Faye had felt when she hugged her. Human life was finite. Moments like this—the four of them, sitting in Faye's cozy but outdated farmhouse kitchen—were numbered and far too precious to waste.

Later, when it came time to leave, Marilee promised herself she would make sure that she and Joe came back soon. As Joe backed the Honda from the driveway, she blew a kiss to his mother, who stood on the porch to wave them out of sight.

"We need to do this again, Joe. Maybe we can make Sunday dinner over here a weekly ritual."

He cast her a surprised look. "I thought Sunday was a big thing with your family. A midday meal after noon Mass. I don't want to screw with that."

"Well, maybe we can come here afterward. We usually eat fairly early at Gerry and Ron's place. We could enjoy another meal here later in the day. I think it'd be fun. You and I can do the cooking and cleaning up while your mom supervises. Then afterward we can watch a movie or play a game."

He rolled his eyes. "Somebody better supervise if I'm cooking. Otherwise we'll have a disaster."

"A bad one!" Zachary chimed in from the backseat.

"You sure you want to make a commitment like that?" Joe asked. "Once Mom starts to expect us every Sunday evening, it'll be too late to back out."

"Why would I want to back out? I love your mom. I enjoy being around her."

"Yeah?" He smiled and nodded. "Same goes for me with your folks. I've always thought highly of them, and I look forward to spending lots of quality time with them."

Considering the way her father had behaved, Marilee thought it was big of Joe to say that. Guilt stabbed through her, and she fixed her gaze on the passing scenery, her mind circling the problem. She needed to tell her dad the whole truth so he'd no longer resent Joe so much. But how could she possibly do that? She'd be opening herself up to dozens of questions, the answers to which might be far more hurtful to Joe than her dad's disapproval.

Joe managed to get Marilee an appointment to see a Bedford psychiatrist the following Wednesday afternoon. Immediately after securing the appointment, he called Sarah Rasmussen to ask if she might be able to help out at his mom's so Zachary could stay there. Then he asked for time off from work so he could drive her himself. He was afraid she might be so upset that she wouldn't be safe behind the wheel.

Marilee was as white as a sheet when she finally emerged from the clinic. Watching her as she approached the car, Joe noted the dark circles that had appeared under her eyes in the space of sixty short minutes. When she slid into the Honda, he reached out to take her hand. It was ice cold.

"Hey, you okay?"

"Fine. Really." Even as she spoke, she refused to look directly at him. "She gave me a prescription. I'm supposed to get it filled on the way home and start taking it immediately." Hands shaking, she unfolded the paper. "Something called Paxil? She says they've used it with great success to treat panic disorders, and if it works on me, it may help control or completely eliminate my attacks."

"Mari, that's great news. Right?"

She nodded but still didn't look at him. "Yeah, if it works. She says it'll take about three weeks before I see any real difference."

"Three weeks is doable." He gave her fingers a squeeze. "Honey, why won't you look at me?"

She finally turned her gaze on him and flashed an empty smile. Joe's heart caught. There was something in her eyes—a coolness and remoteness. It was as if she had shut down inside and was no longer connecting with him. He was reminded of the early days immediately after his confrontation with her on the deck, and he couldn't shake the feeling that she had erected an impenetrable wall between them again.

"When you were talking with the doctor, did my name come up?"

Her cheeks flushed and she glanced quickly away. "Don't be silly. Why would your name come up? You had nothing to do with anything."

He did now. Joe swallowed the retort. *Patience.* Now wasn't the time to point out the importance of his role in her future or to remind her he was the man with whom she would eventually be intimate. Why *wouldn't* his name come up? As Joe drove home, he sent up a silent prayer that she'd rally and start to feel better soon.

She didn't.

As they marked off the days before her next appointment, she grew even more withdrawn, and not only from Joe. There were times when she seemed not to be aware of Zachary and didn't hear when the child spoke to her.

Separate bedrooms, Joe could handle temporarily. Separateness twenty-four hours a day, especially when it affected his son, was another matter entirely. One evening, he set Marilee down, determined to talk with her.

"Mari, do you know how much I love you?"

"Yes. As much as I love you, I hope."

"More," he whispered. "And it breaks my heart when you shut me out. Remember how we always used to talk when we were young? About anything and everything. Nothing was taboo. You trusted me never to judge you, to always be your best friend."

Her eyes darkened, and she looked guiltily away.

"You need to be open with me now," he urged gently. "Talk to me about that night. Sweetheart, how can I help you—how can I understand how you're feeling—if you won't share with me?"

"That wasn't part of our bargain," she said. "I agreed to go to counseling, but I never said I'd talk with you about it."

"People who love each other don't keep secrets. Especially not when it's destructive. I want to be here for you, and ever since you saw the doctor, you've been shutting me out. Now you're even withdrawing from Zachary. I know something was said about me during the session that upset you. Won't you tell me what it was so we can discuss it?"

"Nothing, Joe. I told you that."

He felt the tendons along the back of his neck draw into aching knots. "Yeah, well, I won't accuse you of lying. But I think you're skirting the truth."

Her face drained of color. "Don't be silly. If your name had come up, which it *didn't*, I'd tell you."

"So my name wasn't mentioned." Joe waited a beat, feeling almost guilty for what he was about to say. He knew her far too well, just as she did him. There could be no lies between them. "So let me guess," he murmured. "I was referred to as your husband, right? Not precisely by name. I see. That's a neat little loophole."

She flattened a hand over her chest and started wheezing for breath. Because she'd had only that one panic attack in his presence, Joe honestly didn't expect her to have one now.

He was wrong.

Before he knew quite how it happened, Marilee fell to the floor, her slender body jackknifing into a fetal position, her hands clutching her throat. Joe dropped to his knees beside her. This was bad. Really bad. Her lips turned purple, then a frightening blue. And still she couldn't breathe.

He gathered her thrashing body into his arms, forcing her to sit up with her back against his chest. Rocking her as he might a child, he trailed a fingertip under her nose and whispered reassurances, uncertain what he said, his only thought to calm her.

When the attack finally subsided, they were both wringing wet with sweat, his running in steamy rivers down his body, hers clammy and cold. Joe cradled her in his arms and vowed he would never again press her to reveal what had been said between her and the psychiatrist. He could only pray the doctor knew her business and Marilee would soon start to make progress.

The following week when his wife became even more withdrawn and less talkative after her counseling session, Joe told himself not to worry. Marilee's greatest fear about seeking professional help had always been that she might get worse before she got better. This was probably a common occurrence and would pass. The sessions forced her to dredge up old memories, making them fresh in her mind. Naturally it was a difficult time, and anyone might become self-absorbed for a while. She'd get better soon.

Soon. The word became Joe's mantra. Soon, she would start to smile again. Soon the smudges of exhaustion under her eyes would start to fade. Soon she would open up to him, and together they would bury her ghosts. *Soon.* She would get well. He had to believe that. The alternative, that he'd pushed her into doing something that had made her worse, was unthinkable.

Then he noticed that she'd stopped eating. The weight began to fall off of her at an alarming rate. Growing concerned, Joe called her doctor from work. The ensuing conversation was an eye-opener. Judging by things the doctor said, Joe gathered that she believed Marilee had been talking openly with him, relating to him in detail what had happened that night ten years ago.

"This is a hard time for her, Mr. Lakota. Marilee has made herself very vulnerable by talking about all this with you. Many women harbor a deep-rooted fear that the men they love will hold this sort of thing against them somehow, that even though a man might never admit it, he casts blame on her and feels a certain degree of repulsion. Do you understand what I'm saying? Societal judgments. We've all heard them. Even today, that way of thinking lingers."

Joe rocked back in his chair and closed his eyes. He didn't know what Marilee had told the doctor, but he needed to set the woman straight. Working under the assumption that Marilee had talked with him, she was perilously close to violating doctor–patient confidentiality. Only what about husband-wife confidentiality? If Marilee had been lying to her doctor, Joe hated to tell on her.

"Doctor Patterson, we're in a spot here," Joe finally said. "And I'm not sure what to do."

Silence. After a moment, the doctor sighed and said, "I see."

Joe knew by her tone that she had put two and two together. He was relieved. The physician's astuteness had saved him from having to betray his wife.

"Well, that puts a whole new light on things," she said. "I appreciate your candor, Mr. Lakota." Paper rustled at her end. "If Marilee is losing weight and apparently not sleeping, I should see her as quickly as possible. I have an opening tomorrow afternoon. Will that work for her, do you think?"

Joe would see that it did. "I'll have her there."

*   *   *

When Joe came home that evening and informed Marilee that he'd made an appointment for her with the psychiatrist the following day, her stomach dropped. He'd been on the phone with her doctor? Initially she was dismayed. That feeling was quickly eclipsed by fear and anger.

"How dare you?" she cried. "She's *my* doctor. I made it clear from the start that I didn't want you involved. How *dare* you contact her behind my back!"

A terror ten years in the making mushroomed within Marilee, fueling her outrage. Oh, God. What had Doctor Patterson told him? Oh, God, oh, God! If Joe found out, he'd do something crazy. She just knew it. What would happen to him then? And, more importantly, what would happen to the son he loved so much?

Frustrated, frightened, and angry beyond words that he'd called her doctor behind her back, Marilee swung her arm over the top of the kitchen counter, knocking everything in its path to the floor. She didn't hear the crash of her pig cookie jar. She couldn't even remember seeing it land. When awareness returned to her, the ceramic container lay shattered at Joe's feet.

She blinked and stared, barely able to credit her eyes. Then she heard a whimpering sound and saw Zachary huddling against the louvered doors of the utility room. The child's face was pale, his frightened eyes as big as quarters.

Joe said not a word to her. He simply shot her a look that could have pulverized granite and went to pick up his little boy. "It's all right, tyke. Mari's just having a bad day. Don't be afraid."

Stunned at what she'd done, Marilee cleaned up the mess after they left the room. Then she followed them, hoping she might talk to Zachary and make things better. She found father and son in the living room. Joe sat on the sofa with his back to her, holding his son in his arms.

"How come mommies always yell and break stuff, Daddy?" she heard Zachary ask.

"Mari's just not feeling very well. That's all," Joe murmured.

"Is she getting sick like my other mommy?"

Joe hesitated before he answered. "Not the same kind of sick, sprout. But she hasn't been feeling very well."

"Is she gonna get better?"

Joe cuddled his son closer, his voice hoarse with worry as he replied, "I hope so, Zachary. I hope so."

"I don't like it when she's sick."

"Me neither."

"She makes me scared when she screams at you, Daddy."

"I know."

"Did you feel scared?"

"No, not for myself," Joe said softly. "I do feel scared for her, though. She's feeling really bad right now."

"If I do a nice thing, will it make her better?"

"Maybe tomorrow. Tonight I think she just needs space, and we probably shouldn't bother her."

Marilee clamped a hand over her mouth and slipped away to her bedroom, managing to stifle her sobs until she closed the door. Then she sank onto the edge of her bed and wept. What was happening to her? She loved that little boy so much. So very much. She would never deliberately do anything to make him feel frightened, yet she had. Zachary was fragile. What could she have been thinking? She'd known he was in the kitchen. How could she have behaved so maniacally in front of him?

Maniacally, maniacally, maniacally . . . oh, God . . . she really *was* crazy, and now her lunacy was poisoning the lives of those around her, just as she'd always feared it might. *Zachary.* He was such a precious little guy. *She makes me scared when she screams at you, Daddy.*

Marilee had never felt so ashamed in all her life.

A few minutes later when Joe tapped on her door, she braced herself, for she knew he was furious with her, and she couldn't blame him. After wiping her cheeks, she called out for him to enter. When he stepped into the shadowy bedroom, his dark face looked as gray as the twilight outside the window.

He closed the door and leaned against it, his gaze offering hers no quarter. "Mari, I had no right to call your doctor behind your back, and I'm sorry I took that liberty."

Marilee couldn't bear to look at him. She bent her head.

"I'm concerned about you. You look as if somebody's punched both your eyes, and you're thin as a rail. I love you, and I don't want this marriage to be the death of you. So I called Dr. Patterson, and I shouldn't have. It would have been better to confront you with my concerns and insist that you call her yourself.

"That said, on to another concern, namely my son. I know I stepped over the line, and that you had every right to be angry with me. But after this, I'd really appreciate your waiting to have it out with me until after Zachary is in bed."

She nodded.

"If we fight—and we're bound to—we'll do it out of his sight and earshot."

He punctuated that edict by leaving the room. She almost wished he would slam the door. Instead he closed it so softly she barely heard the latch click.

After finally getting Zachary put to bed, Joe settled down on the sofa. The instant he began replaying in his mind the words he'd said to Marilee, he got upset all over again. He loved her so much, and he desperately wanted to ease her pain, but how could he when she lied to him?

He sighed and rubbed the bridge of his nose. A bitch of a headache had taken up residence behind his eyes.

"Joe?"

He nearly parted company with his skin at the sound

of her voice. He whipped his head around. She stood just a few feet behind him, her hands clasped before her, her eyes huge and pleading in her pale face. In a glance, he knew she'd been crying all evening. Even her cheekbones looked swollen. He felt the tug on his heartstrings and wanted to gather her close for a hug.

She wrung her hands. "I know you're very upset with me right now and that it's not the best time in the world, but I, um . . ." Her voice trailed away, the last quavering note lingering in the air. "I need to speak to you." She glanced over her shoulder. "I was wondering if you'd step outside with me."

"Outside?"

"To the backyard. I'm afraid this exchange may end in unpleasantness, and I, um . . . don't want Zachary to hear. I, um . . . did something. Something you're going to be very angry with me about. I need to tell you about it now."

Judging by her pallor, she wasn't looking forward to it, but she turned and led the way from the room anyway, apparently determined to get it said.

Once in the backyard, she wandered in an erratic circle around him, kicking at the grass one second and then sighing as she leaned her head back to gaze at the sky the next. Joe watched her for a couple of minutes, wondering what on earth she was about to say.

Then she turned a luminous gaze on him. Even with only the light of the moon to illuminate her face, he could see that her eyes were full of tears and that her mouth was quivering. He ached for her. What had happened to the Marilee he'd once known—the spirited girl, nine parts angel and one part imp, who had never hesitated to stand toe-to-toe with him?

He moved toward her. "Honey, nothing you did can possibly be *that* bad."

Just before he reached her, she turned away and started cutting circles in another direction. "It's not *bad*, exactly. I just don't know how to start."

"Maybe I can help you out. At your first appointment, your doctor advised you to tell me exactly what happened that night, her reason undoubtedly being that I could play a big role in your recovery. Rather than do that, you put her off by lying and claiming you told me." He paused. "How am I doing so far?"

"I'm sorry you found out from the doctor that I've been lying to her about talking to you." She gave a nervous little laugh. "That's the whole problem with lying, don't you know? It always catches up with you."

"No matter how I'd found out, I'd be upset. Not so much about you lying to me, although that hurts because you don't trust me enough to confide in me. But what really upsets me is your lying to your doctor. How can she help you, Mari? She thought we were talking openly."

Joe rubbed his jaw, watching as she fell back into a walk, going first one way and then another. "Mari, would you stop? I'm getting dizzy watching you."

"I'm sorry." She pushed at her hair and then kicked at the grass again. "Oh, Joe . . . I know I have to tell you this, but it's just so *hard*."

"There's more?"

"A *lot* more."

"Just take it from the beginning."

"I *can't*! That's the whole problem, don't you see?" She wheeled to look at him. "Do you remember when I played spokeswoman for Zachary and got you to promise you wouldn't blow up and do something stupid if he opened up and talked to you?"

He swung the sole of his running shoe in a wide arc, barely grazing the blades of grass. "Of course I remember. It wasn't that long ago."

"Would you make that same promise to me?"

Joe was starting to get an uneasy feeling. "You're afraid I'll blow up at you?"

"I can't say anything more until I have your solemn promise, Joe."

"I promise."

She began to circle him again, kicking up sprays of grass with the toes of her sneakers. After making several turns, she finally said, "Do you remember the last game you ever played between Simon Benson and Pettigrove State?"

That night was indelibly engraved on his brain. Paul Myric, one of his college buddies and a Simon Benson University linebacker, tackled Pettigrove's running back, Keith Lesterson, after the whistle blew. Myric never intended to take a cheap shot. It was simply one of those moments in football when a player's momentum and the referee's call weren't in sync, and as sometimes happens in such a rough game, the resultant hit injured Lesterson's spine, paralyzing him from the neck down.

"Sure, I remember," Joe said softly. "Why are you bringing that up?"

She just kept circling him, her head bent to stare at her feet. "You remember that the next week, Stan Salisbury and four other players from Pettigrove drove to Eugene, waited outside a bar, and jumped Paul Myric when he was crossing the parking lot, their intent to seriously hurt him to get even for what he'd done to Lesterson."

"Marilee, I was there. I jumped in to help Paul out."

She finally looked up. In a shadow cast by the roof of the house, her features were cloaked, only the shimmer of her eyes reaching out to him from the darkness. "That's my Joe, always jumping in to fight someone else's battles, mine more than anyone's, I think. You dislocated Stan Salisbury's shoulder that night."

"Yeah, well, he came to Eugene looking for trouble, and he found some. I never meant to hurt him. You know that. It wasn't my fault he was drunk. When I shoved him, he fell and hit his shoulder on a parking curb. Why are you dredging all that up? It's water under the bridge."

"It's not entirely under the bridge," she said hollowly. "Stan still lives here in town. He sells real estate now, has his own brokerage. Did you know that?"

Joe nodded. "Yeah, I ran into him shortly after I moved back. Bought him a cup of coffee." He tugged on his ear. "He's an okay guy now that he's matured out a little. Sort of fidgety. He ended up marrying Susan Holmes. You remember her. She was in your—" Joe broke off, watching her as she stepped into a swath of moonlight. Her facial muscles were drawn so tightly over the underlying bone that her face had become a twisted caricature. "She was in your sorority," he finished softly.

She lifted her chin and squared her shoulders, her eyes filled with pain and an underlying hatred he couldn't miss. "Did you and Stan have a nice chat and do a little male bonding?" she asked. "I suppose after all these years that he's over hating your guts."

Joe's stomach was somewhere around the vicinity of his knees. "Where are you going with this, Mari?"

"Joe Lakota, the golden-haired boy." She gave a brittle laugh. "All through high school, until you graduated, poor Stan never got to play first-string quarterback. It wasn't until his senior year that he finally got to play and get noticed by the scouts, and even then, his scholarship wasn't all that great. Can you imagine how he must have resented you?"

Joe could only stare at her.

"He played really well once he got in college. Finally, he was out of your shadow, a star quarterback in his own right. Then, low and behold, his junior year at Pettigrove, what happened? They were having a winning season until Lesterson, one of their key players, got his spine snapped. Then the following week, you knocked Stan off his feet during a fight and screwed up his throwing arm. All his dreams of playing pro, down the tubes. Rightly or wrongly, can you imagine how he *detested* you? Or how it rankled, watching you and Myric go on to glory, knowing your team would probably win the bowl game?"

Joe felt as if ice water was trickling down his back. "Oh, Jesus," he whispered.

Her face looked as if it had turned to a carving of salt.

"Good old Stan. He's an *okay* guy. All he ever really meant to do was screw up Simon Benson's season by making damned sure you couldn't play in the bowl game. Without you, they would have lost, with the added benefit that if they hurt you badly enough to keep you out of the game, you probably wouldn't make the pro draft, either. An eye for an eye, so to speak. With a little help from Myric, you totally destroyed his football career. Why not do his best to ruin yours?"

Joe wasn't sure his legs would continue to hold him up. He lifted a hand. "Wait a minute. Give me just a minute."

"I can't," she whispered, her tone tortured. "I have to get it said, Joe. Stan and his buddies had already caused trouble in Eugene. The only reason they weren't thrown in jail was because Myric didn't want to cause more bad feeling between the teams by pressing charges. They were afraid to go back to pick a fight with you. To get to you, somehow they had to lure you onto their turf. Only how could they possibly do that?"

Joe was shaking. He stared hard at her, his hands clenched into throbbing fists. "Dear God, what are you saying?"

"You know what I'm saying."

The earth felt as if it shifted beneath him. A loud pounding began in his ears. "I'll kill him. I swear to God and all that's holy, he's a dead man."

She closed her eyes. "No," she said softly. "You promised, and I'm holding you to it."

Joe took a step toward her. "You kept this from me? All these years, you kept this from me? Oh, Marilee. I had a right to know! I sat down and drank coffee with the no-good son of a bitch! You should have told me! Fidgety? Now I know why he was so nervous! He thought I knew."

She flinched and opened her eyes. "Look at yourself. Ten years later, Joe, and just *look* at yourself. If I'd told you right after it happened, could I have held you back?

No. You would have gone after them, and you would have killed one of them. Your whole life would have been destroyed. For what? For what, Joe? Would telling you have undone what they did? Made me whole again? No."

"Like I would have cared?" he yelled at her. "Like football was the only thing in my life? I *loved* you! You were my girl, and the bastards *used* you to get at me? Name me a guy who wouldn't go after them for that, and I'll show you a spineless excuse for a man who isn't worth the powder it'd take to blow him straight to hell!"

"You promised," she said and grabbed his arm. "You promised me, Joe!"

"You tricked me into it! I thought this was about something you did!"

"It was, in part. I didn't tell you!"

"No, and I'll never forgive you for it, either. I had a right to know."

Her nails dug into his skin. "To what end? So you could be in prison right now? Or on death row, awaiting execution? They *wanted* me to tell you! When they were done, they said, 'Run to Joe, little girl. Tell him we'll be waiting for him!' The *fools*. I knew you! One guy, five! You wouldn't have cared, and you would have killed one of them! What was I supposed to do, let that happen? Well, it's not always about you!"

"Me?" he whispered incredulously.

"Yes, about *you*. You're not the only one with a God-given right to protect the people he loves. I loved you, too, and I protected you the only way I knew, by keeping silent. Not telling my folks. Daddy would have made me file charges if he'd found out, and then all hell would have broken loose! No way could we have kept it from you then! Do you think keeping my mouth shut was easy?"

Joe shook her off and headed for the house. Salisbury still lived in town. His address would be in the phone book. That was all he could think.

Marilee ran up the deck steps after him. "Joe, please. Don't do anything. Promise me you won't do anything! If not for me, for Zachary!"

Unable to get the pictures out of his mind, Joe shoved his way into the house. *Rage.* A murderous, mindless rage. *Tell him we'll be waiting for him.* Oh, God. Five of them. *They were holding me down, and I couldn't move his hand. He was suffocating me.* Oh, Jesus. Only animals would do something like that.

Joe strode straight to the phone and grabbed up the phone book. Marilee followed him into the kitchen. "So now what?" she asked thinly. "You asked me to tell you, and what happens when I do? Joe, *please.* If nothing else, wait a few minutes. Just *five.* Give yourself time to calm down and think. Please?"

He turned from the counter. When she stepped into his path, he caught her by the shoulders and set her out of his way. "You handled it your way, and ten years later, it still isn't finished. Now it's my turn."

"So it's all been for nothing? Everything, all for nothing!" she cried. "Just like that, and you're going to throw your life away."

"No, I'm going to get yours back!"

With that, Joe stormed from the house.

Twelve

*J*oe drove directly to the Salisburys' residence. Once there, he parked at the curb across the street, and then sat in the car under blanket of darkness, his hands knotted over the steering wheel while he glared at the well-lighted front windows of the tidy ranch-style rambler. Next to the front door below the porch light hung a welcome wreath, gaily decorated with roses and mauve ribbon. To Joe, that wreath represented everything Salisbury took for granted—love, laughter, and normalcy, things he and his friends had heartlessly stripped from Marilee's life.

It was early yet, not quite nine. Salisbury was probably cuddled on the sofa and watching a favorite sitcom with his wife. *Hatred.* Joe had never before detested anyone enough to kill him. He did now. He trembled with the need to smash his fists against something, preferably the bastard's face. *Mari.* Salisbury and his buddies had destroyed her, and for what? To exact revenge by sabotaging a bowl game and destroying a competitor's future in football?

Joe had seen all kinds of insanity over the course of his career—young athletes risking their health by shooting up with steroids to gain bulk, key players injecting injured joints with cortisone to be in a game, not caring that they might end up crippled for the rest of their lives. He'd even seen coaches perpetuating the madness, as consumed with the need to win as their players. There was no explaining or understanding it. The desire to win, to be in the limelight, became a monster. But, dear God, there were limits. Self-sacrifice was one thing, and at least forgivable. Victimizing a young girl and ruining her life was not.

Now Marilee's victimizers had moved on, their villainy neither disclosed nor punished. Oh, yeah, a real upstanding citizen, that was Salisbury, the successful real estate broker who had it all, a pretty wife, three cute kids, and a brand new minivan. How was that fair? More importantly, how could any man who called himself a man let this go? Joe couldn't. Rightly or wrongly, he just couldn't.

He felt badly about running out on Marilee. Ideally, he should have stayed with her, held her in his arms, listened to her talk. *Ten years.* She'd kept this from him all that time, and when she'd finally worked up the courage to tell him, what had he done? Exactly what she'd always feared he might.

He'd make it up to her, he promised himself. But he could be no use at all to her while he was shaking with rage, and there was only one way for him to rid himself of the anger—up close and personal with the son of a bitch who had hurt her. Just going to the grocery store had to be a trial for her. Even after all these years, she must worry that she might run into Susan or Salisbury himself if she went to town.

Joe closed his eyes for a moment, feeling sick. Pizza pans in front of her doors. Strings of bells hanging all over her house so no one could sneak up behind her. She'd called her past behavior irrational, and deep down,

Joe had agreed. What normal person lived like that? *You need help, Mari.* How many times had he told her that, unable to understand why she so stubbornly refused to get any.

He swore under his breath and climbed from the car. There was more than one way to skin a cat, by God. He'd promised Marilee that he wouldn't do anything stupid, but that didn't mean he could do nothing at all.

Joe strode across the street and up Salisbury's front walk onto the porch. He pounded on the door with such force that the framework shook. When Salisbury answered the knock and saw his caller, he turned pale. "Hey, Joe. How's it goin'?" he said, glancing nervously past him to scan the darkness. "What brings you by?"

Joe blasted the man with a glare. "Funny you should ask how things are going, Stan. The answer is, not worth a shit. Marilee and I just had a long talk, and you'll never guess what she told me."

Salisbury skimmed a hand over the top of his head, the gesture revealing his nervousness. Joe was pleased to note that the son of a bitch was going prematurely bald. He was also developing a paunch. Richly deserved deterioration. Soon he'd resemble the fat slug he really was.

"I'll cut right to the chase, Salisbury. You're a worthless excuse for a man and not worth getting slime on my hands to kill you. That said, leaving you alive causes a problem. You're not fit to breathe the same air my wife does."

Susan, a slender brunette, appeared in the doorway behind her husband. Her green eyes widened when she saw Joe on the porch. "What's going on?"

"Stan and I are having a long overdue chat," Joe said sharply. "I learned tonight that he and his buddies gang raped my wife ten years ago, so you'll excuse me if I'm raising my voice and not watching my language. I usually don't curse around ladies, but, then"—he cut Susan a dismissive glance—"the definition doesn't apply to present company."

"Watch your mouth, Joe. She had nothing to do with it."

Susan clutched Stan's shirt sleeve. "What's he talking about?"

Stan ignored the question. "Go back to the living room, honey. This is between me and Joe."

Joe snorted. "Susan lured Marilee into the trap you set up. I'd say she had plenty to do with it. Just because she didn't hang around for the fun doesn't excuse what she did."

Susan looked bewilderedly at her husband. "Rape, Stan? What's he saying?"

Joe held Stan's gaze. "Listen carefully, Salisbury. I'll only say this once. In the morning, you'll start making arrangements to get the hell out of here. Sell the house, dump the business. Relocate wherever you like as long as it isn't within a five-hundred-mile radius of Laurel Creek. I'll give you thirty days, and if you've cleared out in that time, I'll let this go. When you leave, don't ever come back. I know you have family here. Too bad. If they want to see you, they can drive to you, not the other way around."

Stan laughed. "You can't make me move. What are you, nuts? I've got a life here."

"Life here, as you know it, is over," Joe said softly. "Clear out, or I'll ruin you. Everyone in town will know. You reading me loud and clear? Your folks, your kids, your friends, your business acquaintances, the people in your church. *Everyone*. You won't be able to hold your head up in this town. I'll make damn sure of it."

"That's slander!"

"No, just the dirty truth." Joe allowed himself to smile. "Frankly, I hope you're dumb enough to stay. I *want* to ruin your life, Stan. It'll give me no end of satisfaction."

"You're bluffing! Marilee will never tell what happened that night. Her reputation would go down the drain right along with mine."

"If I'm forced to disclose this, I'll take her somewhere

new. Her family will still love her if they learn the truth. The question is, will yours? I doubt it. Not even a mother loves a rapist."

"You mean it's *true*?" Susan cried, her eyes filling with revulsion. "Oh, my God, Stan. You said you were just going to scare her!"

"Shut up!" Stan fixed his gaze on Joe. "You can't mean this," he said reasonably. "I don't know what Marilee told you, man, but she's lying."

"Marilee doesn't lie, and if you say she did one more time, I'll kill you, you worthless bastard."

"All right! All right." Stan held up his hands, his face shining with beads of sweat. "Don't lose it, buddy. Just stay calm. Let's keep this in perspective."

"I'm not your buddy," Joe said softly. "And what, exactly, is the perspective, Stan?"

"That sometimes shit happens. It just does, and there's nothing you can do. I *tried*, man. I tried to stop them. Only she started fighting. Scratched somebody. Tempers flared. Honest to God, Joe, I never meant for it to go that far. Ask Marilee. She'll tell you that. It wasn't my fault."

"You tried, huh?" Joe felt as if he might vomit. Breathing through his mouth, he kept his teeth clenched, unable to shake the thought that there were particles of filth in the air. "You miserable excuse for a human being. Just looking at you turns my stomach."

"It turned ugly, Joe. Things got out of control. They were all drunk, pumped up. They turned on me. I didn't have a choice at that point but to go along. Hey, it happened years ago. All right? A bunch of drunk boys. You don't destroy a man's reputation over something he did as a kid. It's over. Done. We all felt sorry afterward."

"*Boys*? Hardly. You were a grown man, and you knew *exactly* what you were doing. As for it being over? Maybe for you, but not for Marilee. When a woman's violated, it's never over for her. *Never*."

Salisbury knotted his fists and jerked his sleeve from Susan's grasp. "So now you're going to ruin me? All these years later? I got a wife and kids, and you want me to turn their lives upside down?"

"Lots of families relocate," Joe retorted. "You're getting off easy. Grab your hat and thank God. If I had my way, you'd be a dead man. She knew you and trusted you, you rotten son of a bitch. How can you live with that? She was only eighteen, for God's sake, just starting her first year of college and green as grass."

"Yeah, we noticed," Salisbury said with a sneer. "Surprised the hell out of me. Hotshot Joe Lakota, and his girl still had her cherry."

Joe nearly lost it then. Adrenaline surged through his body, snapping every muscle to a throbbing tautness. He was about to spring when Susan cried, "Oh, my *God*! Oh, my God. How could you, Stan? How could you?" She flew at her husband, scratching at his face, kicking his shins. "You *bastard*! You *lied* to me, said you never touched her! How could you do that, and then come to *me*?"

Joe fell back, watching in stunned disbelief as Stan struggled to protect his face. Susan shrieked when her husband grabbed her wrists. She brought up her knee, jabbing him hard in the crotch. *Score.* Stan grabbed himself and staggered against the door jamb.

"You came to me *afterward*!" she cried, pounding on him with her fists. "We were together later that night. After you were with *her*, you came to *me*?"

Joe backed off the porch, shaking his head. He couldn't believe these people. Susan wasn't upset over the fact that her husband had raped a young girl. Oh, no. All she cared about was that he had been *with* someone else? *With*? She was as sick as he was, and as far as Joe was concerned, the pair of them deserved each other.

"Pack it in, Stan," he called as he left the yard. "You're finished in this town."

All the way to the car, Joe could still hear Susan screaming at her husband. Some of the names she called him were so creative they even made Joe's ears burn. He'd called it right. She was no lady.

Before climbing into the Honda, he paused for a moment to observe the show. Porch lights were coming on up and down the street, and people were opening their front doors to see what was going on. Stan was hunched over at the waist, his arms folded over his head to shield himself from his wife's blows.

Joe smiled grimly as he climbed in the car. Salisbury didn't need any help ruining his life. He'd already done a fine job of it all by himself.

Marilee's Taurus was gone and the house was as dark as a tomb when Joe pulled into the driveway. He sat there for a moment after cutting the engine, then he pocketed the keys and exited the car. What had he been expecting, for her to be waiting with open arms? When he recalled some of the things he'd said to her this evening, he wouldn't blame her if she never spoke to him again.

His gaze shot to the dark windows of what was now Zachary's room, and for the space of a heartbeat, he worried that she might have left the child in the house alone. The thought no sooner took root than he plucked it from his mind and tossed it away. Marilee would never do that, not even to a child she didn't love. Wherever she had gone, she'd taken the boy with her, and his welfare would be her first concern.

Boo met Joe on the walkway that cut between the house and garage. Joe stopped to scratch the hound's ears. "Hey, buddy," he said softly. "You mind if I sleep in your doghouse tonight?"

Boo snuffled Joe's forearm, smearing his skin with drool. Joe gave the dog a final pat and then moved past him to sit on the side steps of the deck. That brought back memories. He'd been sitting exactly here that first afternoon. His heart caught when he remembered the wariness he'd seen in Marilee's eyes that day. And God forgive him, he'd been angry with her. Granted, he'd had good reason. She'd allowed people he cared about to think badly of him, after all. But she'd had good reason for keeping quiet, too. Knowing her as he did, he should have reserved judgment until he learned the truth.

Joe sighed and gazed solemnly between his spread knees at the moon-washed step. *Marilee, Marilee, where are you, Marilee*? He supposed she was over at her parents' place, undoubtedly so upset she didn't want to see him right now. No big surprise. He could go after her, he guessed. Despite the fact that they disapproved of the marriage, her folks wouldn't turn him away. They were very old-fashioned in their thinking and wouldn't interfere if he barged in, demanding to see his wife. But what then? He could toss her over his shoulder and carry her home against her will, but what would that prove? That he was bigger than she was?

Joe rubbed a hand over his face and looked up at the patch of sky that showed between the adjacent eaves of the house and garage. Stars twinkled against the swath of bluish black, reminding him of diamonds on dark velvet. Seventh heaven was a long way off tonight, he thought morosely.

Sadness swamped him. He'd spent well over half his life wishing on stars, and every one of those wishes had Marilee's name on it. He'd never really wanted anything but her. Oh, sure, he had been passionate about football. But compared to his love for Marilee, even his dreams of one day playing pro had been secondary. She'd come first. *Always.* That being the case, how had he managed to fail her so completely?

It hurt, knowing that. He kept recalling the things Ron had told him. How she had withdrawn from everyone after the breakup. How concerned they'd all been for her health. She had needed Joe then, and he hadn't been here for her. *If only.* Things might have turned out so differently—*if only*. If only he hadn't been such a hothead, always ready to fight to defend her. If only he hadn't been so self-absorbed the night she broke up with him, he might have seen the fear in her eyes. He would have stayed with her then—been there to help her through that time. He could have taken her for long walks, just holding her hand, if nothing else, and listening while she poured her heart out.

Instead, she had weathered the storm alone, and she'd never taken all those steps back to wellness. *Forever, Joe. You win.* Knowing what he knew now, he wanted to die when he remembered her saying that. Tonight he'd looked at her and wondered where her courage had gone. Ah, God. Bless her heart, she had more courage in her little finger than he did in his whole body.

Joe's chest went tight, and then and there, he promised himself that if she gave him a second chance, he'd somehow turn back the clock. This time, he'd take her for those long walks, and he'd content himself with just holding her hand for as long as it was necessary. *I can't play by your rules*, he'd told her. *Ten minutes, that's all I need.* Now he wondered how she'd ever had the nerve to run after him. Her feelings and fears couldn't be erased in ten minutes. From now on, he'd put her first, to hell with how he felt or what he wanted. She was all that mattered—all that had ever mattered, and somehow he would prove it to her.

They'd get through this and come out on the other side to realize the dreams they'd once had. They *would*. The alternative, that something so very precious would be lost, was unthinkable.

Resolved to rectify matters, Joe tried to concentrate on the beauty of the night. When she came back—*if* she came back—he wanted to be calm and clearheaded. Along the walkway between the garage and house, the glossy-leaf camellia bushes rustled softly in the breeze and from out of the surrounding darkness, the harmonious voices of crickets chanted an erratic refrain, the symphonic effect forlorn.

A flare of bright light suddenly played over him. He

cocked his head to listen. From out in the drive, he heard a car engine sputter out and then a door slammed. Marilee was home. He sent up a silent prayer of thanks, trying to think what he should say to her, and decided the first order of business was to beg her forgiveness for telling her he'd never forgive *her*. How could he have said that to her? It was going to haunt him for the rest of his life. She'd kept silent to protect him.

She gave him no chance to speak, let along phrase a heartfelt apology. Instead, she came around the corner of the garage at a dead run, her purse dangling by its strap from one hand and swinging wildly at her ankles. When she saw him, she staggered to a stop.

"Joe? Oh, God, Joe, I'm so sorry. I saw the cop car at Stan's place! Forgive me, forgive me."

He stood and stepped off the porch. "Cop car?"

"I should *never* have told you. Stupid, stupid, stupid. I knew what would happen. I *knew*."

"Mari, I—"

"How bad did you hurt him?" She clamped a hand to the top of her head. "Oh, God. I can't think. You need to leave. I'll go to your mom's and pick up Zachary while you pack a few clothes for each of you. Do you have a passport for him?"

"Mari, would you put on the brakes for a minute and listen to me? I didn't hurt Stan. I kept my word to you and never laid a hand on him. If there's a cop car over at his place, it's because Susan raised such a ruckus that a neighbor called the police."

She peered at him through the shadows, her expression disbelieving. "You didn't hurt him?"

"I kept my word. Stan's fine." As quickly as he could, Joe told her what had transpired and that Stan Salisbury would soon be leaving Laurel Creek. "When I left their place, Susan was pounding the crap out of him, but I never touched him."

She moved past him to sit on the second step, for all the world as if she couldn't stay standing a second longer.

Joe saw how violently she was shaking, and regret formed an aching lump at the base of his throat. He groaned and hunkered before her.

"Oh, honey, I'm sorry. I didn't mean to give you such a scare. I never laid a finger on him, I swear."

She continued to gape at him. "Do you really think he'll leave town?"

"I know he will. He's a spineless worm. Always has been, always will be."

She started to laugh, a high-pitched, hysterical laughter that quickly turned to sobs. Joe couldn't bear it. He joined her on the step and gathered her into his arms. "Oh, sweetheart, don't. It's all right. Everything's going to be all right now."

She continued to cry. Deep, tearing sobs shuddered up from her. Joe held her close, rocking her, trying to soothe her with light strokes of his hands. And still she wept. He had a feeling this was ten years overdue, that she needed to let it all out.

When at last she ran out of tears, she leaned limply against him, the brace of his arms all that seemed to be keeping starch in her spine. Smoothing wet tendrils of hair from her face, Joe swayed slightly, letting the silence and the rocking motion soothe them both. There were so many things he wanted to say to her—needed to say to her—and he couldn't even think where to start.

"I'll be so glad to have him *gone*," she whispered. "So glad, Joe. You just can't know."

He had an inkling.

"Right after I bought the house," she went on faintly, "I decided to get some counseling. I knew I could do it then without my folks finding out."

"You went for counseling?"

"I tried. I'd been having nightmares—terrible nightmares—and they were getting worse. I needed help. I finally realized that. So I called to make an appointment at county mental health. Back then, I still didn't make all that much with my stories, and the house payment had me strapped. The county charged according to income, so I figured I could afford to get counseling there."

Joe didn't know where this was going. He supposed it didn't matter. She was talking to him, telling him stuff she'd never shared before. That was all that counted.

"Two days later—on a Saturday afternoon—I was out in the yard raking leaves, and when I turned around, there stood Stan. You've heard people say they nearly died of fright? Well, I almost did. I swear my heart stopped. I couldn't move, couldn't scream. I just stood there, Joe. I was holding a rake. I could have beaned him with it. But I just *stood* there."

Joe tightened his hold on her, picturing the scene. He could almost taste the terror she must have felt—an awful, metallic coldness at the back of his tongue.

"He told me he'd gotten wind of my appointment," she whispered. "And there was no way he'd let me keep it. The first thing a counselor would do was insist I give him the names of my assailants, he said. And then I'd be encouraged to file charges. Gossip travels like wildfire in a small place like Laurel Creek. No way was he going to let me drag his reputation through the dirt."

Joe closed his eyes and clenched his teeth.

"He said two things were going to happen if I ratted on him, the first that he and his friends would all testify against me and swear that I was willing. It had been months. How would I explain keeping silent for so long? It'd be their word against mine. I'd be a laughingstock when they got finished with me. And afterward they'd make me wish I'd kept my mouth shut. All five of them would pay me a visit, and it'd be just like old times."

It took all Joe's self-control to remain sitting. He wanted to drive directly back to Salisbury's place and commit murder this time. But, no. This was only the beginning, the first of many things Marilee would tell him. If he wanted her to trust him and confide in him, he absolutely had to get past this and stay calm.

"How did he find out you'd made an appointment?" he forced himself to ask.

"His mom. She did some kind of social work. I can't remember what, exactly. Somehow she found out. Probably saw my name in the appointment book or something. Stan never said, and I could only guess, but I think she told him. An interesting bit of gossip, Marilee Nelson, going to a shrink. When I made the call, I never even thought about her working there."

Joe took a deep breath and slowly released it. "Ah, Mari. No wonder you put pizza pans in front of the doors. You must have been so scared."

She dried her cheek on his shirt. "Scared? Scared is when your heart leaps and your knees go watery, Joe. I went way beyond that. Stan had moved back by then. He and Susan lived just a few blocks away. And there he was, in my yard. You can't know—you just can't know. Oh, God. I was so terrified, I couldn't even *think*."

"Oh, honey . . ."

"I look back on that time and you know what I feel? *Outrage*. Of all the unmitigated *gall*. He knew. Don't you see? He *knew* why I didn't tell. That I was protecting you. He knew he could push me, that he could intimidate me, and I'd do nothing. Their word against mine. That was their plan all along—to lure you onto their turf, incite you to do something crazy, and afterward, they would all swear they did nothing wrong, that I was a willing partner and you flew into a jealous rage.

"When he showed up in my yard, I should have done something immediately. Told my folks. Called the police. Things had gotten way out of hand at that point. Way out of hand! He was threatening to come back and do it *again*! Instead of calling the police, you know what I did?"

"No, what?" he asked, his voice grating like a fingernail over coarse sandpaper.

"I ran in the house. Locking windows. Barricading doors with furniture. '*He's coming back.*' That was all I could think. I got a kitchen knife and hid in the closet. In the *closet*, Joe. Like a little kid hiding under the blankets. Was that rational? *No.* I just—lost it."

Joe threaded his fingers through her silky hair and made a tight fist. "Sweetheart—out in the yard—did Stan do something? Besides just threaten you, I mean?"

A shudder ran through her body, and she smashed her nose against his shirt. *Silence.* A long, horrible silence. When she finally spoke, her voice was little more than a squeak. "He pushed me up against the garage and—oh, *Joe*—don't ask. Even now, I feel so ashamed."

"*Ashamed?*"

"I was still holding the rake. The whole time, I was still holding the rake. All my life, I'd been a brat, giving back as good as I got. If someone pushed me around, I never thought twice about pushing back. So what if they were bigger than me? And suddenly there I stood, so scared all I could do was sweat."

"Mari . . . Mari. You're not a coward. That's not what you're saying, I hope, because if it is, we're going to butt heads."

"I should've clobbered him. Instead, he put his hands on me, and I just—let him!"

For a moment, Joe couldn't breathe, and for the first time, he really got a taste of how Marilee must have felt as one of her attacks came on. When his lungs finally grabbed for oxygen, he gulped and exhaled raggedly. "When he put his hands on you, did he—you know— hurt you?"

"There are all different kinds of hurt," she whispered. "He only touched me up top—over my clothes. Nothing else. He was bullying me—trying to frighten me, that's all. And I let him. Something in me just snapped, Joe. Up until that moment, as sick and frightened as I was, I'd made a choice. You know? I was determined not to let them use me to hurt you, and somewhere deep, under all the fear, I felt brave. After that, I no longer did. I came face to face with who I really was, a sniveling coward."

"No."

"Yes! I hid in the *closet*! For *hours*!" she wailed. "You know what I realized then? Do you? That I'd *never* been brave. Never! I always had you to fight my battles. In the back of my mind, I always knew you'd come to my rescue if I got in a fix. I went through half my life, patting myself on the back, thinking I had grit. What a joke. Left on my own, I had the spine of a jellyfish.

"I telephoned you that night. Did you know that? When I finally worked up the courage to crawl out of the closet, I called Gerry and Ron on the bedroom extension and got your number."

"You called me? I don't remem—"

"Your roommate answered. He hollered for you to come to the phone. I heard him tell you he thought it was me. You picked up, and you said, 'Hello?' in a funny-sounding voice. Then you said, 'Mari, is that you?' "

"And you didn't answer." Joe closed his eyes as the memory came back to him. "I listened for a long time, praying it was you, but you never answered. I finally hung up, thinking it was a crank call."

"It was me," she said hollowly. "I never hung up, not even after you broke the connection. I slept with the receiver in my arms all night. It made me feel closer to you somehow. Safer. Isn't that silly?"

Tears filled Joe's eyes. "Ah, God, Mari, why didn't you say something? I could have caught a flight home and been here in a few hours. Why in the hell didn't you ask me to come? Maybe I am a hothead. But I loved you so much. Why didn't you say something?"

"Because." Just that one word, *because*. But it conveyed a world of hopelessness. After a time, she added, "There was too much between us. The thing with Stan wasn't all of it. When I heard your voice and imagined you racing home to be with me, I knew I couldn't."

"Couldn't what?"

"Be *with* you. I was too messed up by then. It was like getting turned around in a mirror maze, Joe. I couldn't find my way out, and everything was distorted. You know what I mean? Looking back, I realize now that I wasn't thinking straight from the very start. I made stupid decisions, and those decisions led to more stupid decisions. You can't allow someone that kind of leverage over you. It's always a mistake. By keeping quiet about that night and waiting, I damaged my own credibility. If I'd gone forward later and accused them, who would've believed me?"

Joe rested his chin atop her head. *A mirror maze.* That description created such a clear picture in his mind of how she had felt then and might still feel now. Confused, panicky, uncertain where to turn.

"Oh, honey, I wish I had been here."

She stirred and curled a slender hand over the nape of his neck. "At that point, you probably couldn't have helped me, Joe. It took time, and I got worse before I started to get better. We can think, 'What if?' We can tell ourselves things would have gone differently, if only this had happened or that had happened. But the fact is, things happened the way they did. It's done. We can't change it. I'm just thankful I came through it with my sanity."

"Me, too."

"But there were times when I swear I felt it slipping away from me. It was as if I stepped up to the very edge of a high cliff and looked down into a dark, horrible abyss. It was only by the grace of God that I was able to take one step backward to keep from falling into it. When I started to get better, I had this favorite day-dream—that I'd get completely well, have my life all straightened out, and then you'd come back home. In my dream, when you saw me, you realized you still loved me." She fell quiet for a moment, her fingers toying nervously with his ribbed collar. "Only when it really happened and you moved back, I wasn't well. I was better, but not well, and there you were, ready or not. Even worse, you'd guessed my secret. Not all of it, but you'd guessed enough to scare me half to death. I was terrified I'd do or say something, and you'd figure out the rest."

Joe sighed. "No wonder it was so easy for you to understand Zachary. You were both in the same spot. I've made a lot of mistakes, Marilee. With you, then with my son. Maybe I've learned my lesson a little late, but I have learned it. You never need to worry that I'll go off half-cocked again. I give you my word on that."

She said nothing.

"As for that favorite daydream of yours? I'm still here, and I'm not leaving. Being with you is my favorite dream, too, awake or asleep. How's about if we make it come true together?"

"I'm not sure how. Just when I think I see a way out of the maze, I bump face-first into myself. Does that make any sense?"

"I know the way out. If you'll trust me, I'll show you."

"By having sex, you mean?"

He tightened his arms around her. "No, not sex. Do you really believe that's all I think about?"

"Yes."

He chuckled. He couldn't stop himself. He did think about it a lot, as in every time he looked at her. "You're not quite ready to make love yet. When you are, you just holler, and I'll take it from there. All right?"

"I think you should know that I'm beginning to wonder if I'll ever be ready. Every time I think about it, I freeze inside."

"Why is that, do you think?" He waited a beat. "I'll tell you why. You aren't thinking about what it'll be like with me. You can't possibly know because you have only one point of reference, a really bad one. I wish now that we hadn't waited. That we'd made love a hundred times. Then you'd be able to look back and remember good things. Instead you've got only horrible memories."

"Yes," she admitted hollowly. "Really horrible ones, Joe."

"I'd like you to share those memories with me."

"Share them with you?"

"That's right. Tonight. Talk to me, Mari—the way you should have been able to talk to me ten years ago. Bad memories lose power when you share them. Don't you know that?"

"Sharing them with Doctor Patterson hasn't made them lose power."

He smiled sadly and pressed a kiss to the tip of her nose. "That's because Doctor Patterson can't help you replace all the horrible memories with beautiful new ones. Trade me? Straight across, old memories for new memories. Do we have a deal?"

Thirteen

*O*ld *memories for new memories.*

Joe's plan sounded crazy to Marilee. Every detail about that night was indelibly engraved on her brain, and the memories wouldn't lose power merely because she had shared the experience with him. Nevertheless, share it she did. Joe could be very persistent when he set his mind to something, and for the remainder of that evening, he applied himself to the task of digging the entire story out of her.

At first Marilee resisted, preferring instead to give vague descriptions. The things she had endured were shameful and degrading, and she had never been able to shake her feeling that the incident had left her tainted. Even worse, it was the kind of filth a woman could never wash away. God knew she had tried, scrubbing her skin nearly raw on several occasions. Afterward she still felt dirty, and deep in her heart, she feared Joe might feel the same way.

She had no intention of telling him that, of course. But, then, it wasn't her intention to start crying again, either.

"I'm sorry," she said, swiping angrily at her cheeks. "I don't know what's gotten into me tonight. I think the dike has sprung a gigantic leak."

"Good. Stop apologizing and just let it out."

For some reason, that only made her cry harder. Embarrassed but unable to make herself stop, she cupped a trembling hand over her eyes. "Just—give me a—minute."

"I've given you ten years." He hooked an arm around her waist, his muscles drawing taut to form a relentless circle. "Come here, honey."

"No . . . no, I just need—"

"This is what you need," he said, his voice a rumbling growl. Before she could anticipate what he meant to do, he lifted her onto his lap. "And what I need. Ah, God, Mari. When I think of you going through that alone, I want to cry with you." One arm still locked around her, he began to stroke her hair and back. "I should have been there. I wish with all my heart I had been. I should have been there."

"Oh, Joe . . ."

Marilee wasn't sure what she told him after that. Nothing . . . everything. Words rushed out. They came in bunches, making no sense. She expressed thoughts and feelings she wasn't even aware she had. She heard herself describing things that had happened in graphic detail, a part of her horrified and ashamed, another childlike part of her needing to tell him.

Whenever she faltered, he prodded her on with leading questions, until finally she'd told him everything. The strangest feeling came over her then—an emptiness way deep within, as if a festering wound inside her had been lanced and drained. She lay limp against him, one shoulder tucked beneath his arm, her cheek resting over his heart. The cup of his body and the clasp of his arms created a cradle of strength and warmth around her.

"Somehow I kept it together until after I saw you," she whispered. "Sort of like during a disaster—how people do what needs to be done and then fall apart later. It was like that for me. I knew I had to do that one thing first— see you, give back the ring, and convince you it was over."

"Oh, Mari. I understand why now, but, oh, God, how I wish you hadn't done that."

Silence. A long, wistful silence.

"After I left—what happened then, honey?"

"Everything's a blank. I drove back to school and packed my stuff, but I've no recollection of doing it. I only know I did because my family has mentioned it now and again. It's sort of scary to me now, knowing I drove all that way on autopilot. I don't recall anything about it."

"Jesus . . . you might have had a wreck."

"My first clear memory, I was already back home. Lying in bed with the sheet pulled over my face. Hours and hours, staring at the whiteness. I pretended it was snow. Isn't that crazy? I was cold. So horribly cold, and I couldn't get warm. Even my mind felt frozen. Buried under snow. That was how I felt. And I begged God to just let me stay there. I remember Mama coming in and pulling away the sheet. It was like—you know that feeling you get, watching a movie too close to the screen? The way everything races at your face? That was how I felt—like everything was coming at me. Mama, the walls and furniture. It was *horrible*, and only the sheet over my face made it stop."

"Oh, Mari. You should have been under a doctor's care. Shock, maybe. Or a nervous breakdown. Dear God. Why didn't she call somebody?"

"She did. One time, she did. Then Daddy came home, and I begged him not to make me go. I knew they'd find out. That a doctor would take one look at me and *know*. I still had bruises and scratches, and I was hurt inside. Just the thought of being examined and touched made me panicky. I didn't want a stupid doctor. I just wanted to be left alone."

"And your dad gave in?" he asked, his tone incredulous.

"He told Mama I was a big girl and knew if I was sick or not. I didn't have a fever or anything. If I didn't want to see a doctor, I didn't have to. It wasn't until later when he saw that I'd lost so much weight that he forced me to go."

"And by then the telling evidence was gone," he finished for her.

"Yes, all gone. And by then I didn't need the sheet over my face. I had it inside my head."

"*What*?"

"Inside my head—the whiteness. I can't explain. But for a while, that's how it felt—like the sheet was still there inside my head. I could see and hear. But I didn't feel anything. I could leave my room. Talk to people. Eat. Watch television. Go to church if they made me. I no longer felt anything, and I needed that. It held everything away until I was ready for it. You know? After that, I slowly let my feelings back in, and I began to get better. That was when I started sketching and drawing, doing stories for Gerry's kids. Everybody said they were good enough to publish, so I made a submission, and before I knew it, I was getting paid for working through my feelings."

She felt his mouth curve in a slight smile. "Working through your feelings?"

"Children's stories were my catharsis. Reflections of me, of my life and what had happened. Simplistic allegories, basically. In my stories, I could make things happen the way I wished they could happen." Marilee closed her eyes, feeling suddenly uncomfortable. "It gave me a source of income, and it helped me cope as well. It was the perfect job for me. Not long after, I got the brilliant idea to buy this house, and then my nightmares grew worse. I called to make an appointment for counseling, Stan showed up, and I went downhill from there. Panic attacks, agoraphobia, paranoia. It took me a long time to get better."

"It took a lot of guts. That's what it took."

Marilee surprised herself by laughing softly. It was the most incredible feeling, being able to laugh so soon after talking about those dark years of her life. She felt as if Joe had opened heavy curtains inside of her and let in sunshine. "I don't see myself as being particularly courageous."

"Yeah, well, we're always our own worst critic. For example, you asking me not to feel differently about you. As if what happened was somehow your fault, and I'm going to think less of you?"

"I don't remember saying that."

"You said that," he assured her. "And it breaks my heart to know you feel that way. Can you explain why, Mari?"

She smoothed her hand over his shirt, listening to the rasp of his breathing and the muted thud of his heartbeat. "It's a silly thing. Not important, really."

"It's important to me."

"You waited," she whispered.

"Waited?"

"Until we could get married, you waited."

"And that's significant?"

Marilee cringed inside, her fingers clenching into a fist. "You were waiting until we got married, and they—*ruined* that. I know it mattered to you. Please don't lie and say it didn't. I know better. You'd been with other girls, but you never touched me that way. You wanted us to be married first."

When he finally answered the charge, his tone was scolding. "You think that I—*Mari*, you sweet, silly love." He ran his fingers into her hair, his broad palm pressing hard against her scalp. "I wasn't waiting until our wedding night because I cared one way or another if you were still a virgin." He broke off and swore under his breath. "I waited because that was who you were."

"Who I was?" she repeated confusedly.

"Before we went out on Saturday nights, I had to take you by the church for confession. Remember that? What kind of guy deflowers a virgin in the backseat of his clunker Chevy when she still hasn't finished her penance?"

Marilee couldn't see how her penance in high school had anything at all to do with her being a virgin on her wedding night.

"You *liked* the way I was," she squeaked, "and after that, I was—changed."

"No." He kissed the end of her nose. "When you walked out of that fraternity house, you were as pure and sweet as you were when you walked in."

"How can you *say* that?"

"Because it's true. It was their wrongdoing, Mari, not yours. As for waiting until our wedding night? Sweetheart, how could I have done otherwise and lived with myself? No matter how much you loved me—or how wonderful it might have been between us—I knew you'd be eaten up with guilt. In your mind, even petting was a sin." He sighed and settled more of his weight against the cushion, drawing her with him. "You carried a rosary and a little vial of holy water in your coin purse, for God's sake. I *wanted* to make love to you, only I knew if I did, I'd change all the things about you that I loved the most. Does that make any sense? Making love is supposed to be a beautiful thing, and I knew it wouldn't be beautiful for you until I put a ring on your finger."

"Oh, Joe . . ."

"Do you remember the time we sneaked away to spend a night alone in the woods?" he suddenly asked. "You told your mom you were sleeping over at Patti's. All we had was my sleeping bag and one pillow, and off we went. You'd just turned sixteen."

She smiled again, soothed by the sturdy hardness of his body and the low rumble of his voice. "I remember."

"It was my plan to make love to you that night."

"It was?"

He laughed softly. "You were sixteen. I had it all worked out in my head that sixteen was a landmark age. You were finally *old* enough. I asked you to sneak off with me, and you never even hesitated to say yes. All that week, I was so excited I could barely think straight, and I counted the minutes until I could get my hands on you."

"I had no idea."

"Marilee," he said, his tone laced with tender exasperation, "when a nineteen-year-old guy invites the girl he adores to sneak away with him for an interlude in the forest, what, *exactly*, do you suppose he has in mind, roasting his-and-her marshmallows on the same stick?"

"Well . . . I suppose if you were to suggest it now, I might be highly suspicious of your motives."

"You should have been then, but God help me, you weren't. All you were worried about that night was the lie you'd told your mom. Lying, you informed me, was a *mortal* sin, and if you got eaten by a bear before morning, you would go straight to hell." He gave a low laugh. "Being nineteen and oozing testosterone, I figured we might as well have fun if we were going straight to hell, fun being passionate sex in my sleeping bag. *Not.* When I got you zipped in, you poked me in the eye making the sign of the cross, and then you said your bedtime prayers. Your *prayers*, for God's sake! My week-long condition, politely termed unflagging readiness, fizzled and bit the dust. The next thing I knew, I was digging in the trunk, looking for the damned marshmallows, and I ended up taking you back to town so you could spend the night at Patti's like you'd told your mom you were going to."

Marilee laughed. She couldn't help herself. He sounded so thoroughly disgruntled.

"You think that's funny, do you?" He laughed as well and then groaned. "If you ask most guys to name the moment they made their passage from boyhood to manhood, they'll usually cite a hot sexual exploit. Not me. I became a man *that* night—somewhere between 'Hail Mary' and 'pray for us sinners.' It wasn't until that moment that I realized."

"Realized what?"

He drew her closer. For a long moment, he said nothing, and when he finally did speak, his voice had dipped to a husky, throbbing tenor. "That my forever girl was worth waiting for." He pressed a kiss to her hair. "And you know what, Mari mine? You're still worth waiting for."

After seeing Marilee off to bed, Joe headed straight for the spare fourth bedroom she used as an office. Every book she'd ever written was on the top shelf of her bookcase. Joe piled the entire collection, numbering nearly thirty, in the crook of his arm and carried them to his bedroom, where he planned to have a reading marathon. After checking the copyright dates, he determined that the earliest publication was entitled *My Friend Moe*.

Feeling vaguely guilty, Joe stripped down to his boxers, then stretched out on the bed with his shoulders and head supported by two pillows. It wasn't as if he was reading her personal diary or anything, he reminded himself. He could buy any one of these books downtown. If the story content reflected her thoughts and feelings, and she didn't want him reading it, then she should never have allowed it to be published in the first place. He had no reason to feel like a snoop.

He had read only a few lines when his scalp began to prickle. The story was about a little girl named Bethany whose best friend in the whole world was her loyal dog, Moe, a big and boisterous dark-brown mongrel with a penchant for playing ball, chasing the mailman, and tipping over the neighbor's trash cans. An intractable rascal, Moe had one saving grace, his absolute devotion to Bethany. The girl and dog were nearly inseparable, the only time they were ever apart when she was away at school.

Joe frowned. The only time he and Marilee had ever been apart as kids was while they were away at college. *Moe*? Change the first letter, and what did you have? *Joe*. This *was* their story.

A mischievous mongrel? She might have at least made him a purebred—a handsome golden retriever, maybe. She'd nailed Joe perfectly otherwise, though. A passion for playing ball. Big and boisterous. Full of mischief. Those phrases perfectly described him as a teenager and young man.

Sighing, he read on and soon started to smile. Rapscallion though he was, Moe was a great dog, his most prominent trait a fierce protectiveness of Bethany. When the neighbor boy pushed Bethany down, Moe pinched him on the leg and tore his jeans. When Bethany awoke from bad dreams, Moe lay between her and the closet so no imaginary monsters could sneak out and get her. When things went wrong at school and Bethany came home in tears, it was Moe who always licked her face and made her smile again. Moe, always Moe, Bethany's shaggy canine prince.

Tears stung Joe's eyes when he came to the dark moment in the story. On her way to the bus stop one morning, Bethany didn't walk with the other girls, as her parents had told her to do. She decided to go a different way instead and soon found herself in a strange neighborhood. Big bushes grew along the sidewalks, and tall trees shaded both sides of the street, making the way seem dark and spooky. Bethany began to feel afraid, so she walked faster, anxious to be back with her friends.

About halfway up the block, a huge, shaggy dog leaped at Bethany from the bushes. To escape, she darted into an alley and squeezed behind a garbage bin. The huge dog, too broad at the shoulders to follow, lunged and snarled, snapping the air before her face with its huge teeth. After a while, the garbage bin moved slightly under the force of the dog's weight, and Bethany knew she was about to be eaten.

She screamed and yelled at the beast to go away. He only inched closer, his snarls terrifying her. Minutes crawled by and mounted into hours, and still she was trapped, knowing with every breath that the dog might hurt her if he got closer.

Finally a policeman heard the ruckus and came into the alley. The dog heard him coming and ran away. Bethany was rescued and taken to the police station, where her father was called to come collect her. When she finally got home and her loyal friend Moe came racing out to greet her, Bethany stared at his huge, shaggy body and his great big teeth. She was frightened and clung to her father's leg.

Bethany had become terrified of her very best friend in the whole world.

Joe's throat went tight as he read that line, for he knew it was a reflection of how Marilee felt. He smoothed his fingertips over the page, seeking a connection with the girl who'd penned those words. *Mari, his sweet Mari*. In reading this, he could finally understand her torment back then.

Joe sighed and refocused on the story. Bethany—Marilee. As he read on, the two became one in his mind, and he no longer pictured Moe as a shaggy dog. Instead he saw himself at twenty-one—a tall young man with a bull neck, broad shoulders, and a body sculpted with muscle from working out with weights.

Bethany tried not to be afraid of Moe. Deep down, she knew that he would never hurt her, after all. He was just so big and boisterous, and when he tried to lick Bethany's face in greeting, she couldn't help but notice that his teeth were long and sharp, just like those of the dog that had nearly eaten her.

Joe sighed and passed a hand over his eyes. *Memories*. He had tried to kiss Mari hello when he saw her that night, never dreaming she might feel afraid of him. She'd pushed against his chest and averted her face. *What's wrong*? he'd asked her. *Aren't you glad to see me*? She had never answered, and before he could pursue the matter, she'd handed him the ring. From that moment on, he'd been blind to everything but his own pain.

Joe forced himself to keep reading. When Bethany's fear of dogs didn't go away, her father found Moe a good home with another family. Moe was miserable with his new owners, and despite her fear of dogs, Bethany missed Moe dreadfully. She never played with the neighbor boy anymore because Moe was no longer there to defend her. She never went for walks because she was afraid the vicious dog might leap out at her from the bushes. She needed Moe to make her feel safe again, but she was afraid to ask her father to bring the dog back.

Moe eventually ran away from his new home, and one afternoon he magically appeared at Bethany's front door, scratching to come inside. Badly frightened when she saw the dog, Bethany ran and hid in her bedroom. Moe's feelings were badly hurt when Bethany ran away from him, but he loved her too much to let that discourage him. He hooked the screen door open with his nose and let himself in the house. Then, using the big, sharp teeth that Bethany so greatly feared, he turned the knob on her bedroom door. Once inside the bedroom, Moe lay between her and the closet.

Bethany realized then how foolish she had been. Even now, when she was treating him so badly, Moe was trying to make her feel safe. She jumped off the bed, threw her arms around Moe's neck, and started to cry, saying how sorry she was for sending him away. It wasn't Moe's fault that she'd walked a different way that awful morning, and just because she'd been chased by one bad dog, that didn't mean all other dogs were bad as well, especially not Moe, who loved her so much.

Moe understood and wasn't angry with Bethany. He was her best friend in the whole world, after all, and best friends understood when no one else could. As Moe had always done when Bethany grew sad, he just licked her face and made her smile again.

After reading the ending, Joe closed the book and angled an arm over his eyes. *Ah, Mari.* There was nothing he wanted more than to make her smile again.

Just like Moe, he had magically appeared on her porch one afternoon and followed her right into the house. The world beyond these walls was her closet, filled with very real monsters, and he'd been doing his damnedest to make her feel safe ever since.

Setting the book aside, Joe reached over to turn out the light. As darkness enfolded him, he smiled. He wasn't lying on her bedroom floor, but he was only two doors up the hall, which was as close as he could manage for the moment. No monsters, real or imagined, would get within a hundred yards of her, that was for sure, and in thirty days, the vicious dog three blocks over would be leaving town.

For never having read that story until tonight, he'd done a damned good job of living up to her expectations, he decided. Now it was only a matter of time and waiting her out. She was almost there now. He saw it in her eyes every time she looked at him. It wouldn't be long before the last obstacles between them fell away. A few days. Maybe as much as a few weeks. It didn't really matter.

His forever girl was worth waiting for.

Fourteen

You're still worth waiting for. For Marilee, those words became a litany, a phrase she whispered to reassure herself when she felt unsettled—which, around Joe, seemed to be most of the time. He was so exasperatingly *male*. Even the simple act of taking an evening walk drove home to her the contrasts between them.

To Marilee, a stroll along the banks of Laurel Creek as the sun set was an opportunity to admire nature. It was well into September, and the hillsides were resplendent with the first vibrant shades of autumn, oranges and yellows providing brilliant splashes of color against the backdrop of forest green. She loved the crisp edge in the evening air that heralded the approach of winter. Visions of jack-o'-lanterns, Thanksgiving turkeys, and Christmas lights filled her mind. As she watched Zachary romp with Boo along the edge of the stream, she imagined how much fun it would be to decorate the house this year and how the little boy's eyes would sparkle with excitement.

On one such excursion, Marilee gazed reverently at

their surroundings and said, "Oh, Joe, isn't this the most beautiful sight you've ever seen?"

"Yes," he agreed. "Absolutely the most beautiful, barring none."

Something in his tone made her look at him. Instead of admiring the hillside, he was gazing directly at her with a speculative and mischievous twinkle in his eyes.

"*Joe!*" she said, thoroughly exasperated. "You aren't even looking."

"Oh, I'm looking, all right, and I love what I see," was his reply.

Marilee began to fidget then, afraid that a button on her blouse might be unfastened or that her jeans had come unzipped. As she made anxious forays over her clothing with her hands, Joe chuckled.

"What are you doing?"

"Making sure I'm still put together."

At that, he winked and said, "Trust me, you're put together as nicely as any woman I've ever seen."

And so it went, his teasing repartee keeping her flustered and off balance for the remainder of the walk.

"You're doing this to me on purpose," she accused one evening.

"Uh-huh," was his response, his gaze warm on hers and his mouth tipped in a slight smile. "Remember what I told you. When you're ready, just holler, and I'll take it from there."

"Why do I have this feeling you aren't talking about roasting his-and-her marshmallows on the same stick?"

He gave a rumbling laugh. When his mirth subsided, he said, "Because you're an intelligent lady who knows when she's being hit on?"

"Like you're subtle and I need to be particularly astute?" When he only laughed again, Marilee playfully punched his arm. "You're making me very nervous."

He looped an arm over her shoulders and drew her close to his side. "You shouldn't feel nervous. I'm your best friend in the whole world, remember?"

For some reason, those words and his tone of voice struck a chord, but before she could pursue the thought, he bent to nibble lightly on her ear. Goose bumps popped up all over her with the first graze of his teeth. She glanced anxiously around, half wishing they were closer to the park where there were other people. *Silliness.* If he were going to try something, he had plenty of opportunity at home. He wouldn't wait until they were walking along Laurel Creek, especially not with his son playing nearby.

His voice was a low rumble that coursed clear through her when he whispered, "Forever is worth waiting for. Don't feel nervous. All right?"

Despite his reassurance, Marilee knew his patience with her was wearing thin, and she couldn't really blame him for that. What was wrong with her? He was drop-dead gorgeous. He was sweet and wonderful. On top of all that, he really was her best friend in the whole world, and she loved him so much she ached. All he wanted was what millions of other men took for granted, what millions of other women freely gave. Why couldn't she be what he needed her to be?

At her next weekly session with Doctor Patterson, Marilee complained bitterly about the constant tension she was under. "He never lets up now. No matter what we're doing, there are undercurrents. He lets me know in a hundred different ways that he's thinking about it. Honestly, Joan, don't men ever think about anything *else*?"

Joan smiled and leaned back in her chair to prop her feet on her desk. "Studies indicate not."

Marilee found that revelation startling. "Oh, God. *Never*?"

"Most men say they think about sex throughout the day, even if they're concentrating on something else."

"That must make life slightly complicated."

"They seem to handle it all right. Undoubtedly something to do with right brain versus left brain." Patterson shrugged. "Men are sexual creatures. It doesn't sound to me as if you've reason to be alarmed. Joe is obviously willing to wait. He's just letting you know he's eager and that the waiting isn't easy, that's all."

"Oh, Joan. What am I going to do? I love him. Honestly I do. But I'm nowhere near ready for an intimate relationship yet. And I don't know when I will be."

Joan smiled again. "I'm asking *you*, Marilee. What is it you feel must happen before you're ready? What is it you require Joe to do before you'll be ready?"

"I'm not sure."

She glanced at her watch. "Think about it. Perhaps you'll come up with some answers. We'll resume this discussion next week."

One evening Joe came in from football practice shortly after Marilee got home from a counseling session. "You look exhausted," she told him. "What's wrong?"

Still dressed in his school-issue gray sweats and T-shirt, he sauntered across the kitchen, gathered her into his arms, and buried his face in her hair. "Just a rough day," he said tiredly. "How's the story in progress going?"

"Good. I worked about three hours today, and I got quite a lot accomplished." Sensing that he needed a hug, Marilee looped her arms around his waist. "Care to talk about it?"

"Friday night's an important game. We're going to lose our asses, and when we do, the school board will not be pleased. Bedford has already beat this team we'll be playing. If we lose, the handwriting is on the wall that we'll lose when we play Bedford. I'm worried about losing my job."

"You've had a fairly good season. Not a phenomenal one, but a great improvement over last year. Does this one game really matter that much?"

"I haven't performed a miracle. I'm Joe Lakota, remember? They expect me to work one."

"That's absurd."

"Tell it to the board. They want a win Friday night." He sighed. "Ah, Mari. I tore into a kid today. Blasted him. Lost my temper, cussed, threw a helmet clear across the locker room. I'm just sick about it. I swore I'd never act that way, and now here I am, letting the pressure get to me."

She ran her hands up his back and felt the knotted muscles along his spine. "You're so tense."

"My frustration level is clear off the chart. Nothing's going right."

Especially not at home, she thought guiltily. "Oh, Joe."

"What if I lose this job? What the hell will we do?"

She tightened her arms around him. "You aren't going to lose this job. But if you do, so what? You *are* Joe Lakota. Don't forget that. You can always get another job. Even a better job." She snapped her fingers. "Just like that, I'll bet."

"Not in Laurel Creek."

"Then we'll move."

He lifted his head to look down at her. "You'd do that?"

Marilee's heart broke a little, for she could see in his eyes that he truly doubted she would relocate to be with him. "Of course I'd do that."

"What about your house? That's why we have mine on the market to sell instead of this one, because you love it here so much."

She would hate to leave her house. It had been her haven for so long, and the very thought of living somewhere else unsettled her. "I'd adjust."

"I don't want to turn your whole life upside down."

He already had. She smiled up at him. "You know what I think?"

"No, what?"

"I think you've lost touch with all the things you love about football. It isn't all about winning. Is it?"

His mouth twitched. "No, ma'am."

"Is that the message you want to send to those kids?"

"No, ma'am."

"What do you want to teach them?"

"How to be part of a team. To take pride in being the best they can be. To give all they've got and enjoy the game, win or lose."

She nodded. "Go call that boy you yelled at and apologize. While you're doing that, I'll make some sandwiches, and we'll go to the park for a picnic. We can romp on the grass with Zachary. You can stretch out on a blanket and cloud watch. It'll help you to unwind. How's that sound?"

"Better than you can imagine, but no sandwiches. I'll spring for a bucket of chicken."

Zachary came bounding into the kitchen just then. "Yum, chicken!" he piped in excitedly.

Joe scooped his son up for a bear hug. "You up for a picnic at the park, tyke?"

"Yeah! Can I catch salamanders in the creek, Daddy?"

Joe glanced at Marilee. "You think it's too cold out for that?"

She glanced through the French doors at the Indian summer evening. When she looked back at Zachary, she winked. "Not if you take a change of clothes."

"I'll go get some!" Zachary squirmed to get down and then raced off to his bedroom. In less than a minute, he returned to the kitchen, his arms laden with clothing. "Can Boo go, too, Daddy?"

Joe sighed and nodded. To Marilee, he whispered, "Make that *two* buckets of chicken. Damn dog eats like a horse."

Thirty minutes later, Joe and Marilee were walking hand-in-hand along the bank of Laurel Creek while Zachary and Boo played in the water. It was an absolutely perfect evening, the sunset streaking the sky over the mountains with incredible shades of coral.

"This is such a beautiful spot," she said dreamily.

"Yeah, incredibly beautiful. So beautiful I sure as hell don't want to leave."

Marilee glanced up to find his gaze fixed on the horizon. "Are you still worrying about the job?"

"Yeah, I guess I am."

"Let's not borrow trouble."

"If it were only me and Zachary, it wouldn't be as bad. He's better now, and there are dozens of small towns in Oregon, most of them plenty close to come see Mom. I'm sure I could get another coaching job at a school a bit less focused on winning and more focused on the sport itself. I just don't want to upset your life any more than I already have. You know?"

"I'm going to be okay, Joe."

He nodded. "That house is your comfort zone, though. A little world you've carefully created, and it's the only place you really feel safe, even now."

"My bubble?"

His Adam's apple bobbed as he swallowed. "I'm not taking shots, Mari. It's just—hell, I don't know. When did I first show up at your place, sometime in July? In a little over two months, I've commandeered your life. We haven't even gotten the wrinkles ironed out of our marriage yet. It'd be a hell of a note to have to relocate, on top of it all."

She thought of her house, with the carefully selected wallpaper and treasured knickknacks, her paintings and photographs decorating every available spot. Perhaps it was her comfort zone, as he called it. But it had also been very empty and lonely until he and Zachary had come along.

"I make fairly good money," she reminded him. "If you should lose this job, I can keep us afloat until you find another one. If that means moving, then we'll simply take it one step at a time." She met his gaze. "Together."

"Ah, Mari."

"I mean it," she insisted. "Stop worrying about the stupid job. Where you go, I go, and I'm going to be all right with that. Don't coach by their rules, Joe. You love football, and it's never been solely about winning for you. Winning's wonderful, and it's great fun, but that's not what you feel passionate about. If you betray yourself and the game you love for this stupid, two-bit job, you'll be miserable. Tomorrow when you step out on the field, tell the board members to go screw themselves, and coach your team *your* way."

He scratched beside his nose and bent his head. The wind whipped his dark hair, and when he looked back up, lazy tendrils of sable lay over his high forehead. "Those boys are playing their hearts out for me. You wouldn't believe how they've improved since the start of the season."

"Tell them that."

He smiled slightly. "I will." He reached out to touch her cheek, his eyes dancing with amusement. "I can't believe you just told me to tell the board members to go screw themselves. You've been hanging out with me for too long."

Not nearly long enough. She was shooting for a lifetime.

Zachary happened upon a pool filled with salamanders just then. He squealed with delight, his cries interspersed with Boo's excited baying.

"Don't you have crawdads in that can?" Joe called.

"Yup."

"Make a choice!" Joe yelled back. "Salamanders or crawdads. You can't put them together."

"How come?"

"The crawdads may hurt the salamanders."

Zachary reached into his can to pluck out a crawdad, and then jerked his hand back. "Ouch!"

Joe chuckled. "See? They're mean little buggers."

Smiling, Marilee went to sit on a grassy rise overlooking the stream. After a moment, Joe joined her. Once settled on the ground, he curled an arm over her shoulders. They watched Zachary wade to shore, where he emptied his can at the water's edge. Boo barked and chased after a crawdad that spilled out. An instant later, the dog succeeded in catching the crustacean, which earned him a pinch on the nose. He yelped and hightailed it up to Joe and Marilee, who both ducked their heads and cried, "Go away, Boo!"

The cowardly hound was having none of that. He made a beeline for Marilee, his protector. Upon reaching her, he shook himself, covering both humans with creek water and specks of mud. Joe swore under his breath. "Tell me again why you rescued him from death row?"

Marilee giggled. "Because he's irresistibly handsome?"

Joe studied the hound's homely face. After a long moment, he said, "There may be hope for me yet."

Hope for him? Marilee had already lost the war and just couldn't think of a way to tell him. *Holler when you're ready, and I'll take it from there*, he'd told her. Only he'd failed to mention what she was supposed to holler.

He cupped her chin in a big hand and gently wiped flecks of mud from her face, his hard fingertips feathering so lightly over her skin that her toes curled. His gaze held hers for a moment, then he flashed one of those crooked grins that always turned her legs watery and made her wonder how it would be when he finally kissed her again.

"How did I ever get so lucky. You're the most beautiful thing I've ever clapped eyes on, even with hound spray all over you."

She giggled. He settled his arm around her again. They resumed watching Zachary as he splashed through the water, catching salamanders and putting the slippery creatures into the coffee can.

Joe said nothing more. But then he didn't need to. His hand on her arm said it all. He traced light circles on her sleeve, his fingertips setting her skin afire even through the cotton. Marilee closed her eyes, mesmerized by the caresses. When he moved down and began to torture the sensitive skin at the bend of her arm, she tried to imagine how it might feel if he touched her that way all over. Goose bumps, everywhere, no doubt. *Oh, yeah.*

"Joe?"

"Hmm?"

For the first time since the Paxil had begun to take effect, Marilee felt as if her windpipe was starting to close off. "I think maybe I'm ready," she said faintly.

Never taking his gaze off his son, he nodded. "Yeah, me, too." In a louder voice, he called, "Hey, Zachary. Time to get out and change into dry pants. Marilee and I are ready to eat."

Marilee cast him a startled look, convinced he had to be teasing her. He wasn't. He honestly didn't realize what she had just tried to tell him.

"Aw, Daddy!"

"Aw, Zachary," Joe mimicked. "No whining. It'll be dark soon. We need to get back to the park and eat our dinner."

The following Wednesday evening, Marilee was gone when Joe got home, which struck him as being unusual. Most times when he dragged in after practice, he found her in the kitchen, busily preparing dinner. Tonight the only evidence that she planned to cook was a package of ground beef she'd set out to thaw beside the sink. After looking for a note and finding none, Joe remembered that she'd had an appointment with Patterson this afternoon. Probably shopping, he decided. Sometimes she stopped to get groceries in Bedford on the way home.

He grabbed a quick shower, threw on a pair of chinos and a cotton shirt, and then headed back to the kitchen, determined to surprise her by having their evening meal well on its way to completion before she came in. After staring at the meat for several seconds, he decided to err on the side of simplicity. Hamburger patties, baked potatoes, and a green salad would do for dinner. Even a kitchen klutz could manage a meal like that without mishap.

Twenty minutes later when Marilee entered through the French doors, the kitchen smelled of charred ground beef and Joe had to wave a hand in front of his face to see her clearly through the smoke. "Damn, Mari, I'm sorry. I only turned away for a minute to wash some lettuce. First thing I knew, the patties were burned."

Pale and big-eyed, she closed the door behind her, then stepped to the table to set down her purse and two sacks, one small and brown, the other large, off-white and bearing the name of a local department store.

Concerned by the look on her face, Joe said, "Honey, is something wrong?"

"No, nothing."

Joe glanced at the door, saw no sign of his son on the deck, and asked, "Where's Zachary?"

"He's staying the night with your mom. Mrs. Rasmussen's there to help with dinner, and afterward they're going to play board games." She flashed a tense smile. "You and I have the house to ourselves tonight."

"Would you like to go out for dinner?"

She shook her head. "Nah. Let's just have something here."

"I cremated the beef. Any other ideas?"

"Something quick and simple." With trembling hands, she opened the small brown sack and drew out two items, which she set in plain view on the table. "I was, um . . . thinking we could just skip making a big meal tonight and—well, you know—be creative." Her cheeks went crimson. "Dr. Patterson thought I might get your attention with these."

Joe's gaze became riveted to the can of fat-free whipped cream and the small jar of maraschino cherries sitting beside it. For several endless seconds, he could scarcely think, let alone speak.

"Joe?" she said nervously. When he didn't answer, she

quickly added, "Aren't you going to say something?"

He swallowed in an attempt to regain his voice. Then he jerked his gaze from the can to her big blue eyes, in which he read a host of emotions, the most glaringly obvious sheer fright. He swallowed again and finally managed to croak, "Yeah, do you know CPR?"

She gave a startled laugh and then stifled the sound by biting her bottom lip. "I, um, guess I've taken you by surprise."

"Oh, yeah. I'm surprised, all right." Joe took a step toward her. "May I ask what brought this on?"

She averted her gaze and started fiddling with her purse strap. "I think maybe I'm ready, is all. Dr. Patterson says I am."

Joe advanced another step. "Ah, I see." He waited a beat. "And what does Marilee say? Or are you allowed a vote?"

"Oh, of course."

"Of course, what?"

"I have a vote." She drew what appeared to be lacy white lingerie from the department store sack. "I almost got red—or black. Finally, though, I settled on white. The siren look isn't really me, I don't think." She held the creation up. "Do you like it?"

He could count the buttons of her blouse through both layers of nylon, and for a moment, he thought he really might have a coronary. He didn't tell her that, though. "It's—nice. Really nice." He was so stunned, he couldn't think of anything else to say.

Crumpling the gown in her hands, she dropped her arms and sighed. "I'm blowing this, aren't I? It's not the one-hundred-yard dash. On your mark, get set. I had it all worked out. How it would go. What I'd say, and what you would say, and—oh, *Joe!* Why can't I be like other women? This isn't romantic at all, is it?"

"What am I supposed to say, honey? Tell me, and I'll say it."

"Never mind. This was a bad idea."

He wanted to grab her and the whipped cream and make tracks for the nearest bedroom. "It's not a bad idea."

"Yes, it is. I should have just waited."

"For what?"

"For you to—well, you know."

No, he didn't know.

"Only you *haven't*!" she cried, her tone laced with frustration. "Not that I'm blaming you or anything. I know you've only held off out of regard for me. It's just—well, I tried to tell you. Down at the park. So you'd take the initiative. Only you thought I wanted to eat."

Joe vaguely recollected the moment. "You were ready *then*?"

"Iffy, but willing to try."

"And now?"

"Still iffy. But we can't go on like *this* forever. You're making my skin turn inside out."

"I am?"

"You know very well you are. All those touchy-feelies. You do it on purpose."

"It worked?"

She narrowed her eyes.

That was all the answer Joe needed. He moved toward her. She tossed the negligee on the table. "I can't really wear it yet. It was just a white flag of sorts."

And a sweet surrender, it was. If she wore nothing at all, he'd be a happy man.

"Same for the whipped cream," she quickly added.

She was so sweet, he could pass on the topping as well. Joe got close enough to grasp her by the arms. At his touch, she leaped, and her wary gaze became fixed on his. "Mari, relax. It's not the hundred-yard dash, remember? I'm tickled pink that you've reached this decision. Honestly. But making love isn't something you do when the whistle blows. You wait for the right moment."

"If you wait for my right moment, we're in trouble.

And to be truthful, rather than drag out the torture, I prefer to just get it over with."

He smiled. He couldn't help himself. Get it over with? "You're not about to undergo major surgery without anesthetic."

"That's good to know. Do we have any wine?"

He chuckled and drew her toward him. "Oh, no, you don't. I learned my lesson on that one. And I'm not about to rush into this. How about if we grab some cheese and crackers, go to bed, and talk while we eat. If you're still this nervous afterward, we'll pass on having sex until later when it feels right."

"Cheese and crackers in bed? Won't that be messy?"

"Nah, not that messy." He imagined licking crumbs from her navel.

"Joe?" She pressed a staying hand against his chest and gulped, the sound a hollow *plunk* at the base of her throat. "Just for the record. I'm not quite ready for downhill with no brakes. All right?"

Joe wasn't sure if she was ready for downhill in low gear. "Sweetheart, just trust me, all right?"

Fifteen

As Joe laid out munchies on a platter to take to the bedroom, he kept rubbing his hands together and whistling. Marilee didn't think his enthusiasm was inspired by the Ritz crackers.

Oh, God. She nearly dropped the jar of pickles as she pulled it from the fridge. Then, as she began to slice dills, her hands shook so badly, Joe relieved her of the knife. "You're going to cut yourself." He quartered a pickle and tossed the pieces on the platter. "No injuries allowed." He winked at her. "Nothing—and I do mean *nothing*—is going to screw this up."

In other words, she was going to jump off the high dive whether she lost her courage or not.

Once in his bedroom, Marilee stood uneasily at the side of the bed. Joe cleared a spot on the nightstand for the platter. Then he poured them each a goblet of burgundy. That done, he unbuttoned his shirt and peeled it off. Marilee stared, wondering if all men had such defined abdominal and pectoral muscles. He even had muscles that rippled in the small of his back.

"What?" he asked softly, his dark eyes questioning her.

"Um . . . *nothing.*"

"You gonna lose the shoes and jeans?"

She hoped to heaven not. "Actually, Joe, I feel a little funny. I'm usually fully clothed when I do the cheese-and-cracker thing."

His teeth gleamed in a slow grin. "It's not the cheese-and-cracker thing that you're worried about." He held his hands out to his sides. "Think of it this way. If I keep my pants on and you keep your blouse on, together we'll make one fully clothed individual."

"Enough clothes for one of us, thank God there's only two of us?"

He chuckled and scratched his head. Then he shifted his weight onto one leg and settled his hands on his hips, the stance so thoroughly masculine that she nearly ran screaming from the room. "Mari, you know what I think the problem is here? This isn't coming naturally for you."

"That's an understatement."

He laughed again. "What I mean is, you're making a huge thing out of this."

Her gaze dropped. She didn't mean to look there. It was more like his male anatomy had magnetic properties and her eyes were metal shavings. One look was all it took to convince her that she was *not* exaggerating the dimensions of this, and the countdown had begun.

"Don't," he whispered.

"Don't what?"

"Don't stare at me there." He shifted his weight again, apparently to minimize the prominence of that part of himself, only it didn't work. Then he sighed and rubbed his jaw. "Mari, would you stop? I can't control him, you know?"

"Him, who?"

He winked at her. "John Henry. And no smart cracks. Practically all guys name them."

"*Why?*"

"Because—holy hell." He pinched the bridge of his

nose and bent his head for a moment. "I can't believe we're having this conversation. If you had somebody who hung around all the time, wouldn't you name him? I don't know *why*, all right? I just named him, that's all. Don't you have a name for your—"

"*No!*" She sniffed and averted her gaze to stare at the wine. "I need a drink."

"You don't need a drink. A few sips is all, and I'm counting them."

"Please, Joe, don't tell me what I need."

He ran a hand over his belly and sank onto the mattress, turning as he sat to brace his back against the footboard. Bending one leg, he rested a bare foot on the bed, the position concealing John Henry from her view.

"You know, honey, I'm in this shape ninety-nine percent of the time I'm with you. You walk across the room . . . or you smile at me . . . or I look into those beautiful blue eyes, and I'm a goner."

"The way I *smile*?"

"Other things, too." He patted the bed. "Kick your shoes off and sit down. You at that end, me here. Let's just talk."

She toed the heel of each sneaker. In her stocking feet, she sat gingerly on the mattress with her back against the sleigh headboard. Hugging her knees, she gazed solemnly at him. "What'll we talk about?"

"Hell, I don't know. Let's play question and answer. You go first. Anything about me you're dying to know?" He leaned forward to grab the platter off the nightstand and set it on the bedspread between them. Before sitting back, he popped a slice of cheese and a cracker in his mouth. "Ask away."

"How'd you ever come up with the name John Henry?"

He narrowed an eye at her, pocketed the half-munched cracker in his cheek, and said, "Can we leave John Henry out of this?"

"I could go for that."

His eye narrowed even more. He chewed for a moment. "Point made. Okay. You really want to know? The term 'John Henry' is synonymous with a person's signature. When I was a kid and it snowed, I used to sneak out behind our backyard hedge and write my name."

"On what?"

"The snow."

"With John Henry? That must have been a chilling experience."

He snorted and almost choked. When he'd finally worked the cracker down the right pipe, he smiled and shook his head. "The intrinsic differences between boys and girls are amazing. A guy would know exactly what I mean because he would have done it when he was a kid. I *peed* in the snow, Mari. Boys do things like that."

"They do? *Why?*"

He grabbed another piece of cheese. "I have no idea. It's just a thing boys do. At ten, it was of primary importance to me to be able to piss farther than Bobby Miller. Every time we played together, we sneaked off to have a contest." A flush crept up his neck. "You did ask. That's how I came up with the name John Henry, writing my name in the snow."

"Poor Zachary."

He raised an eyebrow. "Why 'poor Zachary'?"

"That's a lot of letters. He'll never be able to get his name written in the snow, and he'll grow to manhood with a complex."

Joe chuckled. "He can shorten it to Zach, and when I catch the little stinker doing it, I'll be sure to tell him I'm impressed. That's one more letter than I had to write."

She giggled and reached for a cracker herself. "Your turn to ask a question."

He thought for a moment. When he finally met her gaze, his eyes had gone serious and questioning. "Why do you love me?"

Marilee's heart caught. She thought about her answer

before she finally said, "Because you never peed on the snow in front of me."

"No, seriously."

"That was a serious answer." She gazed at her tooth prints on the cracker. "There was always a side to you that was rough-and-tumble. You had a wild streak. You drove too fast. You drank before you were of age. I know you had a filthy mouth because sometimes you slipped and cussed in front of me. Half the time you were in some kind of Dutch. But around me, you were always a gentleman. When I was in the car, you never drove crazy, and when I was with you, you never drank, and you never took me anyplace where other kids were drinking."

"I was a master at deception, so you fell in love with me?"

Marilee smiled. "You protected me. *Always.* You made me feel so special. And you weren't deceptive. I knew you were rowdy, and you never tried to hide anything you did when you weren't with me. You just followed a different set of rules when we were together." She set the cracker back on the plate and hugged her knees. "You roasted me a marshmallow instead of pressing me to have sex. At the time, I didn't appreciate that particular sacrifice, but I do now, and that's exactly the sort of thing that made me love you. It's the reason I still love you." A burning sensation washed over her eyes. "You're eating crackers and cheese right now, and I know you'd much rather be doing something else."

He smiled and returned his food to the platter as well. "I guess maybe I need to clean my mouth back up. I swear quite a lot these days."

"I'll take you the way you are. I'm the one who needs to work on things." She hugged her legs more tightly. "I'm sorry I'm being so difficult. I don't mean to be. It's just—" She broke off and searched for words. "I'm mostly okay with everything. You know? And on an intellectual level, I know there's nothing to feel afraid of. Only deep down there's a part of me that can't forget how very painful it was. It wasn't over quickly. The hurting was terrible, and it seemed to me then that it'd never stop. I can't get that out of my head."

He put the food back on the nightstand and came to sit beside her. Looping an arm around her back, he straightened his legs and whispered, "Come here."

Marilee no sooner got settled on his lap than she flashed him a startled look. "You're fine," he assured her.

"You're sure?"

He winked at her. Then he slumped back against the wood, drawing her with him. His hardness throbbed against the back of her leg like a heated length of metal pipe. "When the time comes, I'll never cause you any pain," he whispered, rubbing his chin on the top of her head. "If you experience any discomfort, period, just tell me, and I'll stop. I give you my word on that."

"I know that, Joe. Honestly, I do. I'm just nervous."

"Well, stop feeling nervous. We're not going to do anything for you to be nervous about. Not now. When it feels right, Mari, and not before. It has to come naturally. You can't just decide to do it and start. Later when it's old hat, yeah. People get a few minutes of privacy without their kids, and they decide to make love. But that doesn't work for a woman the first few times, when she's self-conscious. Just taking off her clothes is a major big deal. I need to set the right mood and make you feel mindless before we reach that point."

"Mindless?"

He smiled and kissed her forehead. "It'll happen, and when it does, the intimacy isn't uncomfortable. You won't feel embarrassed. You just sort of float into it, and everything feels perfectly right."

"Oh, I hope so."

"I know so." He squeezed her shoulder. "Now—forgive me for saying this—but if we don't eat, my belly's going to start growling."

"I imagine you are starving. I am, too, actually."

"Off with the jeans. I promise not to touch, but at least let me enjoy looking."

To Marilee's relief, he didn't watch when she stood beside the bed to slip out of her pants. Before she returned to sit beside him, he lifted his hips to shove the bedcovers down. When she had joined him again, he drew the sheet up over their legs.

"You can't see much with the covers over my legs."

He grinned and shoved a piece of cheese in her mouth. "I'll sneak peeks. Eat, lady. I don't want those gorgeous knees to lose their dimples."

"My knees aren't dimpled."

"Wanna bet? Cutest little dimples I've ever seen."

He balanced the platter on their laps and handed her a goblet. They ate their makeshift meal, the crunching noises as they chewed all that broke the silence between them. When their hunger was finally satisfied, they lay propped against the pillows, his shoulder providing a cradle for her head. They talked then, about whatever came to mind, their voices pitched barely above a whisper, their eyes growing heavy from the wine as dusk finally descended outside and darkened the window glass.

When drowsiness drew them into slumber, they slipped into the blackness wrapped in each other's arms.

Marilee woke up shortly after midnight, her senses reeling, but not from sleep. Her back tingled. Her neck tingled. And there was a big, warm hand busily at work, making her hip tingle. She blinked and stared into the shadows, disoriented, yet feeling deliciously languid. *Joe.* The hand was his. She would have recognized his touch anywhere. Big, slightly callous fingers. A hard palm that moved over her skin like the underside of silk, lightly rubbing her the wrong way.

She rolled onto her back, wedging her shoulder against his chest. "Joe?"

In the moonlight that spilled through the lace curtains

at the window, his features were limned with silver, his firm mouth tipping slowly into a grin as he smoothed her hair back from her face and then suspended himself above her.

"Hi, Mari mine."

She returned his smile and blinked sleepily. "What're you doing?" she asked, even as his fingertips trailed over her bare thigh, setting her skin afire.

"Nothing."

It didn't feel like nothing. If felt—*right*. No anticipation. No nervousness. To simply awaken in his arms, already tingling from his touch, was divine. He'd been making love to her while she slept, she realized. Tantalizing her nerve-endings. Making her want. *Clever.* She arched, loving the feel of his hand on her leg. *Sneaky.* He'd slipped past her guard, arousing her on the sly. *Oh, God.* His fingertips traced a delicious, electrical path upward to follow the ridge of elastic that dove between her thighs. The slight brush of his knuckles over that most sensitive place nearly robbed her of breath.

"Joe?"

"I'm right here." He bent his dark head to nibble her throat. She let her head fall back to accommodate him, feeling safe because she still wore her blouse and underwear. Even as she thought that, he slipped a button free and trailed his lips lower. "And right here," he whispered against her sensitized skin. Another button bit the dust. "And right *here*," he murmured as he opened her blouse, his lips following in the wake of parting cotton.

When he slipped a finger under the front elastic of her bra, she stiffened and made tight fists in his hair. "Joe?"

"Yes, and don't forget it. Just keep saying my name. It's me. No one else."

She flinched when he tugged the cup of her bra down and coaxed her breast from the shield of stretchy lace. The cloth retracted when he released it, the gentle squeeze of elasticity holding her softness high and proud.

Cool air washed over her bared nipple, hardening the tip and making the aureole pebble.

He leaned back and gazed at it. "Ah, Mari. It's just like I imagined—as soft and pink as a rosebud."

She cupped a hand over the spot, embarrassed to have him not only look but make comment. He chuckled and tugged the other bra cup down. "You can have that one. I'll take this one."

He dipped his dark head and touched the throbbing peak with the tip of his tongue to lave it with wetness. Then he blew softly, the waft of his breath shivering over her flesh and making it harden. She gasped. He caught the distended nub between his teeth and gently tugged. A whine of shock caught in her throat. Then his warm, silken mouth closed over her. She sobbed, paralyzed by the sensations that ribboned from her breast to her belly.

"Oh, Mari," he whispered against her, even the movement of his lips a seduction. "You're so sweet. I've waited a lifetime for this."

Her sobs turned to moans as her flesh hardened and peaked, straining toward his silky lips, begging for *more*. He flicked the tip of her with his tongue again.

"Give yourself to me," he urged in a throbbing whisper. "*Please*." He flicked her again, teasing her sensitive flesh into a throbbing erection that protruded defenselessly toward him. "Say it."

Marilee arched up as if she were attached to him by an invisible thread. She couldn't think, let alone say what he needed to hear. "Oh, Joe . . . oh, Joe . . . oh, Joe . . ."

He grazed her with his teeth—lightly, torturously. "*Say* it. 'I'm yours, Joe.' I need to hear you say it."

"I'm *yours*," she whispered. "I've always been yours. *Always*."

His mouth closed over her then, drawing so sharply, he emptied her lungs of breath. She cried out, her spine arching as he loved her there with masterful expertise, his lips, teeth, and tongue staking irrevocable claim. He teased her with drags of his tongue until her entire body jerked with each pass. Then he suddenly drew back, his big hands dispatching her blouse, bra, and panties with such speed that Marilee barely realized what he was about. She was completely nude when he leaned over her again, his teeth gleaming in the shadows as his dark face creased in a grin.

"You okay?"

Marilee wasn't quite sure if "okay" described how she felt. But before she could articulate the thought, he bent his head and suckled her other nipple, which had never endured such delicious torture and didn't know quite what to think. Not that it had thinking capabilities. It was just that it *seemed* to be the center of her being at the moment That undoubtedly explained why she so easily deferred to Joe, who seemed to know what he was doing, at least. Try as she might, she couldn't quite recall her name.

He continued the delicious assault, moving from her breasts to her belly, then back up again, his mouth vanquishing every nerve-ending in its path, until she was little more than a puddle of throbbing flesh, goose bumps, and murmurs lying sprawled beneath him.

"How you doing?"

She had been hoping he might know. She struggled to draw in a complete breath and clear her head enough to reply. She'd almost found her voice. Almost. And then he tickled her navel with the tip of his tongue.

"Oh . . . Joe, stop!" she cried. "I can't *think*."

"That's good," he assured her huskily. "I *love* your mind, Mari. I swear to God, I do. But don't bring it to the bedroom."

He circled her navel with little flicks of his tongue again, the result a mindless dizziness that convinced her she no longer had a mind to worry about.

"Mari, don't be afraid. I'm going to kiss you here now. Is that all right?"

It sort of tickled and made her bellybutton feel as if it was fastened to her backbone, but she liked it. Amazing.

She'd never realized until now how very sensitive her navel could be. "Yes, all right."

He sighed and bent his head.

He missed her bellybutton completely.

Marilee's shoulders came clear up off the mattress. He was—oh, angels and saints! She'd heard of this practice. She was twenty-eight years old, after all. But she'd never believed *normal* people engaged in such activities. Then again, maybe Joe wasn't average. He'd always been a mischievous rascal, thumbing his nose at the rules, stepping over the line.

She braced her weight on one elbow and grabbed a fistful of his hair, fully intending to put a stop to this. Only his mouth had already closed over her, and the teasing passes of his tongue on that most sensitive place turned the one arm that supported her weight to the consistency of an overcooked noodle.

She collapsed, flat on her back, and stared in startled amazement at the ceiling, some distant part of her brain appalled. A very *distant* part of her brain. That part of her wanted to be shocked. Scandalized. Offended. The rest of her just wanted to melt in his mouth and cease to care. *Oh*. This was so . . . *Joe*. It was—she had to—*oh, dear God*—what was he *doing* to her?

He drew hard on her then. The man had the suction power of a Hoover vacuum. She had a hysterical urge to giggle. Then every thought in her head was sucked out. Her hips lifted as if of their own volition. Her other fist knotted over his hair to pull him closer. She needn't have issued the invitation. He was right there—as close as a man could get, taking possession in a way that left no part of her inviolate.

And she surrendered, allowing him to take, to give her pleasure. It was beyond her imagination, the sensation building and building, her body's need increasing to a frantic urgency.

"Joe, please! *Please!*" she cried, not even sure what it was she wanted.

He knew, and he gave it to her, increasing pressure and tempo, until release crashed over her in shuddering waves.

Afterward, he rose over her, his eyes glittering in the shadows as he unfastened his trousers. Marilee knew an instant of terror, for this was what she had always feared, the brutal thrust and invasive torture.

"Don't be afraid of me," he whispered huskily as he moved down to her. "I'd rather die than hurt you. Don't you know that?"

She did know that. But he'd never been on the receiving end. She felt the hard, throbbing shaft of his manhood against her thigh. She couldn't help it. She felt half sick with dread, knowing he meant to put that huge thing inside of her. She could almost feel the tearing pain, and then the agony that would never end.

To her dismay, he curled her hand over him. She tried to recoil, but he kept her fingers pressed down. "You do it," he whispered. "Only as much as you can take. Keep your hand on me so I can't go in too far and hurt you."

He wanted *her* to do it? She nearly bolted, only he was above her, and she had a feeling he'd grab her by an ankle to haul her back if she tried to run.

"Go ahead. Just barely inside. See how it feels. I swear to you, Mari, it won't hurt."

He had never broken a promise to her. Knowing that gave her courage now. She directed him toward her, feeling as if she were about to plunge a sword into herself. He nudged forward with his hips. The silky head entered her.

She sobbed and stiffened, expecting pain. *Nothing.* Through the shadows, her gaze sought his. He flashed her a strained smile. "Trust me, Mari mine. Move your hand and let me take it from here."

She moved her hand, and he did. In one smooth forward thrust, he impaled her. Marilee cried out and shoved her hands against his shoulders. He froze, his eyes filled with question.

"You okay?"

Miraculously, she seemed to be. No pain. Not even any discomfort. Just a sense of fullness. He relaxed his weight onto her, the brace of one arm all that kept him from squashing her. "I love you, Mari mine," he whispered, and then proceeded to kiss her. Long, deep kisses. Marilee knew he was trying to arouse her again, that he wanted her mindless. Mindless wasn't an attainable state, not when she was so tense.

"Just finish it," she pleaded.

He sighed and levered his weight off of her, his powerfully roped arms gleaming like polished sculpture in the wash of moonlight, his well-muscled shoulders rippling as he pressed cautiously forward. She gasped at the unaccustomed sensation.

"Tell me if it hurts. I'll stop."

"No, no. I'm fine."

And she was. Wonderfully, incredibly fine. He drove gently forward again, smiling this time when she gasped. "Good?" he asked.

She could only nod.

He increased the tempo slightly, the end of each thrust making her feel bursts of sensation deep inside. Her body quickened around him, and he evidently felt the change.

"Come with me," he whispered to her.

"Where?" she asked, bewildered because she thought he meant in a physical sense.

"Seventh heaven," he whispered. "It's six flights up from regular heaven, the place where only lovers can go. Come with me?"

Her throat tightened. "Oh, Joe, I'm nervous."

"Come with me, and you won't be."

"How?"

He bent to kiss her and whispered against her lips, "Just hold onto my neck, and I'll take you."

She hugged him tight, trusting him as she'd never trusted anyone, and the instant her arms locked, he drove into her, hard and fast, holding nothing back. One thrust, two. Marilee's mind splintered. She brought up her knees, meeting him, jolted by the force with which he entered her, yet glorying in the burn.

Seventh heaven . . . she'd thought he was exaggerating. He wasn't. Six flights up from regular heaven, it was the place where only lovers could go, and Joe Lakota gave her a personal, guided tour.

Sixteen

When Dr. Joan Patterson got to the office at half past nine the next morning, her nurse greeted her with an armful of gorgeous dusky pink, long-stemmed rosebuds.

"Ohmigosh!" Joan cried as she took the flowers. "Aren't these lovely? Who on earth sent them?"

Helen smiled and shrugged. "Somebody loves you. I didn't read the card."

As Joan let herself into her inner sanctum, she inhaled the perfume of the rosebuds, sighed in appreciation, and opened the accompanying card.

> *One for every wasted year. You're worth your weight in rose petals.*
>
> *Joe Lakota*

Joan laughed softly and said, "Way to go, Marilee!"

*   *   *

Joe was already gone when Marilee woke up at ten. Dreamily she brushed her hand over the indentation on his pillow, yearning to feel his big, warm body pressed against her again. The thought made her giggle. What a switch. She couldn't *wait* until they made love again. Only how on earth would they ever manage with a four-year-old in the house?

Zachary. Marilee bolted upright and glanced at her watch. Good grief. It was already a few minutes past the hour. She had to grab a quick shower, throw on some clothes, and go get her son. *Her son.* Oh, how she loved the sound of that. She knew he was fine over at his grandmother's and probably having fun, but he must be wondering by now when Marilee would come to get him. And, too, she didn't want to overtax Faye.

Yawning and rubbing her eyes, she stumbled down the hall to the bathroom, turned on the shower, and then reached to pull off her nightclothes. Then she realized she was wearing none. A foolish grin spread across her lips. She had just streaked down her hallway naked, and she hadn't even noticed.

Hot water. She needed to stand under the spray and wake herself up. She nudged back the curtain and slipped in under the stream of water. *Ah.* She turned her face into the warmth and rubbed her eyes. Then she fumbled for the shampoo in the caddy. A second later, as she ran her fingers through her long hair, trying to work up a lather, something on her left hand caught in her soppy curls. She tugged and winced. Then she reached up to feel. A ring? Curious and already smiling because she knew Joe must have slipped the ring on her finger while she slept, she worked her hair loose from the prongs. What a sweet way to surprise her, she thought.

Squinting to see the ring, she was surprised, all right. She stared through a blur of suds at the solitaire diamond that now sparkled so beautifully next to her wedding ring. *Oh, God.* She leaned against the tile and stared, her heart catching. Not just any ring. *Her* ring. The one she'd returned to Joe ten years ago. Marilee would have recognized the marquis solitaire anywhere.

"Oh, Joe!" she cried.

The next instant, she slid down the tiled wall, plopped butt first on the bottom of the tub, and then huddled there, sobbing her heart out and choking on water that kept getting in her yawning mouth. *Her ring*. He'd kept it. All these years, he'd kept it. She couldn't believe it. He'd been married to another woman. Had a child. But he'd still kept her ring. If ever she'd doubted his love for her, this proved, beyond anything, that his heart had always belonged to her. *Always*.

Joe opened the French door, letting Zachary and Boo enter the house in front of him. As he followed the pair into the kitchen, he ruffled his son's hair and called, "Mari?"

No answer. After ordering the flowers for Patterson and calling in sick at work, Joe had gone to pick up Zachary by himself, wanting to let his wife sleep in and recuperate from their lovemaking last night. Unaccustomed to those activities, Marilee had slept right through the noises he made this morning, stumbling around the bedroom to find himself a change of clothes. But surely she was awake by now.

Joe grinned as he moved through the house to find her. She'd be tickled pink when she found out he'd played hooky and had all of today plus tomorrow and the weekend to spend with her. Throughout the football season, he'd been scheduled to teach history only Monday through Wednesday, with another teacher taking the class Thursday and Friday to free Joe up for the hecticness that preceded a game weekend. Luckily, there was no game scheduled this week, so his assistant coach, Ted, only had to cover for Joe during practice. The team was coming along nicely. Joe doubted they'd win the game with Bedford. That would take nothing short of a miracle. But they'd improved immensely nonetheless and would give Bedford High a run for its money.

Ted had laughed heartily when Joe telephoned him and said in a perfectly normal voice that he had a terrible case of laryngitis. "It's about time you had a honeymoon!" Ted said. "Not to worry. I heard how hoarse you were all week, and I'll back you up with the big cheese. Only one thing for a coach to do when his voice goes out, and that's to give it a four-day rest."

"You're a champ, Ted," Joe told him with heartfelt sincerity. "I really appreciate this."

"Just be sure you return the favor come deer season. I'd like to take the whole week off if you can handle things without me."

Joe chuckled. "You got it, buddy."

"Enjoy the time with your wife," was Ted's parting advice. "You're only newlyweds once, you know."

As honeymoons went, four days wasn't much, but Joe planned to make the most of them. After speaking with Ted, he called his mom's doctor to ask if watching Zachary for four days would be too much for her. "I know you've already given the green light for overnight stays if she has someone to help her, but I thought I'd better check with you before I left Zachary there for a longer period of time."

"Will her neighbor lady be helping her out?" Dr. Petrie asked.

"Yes, she will."

"Not a problem, then," Dr. Petrie assured Joe. "In fact, it'll probably do your mother a world of good to have him. She's much stronger now, and as long as you make sure she doesn't overtax herself physically, she'll be fine. Normal activity, within reason."

Joe's mom was delighted when she learned she could have her grandson for a prolonged visit. "Four whole days? The circus is in town. We'll definitely go to that. I'll call Sarah right away. She'll want to rent a scad of children's videos. I don't know who enjoys them more, her or Zachary."

Four days. Joe hoped to take Marilee camping up at Holt Reservoir, the same place he'd taken her twelve years ago right after she turned sixteen. Ron had a tent they could borrow. Joe would roast a few his-and-her marshmallows on the same stick, romancing his bride by the light of the moon and a flickering campfire, and then he'd take her to bed. After she said her bedtime prayers, he'd show her what sleeping bags were made for.

As he walked up the hall toward the bedroom, Joe heard the shower running. He doubled back and went to the bathroom. As he slipped inside and locked the door, he grinned, all thought of sleeping bag escapades fading from his mind as he contemplated the pleasures of inter-rupting his beautiful wife's morning shower. She'd prob-ably get all embarrassed, shriek at him to go away, and grab for a towel to cover herself. Over his dead body. Last night, he hadn't had an opportunity to properly ad-mire her. She'd been too bashful, and he'd been too pre-occupied with certain unveiled parts of her to appreciate the overall view.

Not so now. Given the fact that Zachary was awake and all ears, Joe knew he couldn't do anything but drool over the menu. But, hey. There was no harm in looking. Right? And it was a privilege he'd been denied for too many years as it was.

From here on out, he planned to make up for lost time, and if he had his druthers, it would be downhill without brakes the whole way.

As he sneaked over to jerk the shower curtain back, Joe heard a strange sound. When he poked his head around the curtain, his lecherous thoughts fell away and concern took their place. Marilee was huddled under the shower spray, sobbing her heart out.

"Sweetheart? Dear God, what's wrong?"

She looked like *The Addams Family*'s Cousin It. Her hair hung in curtains over her face, the sopping strands nearly drowning her. Joe punched the faucet to shut off the water and then fell to his knees beside the tub, pushing at her wet hair in an attempt to find her face. Instead of grabbing for a towel as he'd imagined she might, she grabbed hold of him.

"Oh, Joe!" She scrambled onto her knees and threw both wet arms around his neck. A long hank of dripping hair slapped against his shirt. "My ring. You kept it. All these years. Oh, God. It breaks my heart. I love you. I do. I love you so much!"

All this over the ring? He'd thought somebody died. "Mari, sweetheart, don't be sad. I didn't do it to make you sad."

Wet hair smashed against his cheek, and he felt streams of water running down his neck. "I'm not sad. I'm s-so h-h-happy!"

This was happy?

A warm, wet mouth sought his. Little sobs of breath puffed into him. Her tongue made a searching foray over his top teeth, found an opening, and darted in to flirt and tangle. Happy was good. *Oh, yeah.* His hands were full of hot, wet, silky flesh. She flung a leg over the side of the tub to get closer, and as she pushed up onto the porcelain barrier, her mouth wrenched away from his. He barely noticed because a pink nipple was bouncing in front of his nose, droplets of water beading the tip. Given the fact that his mouth was already open, how in the hell could he pass that up?

Joe wasn't sure how it happened, but the next thing he knew, he was lying on his back with his knees jammed against the linen closet and his shoulders wedged between the tub and toilet. Normally he might not have liked getting so up close and personal with the john. One of the bolt covers was poking his ear. But there were compensations. Two dusky rose nipples were down there with him, and they were attached to the most beautiful wet female who'd ever clamped her legs around a guy's hips.

Holy hell.

Happy was great.

If one diamond got this response, he'd get her a whole truckload.

Joe slipped a hand between their pelvises, curled a finger, and found white-hot slickness. Marilee jerked, moaned, and sank onto his finger, her soaked hair spilling in a curtain around his face as he cultivated a passion for rosebud pink.

"Daddy?" Zachary called through the locked door.

Joe froze and quit breathing.

"Daddy, can Boo and me watch Barney?"

Joe struggled to bend one wedged arm and bat at Marilee's wet hair to get it out of his face. "Barney?" He sputtered, sounding like a choir boy whose voice was changing. "Sure, sprout. Go watch Barney."

As he spoke, his lips moved on the throbbing tip of Marilee's nipple, and her breath started coming in soft little pants.

"Can you come put him in for me? I can't work the VCR."

Marilee sat up, the grind of her plump posterior making Joe worry that John Henry was about to leave his signature on the inside of his fly.

"Sure. I'll come put Barney on for you," he managed to croak.

Gulping and shaking, Marilee cupped a hand over her eyes. Joe lay there for a second, watching her beautiful breasts jiggle as she struggled to calm her breathing. "I didn't know he was here," she whispered. "Oh, how *awful*. I'm depraved."

"I'm stuck."

"I'm so sorry, Joe. I didn't—"

"Mari, I'm *stuck*."

She lowered her hand and blinked owlishly at him through wet squiggles of blond hair. "You're what?"

"Stuck. You gotta get off me so I can try to get up."

She dismounted with a swing of one leg that provided

Joe with a panoramic shot of the sweetest scenery he'd ever clapped eyes on. *No way.* He had a son standing out there who had ears the size of Dumbo's. John Henry was shit out of luck.

Marilee scrambled to her feet and leaned over the toilet to peer down at him. "Heavens! You *are* stuck. How on earth did you get in there?"

He had been attacked by a wet, gorgeous, sobbing, very sweet nymphomaniac. "What I want to know is what lunatic put the damned toilet so close to your bathtub?"

"Daddy. He installed it for me when I remodeled."

Joe groaned. Karl Nelson had finally gotten even. "Can you give me a hand?"

Marilee reached down, he grabbed hold, and there followed a brief struggle, with one hundred and ten pounds of wet woman trying to dislodge over twice her weight in damp male from the foot-wide space between the john and tub.

After two tries, she said, "Oh, Joe! Do you think I should call the fire department?"

The very thought lent Joe strength, and using his abdominal muscles, he put Herculean effort into a sit-up, finally managing to extricate his shoulders from the narrow space. When he'd pushed to his feet and took measure of the area where he'd been lying, he decided sleeping bag escapades might be a hell of a lot safer.

Zachary spent the next ninety minutes watching Barney cavort on video. Joe made damned sure the volume was turned up to ear-shattering decibels. Then he spirited Marilee away to the bedroom to show her how he imagined love scenes had been done in the silent film era.

Shortly after lunch hour that day, another bunch of dusky-pink rosebuds were delivered to Joan Patterson's office. This time, she didn't need to read the card. She took one look at the flowers and burst out laughing.

*   *   *

Moonlight and firelight.

Sitting on a log beside her husband, Marilee snuggled close to his side, her head resting on his shoulder, her gaze fixed dreamily on the dancing flames. Though slightly chilly, the night was perfect, the scents of fir and pine drifting gently on the breeze. In all her life, she'd never been this happy. *Joe.* She'd loved him since early childhood, and now she could look forward to a future with him.

"What are you thinking?" he asked.

"About babies and our chalet on a hill overlooking the valley. Remember how we used to dream together about the house we'd build?"

He pressed a kiss to her hair. "Forget the house. Did you mention babies?"

"Mmm. Bunches."

"You sure you want a bunch of Lakota papooses cluttering up your life?"

"I'll see how it goes after we've got a half dozen or so. If they're bothersome, then maybe I'll rethink the situation and not have any more."

She felt his lips curve in a smile. "Only six? A good Catholic girl like you? You threatened me with a dozen once. I figured you'd want more."

"Good grief. How many are you thinking?"

"Let's go for ten, one for every year we lost."

She sighed. "Remember Mandy and the soap. You got sick. Are you sure you can handle ten babies?"

"The truth?" He was quiet for a second. "I think two kids is aplenty, and I'm convinced Ron is out of his mind for having eight. Just buying shoes could bankrupt a guy."

"Oh, dear."

"What?"

"Our first fly in the ointment. I don't believe in using artificial means of birth control."

"Aren't there other ways?"

"Gerry says abstinence is the only surefire method."

Long silence. "*Abstinence*? No wonder Ron has eight kids."

"Regrets?"

"Not a one," he said emphatically. Then, "I don't suppose you've ever considered becoming a Lutheran?"

She giggled. "It's a wonderful religion. Unfortunately I'm a dyed-in-the-wool Catholic."

"We may have to raise sheep and dye our own wool if we make ten babies."

"What's your solution?"

He bent his dark head close to hers and, in a low tone, bleated like a sheep in her ear. Marilee was still laughing when he carried her to the tent. They knelt on the sleeping bag facing each other.

"We're running way behind schedule," Joe whispered as he peeled the windbreaker off of her and tossed it aside. "I've got my work cut out for me if you want ten little Lakotas." He dipped to kiss her nose and began unbuttoning her blouse. "No time to waste."

He'd left the tent flap up, and firelight played over them. Marilee felt suddenly self-conscious. "Can you let down the flap, please? It's sort of *bright* in here."

"It's perfect in here."

"It's *bright* in here."

As he drew off her blouse, he whispered, "Don't mind me. Just get your prayers said. Once your jeans are off, God goes on hold, and the rest of the night is mine."

He unsnapped her jeans and tugged down the zipper. His big hands skimmed her hips as he pushed at the denim. When it was heaped around her bent knees, he reached behind her, unfastened her bra, and drew the straps down her arms as he sat back on his heels.

Marilee gasped as the cool night air washed over her bare breasts. "I can't *pray* while you're doing this."

He cupped her softness in his hands. "I can," he said, his voice husky and throbbing. "I'm thanking God for giving you back to me."

"Oh, Joe. You say the sweetest things." She crossed

her arms over herself. "I love you oodles."

He grinned and drew down her arms. "Don't be shy," he whispered. "You're so beautiful, Marilee. I could spend the whole night just looking at you."

"Kiss me instead." She leaned toward him in hopes that he wouldn't be able to see as much of her. "It makes me nervous when you stare."

He caught her by the shoulders and set her back from him. "No way, lady. I'm seeing it all tonight. I've been waiting twenty years for this moment, and I'm going to savor it." He set her down to jerk off her shoes and the jeans. Then, with a gentle shove, he flipped her onto her back and peeled her panties off. When she lay nude, he said, "Don't move," and then he sat back and took slow inventory of her.

Marilee cupped her hands over her breasts and closed her eyes. "This is *torturous*."

"What are you so shy about?"

"I have fat legs."

"Your legs are plump and soft, not fat. I think they're perfect, and my opinion is all that counts."

"When I lie on my back, my boobs slide sideways into my armpits."

He chuckled. "Really? I gotta check that out." She heard a rustle of movement, and the next instant, his long body stretched out beside her. "Ah, Mari. That ring looks so perfectly right, being on your finger again."

Marilee opened her eyes to look. The solitaire twinkled in the flickering light as only a diamond can. A lump came into her throat, and she forgot all about feeling modest as she lifted her hand to admire it. "It's so beautiful, Joe. Do you know what makes it sparkle that way?"

He jerked his gaze to the ring. "No. What?"

"Promises. And as long as we never break them, it'll always sparkle."

"I'll never break my promises to you," he whispered as he bent to kiss her lips. "Never, Mari mine. When I give you my word, it's for keeps. Always remember that."

Marilee gave herself up to the kiss and her husband, content in a way she'd never been and had never hoped to be. *Joe*. He was all she'd ever wanted, and now, at long last, he was hers.

The following Wednesday evening, Joe came in late from work. Marilee met him as he stepped in the French door. Looping her arms around his neck, she gave him a scolding look. "Okay, out with it. What's her name?"

He grinned and bent to kiss her. "Marilee's her name, ask me again, and I'll tell you the same. I ran over to Bedford tonight to watch their team practice. Our game with them is fast approaching, and I thought I might pick up on a few of their weak points. Sad to say, they don't have many."

"I'm surprised the coaches didn't tar and feather you, then ride you out of town on a rail. Infiltration of the enemy camp? Sneaky, very sneaky."

"I went in disguise." He lifted the baseball cap in his left hand. "Pulled it low over my eyes and wore Ted's bowling jacket. I stayed in the bleachers, so no one recognized me."

"That *is* sneaky. How fun! I want to go next time. I'll wear a black wig and sunglasses."

Joe laughed. "And a slinky red dress? Oh, *yeah*. I'll take you on a spy mission any time. I probably wouldn't pick up much information, watching the other team play, but a guy has to make occasional sacrifices for a greater cause. Right?"

"Right. Go wash up for dinner, Double-O-Seven. Pork loin and biscuits."

"And you for dessert?"

Marilee drew away, and then she snapped her fingers. "I almost forgot. I saw Joan today. She sent you a message." She raised her eyebrows at him questioningly.

"For some reason, she wants me to tell you she isn't fat."

Joe frowned bewilderedly. "She isn't fat? That was the message?"

Marilee stepped to the stove to check on the pork loin. "Well, not verbatim. Actually she said, 'Tell Joe I only weigh a hundred and thirty pounds, and if this keeps up, I may be offended.' "

Joe chuckled.

Marilee glanced back over her shoulder. "Okay, what's the joke?"

He gave her an innocent look that didn't fool her. When she narrowed her eyes, he lifted his hands. "You don't want to know."

"Yes, I do."

"In the cards, I said she was worth her weight in rose petals, and I guess maybe she's trying to tell me I've already sent her more than she weighs." He sniffed. "A slight exaggeration. I haven't sent *that* many."

"All those roses? *You* sent them?"

He shrugged. "By way of appreciation, is all."

"For what, exactly? There are so many roses, she's run out of vases and is using quart fruit jars."

"That's the part you really don't want to know."

"Yes, I do."

"You *say* that, but I know you, and you'll get all upset. There was nothing to it. All right? Just my way of letting Joan know her treatment was a fantastic success and that I'm very grateful to her."

Marilee turned with the long-handled fork still in her hand. "You *didn't*." She thought back, determined how many times they had made love since she'd seen Joan the previous Wednesday, and cried, "You *did*! She's got *eleven* bunches of roses in her office."

"Now, Mari. Joan doesn't know I sent them each time we had se—"

"Don't say it!" She gestured toward the living room where Zachary was watching a learning video. "We have a four-year-old in the house."

"I didn't use that word in the cards, either. A tasteful thank you, that's all. I was really grateful for all her—"

"I can't believe you sent my doctor roses every time we had—"

"Don't say it!"

Marilee just stood there, hissing the first letter of the word with prolonged, serpentlike sibilance. Finally she said, "She *knew*. That's why she wanted to hear all the details. 'All this buildup,' she said. You were sending her *roses* every time we—"

"Don't say it."

"I'm so *embarrassed*. Why don't you just take out a personal ad and tell *everybody*?"

"I'd never do that. Mari, come on. Joan isn't just anybody. Roses seemed a perfect way to thank her without— you know—actually thanking her. I couldn't very well telephone her and say, 'Hey, Joan, you'll never guess what.' So I let her know that way. You have to admit, roses say it all. You had a *fantastic* turnaround, and I only did it the first week. No roses tomorrow, I promise."

"How do you know you'll even have occasion to send some tomorrow?"

He got a blank look on his face. Then he frowned and rubbed his jaw. "You aren't *that* angry, are you? Damn. Let's keep our perspective."

Marilee struggled to keep a straight face instead. "If it was so fantastic, why didn't I get any?"

"Any what?"

"Roses."

"You want roses? Sweetheart, if you want roses, I'll happily—" He glanced at the fork she was wielding. "Marilee Nelson Lakota, don't even *think* about it."

She giggled and lunged at him. Even with a bad knee, Joe was lightning quick. He grabbed her wrist, then spun her around with her back to his chest and locked her against him with a steely arm. "Now what're you going to do, Mrs. Lakota?"

She leaned her head back. "Nothing. I'm right where I want to be."

He growled and nibbled on her neck. "I'm sorry if I embarrassed you," he finally whispered. "I'm just so happy, Mari. I needed to tell her thank you for helping you, and it was the only way I could think of to do it."

"I understand." Tingles ran down her spine as his teeth grazed her skin. "But continue to grovel. I really like this."

"When we get Zachary down for the night, I'll show you some real groveling. And I promise, no roses to Joan. After this, I'll send them to you."

"I don't want roses. I'd rather we go into overtime."

He laughed. "Overtime? You're starting to sound like a coach's wife."

"I am a coach's wife. And I want overtime."

"Are you going to be a demanding lover?"

"Yes."

"Hmm." He leaned around to kiss her. As their lips parted, he whispered, "Maybe I'll send Joan roses one more time."

An hour later, Joe and Zachary were helping Marilee to clean up the kitchen, Joe scraping and rinsing dishes, then handing them to his son, who put them in the dishwasher in such creative fashion that Marilee had to bite her tongue.

She smiled and shrugged. They were having too much fun for her to ruin it by being fussy. Joe was singing his version of "Baa-baa, Black Sheep," making up his own words as he went along, occasionally slipping in a line that reminded Marilee they had a date in the bedroom later to work on the first of all those babies she wanted.

"Baa-baa, black sheep, give me all your wool. We're going to need that, and ten bags full!" He flashed her a lazy grin and winked.

Marilee blushed and bent to flip a cup over. She kissed Zachary's forehead. "My goodness, Zachary, you're such a good kitchen helper. I had no idea you could load the dishwasher. You're in trouble now!"

Zachary beamed. "My dad taught me."

Marilee could believe it. Ah, well. She'd get his father trained. They could think of it as an equal-time trade-off, Joe teaching her boudoir techniques, she teaching him kitchen arts. Eventually the two of them would be all-around experts in every room of the house.

The doorbell rang just then. Marilee quickly dried her hands and ran to answer the summons. Boo took care to remain one step behind her as he played his part as the household watchdog, emitting a low *woof* every few paces. Through the paned glass of the double front doors, Marilee saw two uniformed police officers standing on the porch.

"What on earth?" As she reached the slate entry, she heard Boo's toenails grab the floor as he applied his brakes. For reasons beyond Marilee, anyone in a uniform, even a pint-size cub scout selling cookies, scared the poor hound half to death. The dog ran in the other direction as she opened the door. "Yes, may I help you?"

The older of the two policeman, a plump-cheeked man of about thirty with brown hair and kindly gray eyes, tipped his hat to her. "Good evening, ma'am. We're looking for Joseph Lakota. Is he here?"

Marilee's heart caught. Then she silently scolded herself for being silly. Life wasn't really a gigantic roulette wheel, and the anxieties she'd mentioned to Joan that afternoon about something happening to ruin her happiness were foolish. The police could want to speak to Joe for any number of reasons. One of the boys on his team might be in trouble—or missing. Or perhaps the police department was holding a fund-raiser, and they wanted to ask Joe to donate or be their spokesman. Beyond the world of Laurel Creek, her husband was a celebrity, after all.

"Yes, Joe's here."

Marilee was about to run get him when he spoke from

directly behind her. "Hey, Pete!" he said warmly. "How's it going?" Curling a hand over Marilee's shoulder, Joe stopped beside her. "This is my wife, Marilee." To her, he said, "You remember Pete Mueller, honey. His folks used to own the fruit stand out on Old Highway 99. We were in the same graduating class."

Marilee smiled. "Oh, yes." She gestured at his hat. "The uniform. I didn't recognize you, Pete. My apologies."

"Not a problem." Pete shifted his weight from one foot to the other, looking uncomfortable. The younger officer beside him, a lanky redhead with freckles, appeared to be equally tense. "This isn't a social call, Joe. We have to take you downtown for questioning."

Joe's grin vanished. "What about?"

Pete turned his gaze on Marilee. "What time did your husband come home tonight, Mrs. Lakota?"

Marilee threw Joe a bewildered look. "I, um . . . gosh, about a quarter after seven, I think. Why do you ask?"

Pete Mueller met Joe's gaze. "That's a little late to get in, isn't it, Joe? Did you have to stay over at the high school?"

"Occasionally my job involves more than just coaching." A muscle in Joe's cheek started to tic. "What is this, Pete?"

"Where were you tonight? When we went by the school to talk to you, Ted told us you missed practice. Isn't that a little unusual?"

"I drove to Bedford this afternoon to scope out their team. The big game is in two weeks."

"I see." Pete nodded and glanced over to make sure his partner was taking notes. "And is that where you picked up all the red mud on your car, over at Bedford?"

"No, we went camping at Holt Reservoir this weekend."

"When you were in Bedford, did you speak to anyone who can verify that you were there?"

Joe's hand tightened over Marilee's shoulder. "I'm not

answering any more questions until you tell me what this is about."

Pete's expression went stony. "Stan Salisbury has been murdered. His wife, Susan, claims you made threats on his life three weeks ago. Is that true?"

Joe's face went gray. Marilee felt as if she might faint.

"Yes, it's true," Joe said softly. "I was pissed off, though. I didn't mean it. *Murdered*? Oh, sweet Christ."

Seventeen

A gigantic roulette wheel. Over the next hour, Marilee kept trying to reassure herself. Joe's number hadn't hit. In a few hours, he would come home, laughing over the misunderstanding. The police would apologize and feel terrible for putting them through this. *Murder.* Oh, please, God.

Huddling on the sofa, Marilee held Zachary on her lap while the police searched the house. They even dumped out the Cream of Wheat in search of heaven knew what. If they kept this up, what on earth would she feed Zachary for breakfast?

"What are you looking for?" Marilee asked, hoping she might expedite matters by locating the item for them. They ignored her question. A few minutes later when an officer began taking apart all her picture frames, she cried, "Would you please *stop*! Some of those photos are irreplaceable. I've no negatives!" Her plea was ignored.

A few minutes later, another officer came in from searching Joe's car. He cast a meaningful glance at Zachary, who cowered in Marilee's arms. "Mrs. Lakota, I know the little boy is very upset, and I hate to ask you to leave him. But can you step out onto the front porch for just a few minutes without him?"

When Marilee set Zachary off her lap, he curled into a fetal position and covered his head with his arms. "Hey, sweetkins," she whispered. "I'll only be gone a few minutes. All right? You stay right here, and I'll run all the way to the porch and all the way back. You'll barely miss me."

"I want my daddy!" Zachary said fiercely. "Make them bring him back, Marilee. He didn't hit anybody this time! How come they took him away in a police car again?"

Marilee almost clamped her hand over the child's mouth to hush him. She looked nervously at the officer who waited for her. When he saw her expression, he said, "We've checked Mr. Lakota's police record. The little boy isn't telling me anything I don't already know."

Marilee's legs went watery. "What does that mean?"

The officer's mouth hardened. "That we're aware of your husband's history of violent behavior," he said softly.

Oh, God . . . oh, God. It was the best Marilee could do by way of a prayer as she hurried to the front of the house. When she stepped out onto the porch, another police officer was standing on the top step waiting for her. With a gloved hand, he gingerly held what looked like a very short baseball bat by the tip of its handle.

"What on earth is *that*?" Marilee whispered, her gazed riveted.

"Have you ever seen this before, Mrs. Lakota? We found it under the front seat of your husband's Honda. It's commonly called a billy club, among other things. Here in Oregon, recent legislation forbids ordinary citizens to carry them in their vehicles."

There was *stuff* all over the hitting surface of the bat, a blackish red goo with strands of sandy hair poking out. Marilee's gorge rose. Black spots danced before her eyes. Stan had sandy-colored hair.

"Mrs. Lakota?"

The officer's voice seemed to come from a long way off. Marilee knotted her hands into fists, fighting for self-control. She absolutely could not faint. This wasn't really happening. She was having a horrid nightmare. Here pretty soon, she'd wake up, and she'd never even mention the dream to Joe because it would hurt him to know she'd believe him capable of such an act, even in her sleep.

"I . . . um . . ." Her voice sounded weak and stuttering. "No, I've never seen the awful thing before, and it doesn't belong to my husband."

"Perhaps he kept it under the car seat without your knowledge."

Marilee blinked and tried to focus. She wanted to say that she'd looked under the seats of Joe's Honda a hundred times and never seen that horrible bat. But the truth was, she'd never had reason or inclination to search his car. "It *isn't* his!" she settled for saying. "We took the Honda camping just this weekend. I guess I would know if he'd carried such a thing in there."

"Did you look under the driver's seat?"

Marilee searched the policeman's eyes, and she knew in that moment that this wasn't a bad dream. Stan Salisbury had been bludgeoned to death, and the murder weapon had just been found in Joe's car. God forgive her. This was her fault. For ten years, she'd kept silent, never telling Joe what Stan had done because she'd known he would fly into a rage. Now her worst fear had come to pass.

Joe hadn't been able to bear it, and he'd killed Stan Salisbury.

"Yes," she finally said, her voice steady and unnaturally loud. "I *did* look under the driver's seat. And under all the other seats as well. And in the *trunk*! That horrid *thing* was not in my husband's car."

The officer nodded. "May I ask what you were looking

for, Mrs. Lakota? People don't usually search under all the car seats."

"I was looking for the can of bug spray!" Marilee had no idea where that had come from. She only knew she had to lie to protect Joe, and she had to be convincing. "You know those little things that buzz in the night and bite you through your clothes? Commonly called mosquitoes, among other things. Oregon hasn't passed recent legislature outlawing those, and that being the case, I needed the bug spray."

"I wasn't questioning your word, Mrs. Lakota."

"Weren't you?" Marilee started to hug her waist but stopped herself. *A defensive posture. Classic.* The memory made her want to sink to her knees and sob. "I think you *were* questioning my word, officer." She heard Zachary wailing in the living room. "I want all of you out of my house. You're upsetting my child. Isn't it bad enough that you've hauled his father away to jail?"

"Not to jail, ma'am. We're only questioning him." He shuffled his feet, looking uncomfortable. "Is it true that Stan Salisbury and four other men raped you ten years ago, Mrs. Lakota?"

The world around her did a quick revolution, the ground up, the sky down, the trees in her yard doing a mad dance. She struggled to right her vision, to clear her head.

"We understand that you recently told your husband about that incident and implicated Stan Salisbury as one of your rapists. Afterward, your husband went to Salisbury's residence. There was a heated exchange, during which your husband told Salisbury to clear out of town and, at one point, threatened to kill him. Is that true?"

"I refuse to answer any more questions until I've retained a good defense attorney for my husband." Marilee glanced at the bat. "Say what you like about only taking him in for questioning. I have a feeling an official charge of murder isn't long in coming."

"Obstructing justice is a crime," he reminded her. "If

you withhold evidence that may lead to an arrest or conviction, you can be prosecuted. Besides that, if you believe your husband is innocent, what have you got to hide? Refusing to answer my questions only makes him look more guilty."

"What you think is irrelevant. It'll be a jury's opinion that counts, and every word I say to you may be used against my husband. Isn't that correct?"

"Essentially, yes."

"I can't be forced to testify against him. He is my husband."

"That's true."

"That being the case, even if I am withholding evidence, which I'm not saying I am, I doubt you could make a case against me for obstruction of justice. I also believe I'm entitled to legal counsel myself, since you've made mention of pressing charges against me."

He sighed. "You're making a grave mistake, Mrs. Lakota."

"I'm exercising my right to remain silent until I've received legal counsel."

"By refusing to answer my questions, you're only convincing me that Susan Salisbury's allegations are true."

"I'm exercising my right to remain silent until I've received legal counsel," Marilee said again.

The officer snorted in disgust and then smirked at her. "You better get your husband some legal counsel first, lady." Very carefully, he slipped the bat back into a plastic bag that had already been tagged as evidence. As he removed the latex gloves, he glanced at Marilee. "Until we run this through forensics in Bedford, we won't know for sure. But I'd say we've found the club used to kill Salisbury. And it was in your husband's car."

Right after the police left, Marilee stood in the middle of her destroyed home, holding a sobbing Zachary tightly in her arms. "It's all right, punkin. Please, don't cry. It's all right."

"They took my daddy! They took him! I want him back. Who's gonna read me my story and chase the boogeyman out of my closet?"

This was the first Marilee had ever heard of Joe's nightly battle with Zachary's boogeyman. But, oh, how very like Joe that was. She could almost picture him performing the ritualistic exorcism, throwing open the closet door and rousting out the spooks. *Silly*? Absolutely. But Joe wasn't the type to care how silly it might be. Real or imagined, his son's fears would be important to him. No matter if he was tired after putting in a long day. No matter if he had still more work awaiting him before he could call it a night. He would talk to Zachary, then read to him, making him feel safe and loved, because that was who Joe Lakota was, a big bear of a guy with a soft center who always put the people he loved first.

Tears burned Marilee's eyes. *Joe*. How could this be happening? He was so wonderful and good. She closed her eyes and took deep breaths. She couldn't fall apart. For Zachary's sake, she had to stay calm.

"I'm a fair hand at chasing away the boogeyman," she said, injecting a note of cheer into her voice.

"Nuh-uh! You're not big and strong like my dad."

"That's true. Hmm. Maybe I'll recruit Boo to help me. How's that?"

"Boo's a big chicken. He's hiding under your bed. He doesn't like policemen, and I don't, either!"

Marilee couldn't say she was overly fond of them herself. She panned the destroyed room. It would take her days to get the house put back together. The thought no sooner took root than she wondered what on earth she was thinking. The house? Who cared? Her husband was in jail. And not for a piddling little offense, but *murder*. Oh, dear God. What was she going to do? Joe needed her. She had to do something, only what? Call a lawyer. Yes. That would be the first thing. Only what lawyer?

She needed to find someone really good, really shrewd.

She sat in the rocker and cuddled Zachary close. It was what Joe would want, she knew. Most important things first. Smoothing a hand over Zachary's soft hair, she kissed his forehead and whispered, "Maybe I'm not big and strong like your dad, but you know what? I love you as big as a mountain, Zachary Lakota. Nothing on earth is going to hurt you, not as long as I'm here."

Zachary hugged her neck so tightly he trembled. "I'm scared, Marilee. I'm so scared! They're gonna put my daddy in jail. He didn't hurt that man. I *know* he didn't. I heard them policemen talking. They said my dad bashed his brains with a club. My dad didn't do it! I know he didn't."

Oh, Zachary. He was only four, far too young to even know about such things, let alone be worried about them. How could those men have made such heartless accusations in front of him? Marilee clamped him more firmly to her. "Of *course* your dad didn't do it," she whispered. "Your dad would *never* do such a thing. You're absolutely right."

As Marilee uttered the reassurance, a sense of rightness filled her, and she realized she truly believed what she'd just told Joe's son. So what if they'd found the murder weapon in his car? So what if he had, oh so conveniently, come up with an excuse for disappearing for several hours this afternoon? Way down deep, where fear couldn't reach and reason held no sway, she couldn't believe Joe had done such a thing. *I'll never break my promises to you,* he'd vowed to her the other night in the tent. *Never, Mari mine. When I give you my word, it's for keeps. Always remember that.*

Now those words seemed almost prophetic. They also comforted Marilee as nothing else could. Joe Lakota had his share of faults, a hot temper when it came to protecting the people he loved ranking at the top of the list, but he wasn't a liar. He'd given her his word he wouldn't lay a hand on Salisbury. *You never have to worry again that I'll go off half-cocked.* It made no sense that Joe would make promises like that, only to break them.

Marilee remembered the very first day she had watched Zachary. *Tell him I'll call, every hour on the hour*, Joe had whispered before leaving. And just as he'd promised, he'd called his son every hour, on the dot. At the time, she'd marveled at how extraordinary that was. Worried as Joe had been over his mom, he hadn't forgotten, though, and despite all the demands on his time, he'd wasted precious seconds explaining to Zachary how to watch the clock and determine when he would call again.

She took another deep breath and slowly let it out. *Keep to the basics.* What was the one absolute in her life? *Joe.* He had never let her down. Not once. When everything else went to hell in a hand basket, she could count on him. Always. To her knowledge, he had never lied to her, never even so much as colored the truth. And she couldn't remember a single instance when he had failed to act in her best interests. The same went for his son.

Killing a man and ending up in prison was not in her best interests, and it would leave Zachary horribly vulnerable as well. Joe simply wouldn't do something to jeopardize either of them.

"Zachary," Marilee said more loudly, "you are absolutely right. Your dad didn't do it!"

"I know," the child agreed.

Marilee pressed her face against his hair and laughed. *Relief.* She didn't know where her head had been at— possibly bouncing around that imaginary roulette wheel called life that she'd told Joan about. Anxiety, yet another stage of recovery. She'd been expecting something awful to happen, and low and behold, it had. That didn't excuse her for jumping to conclusions, of course, and she regretted that she had. But mistakes could be rectified, and she'd nipped this one in the bud early on.

Joe was innocent. He had to be.

She gave Zachary a little jostle to get his attention. "Orders from your new mom, big guy. From this moment on, feeling scared isn't allowed. Your daddy may be in jail, but they aren't going to keep him. You and I are going to get him out."

Zachary drew back, rubbing his eye with one fist. "We are?"

"You bet we are." Marilee helped dry his cheeks. "I'm going to need lots of help to do it, though. Can I count on you?"

"Yup. I love my dad a lot!"

Marilee blinked away tears. "So do I. And together, we're going to set the Laurel Creek police department on its ear."

Zachary nodded. Then he peered out around his knuckles and said, "How?"

Marilee's stomach knotted. "First, we shake." She offered her right hand. "I promise to be brave and fight like a trooper to get your dad out of jail. Do you promise to be really, really brave and help me?"

"Yup." Zachary put his small hand in hers. "What do I got to be brave about?"

Marilee shook his hand. "First of all, if your dad has to stay in jail for a teeny little while, you have to help me chase the boogeyman out of your closet at night."

Zachary's eyes went wide.

"We'll use the broom and my great big pan lid. Not a problem. When he comes out, I'll whop him and you can slap him up alongside the head with the lid. You don't have to be big to whip the boogeyman. You just have to be creative."

"I wish we could just let my dad do it."

Marilee nodded. "I know. But we'll do the next best thing, and talk to your dad about it on the phone. He can tell us *exactly* how to handle the boogeyman. He's been running him off for quite a while."

"Yup."

"Well, then? Problem solved. Your dad's a great coach."

"Yup." Zachary gave Marilee a wary look. "What else do I gotta do?"

"Well." She took a deep breath. "You have to be really brave and hold my hand to help me be brave while I make a phone call. I think it's time to summon the cavalry."

"Who's the cavalry?"

"My family."

Zachary's eyes went even wider. "Is that lady with lights on her ears and pink hair gonna come over here?"

"Aunt Luce." Marilee smiled. "Actually, Zachary, she's the nicest one of the bunch. I know she looks really weird, but she's the best friend I've ever had. Well, actually, my third best friend. Your daddy is my first best friend."

"Who's your second?"

Marilee gathered him up for a hug. "You are, you silly boy."

After placing a call to Gerry, Marilee telephoned Sarah Rasmussen, told her the awful news, and asked her to gently break it to Faye Lakota. "Please tell her that as soon as I can, I'll come over to give her an update. All right?"

Sarah sighed. "I can't believe Joseph would do such a thing."

"He didn't," Marilee calmly asserted, "and I'm sure everything will come right soon. The police have just made a terrible mistake. Please tell Faye I'm positive Joe will be home sometime tomorrow."

After breaking the connection, Marilee contacted the police department. The female who initially answered her call soon handed Marilee off to a senior officer who was rude, evasive, and explained, only when pressed, that it simply wasn't possible for Joe to speak with his son on the phone.

"We already booked him, and he's in lockup. Come morning, he'll get one phone call. If he chooses to waste it calling his kid, fine by me. But that's all he gets."

"I'm sorry," Marilee said politely. "I don't mean to be difficult. Really, I don't. I understand you have procedures to follow, but this isn't an ordinary situation. Mr. Lakota is this child's sole custodian, and the little boy is very distressed."

"That's too bad, ma'am."

Too bad? Marilee started to get angry. Instead of revealing that, she decided to try wheedling. "Do you have kids?"

"Yes, ma'am."

"Then you know how easily small children can be upset, and that certain experiences, if handled incorrectly, can be emotionally devastating to them for years."

"That really isn't my problem, lady. I'm sorry if the kid's upset. But, hey, his old man should have thought about that before he bashed Salisbury's head in."

Marilee didn't take time to count to ten. She did, however, make it to three, whereupon she said, "Have you heard the expression 'innocent until proven guilty'?"

"Yes, ma'am."

"Going on that premise, can't you find it in your heart to make an exception for a small child?"

"No, ma'am. We can't make exceptions for every Tom, Dick, and Harry. The place would be a zoo."

"I realize that the accommodations in your jail probably don't come equipped with telephones. However, I find it very difficult to believe that you've no cell phone there."

"So?"

"Do I take that to mean there is a cell phone available?"

"Our phone system is none of your concern."

"What is your name?" Marilee asked.

"Brandt."

She asked how it was spelled.

"Why?" Brandt asked.

"I want to have the right spelling when I give your name to my husband's attorney."

"Are you threatening me with a lawsuit?"

Marilee glanced down into Zachary's big, worried eyes. "Do you know who my husband is, Officer Brandt?"

"Yes, ma'am. He's Joe Lakota, the football player. So?"

Marilee squared her shoulders. "Imagine, if you will, the three-ring circus that will soon erect a tent in Laurel Creek. A sports figure, arrested for murder? Oh, man. The headlines will be in every paper across the country. Reporters, crawling out of the woodwork, just for starters. The first thing I intend to scream when they interview me is that Officer Brandt, one of Laurel Creek's finest, refused to allow a frightened four-year-old boy talk to his daddy, who, I might add, is innocent. You're going to look like a hard-nosed jerk when that fact is brought to light. So, in answer to your question, no, I'm not threatening you with a lawsuit, Officer Brandt. I'm promising you that if you don't let my husband reassure his son, I will personally destroy your career. Joe Lakota doesn't have some two-bit, backwater attorney. He's got the best in the country, and I'm going to say two words to him. 'Sic 'em.' "

Long silence, and then, "Captain Croise may be able to help you."

"By all means. Croise, did you say? How is that spelled?"

Ten minutes later, Joe telephoned his son on a cell phone that had miraculously been delivered to him by an officer named Brandt. Marilee got on her bedroom extension to listen

"Hey, sprout. How's my favorite boy?"

"I'm scared, Daddy. How come did they take you away in a police car?"

Joe chuckled. "Well, now, that's simple. They made a big mistake."

Marilee broke in just then. "Hello, Joe."

"Hey, Mari mine." His voice dipped to a husky tone. "I'm so sorry about this. I know it threw you for a loop, and you weren't sure what to think."

Marilee's throat went tight. "Yes, well, I'm okay. The reason I finagled this call is because Zachary needs your advice."

"Hey, sprout, what kind of advice do you need?"

"You're not gonna be here to chase away the boog-eyman tonight, Daddy."

"Ah." Marilee could almost see Joe scratching his head. "That's a problem."

"Yup."

"You know, Zachary, I'm not there to chase away the boogeyman when you stay all night at Grandma's."

"The boogeyman isn't over there."

"He isn't? How come?"

"I don't tell him I'm gonna stay all night."

Judging by the silence at Joe's end, he was attempting to make sense of his son's reasoning. To Marilee's surprise, she found herself grinning. It was sad testimony to her mental state that Zachary's thought processes made perfect sense to her.

"Evasion tactics," she inserted, by way of explanation. "The boogeyman gets fooled into staying at home."

"Oh." Joe sounded nonplussed. Another brief silence elapsed. "Of *course*. Very clever of you, Zachary."

"What am I gonna do, Daddy?" Zachary asked in a quavering voice. "Marilee isn't big enough to scare him away."

"She isn't very big. That's true."

Marilee listened for a few moments while father and son discussed her physical inadequacies. Zachary complained that she had skinny arms with no muscles and a bony neck. She heard laughter in Joe's voice when he concluded, "Yeah, you're right, she's kind of scrawny."

"Yup, and I think she's kind of chicken, too. She says I gotta help scare him away."

Joe chuckled. "Well, now. You guys definitely need a good plan of offense."

"Boo is no help," Marilee enlightened him. "The cops scared him, and he's still hiding under my bed."

"That damned dog." Joe chuckled again. "Hey, Zachary? Mari can be pretty scary sometimes, even to me."

"She can?"

"You should see her with the long-handled fork."

Marilee smiled even though tears were dripping off her chin. "Oh, yes, the *fork*. Why didn't I think of that?"

"The fork will do the trick," Joe assured his son. "No boogeyman in his right mind will mess with her then, and you won't have to help her chase him off."

"What do you say, Zachary?" Marilee asked. "If I scare him away with my fork, will you feel safe?"

"Yup, if my dad says."

"Trust me, Zachary, she even scares me with that fork." Joe sighed. "You okay, sprout?"

"Yup," the child replied in a wobbly voice. "I just want you to come home."

"Me, too, and I will. I'm wearing my magic necklace. Nothing can hurt me. Remember?"

"Don't take it off, Daddy."

"I won't." Joe fell silent for a moment. "Hey, sprout, remember when I used to send you hugs over the phone? I'm going to send you a great big one now. You all ready?"

Zachary giggled. "I'm ready."

Joe made a prolonged grunting sound. The next instant, Marilee held the phone away from her ear because Zachary dropped the extension. "You knocked me over!" the child cried, his voice faint.

"I told you to get ready."

The little boy picked up again, giggling as only a child can. "That was a really *big* one, Daddy."

"My hugs for you will always be big ones, no matter how far away I am."

Listening, Marilee knew this was a game often played in the past by father and son. It nearly broke her heart to think that Joe might never actually hug his son again. *No.* She wouldn't allow herself to think that way. Life wasn't a gigantic roulette wheel.

"What story are you going to request tonight?" Joe asked the child.

"I don't know."

"When I go to sleep tonight, I want to imagine reading it to you in my head. Run to your bedroom and look through your books. Don't come back until you've picked one out."

The phone clattered again, and Marilee heard Zachary racing through the house. She smiled. "Very sneaky, Mr. Lakota."

"Yeah, well, there are some things I don't want him to hear. I'm in one hell of a fix, Mari mine. I'm not sure I can beat this."

"Don't talk that way. It frightens me."

"I don't want to frighten you, but we've got to face facts. This doesn't look good. Salisbury was murdered around five o'clock at Laurel Bend. They found his body down by the creek, and from what I gather, it was ugly. Whoever did it was flat pissed and didn't stop pounding on him until there wasn't much left to pound."

"Oh, dear God."

"There's red mud down there, Mari, and I've got red mud all over my car from Holt Reservoir. Three weeks ago, I went over to Stan's all steamed and threatened at one point to kill him in front of his wife. Toss in the murder weapon, and my ass is grass."

"Someone *planted* that bat in your car," she cried.

"Yeah, but who? Somebody who knows I threatened Stan. Who's that leave us with? Susan. A woman couldn't have done this, Marilee. Not a woman Susan's size, anyway."

Marilee pushed up from the bed to pace back and forth, the phone cord acting as a short leash. "Why don't they run tests? If you killed him, you'd have blood somewhere on you. You weren't bloody at all when you got home."

"I could have washed up, changed clothes, ditched the evidence."

"And kept the bat? How does that make sense?"

"It doesn't, but a killer can get upset, do something dumb. As for forensics, this is Laurel Creek, not Los Angeles. They don't even have a full-time coroner here."

Marilee sank back onto the mattress. "Well, too bad for them. Lack of evidence is a great defense. I'm going to get a fantastic lawyer—a really good one, Joe. Don't you worry. I'll get you out of there."

"Sweetheart, really good lawyers cost a fortune. You've got what—sixty, maybe seventy grand in savings, and I've got about five. There are monthly expenses to consider. With me in here, you'll have to use that money to live on. It could be months, maybe more than a year, before you get another check."

Marilee didn't want to hear this. "I'll manage somehow. I can get cash on credit cards. Maybe borrow on the house."

"Jesus! No. Don't do that. We have to be rational about this. Even a fantastic lawyer can't perform miracles. Somebody's framed me for this, and the way things have played out so far, it could stick. Nobody at Bedford High noticed me in the bleachers tonight. I don't have an alibi. You can't waste all your money. Chances are, I won't be around to help replenish the capital."

"Don't *say* that!"

"I have to. Damn it, Mari, you could be pregnant. Do you think I want my wife, baby, and little boy destitute while I'm cooling my heels in prison?"

Pregnant. Marilee pressed a hand to her waist. The thought should have terrified her, only she prayed he was right instead. A baby. Joe's baby. In her book, that would be a gift from heaven. "I won't be destitute. I have family to help me, remember, and a successful writing career to eventually restore my depleted capital."

"And what about Zachary? We've still got the custody issue hanging over our heads. Lose the house, and Valerie will be all over us." Silence. Then, "Oh, Christ. I hadn't thought of that. She gets wind of this, and she'll come after my kid."

Marilee squeezed her eyes closed. "She'll play hell. Don't even worry about that. Your son isn't going anywhere."

"Oh, God, Mari."

Marilee had never heard Joe sound so scared. Her heart caught, and she held tight to the phone. How like him it was to be in jail, worrying about her, Zachary, and a baby he wasn't even sure had been conceived. "You listen to me," she said fiercely. "I'll protect Zachary with my life. If she comes sniffing around, trying to take him, I'll use every legal obstacle at my disposal to foil her, and if that fails, I'll run with him. As for this house and the money, screw it all. Without you, what's it all worth? I'll do what I have to do, and happily go broke doing it, end of subject."

"Marilee, I'm counting on you to be rational."

"Hello? I'm crazy, remember? I don't have to be rational. I love you. That's the bottom line. I'll live out of a paper sack, if that's what it takes."

"Oh, sweetheart."

"I'll take care of this. I called my family. They'll be here any time. I'm counting on them to help me make sound decisions. Please, don't worry. All right?" She heard Zachary running through the house again. "As soon as I can get the ball rolling, I'll be doing everything possible at this end. Maybe I can come see you tomorrow."

"No. I don't want you here. It's a hellhole."

The other phone clattered in Marilee's ear, and then

Zachary cried, "I picked my story, Daddy!"

"That's record time. Which one did you pick?"

"G'night Moon."

"You're kidding. Again?"

Eighteen

amily. Marilee's kitchen was full to bursting. Her parents, her sister and brother-in-law, and Aunt Luce and Charlie raced over to lend moral support the moment they received word of Joe's arrest. Blessedly, Marilee managed to rock Zachary to sleep before they arrived, and despite the commotion, the little boy continued to snooze on the living room sofa.

Gerry, who'd just climbed from the shower when Marilee called, still had wet hair and wore no makeup when she got there. Her blue eyes were as round as flapjacks. "I got the neighbor girl to babysit, Marilee. I can stay as long as you need me." She pushed back a curly lock of damp blond hair as she glanced at the infant in her arms. "I had to bring slugger along. Right now, I'm a walking, talking fast food joint."

Weighted down with baby gear, Ron entered behind his slightly built wife. His green gaze met Marilee's over the top of Gerry's bent head. His freckled face looked pale by contrast to his dark red hair, and his features were drawn into a solemn scowl. "Don't you worry, sweetheart. I know a fairly good attorney. We'll get Joe out on bail, and by tomorrow afternoon, this will all be cleared up. It's total madness. Joe would never kill somebody."

Marilee felt strangely numb. "Actually, Ron, a fairly good lawyer isn't what I've got in mind. This is a nasty situation, and Joe's going to need the very best representation I can find." She managed a smile for her parents, who had just slipped in behind Ron and Gerry. "Hi, Mama, hi, Daddy. Thank you for coming."

Karl stepped over to hug his younger daughter. "I'm so sorry, honey. Of all the things to happen. That damned man has brought you nothing but heartache."

Marilee extricated herself from his arms. "That isn't true, Daddy. Please reserve judgment for a bit and don't say anything more. There are things I need to tell you, and once I do, you'll only regret anything you say."

Marilee turned to hug her mom, who looked the very picture of a 50s sitcom grandmother in her prim navy dress with white collar, her silver hair laying in perfectly coifed curls. "Oh, Mama."

Emily patted Marilee's shoulder. "Now, now, dear, everything will be fine. Have faith."

Marilee drew back, wishing she had more of that particular commodity. *Faith*. Right now, mostly all she felt was sick fear.

Aunt Luce sailed in the door just then, Charlie heeling behind her like a well-trained canine. She wore a brilliant crimson dress that looked like a scarf rack in a high wind. Miniature traffic-lights dangled from her ears, which made Marilee smile and think of Zachary. The lady with lights on her ears had arrived. Tonight the effect was flashing red stoplights, and unless Marilee missed her guess, the attentive Charlie was permanently held up in traffic.

Lucy tottered across the kitchen to Marilee on black stiletto heels. "Ah, honey!"

When her aunt hugged her, Marilee was enveloped in

a floating cloud of red nylon and Chanel. "Hi, Aunt Luce."

"You poor dear!" Aunt Luce crooned. "You just got him back, and now you've lost him again. Well, not to worry. He'll be home before you know it, making messes and saying he's hungry. Just you wait and see."

"Oh, I hope so."

"I know so. Men are like grease spots. You think you've gotten rid of them, and they pop back out again."

Marilee giggled and wiped her cheeks. "Aunt Luce, that's *awful*."

"I've got you smiling, though, don't I?" She pinched Marilee's cheeks. "Trust me, he probably eats too much for them to consider keeping him. A guy that size has to be high maintenance."

Still smiling at her aunt's nonsense, Marilee directed everyone to sit at the table, poured coffee all the way around, and then sat beside her mother with a steaming mug cupped between her hands. "I have something I need to tell all of you," she announced.

Later Marilee could never recall exactly what she said to her family. She only knew she'd said enough, for when she fell quiet, every face around the table was a mask of stunned disbelief.

"Why didn't you tell us?" was her father's first question.

Marilee's eyes felt dry and grainy as she met his even gaze. "I wish I could give you a cut-and-dried answer to that question, Daddy, but so much played into the decisions I made then. I was frightened and ashamed, confused and intimidated. Standing on the outside, looking in, a person can't begin to grasp how a woman feels in a situation like that, and I was so very young when it all happened. It's difficult to put it into words. A sense of *guilt* I can't describe. Feeling so *stupid*. And terrified. I was absolutely terrified. There were so many people who would have been hurt if I'd told. Joe, especially, and possibly even Ron and Gerry, if Ron had gone with Joe, gunning for those guys." Marilee shrugged, at a loss to explain. "Maybe it was simply a case of making all the wrong decisions for what seemed like right reasons. I don't know. I hurt Joe. I nearly destroyed myself. At the time, I saw no way out. That's all I can say. I looked at all of you—the people who loved me so much—and you seemed a million miles away."

Karl bent his head and stared for a long moment into his coffee mug. When he finally looked back at her, his expression was filled with pain. "I feel like your mother and I failed you."

"Oh, Daddy." Tears filled Marilee's eyes. "One thing I learned in counseling is that blame and self-reproach are fruitless and destructive. You know that saying, 'Shit happens.' How very true it is. I was a *victim*. I reacted to hurt. Maybe I was in shock. I know I wasn't thinking straight. We can analyze it all night. I can blame myself. You can blame yourself. What good will it do? I did what I did, rightly or wrongly. It's over now and unfixable. All we can do is move forward and put it behind us."

Aunt Luce broke in with, "I think Marilee's right. That is all we can do." She glanced at Karl. "You and Em were good parents, Karl. You did the best you knew how to do. Cling to that thought, and forget the rest. It's far more important now for all of us to concentrate on the present. It sounds to me as if our Joseph is in a pickle, and it may be up to us to get him out of it."

"Yes," Marilee said in a tight voice. "A terrible pickle, Aunt Luce. As I just said, I was afraid for Joe to find out what happened, and it wasn't until three weeks ago that I finally told him." She quickly related the events of that evening. "Susan was present when Joe threatened Stan that night, and it was Susan who told the police that Joe might be her husband's killer."

"And the club was found in Joe's car?" Ron asked.

"Yes, and after seeing it, I've every reason to think it was the implement used in the bludgeoning. There were smears of blood and hair on the surface."

"Oh, dear Lord," Gerry whispered. "Joe killed him, then?"

Marilee was about to protest, but Aunt Luce saved her the trouble. "Don't be a ninny, Gerry. If Joe were going to kill one of them, do you think he'd use a bat?" She shook her head. "Not his style. In a blind rage, Joe would jump in swinging. He'd never think to grab a weapon."

A little color returned to Ron's cheeks. "Aunt Luce is right, honey. I know Joe. He's a toe-to-toe, nose-to-nose kind of guy. I'm not saying he's a saint, or that he couldn't be pushed into a rage, but he'd never use a bat."

"Then how did it get in his car?" Gerry said.

Aunt Luce rose from her chair. "My, my, this *is* a fascinating tangle. How, indeed? Someone must have put it in Joe's car, obviously to throw suspicion on him." She began to pace around the table, a perplexed frown creasing her forehead. "Susan, perhaps?"

Marilee suppressed a shudder. "Joe says a woman couldn't have killed Stan, that it had to be a man. A great deal of force went into the blows."

Emily drew her rosary from her pocket. "Holy mother," she whispered.

"Lucille and I are avid mystery readers," Charlie inserted. "I'm a whiz at solving puzzles." He thought for a moment. "Susan is the common denominator and the logical place to start."

"To start what?" Karl asked.

"Solving the crime," Charlie said, his eyes gleaming.

"Isn't that a job for the police?" Emily pointed out. "Only bad can come from taking justice into one's own hands."

"Oh, Em," Aunt Luce said with a snort. "Can it, would you? We're not taking justice into our own hands, we're trying to help Joseph. The police think they've got their killer. It may be up to us to make them realize they don't."

"Oh, my . . ." Emily ran the beads through her fingers, her worried gaze fixed on her twin sister. "This is *awful*.

Marilee's husband, in jail for murder. I just can't believe we're sitting around her table, talking about a bludgeoning as if it's a common, everyday occurrence."

It was a sobering thought. Marilee rubbed her arms. "We have to try to help Joe, Mama."

Emily patted her younger daughter's hand. "I know, dolly. I'm just appalled. This is Laurel Creek. Bad things never happen here."

A bad thing had happened now, Marilee thought morosely, and unless a miracle happened, Joe could be blamed for it. She took a steadying breath and looked up at her elderly aunt. "Susan is the only person who witnessed the exchange between Stan and Joe. Charlie may be right. Whoever planted that club in Joe's car must know Joe threatened Stan, and the only way that person could possibly know that is if Susan told him."

"Which tells us exactly what?" Gerry said. "Come on. In this town? Susan could have told one or two people, and within a half day, the whole town would know. Granted, the information came from Susan, and someone used it to throw suspicion off himself and onto Joe, but who? May I point out that Stan was a creep, and a lot of people probably wanted to kill him? I think he cheated a quarter of the population in shady real estate deals, and before that he sold used cars. Need I say more?"

"God rest his soul," Emily murmured, kissing her rosary.

"Mama, *please*," Gerry scolded. "If you're going to say a rosary for Stan Salisbury's soul, don't do it in Marilee's kitchen."

"The poor man *is* dead. Someone should pray for his soul."

Gerry rolled her eyes. "Yeah, well, not you, Mama. I mean it. The bastard *raped* my sister! If you pray for him while we're all sitting here watching, I'll never forgive you."

Emily flashed a startled look at her husband. Karl tugged the rosary from her hands and slipped it in his pocket. "Gerry's right, honey. Pray for the son of a bitch's soul later, if that's what flips your skirt."

"*Karl!*" Emily said with a horrified gasp. "For shame!"

Marilee struggled not to laugh and dimly realized she was inching close to hysteria. Her family! She wished Joe were here. Right now, he'd be looking at her with one eyebrow raised, his brown eyes twinkling. Oh, how she missed him.

Marilee's dad ignored his wife's chastisement and held up a hand. "The bottom line is that Joe did threaten Stan and he had a motive for wanting the man dead. Not only was the murder weapon found in his car, but he also has no alibi to prove his whereabouts at the time of the killing." He glanced over at Marilee. "You're right, honey. Your husband needs a damned good lawyer, not some ambulance chaser from Laurel Creek."

"Who? I don't know any really good lawyers," Aunt Luce said. "And hiring one's going to cost a lot of money."

"I've got that covered," Marilee inserted. She glanced at her father. "I was thinking, Daddy. Joe has some pretty famous friends. One of them may be able to recommend an attorney."

"Getting in touch with pro ball players may be a trick," Karl said.

"Not with Joe's address book at our disposal. I glanced through it earlier, but I don't know the names of any of the players. To make matters worse, Joe just jotted down initials and nicknames." She looked at Ron. "I was hoping you might recognize some of them."

"Why can't we just ask Joe who to contact?"

Marilee sighed. "Because he doesn't want me to hire him a highfalutin lawyer. He says we can't afford it."

"Can you?"

Marilee squared her shoulders. "Yes. I'm going to sell my house."

To her surprise, no one objected to the plan, not even her dad. Karl just looked at her sadly. "Most of our money is invested. It'll take me a couple of days, but I can liquidate some stock."

"No, Daddy. You and Mama need your investments to live off of. Let me sell the house first. If I go through that money and what I have in the bank, then perhaps I'll ask you for a loan. All right?"

"I said some pretty awful things to Joe when you came back from Reno. Lending him some money for a lawyer would go a long way toward making me feel less guilty about that."

"Oh, Daddy. Joe wouldn't want you to feel guilty. If he were going to blame anyone for the things you said to him, he'd blame me, and he doesn't. But I really appreciate the offer."

Ron located Joe's black address book by the phone and returned to the table with it. For the next thirty minutes, the family tried to make sense of Joe's notes, which were, more times than not, merely initials paired with phone numbers.

Finally Marilee glimpsed a name she recognized. "*Mac*. I distinctly remember Joe talking about him. I don't know what position he plays, but he's with the Bullets."

Ron circled the phone number. "Mac it is. Do you mind if I call him?"

Marilee shook her head. "I'd rather you talked to him, actually. I'm so upset, I may forget half of what he says."

Ten minutes later, Marilee was on the phone with a man named John Swenson, who Mac claimed was one of the sharpest defense attorneys on the west coast. Toward the end of the conversation, Marilee asked Swenson if she could pay seventy-five percent of his retainer fee now and the remainder in a few days. The attorney agreed to that arrangement and told Marilee he would arrive in Laurel Creek late the next afternoon or the following morning, depending upon flight availability. Until then, she was to speak to no one, especially not to any reporters.

"Reporters?" she echoed, recalling her conversation with Officer Brandt. "This is a pretty small town, Mr. Swenson. We aren't usually overrun by the press."

"Trust me, they'll be there in droves by morning," the attorney assured her. "Be prepared. The only two words I want you to say are, 'No comment.' Is that clear?"

"Yes."

"I'll consult with your husband as soon as I get there tomorrow. No worries, Mrs. Lakota. I've lost four cases in twenty years. I'm not angling for a fifth."

After breaking the connection, Marilee turned to her family. She sought her father's gaze. "Daddy, how fast can you get your hands on twenty-five thousand?"

"Twenty-five *thousand*?" Gerry said incredulously. "You're kidding. Right?"

Marilee pressed a hand to her lurching stomach. Joe was going to be furious with her over this. "I have to get my house sold, fast. Swenson wants a hundred grand up front."

After her family went home, Marilee gathered Zachary into her arms and carried him to Joe's room. *Foolishness.* But she felt a connection with Joe, lying in the bed where they'd made love. She cuddled his son close, kissed his hair, and drifted to sleep whispering frantic prayers, her fear for her husband following her into tangled dreams.

The following morning when Marilee let Boo out to go potty, the hound immediately raised a ruckus and came clambering back onto the deck, frantic to be let inside. The dog shot past her when she opened the French door. Bewildered, she stepped out in her robe to see what on earth was amiss.

"Are you Mrs. Joe Lakota?" someone yelled.

Marilee's bare feet felt glued to the deck. She stared in horrified disbelief as people converged on her, some scaling the deck's front steps, others the back. *People, hiding in her yard*? Someone shoved a microphone at her face. She threw up an arm and cried out.

"Do you think your husband killed Stan Salisbury?" a man yelled.

"Why did he do it, Mrs. Lakota? Were Salisbury and your husband enemies?"

Marilee was taken so off guard that her mind went blank. She couldn't move, couldn't reply. She squinted in a frantic attempt to see past the mikes in front of her face, her heart galloping wildly.

"Go away!" Zachary charged out onto the deck and grabbed Marilee's hand. "You go away and leave my mom alone!"

Zachary's voice jerked Marilee to her senses. She glanced down, about to wrap her arms around the little boy to make a mad dash back into the house. Only just then a reporter stepped too close, and Zachary slipped past her to plant his tiny self between her and the interloper.

"Get off our deck!" Zachary cried, his small hands clenched into fists. "Right now! You get *off*! You're scaring my mom."

"Zachary? Are you Zachary Lakota?" a reporter cried, shoving a microphone at the child's face. "Are you Joe Lakota's boy?"

Zachary slapped the mike away. "You get *off* our deck, or I'm gonna make you sorry!"

Marilee grabbed Zachary by the arms. He was rigid and trembling with outrage. Her first instinct was to pick him up and escape. But, no. It struck her in that moment that Zachary was not only facing his own demons, but he was defending her against them. Joe had told her how terrified the little boy was of reporters. That he would stand here now, yelling at them, was an amazing transformation, and something told her she should allow him this moment, that it was something he needed to do, and she would ruin it by interfering.

So instead Marilee stood behind him—once again

playing helpless female while a Lakota male did battle for her. Zachary was definitely Joe Lakota's boy. Tears nearly blinded her as she watched him. He had always reminded her so much of Joe, but never more so than now. He looked ready to take on those reporters with one hand tied behind his back—a little Sioux warrior in Barney pajamas.

"Did your father kill Stan Salisbury?" a woman asked.

Zachary sent her a look so scathing that even Marilee felt the burn. "Get out of our yard or I'm gonna call the cops. Stay on the sidewalk! If you scare Boo again, you'll be sorry."

Zachary turned and pushed Marilee ahead of him into the kitchen, whereupon he slammed the French door and turned to lock it. "Dumb reporters," he mumbled. "Don't be scared, Marilee. They won't hurt you. My dad says."

Marilee sank onto a chair, aware in a distant part of her mind that tears were streaming down her cheeks. Zachary came to her. He reached up to wipe away the wetness, his stubby fingers gentle but clumsy, reminiscent to Marilee of his dad's. "It's okay. They only hide so they can talk to you. They didn't jump out to be mean, like at a party or anything. After this, don't go outside without me. Okay? I'll make 'em go away."

"Oh, Zachary." Marilee gathered him into her arms. "Thank goodness you came to my rescue. I didn't know what to do!" She pressed her face against his pajama shirt, purple splotches swimming before her eyes. Joe would be so happy when she told him about this. So very happy. His little boy was coming out of his shell, swinging both fists. "You were so brave, Zachary. Just like your dad. He'd be so proud of you."

He hugged her neck. "Don't be scared. I been with my dad lots of times when they come. I know what to do. We'll be all right until Daddy comes home, and then he'll chase 'em away for sure."

We'll be all right until Daddy comes home. Marilee returned his fierce hug, convinced that he was absolutely right. They were going to make it through this, and soon the three of them would be together again. It simply couldn't happen any other way.

It was their turn to be happy.

Nineteen

*M*arilee felt like a monkey in a cage, scrambling to stay hidden from the people peering in at her as she drew the curtains and blinds on every window of the house. John Swenson, the big-time attorney, had not exaggerated. The press had descended on Laurel Creek in droves, drawn by the titillating news that Joe Lakota had been arrested for murder.

The first thing Marilee did was call Faye Lakota to forewarn her. Just the thought of the old lady being startled by the press and having a heart attack made her blood run cold.

"I'm so afraid for him," Faye admitted shakily. "How on earth did that bat get in his car, Marilee? Someone's trying to make my boy look guilty."

"I know." Marilee wished she could think of something reassuring to say, but she was so frightened herself that positive thoughts came hard. "I've hired an excellent attorney that a friend of Joe's recommended, Faye. We're going to beat this. I promise you that. Meanwhile we have to keep calm and do what has to be done."

"Can you afford some big-city attorney?"

"I'm afraid I'll have to sell the house." Marilee glanced around at the destroyed kitchen, compliments of the police search last night. "As soon as we hang up, I'm calling a realtor and setting up an appointment to get it listed."

"The house? Oh, honey, let's not jump the gun. You don't want to sell your house. Where on earth will you live?"

Marilee sighed. "Well, actually, Faye, I was sort of hoping you might invite us to live with you. My folks are the salt of the earth, but Mama's a little fussy and regimental. I'm not sure she could handle a four-year-old and a slobbery hound in her tidy little house. And my sister Gerry has eight kids. Need I say more?"

Faye laughed. "I'd *love* it if you moved in here. But selling your house probably isn't necessary. Joseph was always very generous when he was getting those big contracts. I have quite a bit of money set aside."

Marilee imagined Joe sending his mom a few hundred dollars now and again. "This attorney is really expensive, Faye, as in beyond my comprehension."

"I can probably cover it."

Marilee smiled. Faye probably couldn't conceive an attorney who wanted a hundred grand up front. "That's really very sweet of you. But you may need the money you set aside for your old age."

"You sound just like Joseph," Faye protested. "In case you haven't noticed, dear, I'm already *in* my old age. I don't need all that money he sent me. Why, I told him just this summer when he was buying the other house that he was welcome to whatever he needed or wanted. He refused to touch it, and instead he put a minimum down."

Marilee already knew Joe had little equity in the house he was trying to sell. She only hoped hers sold more quickly and that she got oodles of cash in the bargain.

"I'll tell you what," she put Faye off by saying, "if I get in a pinch, I'll be on your porch with my hand out. But let me try to swing it on my own first. All right?"

"Young people." Faye let out a long-suffering sigh. "It seems silly to me for Joseph to be tight for money when he'll get all mine when I die, anyway."

"Not for many, many years, I hope."

Marilee no sooner ended the conversation with Faye than the phone rang again. When she picked up, a woman said, "Hello, Marilee. This is Valerie, Joe's ex-wife."

Marilee's body went instantly cold. For an instant, she couldn't think what to say. Then she gathered her wits. "Hello, Valerie." She glanced over her shoulder to make sure Zachary wasn't in the kitchen. "If you're calling for Joe, he isn't here right now."

"I know where Joe is. Big news travels fast."

"I see." Marilee turned to stare at the water faucet over the double sink, which had a slow drip. She really needed to get that fixed, she thought inanely. "I don't mean to sound unfriendly, Valerie, but if you haven't called for Joe, to what do I owe this honor?"

"I'm coming to get Zachary out of there. I'll be arriving tomorrow afternoon. Please, have his clothing packed."

Marilee's pulse quickened. She swallowed, hard, and curled the retractable phone cord around her fingers, applying pressure until her knuckles ached. "Joe is temporarily in jail over a misunderstanding," she finally managed to say. "Correct me if I'm wrong, but until you pursue the matter through the courts, he still has custody of his son. You're not taking Zachary anywhere."

"Joe's in jail for murder!" Valerie cried. "You can't keep my son away from me."

"Want to bet? Joe has custody, and until that changes, Zachary will stay right here."

"I'll get a special court order. I'm not leaving my kid with a murderer, and no judge in his right mind will expect me to."

Marilee's heart felt as if it was in her throat. "No judge in his right mind will assume Joe is guilty until he's proven to be. That's the law. You're welcome to petition the court, of course. If you want to waste your time and money, that's your business. But until you are accompanied to my door by a representative of the court or the county sheriff and I'm served papers, Zachary isn't going anywhere."

Marilee slammed the phone down and then stood there, shaking. What else could possibly go wrong? she wondered. She was beginning to feel as if she'd climbed onto a wildly erratic roller coaster. *Joe.* She needed to see him. Just for a few minutes. He'd asked her not to visit him at the jail, and he might be upset with her if she ignored his wishes. But that was a chance she'd have to take.

By the time Marilee had battled her way through the reporters in front of her house to reach her car, she was already starting to wish she'd stayed indoors. Her hands were wet with sweat before she got her Taurus backed from the drive and onto the street. In her opinion, these news people were nuts, leaping into the path of her car, pressing close to the windows, snapping pictures through the glass.

Instead of remaining in safety restraints, Zachary sat forward on the backseat to lean his elbows on the lowered center armrests next to Marilee. "Don't stop!" he cried when reporters ran into the street in front of the car. "Pretend like you're gonna run over 'em, and they'll get out of your way."

Marilee imagined a squashed, bloody reporter lying on the asphalt after she mowed him down. She honked her horn and lowered her window a couple of inches to yell, "Get out of the street!"

"Mrs. Lako—"

She cut the reporter's question short by rolling the window back up.

"You gotta just *go!*" Zachary cried. "Daddy does it all the time. Just *go*, Marilee. Don't be scared. They'll jump out of the way."

"Oh, God!" Marilee stared at the men who were all but leaning over the hood of her car. She blared the horn one last time in warning, closed her eyes, and tromped on the gas. "Oh, *God!*"

Zachary giggled. "Scramble! That's the way, Marilee. Just like my dad."

She was picturing scrambled brains. She cracked open one eye. Miraculously, the reporters had jumped to each side of her car, and she hadn't run over anyone. The breath rushed out of her. Zachary laughed again and leaned through the seats to jab his middle finger at a newsman who was flashing their picture through the windshield.

"*Zachary!*" Marilee cried in a scandalized tone. "Where on earth did you see someone do that?"

The child drew in his finger, flashed her a wide-eyed look, and said, "It's what my dad always does."

"Oh." Marilee checked her rearview mirror, for fear they might be followed. She was relieved to see that no reporters were running up the street after them. "Well, I'll have to speak to your father about that." She halted the car at the corner stop sign to check for traffic before she proceeded into the quiet intersection. "That's an obscene gesture, and a boy your age shouldn't see such things."

"You better go faster," Zachary said, straightening to look back. "They'll come after us in cars."

"They *will?*"

As Marilee turned left, she saw a car speeding up the street. To her dismay, the sedan never even slowed down at the corner. The driver ran the stop sign and fell in behind her Taurus in hot pursuit. "Why are they *doing* this?"

"To get more pictures. Drive *fast*, Marilee. Go every

which way. That's what my dad does. You gotta trick 'em."

Marilee stepped harder on the gas. "Zachary James, buckle up."

A few minutes later, Marilee backed her Taurus up someone's driveway and parked under their carport.

"Who lives here?" Zachary asked.

"I have no idea."

"Will the people who live here get mad?"

"I hope not."

"How come are we sitting under their thingy?"

Marilee let out a shaky breath. "To trick the reporters, lady style. Your dad speeds and goes every which way. I drive a little slower and just borrow someone else's carport. We'll simply sit here until all the reporters drive past, and then I'll take you over to your grandma's house, going a different way."

The sedan whizzed by on the street just then. Zachary giggled and jabbed his middle finger again. "You're real good at this, Marilee. Wait till I tell my dad this trick."

The child was having so much fun, Marilee couldn't help but smile. It was a pretty good trick, at that. Big-city dudes. They were no match for a Laurel Creek girl. When another car went by, Marilee couldn't resist. She gave them the finger, right along with Zachary.

Marilee had to go through so much rigmarole at the city jail that she was ready to chew her way through the cell bars by the time she finally got to see Joe. Just like in the movies, they sat on stools facing each other at a counter divided lengthwise by thick plate glass. To speak to each other, they had to use black telephones with smudges all over the handgrips. It was *awful*.

"Oh, Joe, you look exhausted," she blurted.

It was true. He was wearing a wrinkled orange jump-suit with a gray laundry tag sewn on the left breast pocket. His hair was mussed, as if he'd been running his fingers through it, and he had dark smudges under his eyes.

"Mari, what the hell are you doing here?" he asked, his voice sounding like granite scraping over a cheese grater.

She wanted so badly to touch him. She flattened her free hand against the glass, straining toward him. "You're here."

"Oh, Mari, Mari . . ." He sighed and pressed his hand to the glass as though to touch his palm to hers. Only they couldn't touch. Thick glass and a murder charge separated them. "I don't want you in this place. Please, sweetheart, go home. I'm afraid you'll run into some creep on the way out or something."

"I won't. Laurel Creek doesn't have any hardcore creeps. All we've got around here are petty criminals."

"Laurel Creek has at least two hardcore creeps. One is in the morgue, and the other one's walking around out there with blood on his hands. Don't talk to me about how safe and idyllic it is here."

"I'll be careful, Joe."

"You'll stay home." His hand tightened over the phone receiver. "I mean it, Marilee. I don't want you touched by this."

He didn't want her touched by this? She felt as if her insides had been ripped out. Seeing him like this, knowing he might never walk out of here a free man—oh, God, how could she help but be touched by this?

"I love you, Joe. What happens to you, happens to me."

His jaw muscle started to tic. His lashes drooped low over his eyes. "If you love me, stay home, look after my son, and just wait it out."

"Wait what out?"

"This mess. It'll shake down eventually. They've provided me with a public defender. I'll see him after lunch. It'll shake down."

An awful coldness seeped through her as she searched

his gaze. She knew in that moment that Joe didn't believe he would beat this. "Joe, listen to me. I know it looks bad right now—what with the murder weapon being found in your car and all that—but things can only get better from here on out. The worst has happened. Right? Now we'll just prove you're innocent, that's all."

"How, Mari? They've already got me tried and fried. They aren't looking for the killer. I'm their man."

This was so totally unlike him. He had always been the upbeat one, making her smile, giving her hope. For the first time in her recollection, he looked whipped. She pressed her fingers harder against the glass. "Oh, Joe, *don't*. Please, keep heart."

"They're moving me to the county jail in the morning," he said, as if he hadn't heard her. "That's where they put killers. City court doesn't handle big-time murder cases."

"You listen to me," she said sternly. "I don't know what they've been saying to you in this place, but here are the facts. Ron called your friend Mac last night, and he recommended a fantastic defense attorney, a guy named John Swenson. He'll be here this afternoon or in the morning to speak to you. He says he's only lost four cases in his entire career, and yours isn't going to be the fifth. He'll set this two-bit police department on its ear."

"You hired *Swenson*?" His face contorted with anger, giving Marilee cause to be thankful he was held back by plate glass. She had a feeling he very much wanted to get his hands around her neck. "God *damn* it, Mari! Did I or did I not specifically tell you to forget hiring a lawyer, that we couldn't afford it? You've deliberately gone against my orders!"

Even with the glass to separate them, Marilee drew back slightly as she said, "Your *orders*? Excuse me. You're not my superior officer or anything."

The hand he held pressed to the glass curled into a fist. "I sure as shit am. You see that ring on your finger?

When push comes to shove, you're the red shirt in this operation, and I'll call the plays."

She blinked. She'd seen Joe mad a few times, but never quite this mad. "I beg your pardon? Marriage isn't a football game, and even if it was, I'm no rookie to run your plays and take orders. I *married* you. I didn't *indenture* myself to you. This *operation*, as you call it, is a partnership."

"It's a partnership until I say otherwise." He sat back, closed his eyes, and released a slow breath. She had a feeling he was either counting to ten or considering ways he could dispense with the glass in order to strangle her. When he looked at her again, he said, "I told you not to hire an attorney. I *am* your husband. Remember? Where's that Catholic upbringing of yours right now? Conveniently at home in the dresser drawer? In important matters, a wife defers to her husband and lets him make the decisions."

"*This* wife will love you and stand by you, through thick and thin. Your life is on the line."

"It's *my* life."

"No, it's *our* life."

"You will *not* spend all your savings on a one-in-a-million chance of getting me off. Is that clear?"

"Like mud."

"Marilee Sue," he said warningly.

"What, John Henry?"

His eyes narrowed. "What's that mean?"

"That right now you're not thinking with the brains God gave you. I hired Swenson. You can yell all you want, but he's your attorney, end of subject, and until you get out of here, there's nothing you can do about it."

"Swenson charges a fortune. He's like the Lamborghini of defense attorneys. You can't afford him, sweetheart. Please, don't *do* this. The one bright spot in this whole mess is that I know you and Zachary are all right, and that you won't be hurting financially."

"I've got his retainer fee covered."

"With what?"

"Daddy is lending us twenty-five to go with our seventy-five."

He looked as if he was about to rupture a vessel. Veins popped out in his temples. His eyes started to glitter. *"Thousand?"*

"Joe, please, don't be worried."

"What'll you eat, dandelions out of the yard? You'll call Swenson immediately and tell him you've changed your mind."

"No, I won't. He's your only chance."

"If you get a second mortgage on your house to pay him, I'll turn you over my knee."

Marilee reached deep for strength and smiled sweetly. "Promise? That sounds sort of fun. First, of course, you have to get out of here." She sighed with feigned disappointment. "You'll probably be out of the mood by then."

He got a startled look on his face. Then the corners of his mouth twitched. An instant later, he started to laugh. As his mirth subsided, he shook his head and leaned close to the glass to hold her gaze. "Sweetheart, I'm touched. Really. That you'd get a second on your house for me. Wow. I know how much that house means to you."

"Joe, I'll be the happiest woman alive when you get out of here, and you just as much as admitted you might—with Swenson's help."

"You can be the most stubborn, mule-headed, *difficult* person sometimes! You can't jeopardize your whole life on a gamble. Swenson's good. I'll give you that. But, Mari, the evidence is stacked sky-high against me. Don't you see that?"

Yes, she saw that, but never would she admit it. Not to him. He needed her to be strong for him right now. "I don't think the evidence is that damning, actually. They've got nothing conclusive. Did they take DNA samples, or does this one-horse police department even *know* about DNA?"

"They took scrapings from under my fingernails, and they took all my clothes, even my shoes and underwear." He sighed and passed a hand over his eyes. "They also went over my skin with some kind of light. Beats me what the hell it was. I think blood traces show up under it."

"Oh, Joe, that's *wonderful*! Don't you see? You'll check out as clean as a whistle."

His gaze lifted to hers, and in that moment, Marilee felt as if he closed one of those big, brutal fists around her heart. "You really believe I didn't do it," he whispered.

"Oh, Joe, I *know* you didn't."

"I saw the look on your face. When they came to the house." He swallowed and glanced away for a moment. When he looked back, his face was drawn as taut as a drum skin. "You thought I killed him. Even before they found the bat, you thought I did it."

Marilee wanted to die. That short period of doubt. Oh, God, how she wished she could go back and relive those sixty minutes of insanity. She'd hurt him. Until this moment, he hadn't even let on that she had. But she saw the truth of it now, written all over his face. "Yes, I thought you did it," she admitted softly. "For about an hour, I thought you did it."

"What changed your mind?"

"You." Tears filled her eyes, and she yearned to reach through the glass to hug him. "You, Joe. Knowing you as I do. Sure, for a few minutes, sheer terror got the best of me. I'd always been afraid of what you'd do if I told you, that in those first few minutes I wouldn't be able to reason with you and stop you from doing something stupid. When the cops came, the first thing I thought was, 'Oh, God, this is my fault!' My worst fear, realized. A panic reaction. I'm sorry for that. As soon as my head cleared enough to think, I regretted it."

"Maybe you didn't stop me from doing something stupid, after all. Maybe I went behind your back later and killed him."

"You have faults, that temper of yours heading the list." She shook her head and laughed through tears. "You make mistakes. We all do. In short, you're not perfect. But you know what? One thing you've *never* done is break your word to me. *Never*. And I know you haven't started now. You swore to me you wouldn't touch Stan, and once that first flash of anger passed, I know you didn't."

He closed his eyes. A muscle in his cheek convulsed, making the corner of his mouth jerk. She saw his throat muscles convulse again as he struggled to swallow. When he lifted his lashes, he whispered, "I burned to kill him that night, Mari. You know that. I had motive."

"Yes."

"Maybe Stan called me, asked to see me. Maybe he hoped to talk me out of making him leave town, and I went down to meet him at Laurel Bend. He said something, I got steamed, lost my cool." He swallowed again. "The next thing I knew, he was dead."

"Uh-huh. And, of course, you grabbed your handy bat as you got out of your car to go talk to him. That's so *you*. Make sure you've got a club as an equalizer because you're a chicken at heart."

His eyes narrowed.

Marilee shook her head. "You won't shake my faith in you again, Joe. God forgive me for letting myself doubt you even once! *If* you had gone to meet Stan, and *if* you'd lost your cool, you'd have hit him with your fists, not a bat. And even then you would have stopped before you killed him. You might have hurt him, maybe badly, but once he went down, you would have stopped. You're not a killer. Not even in a rage. You're a good man with a good heart, and above all else, you're a fair man. You'd never continue to pound on someone when he could no longer defend himself."

"You're convinced of that?"

"It's engraved on my heart. You've been etching it there all my life, little by little. Convinced, Joe? No. For me, it's unquestionable fact. I think you hated him enough to do him harm—and if you told me right now that you lost your temper, hit him with all your might, and accidentally killed him with one or two blows, then, sure, I'd believe you. You're a big man—a strong man— and that could have happened. But a ball bat? Stan's death was no accident, committed in a flash of rage. Whoever did it battered him. That doesn't have your stamp on it, and nothing on God's earth will ever convince me it does, not even you."

He gestured around them. "*They* believe it. That's the scenario they've come up with. Susan spilled her guts. They know about the incident ten years ago, and that I was forcing Stan to pull up stakes. Even *you* doubted me, Mari. You've known me all your life, and even you thought I did it for a little bit. What's to make these guys change their minds, my honest face?" He pressed his hand against the glass again. "That isn't going to happen. Don't you see that? They're convinced I met him down there, that we got into it, and that I killed him. They aren't even *looking* for the real killer, for God's sake. What do you think's going to happen to save me, a miracle? Or Swenson, maybe? Don't throw away every cent you've got and risk losing your home on a long shot."

"Is *that* what this is about?" Furious, she forgot she was connected to the counter by the phone cord and jumped to her feet. When she reached the end of her tether, she was jerked off balance. Joe came halfway up from his stool as if to catch her from falling. When she regained her footing, they stared at each other. "Make me start to question your innocence, and maybe *then* I'll see reason and forget about hiring Swenson?"

"One of us has to be reasonable."

"Not me. I'm never reasonable. That's my trademark."

"Marilee, calm down. You're losing your temper, honey."

"You're damned right, I'm losing my temper! You nearly broke my heart with that performance, making me feel like a worm for doubting you! And for what? To save that stupid house?"

"That house puts a roof over your head."

"Screw the house. I'm selling it. Forget a second mortgage. I can't get as much cash up front that way."

"Don't you *dare* sell that house!"

"The decision has already been made. It's my house. I'll burn it down if I want."

"You listen here, you—"

"No, *you* listen. We're going to fight this arrest. If it takes every cent I have, and then I have to start borrowing from all our relatives, we're going to fight this, and we're going to win. Quit blubbering your bottom lip and feeling sorry for yourself, Joe Lakota. You've never been a quitter, and I won't let you be a quitter now."

He slammed his phone down, his eyes glittering at her through the glass. When he turned his back on her, she felt for sure her heart really was breaking. He stalked to the door, raised his fist to pound on it to summon the guard. Just before his knuckles connected with the steel-reinforced metal, he glanced back. Then he wheeled around, retracing his steps to the counter with angry strides. He grabbed up the phone, his teeth gleaming as his lips drew back in a snarl.

"I'm no quitter!" he bit out. "And I'm *not* blubbering my lower lip and feeling sorry for myself! I'm trying to do what's best for you because I love you, God damn it!"

"I love you, too," she said shakily. "And what's best for me is to have your arms around me at night. That's what's best. We can live in the tent, Joe. I'm sure Ron will let us have it on long-term loan."

He braced a hand on the counter and bent his head. After a long moment, he sighed and said, "All right, you win." Tears glistened in his eyes when he raised his gaze to hers. "If I can't talk you out of this madness, you leave me no choice but to fight with everything I've got to get out of here so you don't waste your money."

Marilee's heart soared. "Now you're talking. We'll do it, Joe. I just know it. You'll be home soon."

"I hope you're right." He smiled slightly and ran a smoldering gaze over her. "I can't *wait* to get my hands on you."

"Oh, Joe, me neither."

Twenty

*J*ohn Swenson was a thin man with solemn blue eyes, graying brown hair, and ordinary features. He showed up at Marilee's door wearing faded jeans and an old brown-tweed sports jacket over a yellow knit Polo, the outfit finished off with smudged white running shoes of indeterminate brand name. Marilee's heart sank. *This* was the highfalutin lawyer? *This* was what she'd agreed to pay a hundred grand up front for? Oh, God. Joe was going to fry.

"The situation doesn't look good," Swenson told her over a cup of coffee a few minutes later. He sighed and glanced around the living room, his eyes narrowing as he studied disassembled pictures, tipped over knickknacks, and other signs of chaos. "What the hell happened to your house?"

"The police. They searched the place last night."

"Warrant?"

Marilee stared at him. "Well, I guess."

"You didn't ask?"

"No."

He pulled a little scratch pad from his pocket and set aside his coffee to jot a note.

"Is a warrant important?"

"Could be," he said absently. "They find anything?"

"The murder weapon in Joe's car."

"Ah, yes." He nodded and smiled. "Anything else?"

"I, um . . . I don't think so. Unless you count the prize in Zachary's cereal."

He laughed softly. "That thorough, were they? Ah, well, they probably don't get much excitement as a general rule." He pocketed the pad, took another fast sip of coffee, then braced his elbows on his knees and chafed his palms. "Here's the scoop. Your husband has no witnesses to prove he was in Bedford yesterday. The victim's wife heard him threaten to kill her husband. On top of that he's got motive—avenging you—and the murder weapon was found in his car. Not good."

Marilee wanted to weep. "Are you going to be able to help him?"

Swenson smiled. "How would you like to have him home tonight?"

"Oh, I'd *love*—" She broke off. "You're kidding, right?"

"Nope. I'm working on getting him out on bail as we speak."

"Do they let murderers out on bail?"

"*Suspected* murderer," he corrected. "And in answer to your question, it depends on how much conclusive evidence there is. If a judge feels certain the individual is a danger to society, no bail. If he isn't convinced, there's a chance he'll set bail. It's my job to make sure he does."

Marilee was beginning to really *like* John Swenson. He might not look like much, but she had a feeling that only made his dynamic personality all the more powerful because he caught people by surprise. "Can you do that?"

"What do you think you're paying me for, Mrs. Lakota? My good looks?"

"But there's a lot of damning evidence. Right?"

"Not what I'd term a lot." He took a last sip of coffee and then rose. "Where's the blood? Kill a man in that fashion, and you're going to be covered with blood. Did your husband come home and shower? No. Did he shower at the school? No. So where did he shower? He has a well-known face. Has he been placed at a local motel where he might have showered? At a motel in a neighboring town? No. Was he seen at his mother's, where he might have showered? No. So how can they explain that they found no trace of blood on him, not even in his hair?

"Where are the clothes he was wearing when he committed the murder? He couldn't have been wearing the ones he came home in when he committed the crime, because they were clean. Have there been tests run to prove the mud on his car came from—what bend was that?"

"Laurel Bend."

"Ah, yes, Laurel Bend. Does the tire tread of your husband's Honda match the tire tracks found at the scene? Were any traces of blood found on or inside his car? Are his fingerprints on the murder weapon? If not, where are the gloves he wore, which would also be covered with blood?" He shrugged. "Need I go on? I think you can expect your husband to be home tonight. If not tonight, tomorrow."

"Oh, Mr. Swenson, thank you!"

"Don't thank me. It's bail, not vindication. Your husband is in big trouble. The other side of the coin is that I've seen men convicted on less evidence than this."

Marilee walked with him to the front door. After stepping onto the porch, Swenson gazed thoughtfully across her front yard at the reporters who flanked his gray rental car. "Damned press. Thanks to them, I was lucky to get a room in this dinky little burg."

"You're welcome to stay over here. I make a mean steak and salad, and I'd love having you."

He returned his gaze to her and smiled. "I appreciate

the offer, but I never fraternize with clients. You run the risk of becoming friends with them."

"That's a drawback?"

"It is when I hand them my bill."

Marilee gave a startled laugh. "Oh, God. That bad? Tell me, Mr. Swenson, after I pay that bill, will I have my husband at home? Your best educated guess. That's all I'm asking. Is there any chance you can get Joe off?"

"What I need is another suspect. I believe your husband's innocent, Mrs. Lakota. But proving that may be a trick." He scratched his head, his eyes narrowing in concentration. "There *has* to be someone else—one or more individuals who had reason to want Salisbury dead. Someone who hated him enough to bludgeon him. We've got to find out who those people may be. I don't have to round up enough evidence to convict them. I just have to cast suspicion on them. Otherwise Joe will be a one-poodle circus act, and the attention will remain centered on him. Do you understand what I'm saying?"

Marilee nodded.

"Can you think of anyone besides Joe who might have wanted Salisbury dead?"

"Me."

He chuckled. "Aside from you. Salisbury was six-four and close to two-hundred-and-fifty pounds. I don't think you could have killed him, not with a short bat. A long one, maybe."

Marilee could think of no one. She gnawed on her bottom lip. "I know someone who might be able to give me some good leads if I can get her to talk to me. Someone who probably knew most of Stan's friends and business acquaintances."

"Who's that?"

"His wife."

"You know her?"

"Yes. We're not what you'd call friends, but I know her."

"Think you can convince her to open up to you?"

Marilee hadn't spoken to Susan in over ten years. "I can try."

Swenson frowned. "All I need are the names of people who might have had damned good reason to be pissed off at him. I can take it from there, do some digging." He nodded. "Give her a go. See what you can pry out of her. It sure as hell can't hurt. If you hit a dead end, I'll browbeat her for a while myself to see what shakes out."

After telephoning to make sure Faye didn't mind keeping Zachary overnight, Marilee called Susan Salisbury.

"Why would I agree to meet you somewhere?" Susan asked acidly. "You're indirectly responsible for Stan's death. *Why*, Marilee? You kept quiet about it for ten years. Why the sudden need to bare your soul to Joe? I hope it made you feel better, lady, because now my kids don't have a father! Even worse, they can't even remember him with pride. A rapist? Have you seen the papers?"

"No." Marilee strove to keep her temper. "I never would have wished Stan dead, Susan, and I certainly never would have chosen for anyone to know about the rape. I'm very sorry this has happened. I know it must be rough on your children."

"Yeah, I bet your heart just *bleeds*. You think I set you up that night to be gang raped."

Marilee's stomach turned. "Did you?"

"What kind of person do you think I am? They were supposed to scare you, give you a hard time. What kind of woman sets another woman up to be hurt like that?"

"A really vicious one."

Silence. "I've done some shitty things in my life," Susan finally said, "but never something *that* low. God! I wanted to kill Stan myself when I found out. The rotten son of a bitch! He slept with me later that night. Can you believe it? He raped you, and then he proposed to me and took my virginity. How do you think that makes me feel? I thought it was so romantic—something so special.

Damn him. I can forgive all the other women he went through after we got married, but I'll never forgive him for that. To do something that vile, and then come to me like he was oh so in love with me and so caring?" She broke off and sobbed. "The heartless bastard. He never cared about anybody but himself. But that doesn't mean my kids should pay! Me, maybe, for being so damned stupid. And Stan, sure. But not my kids."

Marilee cupped a hand over her eyes, feeling sick clear to the center of her bones. For some reason, she'd never stopped to think about Susan's side of this or how she might feel. What a horrible discovery, to learn you'd given your heart and body to a guy who had just brutally raped another girl. Marilee would have hated to be touched by a man who'd recently been with another woman, period, even if his partner had been willing. The sexual act was so—*intimate*. So invasive. If Joe ever came to her straight from another woman's arms, she would feel contaminated even by his kisses.

"Oh, Susan, I'm—so sorry." She needed information from this woman, but at what cost? She knew that if Joe were privy to this conversation, he wouldn't have the heart to make Susan suffer any more than she already was. "I—this was a bad idea. I shouldn't have called. Joe wouldn't want this. Your husband is dead, and all I can think about is how to save mine. I'm sorry. I don't know what I was thinking. I never gave a thought to your children. I'm sure you can't get away right now anyway. You need to be with them."

"They're at my mom's up north. She and Daddy came and got them this morning," Susan said brokenly. "I'm here all alone." She made a low wailing sound. "The police don't want me to leave t-town yet. In case they n-need to ask me more questions. So I'm h-here all *alone*! Where are all my f-friends? The only people who've called are curiosity seekers. They don't c-care about *me*."

"Oh, Susan . . ." Marilee pushed a hand into her hair. "Would you like me to come?"

"*You?*" she cried. "Oh, that'd b-be dandy. The m-murderer's wife comforting the grieving w-widow?"

"Well, at least you know I'm not fishing for gossip tidbits. I know the inside scoop."

Between sobs, Susan laughed a little hysterically. "Wouldn't the reporters *love* it? They're like vultures out there. I went to get the paper off the porch, and they took a picture of my ass when I bent over to pick it up."

"I have one better. I stepped out on the deck in my robe, and I didn't have the sash tied. They got pictures of me in my Snoopy T-shirt and underpants."

"Oh, *God!*" Susan laughed and then began sobbing in earnest. Marilee listened while the other woman cried as if her heart were breaking. Finally she said, "What're we *doing*? You hate my guts, and I'm not particularly fond of you."

"I don't know. I think we're going over the edge together."

Susan sniffed. "Why did you want to meet me somewhere?"

"To pick your brain. To try to save my husband. Joe didn't kill Stan, Susan. I'm not saying he wasn't mad enough to do it, but Joe isn't the kind of guy to use a bat. He would have done it with his bare hands."

"You'd like to believe that."

"I know that."

"Come on, Marilee. Who else would've bashed his brains out? Give me a break. Name me one person."

"That's why I wanted to talk to you, because I believe, if you think hard enough, you'll be able to give me that person's name."

"Not. Stan was a shit, but nobody wanted to kill him. Except me, occasionally."

"There has to be someone, Susan. Someone who really hated Stan. Someone who might have been angry enough

with him about something to kill him. I'm telling you—
and I swear this to you on my life—Joe didn't do it."

"I suppose he gazed into your eyes and told you he
didn't." She laughed sourly and sniffed again. "God.
Aren't we women pathetic? They lie, and we believe the
assholes. When will we ever wise up?"

"I guess I can't blame you for thinking that way."

"Experience, Marilee. Get enough under your belt, and
you're a cynic." She released a weary sigh. "I've got
some whiskey here. You want to come over and get
drunk with me, you're more than welcome to pick my
brain. It's a dead end, and I should probably tell you to
go screw yourself, but the truth is, I'd rather get drunk
with my worst enemy than be alone right now."

"At your place? What about the reporters?"

"I'm supplying the booze. The reporters are your problem."

Marilee wasn't prepared for the sight that greeted her
when she finally fought her way through the newsmen in
front of Susan's house and knocked on the front door.
The other woman looked terrible, her eyes puffy from
weeping, her dark hair hanging in limp strings to her frail
shoulders. Even worse, along one cheekbone, she had a
purple-black bruise.

"Good heavens, Susan!" Marilee slipped inside and
closed the door, relieved to escape the shouted questions
from the press. "You look worse than I feel. What happened to your face?"

"Stan and I had a big fight a few days ago." Susan's
green eyes welled with tears, and she shrugged. "That's
one thing I can thank Joe for. My old man won't be
knocking me around again."

She turned to lead the way through an open dining
room to the kitchen, talking over her shoulder as she
went. Her black lounging slacks and tunic flowed grace-
fully with her movements. Marilee studied her slender

figure, unable to imagine how it must have felt to be belted by a man of Stan Salisbury's bulk. Poor Susan.

"That's what you get when you marry a rapist," Susan said with bitter sarcasm. "A jerk for a husband." She stopped at the breakfast bar to slosh whiskey into two tumblers. "You want ice?"

Marilee cast a startled glance at the glasses. She really hadn't planned to come over and drink, but that seemed to be Susan's sole aim. "No, I, um, don't need it on the rocks. Straight up is fine."

Susan slid a tumbler toward her. "To men!" she said acidly, lifting her glass. "You can't live with 'em, and you can't live without 'em."

Marilee could agree with the last half of that proclamation. She took a sip of whiskey, hating the taste as it slid down her throat like liquid fire.

Susan touched the bruise on her cheek. "You keep staring. I suppose Joe Lakota would never *dream* of smacking a woman."

"No."

Susan laughed. "Yeah? Oh, honey, give it a couple of years. If he beats this murder charge, he'll eventually get around to popping you. Any guy who can do that to Stan has it in him. Trust me on that."

"Joe didn't do it," Marilee said softly. "I told you that, Susan. You don't really know Joe. He's not a killer."

"I saw enough when he came by here to convince me he could be." Susan poured herself more whiskey and headed for the living room. She curled a leg under herself to sit on the turquoise sofa. Beside her on a cushion was the evening paper, which looked as if it had been crumpled for the trash. She glanced at it and curled her lip. "You seen the spread? We're famous. Ain't it grand? I don't know what we think we're doing. A more unlikely pair, there isn't." She gestured toward the front window. "I wonder what their spin on this will be? 'Wives Join Forces,' maybe. Or 'Murderer's Wife and Victim's Widow Offer Each Other Solace.' " She laughed and sighed. "God, tongues are going to wag about this for years. Laurel Creek, the place where nothing ever happens."

Marilee took a seat in a chair facing the sofa and rolled her glass between her hands. "That's a pretty nasty bruise, Susan. What on earth were you and Stan fighting about?"

Susan took another gulp of whiskey, clearly bent on getting sloshed. In Marilee's inexpert opinion, the distraught woman didn't have far to go. She'd evidently been drinking alone before Marilee arrived. "I was haranguing him," she admitted. "Having to move, jerk the kids out of school so early in the year, leave all our friends." She smiled sadly. "It seemed like the worst thing in the world a few days ago, having to leave here, and I hated him for being the cause." She bit her lower lip. "He, um, tried to get amorous. I couldn't stand for him to touch me, knowing what he'd done to you. I could forgive his infidelities. You know? You get used to that, and it no longer hurts. But after I found out about you, just the sight of him turned my stomach."

"I see."

Susan drained her glass and stood to go for a refill. "I almost got a taste of my own medicine that night. He didn't take want to take no for an answer." Once at the bar, she poured a measure of whiskey, downed it, and then poured herself more, her hands shaking so violently that bottle and glass clinked. "Thank God the kids were gone skating. It got ugly. Really ugly. I slapped him for trying to force me. He got mad and knocked me around. A real gent, that was my Stan."

Marilee felt as if she might get sick. "Susan, I never would have wished that on you. Honestly."

"Yeah?" She returned to the conversation area, carrying the uncapped half-gallon of whiskey. She stopped to add more liquor to Marilee's glass. "Ah, well. I was saved by the doorbell, and he stopped. I guess it would have been poetic justice if he hadn't."

She sat again, swirling the alcohol in her glass, her gaze fixed on the eddy of amber. "I'll bet you thought I didn't give a care about what happened to you. You were wrong." Her mouth trembled. "I felt bad enough, thinking they only shoved you around and scared you. I knew you hated me. Once at the supermarket, you saw me and took off like a scalded dog. Afterward, I felt bad for days, and I didn't even know how far it had gone that night. Now . . ." She lifted a frail shoulder and gulped more booze. "Now I know, and I hate myself. I try to lay it off on my having been so young, not to mention gullible. He said they wouldn't hurt you, and like an idiot, I believed him. They just wanted to rile Joe. Upset you enough that you'd go running to him in a dither. That was all. Or so the bastard told me."

Marilee closed her eyes, feeling curiously numb. "If you didn't know, Susan, you shouldn't blame yourself. We *were* young. What were you, all of nineteen? A wise, older woman in my sorority. You were no more clued in than I was."

"I'd never be involved in something like that now, that's for sure," Susan said softly. "My little girl, Annie, she's six. Since Joe came over and spilled the beans, I find myself looking at her and feeling terrified. I'd die if something like that happened to her in college. I'd just— die. And it's there, in the back of my mind, that seeing her hurt like that may be the way I'll get paid back."

"I think you've paid enough, Susan. I'm sorry about what Stan did."

"You don't know the half of it. He was a jerk from day one." She shivered and took another drink. "Ah, well, our last round was interrupted. At least he never did that to me. A good friend of ours dropped by—an old football buddy of Stan's." Her features softened. "He's Annie's godfather, in fact. A really nice guy—one of the few decent friends Stan ever had. He's been my rock more times than I can count."

"I'm glad someone was there for you."

"Yeah." She sighed wearily. "Me, too. He's been great. Almost from the first, he's been my broad shoulder to cry on. A case of marrying the wrong guy, if you know what I mean. I've wished a thousand times that I'd had the sense back then that I have now, I'll tell you. He begged me to get a divorce. I know he would've married me. But I just couldn't do that to my kids. For all his faults, Stan was a good dad, and they loved him."

"Does this friend live here in Laurel Creek?"

"No, Bedford." She turned her wedding rings on her finger, then lowered her hand. "Who knows. Maybe now I'll finally get my chance with Mr. Right. He really is a sweetie. God, he was so furious the other night when he saw what Stan had done. I thought there'd be a fight. He was just that mad. But instead he got Stan out of here and concentrated on taking care of me."

Marilee forced herself to take another sip of liquor. "You've been through so much, I feel like a worm for trying to grill you for information."

"Grill away. I don't think I can tell you anything. But, you know what? I *wish* I could." She flashed Marilee a look that gleamed like emeralds. "I'd love to find out Joe didn't do it. Not because I give a care about him. It'd just be nice, knowing things turned out okay for you. You talk about what I've been through. Correct me if I'm wrong, but I don't think your life's been any picnic."

Marilee considered the question. "No, definitely not a picnic." She told Susan about the panic attacks, and all the many times when she'd believed she might die for lack of oxygen. "It wasn't fun, but I survived," she concluded. "Now that I've gone through counseling, I'm doing much better. From here on out, I want to look ahead instead of back and have a chance to be happy. There's also Joe's little boy, Zachary." Marilee quickly related to Susan the situation with Valerie. "I'm afraid she'll regain custody if Joe is found guilty."

Susan grimaced. "That's tough. God, why is it that the

kids always suffer? They're so blameless, and the shit always rolls downhill to them."

It wasn't exactly how Marilee might have put it, but she agreed with the statement, nonetheless. "I'd like to stop that from happening to Zachary if possible."

Susan nodded. "Okay. Let me think. Stan's enemies. God, do you have a tablet and pen? I doubt any of them hated him enough to kill him, mind you, but plenty of people didn't like him." She went to fetch a tablet and ballpoint from the hutch. After handing both to Marilee, she began calling off names and relating reasons those individuals may have held a grudge against her husband. "How we doing so far?" she asked some minutes later.

Marilee gazed at her notes with a sinking heart. "There are so *many*. Almost twenty, I think. I was kind of hoping we might narrow it down. Did all these people dislike Stan?"

"Half the town disliked him. Those people are the ones he screwed big-time in business deals, the ones who might, conceivably, have wished him into an early grave."

Marilee lifted her glass to take a drink.

"I guess you can add Don Albin to that list," Susan said with a tinkling laugh. "Not that he'd ever have killed Stan, but he was definitely mad enough at him the other night to clobber him."

Marilee dropped her half-full glass on the carpet. Liquor splashed everywhere, over the tan rug, onto her jeans. Susan jumped up, grabbed some tissues, and started to blot up the mess. When she glanced at Marilee, she froze.

"My God, what's wrong? You look like you just saw a ghost." She no sooner spoke than her eyes darkened. The tissues fell forgotten from her fingers, and in an agonized whisper, she said, *"Don?"*

Marilee could only stare at her.

"No," Susan cried. *"No!* Not Don. He wasn't part of that mess. He'd *never* force himself on a woman. I know he wouldn't." She splayed a hand over her chest. "Please, tell me he wasn't there."

Marilee wished with all her heart she could. "Oh, Susan. I'm sorry. I never—"

"*No!*" she said sharply. "Damn it, no! He'd *never* do such a thing!"

"Susan, calm down."

Susan pushed to her feet. "Get out. *Now*. We've talked enough. I want to be alone now."

Marilee collected her purse, ripped the top sheet from the tablet, and hurried for the door. *Oh, God, oh, God.* Don Albin was Susan's shoulder to cry on, the friend who'd always been there for her?

"He didn't kill Stan!" Susan called after her. "Do you hear me, Marilee? I *know* he didn't. He's a good, kind man. He'd never do something like that. He's a good man, I'm telling you!"

Marilee let herself out onto the porch and closed the door. Not even the reporters who surged forward to meet her as she ran for her car penetrated the haze of horror in her mind. *Don.* She had to get in touch with John Swenson immediately. She thought she knew who killed Stan Salisbury.

In a town as small as Laurel Creek, it didn't take Marilee long to call around and find out where Swenson was staying. Unfortunately the attorney wasn't in his motel room, and all she could do was leave a message for him.

After doing that, she considered telephoning the police herself to give them Albin's name, but she quickly decided against it. Swenson was the legal guru, after all, not her. The information about Albin might be put to more effective use if Joe's attorney chose the right moment to reveal it.

To mark off time, Marilee fed Boo, and then she half-heartedly began straightening the cupboards that the police had left in such a stir. Occasionally when she heard a car door slam, she'd hurry to the front door to peer out at the street, hoping to see Joe climbing from a taxi. If he made bail, instead of calling her to come pick him up, he might want to surprise her.

Each race to the front door ended in disappointment. The press was still camped out in front of her house. The sounds she heard were invariably made by newsmen climbing in and out of their cars. She imagined them, sitting out there in the dark, listening to their stereos and drinking coffee to stay alert. What a horrible job. Even worse, all they got for their trouble were pictures and an angry, "No comment!" She wondered if they had families. Probably. They undoubtedly wished they were home with their spouses, just as she yearned to be with hers.

At eight o'clock, Marilee shelved her hope that Joe might be able to post bail that night. Maybe in the morning—if they were lucky. Swenson had given her no guarantee, after all.

To stave off her crushing sense of disappointment, she focused on the fact that at least she had some information for the attorney that might lead to Joe's permanent release. That was what she needed to be thinking about, positive thoughts, happy thoughts. As difficult as all of this was, at least she had hope that there might be an end in sight. Susan Salisbury did not.

What a tragic person she was—a woman who had loved unwisely, not once but twice. It didn't seem fair. Marilee had made one really catastrophic mistake in her life, and admittedly that had led her to make a series of others that had hurt not only her, but Joe and, by extension, her family. But at least she'd never loved unwisely, giving her heart to a man who had a dark side of which she was blithely unaware. Despite all that she and Joe had endured, they had honesty between them, and their love for each other was genuine. Joe would never strike her or betray her in the arms of another woman.

Thinking of him, Marilee ached to feel his arms around her. Tomorrow night, she told herself. Maybe he'd be home early enough for dinner. She'd buy wine to celebrate. They could spend a great evening with Zachary, and once he was tucked in, the remainder of the night would be theirs. With that thought in mind, Marilee decided to put fresh linen on Joe's bed. And why not some tapers, strategically placed around his room? They could make love by candlelight tomorrow night.

Marilee had just stripped the sheets from Joe's bed when she thought she heard the French door open and close. She froze to listen. A second later, Boo barked softly. Marilee grinned. *Joe.* Only he had keys to the house, so it could be no one else. A giddy delight coursed through her as she ran up the hallway to throw herself into his arms.

"I'll be forever in your debt for this," Joe said as he shook John Swenson's hand. "It's going to feel damned good to be at home with my family tonight. You just can't know. Maybe you'll be worth those astronomical fees, after all."

John smiled and nodded. "Let's just hope we get a break, and you never have to come back here."

Joe scooped his change from the tray on the counter, pocketed it, and then reclaimed his wallet.

"You plan to call your wife, or would you like me to give you a lift home?"

Joe fell into step beside the attorney as they existed the police department, a place he hoped and prayed never to see again. "Would it be out of your way? I'd really like to surprise her."

"I may have spoiled that for you. I told her you might get out on bail tonight."

Joe grinned. "Ah, well, a lift will be appreciated, anyway. She won't know for sure I'm coming home until she sees me. Right?"

*　　*　　*

As Marilee turned the corner into the short hall that led to the kitchen, she braked to a stop so suddenly that her sneakers grabbed on the hardwood floor and squeaked. Don Albin stood just inside the French doors next to the curio cabinet. His gray eyes burned into hers as he returned her stare.

"How did you get in here?" she asked in a faint voice.

He smiled and held up a credit card. "You really should install a better lock on this door," he said softly.

Oh, God. The French doors. Every other door in the house sported two deadbolts, but she'd never gotten around to installing a security lock on the new French doors.

From the corner of her eye, Marilee saw Boo poke his head out her bedroom doorway. The big hound went, "*Whoof!*" and then disappeared again, a coward as always. She was on her own.

Sweat popped up between her shoulder blades. She retreated a step, her gaze fixed on one of the faces that had haunted her nightmares for ten endless years. "Wh-What are you doing here, Don?"

He pocketed the credit card. It was then that Marilee noticed he was wearing gloves. Her stomach clenched with terror, and she could almost hear Swenson say, *Where are the gloves he must have worn?* Oh, God, oh, God. This man was going to kill her. She saw it in his eyes.

Her mind raced wildly. She gauged the distance to the front door, wondering if she stood a chance of making it. The reporters. If she could just make it out into the yard, she'd be safe. Don wouldn't dare touch her in front of all those witnesses.

"You don't want to do this, Don," she said softly. "Think. The press is outside. Someone must have seen you come in."

"No," he said, still smiling. "I parked a couple of blocks over and cut through yards to come in the back way. The reporters are all sitting in their cars, watching the front of the house. They don't know I'm here."

Marilee tensed to run. He lunged at her. She whirled and screamed as loudly as she could, for as long as she could. Running, running. As though caught in a dream, she felt as if her scrambling steps carried her nowhere. Then a strong arm caught her around the waist, the force of it slamming the breath from her lungs. She clawed wildly at his jacket sleeve, trying to get away. Then she twisted, going for his face. Her cry of distress, aborted by his crushing hold, had been reduced to a pathetic whimpering she knew no one outside would be able to hear.

He grunted and released her for an instant to capture her flailing arms. Marilee tried to scream again, but the sound was quickly snuffed out when his arm came back around her, pinning hers to her sides. A big, gloved hand clamped over her mouth. She hung there against his powerful body, her back pressed to his chest, her feet suspended above the floor. His thumb smashed against her nostrils, blocking off her air.

"How's that feel? Huh?" he asked softly. "You remember this, Marilee?"

She wrenched violently, trying to break his hold. Oh, dear God. Oh, dear God. She grabbed frantically, futilely for breath, her chest jerking spasmodically. No air. She couldn't get any air. He was going to suffocate her.

He moved his thumb, laughing softly as she whined to drag in oxygen through her suddenly unblocked nostrils.

"You just couldn't keep your mouth shut, could you?" he whispered. "First you told Joe, and stirred up trouble for Stan. Then you went whining to Susan. She was the only good thing in my whole damned life, and in two seconds, you ruined it. *Why*? Was it satisfying, Marilee? You finally got some revenge. Well, guess what, sweetheart, I'm not getting sent away for murder."

He carried her toward the living room. Marilee kicked, digging her heels into his shins, but her sneakers didn't inflict enough damage to make him let go of her. *Think.*

She had to think. Somehow she had to break free. Make it to the door.

To her horror, he knelt on the living room rug with her still locked in his hold. What was he going to do to her? Terror turned her bones to water. His gloved hand remained clamped over her mouth.

"I never wanted to hurt you that night," he whispered. "We were all just gonna pretend like we might. Nobody really meant to go through with it. Then you turned she-cat, scratched Buckley's face, and everybody went a little crazy. I *knew* it was a bad deal. The minute it started happening, I knew we'd all live to regret it. That you'd scream it to the rooftops and get us all in trouble.

"That was why I blocked your nose. You kept looking at me. Remember? Trying to tell me with your eyes that I was suffocating you? Like I didn't know. I tried to make sure you never talked, you stupid bitch! The other guys would've thought I did it accidentally and helped me cover it up. Sorority girl, tanked up on too much booze. Passes out facedown on something that smothers her. *Easy.* I could've pulled it off, only you kept turning your head, getting a little air, prolonging it. And before I could finish you, Stan started yelling that it was my turn. God, they were all such fools. Like they could do that to somebody and just let her walk out? I *knew* you'd be trouble. And guess what? I was right. You just took your own sweet time to start screaming."

Marilee shuddered at the memories. Oh, please . . . God.

"Well, it's just me you're dealing with this time, and I'm gonna make damned sure you *never* open your trap again. I'm not gonna fry for any of this. No way."

His thumb moved over her nose again. He laughed when she began to buck.

"Go ahead. Struggle. It'll just end it quicker. That's a *good* girl. You fight for all your worth and burn up lots of oxygen real fast."

Her worst nightmare. The cloying fear of suffocating

that had dogged her for so long. She couldn't breathe. Oh, dear God . . .

"They'll think you had one of those panic attacks," he whispered. "Oh, yeah, Susan told me about them before I left to come over. How sometimes you'd even pass out. *Perfect.* I won't leave a mark on you. They'll just find you here on the floor, *dead.* Poor little Marilee. A panic attack finally does her in."

Black spots. Marilee blinked frantically, the airless pounding in her head starting to deafen her. He was still talking. Nothing he said made any sense. What he was doing made no sense. He'd never get away with this. Never. Not that his getting caught would make a difference for her. She'd be dead.

From far away, Marilee heard a strange sound. *Boo.* Barking and baying. Suddenly Don took his hand from her nose and mouth. She hung there, limp in the circle of his arm, gasping frantically for breath.

"Shut up! Get!" he yelled, swinging outward with his arm. "Go on, you stupid mutt! Shut up, I tell you!"

Still laboring for oxygen, Marilee blinked, trying to see. A blur of brown, darting first one way, then the other. As her hearing sharpened, the noises became distinctly recognizable as Boo's barking and baying. *Boo?* Marilee gaped. He was a big chicken, his answer to everything to dive under her bed and hide. She couldn't believe he'd found the courage to come out here and bark, let alone get close enough for Don to swing at him.

Suddenly the dog lunged, capturing Don's jacket sleeve in the huge canine teeth that had, until this moment, never bitten into anything but dog kibble.

"Son of a *bitch*!"

Miraculously, Don loosened his hold on her to fight off the dog. Marilee scrambled away, sobbing. When she gained her feet, she broke into a run.

"Oh, no, you don't!" Don grabbed her by an ankle and brought her down. "You're not—*son of a bitch*!"

Boo attacked in earnest when Don grabbed her, his

bays turning to a high, frantic keening, the cry of a hound going for the kill. Marilee gained her feet again and ran. *Running, running*. The front door. If she could just make it to the front door, all those wonderful reporters would leap from their cars, snapping her picture with their cameras. *Oh, yes*. The front door.

She hurtled herself down the hall, fleeing in a blind panic.

Thump! She hit a brick wall. Fell backward. Big, warm hands closed over her arms to catch her.

"Mari?"

Joe. Marilee saw the blur of his dark face,. She grabbed fistfuls of his shirt and literally tried to run up his legs, she was so scared. Couldn't talk. Couldn't tell him. *Joe*. Oh, thank you, God. *Joe*. She clung to his neck, her chest still whining for breath.

"What the hell? Is that Boo?" he asked. Then, "Son of a bitch!" He set her away from him. "Outside! Get outside, Marilee!"

She fell against the hallway wall, her legs so rubbery with terror that she couldn't move. Joe ran toward the living room, the sound of Boo's growls leading him unerringly to the ruckus.

"Boo!" Joe yelled.

The next instant, Marilee heard Don roar with rage. There was a loud thud. Then the crash of glass. *Joe*. Oh, God. She stumbled toward the living room, terrified for him. What if Don hurt him? Joe had a bad knee. He might not be able to hold his own. Oh, dear God . . . oh, dear God.

Just as Marilee turned the corner in the hall, Boo came streaking past her, his claws losing purchase on the slick hardwood. He slid and bumped into the wall, then regained his balance to resume his dash back to the bedroom. When Marilee saw the two men locked in a brutal struggle in her living room, she almost followed the dog to hide under the bed.

Concern for Joe won out. She ran through the shattered

remains of her crystal lamp, which lay in a spray over the floor. Unable to think of anything else she might do, she grabbed a dining room chair, thinking to clobber Don with it.

Hurrying to Joe's rescue, she raised the chair high and took aim at Don's head. Just as she started to execute a downward swing, Joe flipped the man over his shoulder. Don fell lengthwise on his stomach. Joe dropped on top of him, straddled his hips, and executed a full nelson.

Already in mid-swing with the chair, Marilee nearly clobbered Joe. In the nick of time, she managed to pull off target by a narrow margin, and she hit the floor instead, the impact creating a loud *thwuck*.

Joe threw her a startled look, realized how close she'd come to hitting him, and whispered, "Holy shit."

Two hours later, Marilee and Joe sat crossed-legged on the kitchen floor. Joe held a dinner plate balanced on his crossed legs. It was piled high with bite-size chunks of top sirloin that he'd thawed in the microwave. Boo lay before him, his rheumy eyes drooping, shoestrings of white drool trailing from his jowls.

"I think he's full," Marilee observed. "He's liable to get sick, Joe."

Her husband only smiled and fed Boo another hunk of steak. "It's not often a hound gets the chance to be sick from sirloin. Right, Boo? I owe him this. When I think of all the times I called him 'that damn dog,' I feel so bad. He saved your life tonight. They say the mark of true courage is to face something even when you're scared to death. Poor Boo was pretty damned scared. It's testimony to his love for you that he came out from under the bed to help."

Marilee smiled and got misty-eyed. "He was really something, all right. I've never been quite so surprised, actually. Or *glad*. If it hadn't been for him, Don would have smothered me. I was inches away from passing out." She scratched the hound's ears. "My sweet boy. You came out to save Mom. Didn't you? Yes, you did."

Joe leaned down and made smooching noises at Boo. Watching her handsome husband, Marilee wished he'd make smooching noises at her. He looked so wonderful. Big and Indian dark, his tousled sable hair trailing over his forehead in lazy waves. Her one true love, she thought wistfully. As grateful as she was to Boo, she wanted him all to herself for a little while.

The excitement of the night was finally over, thank heavens. The police were finally gone, and she and Joe had the destroyed house to themselves at last, a fact that seemed to be escaping the big blockhead. Tomorrow it would be back to life as usual, with a four-year-old underfoot. This was their big chance to make wild, passionate love without fear of being overheard, and what was Joe doing, but feeding Boo steak.

Ah, well. At least everything had turned out all right. Joe's name was cleared, and the police had hauled Don off to jail, hopefully for a very long time, charging him with the murder of Stan Salisbury and the attempted murder of Susan Salisbury. According to the last report they'd gotten from the hospital, barring unexpected complications, Susan would recover from the gunshot wound to her chest. When Don realized she was on to him and might turn him in, he'd shot her with the handgun she'd kept for protection in her nightstand drawer.

According to the police, Don had tried to make it look like a suicide—the distraught widow, overcome with grief and unable to bear the scandal, who'd taken her own life. After shooting Susan, he'd slipped out the back, leaving her for dead, a plan that might have worked if the reporters out front hadn't heard the shot and called for help. Fortunately, Susan had been found quickly and rushed by ambulance to the hospital, where emergency surgery saved her life.

It now looked as if Susan would live to raise her children and love again, hopefully more wisely the next time around. It was her turn to be happy, Marilee thought. She was a good person. Truly a good person.

"What's that sigh for?" Joe asked softly as he fed Boo another chunk of meat.

"Oh, I was just thinking. In his twisted way, Don must really have loved Susan. Enough that he couldn't bear what Stan did to her and killed him over it. What goes on in the human mind, that something that could have been so sweet and good became so horrible and out of whack?"

It was Joe's turn to sigh. "Sweetheart, even a rattlesnake probably loves, in its way. Corner it, though, and it'll strike out at its own kind in a blind panic. Don didn't love Susan the way I love you, or the way you love me. It was a sick, twisted kind of love. Probably always was. Something's wrong with the guy. He's not tracking right."

"I know. And that gives me the shivers. Don and Stan. The other three guys involved ten years ago. What happened with all of them, Joe? They were fairly attractive, good in sports, going to college on scholarships. So much going for them, and yet they did something so awful to me that it's inconceivable to most of us. It's like some kind of contagious craziness infected all of them."

"You know that old saying, 'birds of a feather flock together.' There was something not quite right with all of them from the start, and they were drawn to each other because of it, I think." He shook his head. "You see it in gangs and occasionally during wartime—a group of guys who suddenly go berserk and commit atrocities. When you hear about it, you wonder, 'How can that happen? Wasn't there a sane one in the bunch?' It's my theory that they ended up together, in that particular situation, because they sensed the ruthlessness in each other all along."

She shrugged. "I guess maybe I'll never understand, and I should just put it out of my mind."

"Yeah, you should," he said huskily. "They took ten years of your life, damn them. The next fifty are mine."

She smiled. "I like the sound of that. I mean, I *really* like the sound of that. Fifty years. When the cops found that bat in your car, I wondered if we'd ever have another second together, let alone half a century."

"My fault. That'll teach me not to threaten someone's life, no matter how angry I am. I let my mouth get away with me and became the perfect fall guy. What's really frightening is that Don might have pulled it off if you hadn't gone to see Susan."

Marilee nibbled her bottom lip for a moment, eyeing Joe worriedly. "You know, Joe, with the statute of limitations to protect them, the other three guys will never pay for what they did. I, um—" She shrugged and sighed. "I've long since accepted that justice isn't always served, but I know it'll bother you, knowing they're out there, living their lives as though they never did anything wrong."

He smiled slightly. "Not true. They haven't gotten away scot-free, Mari mine. Trust me. They're paying, big time." His mouth twisted and thinned. "That night when I confronted Stan, I went over there burning to ruin his life. By the time I left, I realized he didn't need any help on that score. He'd done a fine job of ruining it all by himself. You can't hurt someone the way they hurt you and then simply walk away from it, untouched. Maybe on the surface it looks as if justice isn't served, and maybe it isn't always by the courts, but we all must answer to a higher authority." He winked at her. "God will get them in the end, and you can bet they're miserable in the interim, everything in their lives poisoned by their own evilness."

"I guess I never thought of it in exactly that way."

"It's the only way for us to think of it. The ultimate justice is meted out by the Big Guy. I'm at peace, knowing that, and I'm determined to move on from here, building a good, wholesome life with you that's untouched by the past. Those guys are damned. You and I are so very blessed. Let's focus on that."

Marilee smiled and nodded, for she believed that she and Joe were blessed. Because of events beyond their control, their lives had taken a ten-year detour, but now they had traveled in a wide circle back into each other's arms, and nothing would ever separate them again.

Boo groaned as he took another bite of sirloin. This chunk he held lightly between his teeth. He was clearly too full to chew or swallow anything more. He gave Joe a morose look. Joe chuckled. "Enough? You sure, fella? Ah, come on. Just one more piece. This is your victory dinner."

Boo lay down his head with the sirloin still caught between his teeth. His wet jowls fanned the floor, making him look even sillier and homelier than usual. Joe sighed. "Well, I guess that's all he can eat." He turned a twinkling gaze on Marilee. "Now, on to other business."

Finally. Marilee smiled as he rose with the plate of steak. After setting it on the counter, he quickly washed his hands and dried them. Then he turned to regard her with that lazy, crooked grin that always made her feel weak at the knees. He proffered a broad hand, then drew her gently to her feet, his dark gaze still holding hers.

Marilee waited for him to kiss her. He bent closer. And then, with lightning quick movements, he crouched, grabbed her around the knees, and pushed erect. Just like that, and she was hanging over his hard shoulder with her fanny aimed at the ceiling.

"*Joe*! What on *earth* are you doing?"

"There's a small matter we need to settle, Mrs. Lakota. Who's the red shirt in this family, and who's the boss. Remember?"

Marilee groaned. "Oh, Joe . . ."

"Oh, Joe," he mimicked. "The palm of my hand's been itching to connect with that cute little behind of yours all day. Now the moment of reckoning has finally come."

He started through the house with her. Marilee hung

there, grinning. He was going to the bedroom. *Oh, yeah.*

"Not only did you hire Swenson against my wishes, which I stated to you in perfectly clear terms, but you defied me about selling the house. *Then*, to make matters even worse, in a life-and-death situation, when I'd told you to go outside where you'd be safe, you ran right into the thick of the fight instead. And then what did you do? You grabbed a chair and came so close to hitting my head with the damned thing, I felt the breeze as it whizzed past my ear."

He settled a big hand on her rump and gave it a squeeze.

"Now, the way I see it, this means we have a serious problem. It would seem that you don't understand that I'm calling the plays. When it comes to important stuff, you're to do what I tell you, when I tell you, and *how* I tell you. Until we get that engraved on your brain, I'm not gonna be a happy guy. Got it?"

"Hmm."

Upon reaching the bedroom, he leaned over the bed, which was still stripped of linen, and dropped her. Marilee squeaked as she hit the mattress. Before she could so much as bounce, he followed her down, catching his weight with his arms. His chest anchored her beneath him, his dark face hovering a scant inch from hers.

"So what do you have to say for yourself, Mrs. Lakota? Are you willing to concede the point and agree to be the red shirt in this operation? Or do I need to drive the point home?"

She looped her arms around his neck. "I'm definitely the rookie when it comes to *this* operation. Just say what, when, and how, Mr. Lakota. Your wish is my command."

"Get that blouse off," he said with a growl.

Marilee quickly peeled her top off over her head and sent it flying. He settled a burning gaze on her chest.

"Now the bra," he said huskily.

She unfastened the front catch, and the lacy cups fell away. "How's that for following orders?"

"Not bad." He lowered his dark head. "Not bad at all. Give me fifty years to work on it, and I may get you trained yet."

His hot mouth closed over her. The jolt of sensation made Marilee gasp. She arched toward him and made tight fists in his hair. Fifty years. *Oh, yes.* He could work on getting her trained to his liking for as long as he wanted. Meanwhile, she'd take the more subtle approach while she trained him.

For a red shirt, he showed a lot of promise.

Epilogue

*J*oe held Marilee on his knee, his hand curled lightly over her swollen belly. It was late Sunday afternoon, and they were to spend the evening with Joe's mom, as they'd fallen into the habit of doing over the last few months. On the scarred oak table before them, Joe had spread out the plans for their dream home, a chalet on a hilltop overlooking the Umpqua Valley. It had become their favorite pastime, imagining how the house would look and discussing how they would decorate each room.

"Which one's my bedroom again?" Zachary asked, leaning over his dad's arm to look.

Joe pointed. "Right there, sprout. That's your bedroom door, opening in off the hall. And over here's your closet. And see those little square things? That's your built-in study area, a desk and bookcases and a computer center."

"For when I start school. Right?"

"That's right. Now that we've won the custody suit, we're stuck with you until you graduate high school." Joe winked at his child. "Longer if I put a lock on the bedroom door so you can't leave us and go to college."

"I'll never move out. I'm gonna live with you and my new mom for always!" Zachary exclaimed. "When we gonna build our house, Daddy?"

Joe kissed Marilee's shoulder. It was summer again, and given the heat, she'd taken to wearing sleeveless maternity smocks. "We'll build it as soon as we can, tyke. We've almost got the money saved."

"In time for our new baby, do you think?"

"No, probably not that soon."

Standing at her breadboard and rolling out pie dough, Faye glanced over her shoulder. "He could build it tomorrow if he wasn't so mule-headed."

"Ah, Mom," Joe said absently. "What's the matter? You feeling cranky today?"

Faye snorted and waved a hand. "Cranky? Frustrated, more like. I know Marilee would love to have her new house when the baby comes. It's just not the same, making do at the other place. She'd like to decorate that new nursery, and take the new baby home to that pretty new house, just like you always dreamed."

"I don't mind the other place, Faye," Marilee inserted. "Really, I don't. We have a spare room. We'll make do."

"When the next Lakota papoose makes his debut, I'll have her in our new house, Mom. That's a promise." The baby suddenly moved under Joe's palm, and he jerked in surprise. "Damn, honey, does that hurt? That boy's gonna be a kicker."

"No, *she* is going to be a soccer champion," Marilee corrected.

Joe grinned and nipped her shoulder this time. "You promised me a football team."

"Well, the sex is determined by the daddy, and according to the ultrasound, Dad screwed up. Definitely a girl papoose. I suppose you can teach her to play football, if you like. But it'll be awfully hard on all your male players, being shown up like that."

He chuckled and smoothed a big hand over her tummy,

his fingers flexing when he felt the baby move again. "If it's a girl, she better look just like her mama."

"She'll look like you," Marilee assured him. "I could see the resemblance in the picture."

"That picture was all a blur."

"Not that much of a blur. I'd recognize that nose of yours anywhere."

"Bite your tongue. If my baby girl has my nose, I'll cry."

"It's yours in miniature, and it looks darling on her, so don't worry. She'll be beautiful."

"Children!" Faye interrupted. "Could we stay on track? Joseph, listen to your mother. I see no reason why you can't use some of the money you gave me to build Marilee a house. I told you at the time that I didn't need it, and that I'd just put it in safekeeping. You said, 'Invest it, Mom. Make us both rich.' So I called that boy you know—that nice young fellow who does stocks and things—and I invested it. Now you won't touch it. How does that make sense?"

"Because, Mama, I gave you that money for yourself. To buy things. To invest for your retirement. You'll need it in your old age."

"How old do you think I'm going to get? Good grief, Joseph, spare me from living that long." Faye sighed in frustration and jerked open a deep drawer. As she pulled out paperwork, she said over her shoulder, "I invested it, just like you said, and now it's just sitting there. Why make your family suffer?"

"We're not suffering," Marilee assured her mother-in-law. "Joe will get us a house soon. We've almost got the down payment saved."

Joe ruffled Zachary's hair. "We're happy enough where we're at, Mom. But I'll tell you what. You keep that money invested, and when you've got a couple of million, I'll take half." He waggled his eyebrows at Zachary. "Right, sprout? We'll go buy camping gear and a lake boat and a—"

"Mountain bike?" Zachary asked.

"Absolutely. The very first thing I'll buy is a mountain bike for you. Just as soon as Grandma's a multi-millionaire."

"Hurry, Grandma!" Zachary cried. "Get to be a millionaire so Daddy'll get me a mountain bike!"

Faye was opening envelopes and looking through papers she tugged out. "How many numbers is that?"

Joe had already resumed his perusal of the house plans. "How many numbers is what?"

"A million," Faye asked. "Six or seven before the cents? I've got lots of sixes, and two sevens. Why can't they just put everything on one piece of paper for me? I can't make sense of all these balances. How much it was last time, and how much it is this time. And they do it for every darned thing. That stock fellow didn't invest it all in one place. Oh, no. He had to stick it here, and there, and God knows where else to make it impossible to keep track of. That's exactly how come I just put it in a drawer. It gives me a headache."

Joe glanced up. Stared at his mother's back. "Mom, you're probably looking at your account number if there's that many numbers."

His mother flashed him a glare, her blue eyes scathing. "Joseph, I'm old, not senile. I think I know the difference between my account numbers and my balances. Easy come, easy go. That was you, back in those days. Making more money than you knew what to do with! I'll happily keep some of it, but I don't want all of it. You're the one who injured his knee to earn it. The way I figure, it's your problem. All these papers are more trouble than they're worth. Before long, I'll outgrow my junk drawer."

Joe lifted Marilee off his knee, pushed up from the chair, and approached his mother. "Mom, I'll be happy to go through it for you if you're confused."

Faye frowned up at her son, who towered over her like a huge Sioux warrior. "You remind me more of your father every day. Do I look confused, Joseph?"

"No, Mama, you look mad."

She nodded. "I've had about enough of you not listening to me. I have a heart problem, not a brain problem!" She gathered up bunches of envelopes and shoved them at him. "You figure it out. And go build your family a house while you're at it. You earned all the money, running around out there in the rain and mud like you didn't have good sense, making homeruns."

"Touchdowns, Mom." Joe opened a sheet of paper, scowled down at it for a moment, and then said, "Mom, this is almost a million dollars!"

Faye twisted around to see. "That's just a six."

"A six?"

"Six numbers before the cents." She plucked another paper from the bunch. "This one's a seven."

"My *God!*" Joe whispered. "Mom, you're rich."

Faye rolled her eyes. "No, Joseph. I saved the money for you. Fool boy. Buying that car with a name like lasagna."

"My Lamborghini, you mean?"

"Whatever. You were too young to have all that money, plain and simple. Tossing checks to me like they were nothing. I said to myself, 'Faye, that boy will need that money someday.' And sure enough, now you do."

"Daddy?" Zachary chimed in. "Is Grandma a millionaire?" When Joe just kept gaping at the stock statements, Zachary tugged on his pant leg. "Daddy, is she rich enough for you to go buy me a mountain bike?"

Joe finally spared a distracted glance for his son. "How many mountain bikes do you want, sprout?"